Heir of Illusion

THE VERRAN ISLES
BOOK ONE

MADELINE TAYLOR

Copyright © 2025 by Madeline Taylor

All rights reserved.

No part of this book may be reproduced in any form or by any electronic or mechanical means, including information storage and retrieval systems, without written permission from the author, except for the use of brief quotations in a book review.

The story, all names, characters, and incidents portrayed in this production are fictitious. No identification with actual persons (living or deceased), places, buildings, and products is intended or should be inferred.

No generative artificial intelligence (AI) was used in the writing of this book. Without in any way limiting the author's exclusive rights under copyright, any use of this publication to "train" generative artificial intelligence technologies to generate text is expressly prohibited.

Cover by Moonpress Designs.

Edited by Maddi Leatherman at EJL Editing.

CONTENT ADVISORY

Violence. Strong language. Sexual content. PTSD. Mentions of self harm. Mentions of grooming. Suicidal ideation. Suffocation. Drowning. Emotional and physical abuse. Murder. Attempted sexual assault. Unwanted touching. Abuse of power. Depictions of grief.

For Carolyn,
I think you would have loved this.

Heir of Illusion

Madeline Taylor

HERPETOLOGY

CHAPTER ONE

I cradle my lover's head in my hands, longing to shatter it against the hardwood floor.

My fingers trail over the smooth marble bust, finding it cold and unyielding. A perfect likeness. Holding his face up to mine, I search his hollow eyes for some kind of explanation or apology. But the only message he offers is an engraving on the bottom.

Long Live the King.

I set the bust back on the display, smiling when I notice the dark red smear I've left behind on his cheek. The blood on my hands tonight is Baylor's fault—it's only fitting that it should stain him too.

Glancing around Darrow's apothecary, I find it hasn't changed much since the last time I was here. He's replaced the chandelier with some obsidian monstrosity. Its shards reflect moonlight onto every surface. A few new mirrors hang throughout the shop, bringing the total up to twelve, and I spot an array of the so-called *healing* crystals he peddles to his clientele.

Lost in this sea of shiny trinkets, it's hard to know where to look. But that's Darrow's genius.

He gives his audience an obvious fool, distracting them with excess and vanity. He never lets them see the sharpness of his teeth or the shrewdness of his gaze until it's too late.

The ceiling creaks in a steady pattern as I listen to his restless pacing upstairs. Despite being the owner of a fine country estate, Darrow sleeps here more often than not. I'd guess that has something to do with the fact that, unlike his country neighbors, Darrow's estate was purchased instead of passed down, and his money was earned instead of inherited.

Though it could also be the proximity to the city's brothels keeping him here in Solmare. I'm told he's a frequent visitor.

I debate with myself whether to ring the bell to alert him of my presence or simply knock over his expensive bust of the king's face. Watching Baylor's head break into tiny pieces would undoubtedly lift my mood.

Reining in my more destructive instincts, I reach for the bell. Most people don't appreciate receiving late-night visits from me. They typically end in bloodshed, like my previous meeting tonight. But if Della knew I was here, she'd want me to at least attempt civility, a perilous feat for someone in my line of work.

The moment the bell jingles through the dark room, Darrow's movements above cease. Several seconds pass before his soft steps pad toward the stairs. He probably thinks he's being quiet, but my hearing is far superior to his.

Darrow descends the staircase with a careless smile carefully painted onto his face. Despite the late hour, he's still dressed in a fine suit made of velvet and embroidered with gold filigree. Not a single one of his honey blond curls is out of place, each of them falling against his shoulders in a way that perfectly frames his strong bone structure.

I have to admire the flawlessness of his facade.

Laughter bubbles out of me at the sight of a jeweled dagger tucked into the waistline of his trousers. As if that would be anything more than a minor inconvenience to me. His gaze narrows as he searches for the source of the sound. Though his brown eyes roam over the spot I'm standing in—he's unable to see me.

As a *wraith*, I can disappear at will.

It's an extremely rare type of illusion magic that makes me a valuable asset. Or a formidable enemy. Even before the war that put Baylor on the throne, before the Goddess of Illusion disappeared, my brand of magic wasn't common.

"Show yourself," Darrow demands, only a hint of fear creeping into his hard tone.

Rolling my eyes, I release the illusion. If he's shocked by my presence in his shop, he quickly covers it underneath a charming smile. I pretend not to notice him unsheathing his ridiculous weapon.

"Lady Iverson," he croons as he saunters down the last step. "To what do I owe this unexpected visit from my favorite *pet*?"

Pet—the king's endearment for me. When I first came to live with King Baylor, he started calling me his little pet. Back then I thought it was sweet, but that was before I realized the name was a reference to how he'd collared and domesticated me.

It turns out I was the last one to be let in on that joke.

Keeping my face blank, I hold Darrow's gaze, not giving him the reaction he's hoping for. Behind the king's back, his subjects often spit the word at me. Similar to Darrow, they wield it cruelly, using it as a slur.

"Perhaps you require my assistance with a difficult matter?" he asks, a seductive grin pulling at his full lips. "I assure you, my lady, you would be in extremely capable hands."

I offer him my sweetest smile in response, one usually reserved for my master, before I brush my arm out and knock the king's bust to the floor. Listening to it shatter is just as satisfying as I'd hoped it would be.

"Oops." I shrug as my smile turns wicked. "Sorry about that, Darrow."

He sighs, staring dispassionately at the shards of marble scattered across the hardwood. "Pity. You'd think by now the king would have you housebroken."

Only a second passes before my blade is at his throat. His hand, still holding his own dagger, comes up on instinct, but I quickly grab his wrist and pin it to the counter next to us. Though his body is tense, his expression is one of boredom, as if his current predicament is of no concern to him.

I tsk, shaking my head in mock disappointment. "Now, is that any way to speak to His Majesty's *wraith*?"

People call me *pet* so often they forget what my owner trained me for.

He maintains his calm expression, but his face pales slightly as he takes in my appearance. When at court, I am dressed for seduction, wrapped in revealing gowns made of silks and satins. But tonight, my trousers and long-sleeved shirt are made from durable leather, and my long red hair is pulled into a simple braid that hangs down my back. Underneath the dark cloak, he can easily make out the gleam from the weapons strapped to my stomach and thighs. And the blood under my fingernails certainly adds a nice effect.

He swallows roughly as his gaze dips to the ruby collar around my throat.

"Did he send you here for me?" Darrow asks softly.

It's a fair question. The king often sends me to kill his enemies. It's what I was doing before I arrived. I shake my head, dispelling the echo of the desperate pleas from the man I murdered tonight. Shutting down my emotions, I force myself to focus on the present.

"Should he have?" I ask. "You aren't doing anything illegal here, are you, Darrow?"

"Come now, Lady Iverson." His flirty grin is back, though it's slightly less convincing. "I would never disrespect His Majesty."

My brows raise. "Really? You were happy enough to disrespect *me*. Did you forget I speak with the king's authority?"

He hisses as I lightly nick his throat with my blade. A drop of blood bubbles up, carving a path down his neck. The faint tease of its copper tang hangs in the air, tempting me to widen the cut, to fill the shop with his blood and send his soul through Death's veil.

Being only half fae, Darrow is more resilient than a mortal, but it's unlikely he would survive a deep cut to his carotid artery. Fractures form in his calm facade as his eyes shoot to the dagger still clutched in his restrained hand. I roll my eyes in exasperation as I release his wrist and lower my blade.

"Come now, Darrow. Do you honestly think I'd kill you?" I laugh as I step back, but we both know if the king ordered me to, I wouldn't have a choice.

He pushes himself away from the display table as his free hand massages his neck, smearing a few drops of blood against his skin.

"Of course not." His lips pull back in some semblance of a smile as he tosses a wayward curl over his shoulder. "I'm too beautiful to be murdered."

I nod to his little jeweled dagger. "Did you truly think that would be enough to stop me?"

"Wouldn't it be enough to stop most?" He chuckles, but it comes off forced.

Darrow has always been far too intrigued by the rumors about me. He often drops veiled comments, hoping to trip me up or trick me into confessing information very few are privy to. There are whispers, of course, rumors that circulate and get written off as conspiracy. But men such as Darrow make it their business to trade in secrets and chase down rumors.

I've no doubt my story fascinates him more than he would prefer.

Forcing myself to relax, I tuck my blade away as I move to the other side of Darrow's display counter, giving him some space. When my foot lands on something hard, I glance down to find the scattered remnants of the king's bust. One side of his face is completely shattered, but the other half held up well. I crush it under my boot, enjoying the way it crumbles.

"His Majesty requires information," I announce.

He tucks his hands behind his back. "On what topic?"

"Your specialty," I say, unable to hide the bitterness creeping into my tone. "Enchantments."

Most fae are not capable of complex magic, typically only gifted long life and rapid healing. But some of us have been granted much more, the nature of it depending on which of the Verran Isles we're from. Someone from the Eighth Isle might be skilled at predicting the future, whereas a person from the First could find themselves able to communicate with all living creatures. But those of us from the Seventh Isle are far trickier.

We specialize in illusion magic. While I'm known as a *wraith*, Darrow is what we call an *enchanter*. They're some of the most feared magic users, with the ability to craft powerful objects and spells. Which is probably why all of Darrow's enemies meet their ruin under mysterious circumstances that can never be traced back to him.

"The king is wondering if you're familiar with any enchantments that bind one person to another?" I ask, sounding bored as I feign interest in his so-called healing gems.

"I would need more to go on. There are many ways to bind two people together. Some temporary and others more permanent." His voice is tense. I wonder if it's because he doesn't enjoy me riffling through his things?

Oh well.

I pick up a pair of emerald earrings from the display and hold them up to my ears.

"Wouldn't these look pretty on me?" I bat my eyelashes at him.

He releases a long breath, pinching the bridge of his nose. "They looked prettier on the display. Be a good pet and put them back where they belong."

Rolling my eyes, I do as he asked. I've learned the hard way not to wear jewels crafted by Darrow. "The king is searching for a long-term binding method."

His eyes narrow with interest. Some of the color he lost earlier returns, along with his confidence.

"Long-term is more complicated," he says, casually leaning against the wall and crossing his arms over his chest. "There are ways of creating a binding potion, but it would need to be ingested regularly to maintain its effectiveness. And it's possible the recipient would build up a tolerance to it over time, meaning you'd need to keep increasing the dosage. It would work well for a few weeks, or even months, but I wouldn't suggest using it for any longer."

He keeps his posture relaxed, the very image of professional interest. But I can tell from the way his gaze watches me too closely, searching for any sign of disappointment over his words, that he's waiting for me to give myself away.

I don't.

"However," he continues, a dangerous gleam entering his eyes, "if he's searching for something that would last years, I'd suggest using an object."

"What kind of object?" I ask as I rest my elbows on the display case between us.

"Oh, anything would do as long as it was something they could wear on their person at all times." He shrugs, motioning to the gemstones in front of me. "Jewels work best. A ring or a bracelet." His lips curve into a wicked smile. "Perhaps a *necklace*."

It's physically painful to stop myself from pulling at my collar, but by the grace of the Fates I somehow manage to stay still.

"Are you sure it's the king who's asking for this information?" He pushes away from the wall and prowls closer. "Or is that collar getting a bit too tight for you?"

My jaw clenches as I force myself to take a deep breath, feeling the air move unrestricted through my windpipe. There's no reason for the collar to be triggered right now.

Darrow chuckles at my discomfort. "And here I thought you were ever the docile little *pet*."

I bare my teeth at him as my fingers itch to claw at my necklace, to rip it from my throat and be rid of its suffocating weight. Like most deadly things, it's beautiful. Dozens of deceptively alluring rubies encased in an intricate silver setting. The largest oval-shaped ruby sits in the center, against my trachea, while a slightly smaller one trickles down to my collarbone.

It's exquisite, yet it hangs around my neck like a noose.

I keep my hands at my sides, reminding myself that pulling at it wouldn't do any good. According to the enchantment placed on the collar, only the king has the power to remove it. When he fastened it around my throat, I was only ten years old. He said it would protect me and make it so no one would ever be able to take me away from him. He promised as long as I was wearing it, he would always be able to find me. At the time, I didn't see anything wrong with that. Actually, I found the idea comforting. But after fifteen years, I no longer find solace in being tied to a master I've outgrown.

When the king explained what the collar would do, there were several things he forgot to mention. One being that whenever I angered him, it would become tighter and tighter until I'm unable to breathe.

Until I suffocate.

I squeeze my fists, trying desperately not to lose my temper. "I'm aware you're the one who supplied the king with my collar."

"Possibly." He shrugs, crossing his arms again. "His Majesty has come to me for many things over the years. You can't expect me to recall every treasure."

I give him a bland look.

"We both know you remember this one well," I remind him. "Fifteen years ago, you opened your little apothecary in Highgrove. A curious place to do business, considering the circumstances of your birth."

Highgrove isn't the same as the rest of the city of Solmare. Money doesn't buy you entrance, blood does. It's controlled by the council, a group made up of members of the ruling families. Only those of noble birth are permitted to own property here. When a spot becomes available in the district, the entire council must approve the buyer.

Despite how hard he's worked to erase his mortal half, it's well known that Darrow is a half fae bastard. That's why the high fae of the ruling class have never fully accepted him. Oh, they're happy to use his services when they have the need, but no matter how fine his clothes or the number of secrets he uncovers, he will never truly be one of them.

They would never willingly welcome him into Highgrove.

He flashes me a sly grin, continuing his performance as a careless idiot. "What can I say? I made a compelling proposal to the council and they saw my value."

I narrow my gaze as my frustration mounts. "Do you honestly expect me to believe the high fae on the council went against hundreds of years of tradition and prejudice to open Highgrove to a half fae bastard merely because they liked your *business model*?"

He shrugs. "Stranger things have happened."

"Not without help," I insist. "This would have cost more than your secrets and backroom bargains. You would have needed royal intervention."

He doesn't answer, but we both realize it's true. The only person who can control the council members is the king.

I lean across the counter, my voice softer now. "I know how generous our king is with those who please him."

Something vulnerable flashes in his eyes, but it's quickly replaced by condescension. "I'm sure you do."

My jaw clenches. "He gave you the deed to this building in exchange for my collar."

"What if he did?" He sighs, pushing a curl out of his face. "What do you want me to do about it now?"

I lift my chin, meeting his gaze head on. "I want you to remove it."

Darrow starts to laugh, but my hard eyes tell him I'm not joking. "That's impossible," he says cautiously.

My hand returns to my blade and his brows shoot up as I remove it once more. A horrible screech fills the room as I drag the tip across the glass display case between us.

"You see, I don't think that's true," I argue, moving to stand before him. "You're paranoid, always careful to keep antidotes for every poison on your premises." His throat bobs as he watches me twirl the knife between my fingers. "You'd never make a deal that could come back to hurt you. You wouldn't have given the king something that could be used against you without knowing how to defeat it."

Every ounce of derision fades from his expression as he pulls his focus away from the weapon and meets my gaze once more.

"Sometimes the risk is worth the reward," he says softly. A faint trace of shame flashes in his eyes as he releases a deep sigh. "Iverson." I flinch at the pity in his tone, but he keeps speaking. "There is only one way to rid yourself of the collar. The king must remove it himself."

No.

Lead sinks into my stomach as my limbs stiffen. This has to work. There are no other options, nowhere else I can go for help. I can't keep living this way. Not after—I cut that thought off, knowing now is not the time to get lost in my guilt.

"You're lying," I insist through clenched teeth.

Unable to stand still, I move through the shop, picking up every item I can find. Glass shatters as I knock several crystal bottles to the floor, searching for something, *anything*, that can help me.

"What are you doing?" he demands as I reach for a vial of purple liquid. Taking it from my hands, he carefully sets it back on the shelf.

"You have to have something that would work," I mutter as I head for the back room, knowing he keeps special items hidden there. "You may play the fool, but I know you. You're too careful to take that kind of risk."

He steps in front of me, grabbing my shoulders and pulling me to halt.

"Iverson, there's nothing here that would help you," he says gently, his brown eyes imploring me to see reason.

But I can't.

A lump forms in my throat, and I'm sure I am choking, sure the collar has seized this moment to strike. I push Darrow away and step back. He nods, his eyes full of unwanted understanding.

I've always felt a strange kinship with Darrow. He may have helped the king destroy me, but we're two sides of the same coin. Both of us bastards who conned our way to the top, occupying spaces we have no right to.

And we're both hated for it.

Forcing air into my lungs, I turn his words over in my mind as I try to spot the lies he's so skilled at hiding.

"You said there's nothing *here* that would help me," I say slowly, watching his face close enough to spot the slight tightening around his eyes. "But what about somewhere else?"

All at once, his sympathy turns to annoyance as his expression hardens.

"Iverson, I think it's time for you to—"

He stops mid-sentence as my head jerks toward the door. An awareness settles over me, making the tiny hairs on my arms stand at attention. The sensation of ice pressing against the back of my neck and dripping down my spine sends shivers racing through me.

Someone is approaching the shop.

Their presence is heavy. Dominant. Oppressive in a way that rivals even the king. As I lick my lips I can almost taste them on the air. Like deja vu, it's familiar in a way I can't place, yet some distant awareness in the back of my mind recognizes the sensation.

Darrow stiffens, looking around for the source of my abrupt change. "What's going on?"

Confusion wrinkles my brow as I turn to face him again. "You don't feel that?"

He shakes his head, sparking a thousand questions on the tip of my tongue, but they disappear as my gaze is drawn back to the door. The presence is getting stronger with each passing second.

They're moving closer.

"Are you expecting anyone?" I demand.

"No," he promises, but the blood draining from his face tells a different story.

I remember how he was pacing upstairs, how restless he sounded. And when he came down, he was fully dressed. Strange for this time of night...

Fuck.

Sparing him a seething glare that promises violence, I wrap myself in an illusion. The feeling of a thousand tiny needles pricking my skin settles over me as I disappear from sight. Envy burns in his eyes as he stares at the spot where I was just standing, but I don't have time to enjoy it. Hurrying past the display counters, I tuck myself into the back corner and whisper silent prayers to the Fates. No one can know I was here tonight. Revealing my intentions to Darrow was already a risk. If this conversation got back to Baylor...

I keep my gaze on the front door, waiting for the source of this strange presence to appear. Unease claws at the lining of my stomach as the room begins to dim. I tell myself it's only a cloud passing over the moon, but then darkness begins creeping up the walls. It covers the windows, leaving only a sliver of light peeking through the glass panes.

Inky shadows slip through the cracks underneath the door as wisps of black smoke push deeper into the room. My heart stutters as they slither out and take the shape of snakes. Their crimson eyes seem to simmer as they turn their heads back and forth, searching for something.

Holy Fates.

Crouching down, I curl into a tight ball and make myself as small as possible. From my new angle, I can no longer see the front door, but I hear it creaking open. A few moments later, heavy boots thud across the hardwood, taking slow, steady steps. I can't see the newcomer, but I still sense their power. It's thicker now that they're in the room—a crushing weight ready to smite any enemy. I have no idea what sort of creature they are and no interest in finding out.

"I like what you've done with the place."

The man's voice is rich and deep, sending shivers down my spine.

"Yes, I apologize for the mess, my lord." Darrow, who is still in my line of sight, glances down at the evidence of my outburst apologetically. "I meant to have it cleaned up before you arrived. I wasn't expecting you for another hour."

His words are steady, but it's clear from the lack of condescension in his tone that Darrow is nervous. The only time I ever hear him this accommodating is with the king.

"No matter," the stranger replies. "I won't be here long."

Marble shards crunch under his boots as he steps forward into my field of vision. Even in the dim light, I can make out his shape. He's tall, staring down at Darrow from a few inches above him. He wears a heavy cloak, black with a fur trim. Despite most of his body being hidden, I can tell he's broad. His dark hair is pushed back, but there's not enough light for me to make out his face clearly.

"Of course." Darrow nods stiffly. "I looked into the matter you inquired about. I'll go get my notes."

He starts to retreat to the backroom, but one of the snakes slips around his neck like a rope. His mouth opens wide as his fingers reach for the shadow, desperately trying to pull it away.

Horror fills me as I watch the ugly scene, replaying the countless times my collar has tightened. Silently counting my breaths, I focus on taking one after another to keep the panic at bay. *I'm not suffocating,* I remind myself. Still, my fingers mimic Darrow's, but both of our actions are futile.

"No need for that," the stranger says. "I'm sure you can summarize it for me."

Darrow responds with an unintelligible noise.

"Ah, my apologies." I can hear the smile in his voice. "Let me loosen that for you."

The shadows remain around Darrow's throat, but they must ease their pressure a bit. He coughs several times before he is able to speak.

"R-right, of course," the enchanter stammers. "I-I can do that."

A fleeting, irrational spark of jealousy hits me. It takes me ages of verbally sparring with Darrow to convince him to do anything at all, yet this man has him cowering in subservience. These wayward thoughts are pushed aside as my attention snags on one of the shadow snakes slithering by the door. If I were to make it that far without being noticed, could I get past the strange creature unscathed? A shiver coils down my spine at the thought of trying.

"I spoke with one of my informants," Darrow says, sounding raspy from the strain. "He was recently reassigned from a low-level job on the wall-"

"The wall?" that deep voice cuts him off.

"The one that surrounds the palace grounds," Darrow explains quickly. "He was one of the guards that used to patrol it."

"Ah. Continue."

Darrow swallows, his eyes flickering to the shadow snake still wrapped around his throat. "He works in the tunnels beneath the palace now. I think what you're searching for might be there."

My brow furrows. Hearing Darrow admit to committing treason and betraying the king doesn't shock me, but I tuck the confession away to use against him later. What does surprise me are these supposed tunnels. I've explored my home thoroughly over the years and have never found anything close to that.

The stranger shrugs. "Perhaps. Is he guarding something specific down there?"

Darrow nods. "A weapon he calls the *whisperer*."

A hiss escapes from one of the shadow snakes, sending a fresh wave of fear pulsing through me.

"Interesting." His tone turns thoughtful. "And did he mention anything else about this whisperer?"

"No. Nothing, my lor—" Darrow chokes again, clutching at the shadows as he tries to loosen them. This continues for several seconds before I hear him inhale a deep breath.

"You were saying?" the stranger asks.

"Only the price!" Darrow cries.

"What price?"

"My informant said they were warned never to touch it! Whoever wields it pays a steep price, but I don't know what it is. That's all! I swear!"

The man steps closer to Darrow, leaning over him.

"I believe you." His voice is soft now, almost bored. For a moment, I believe the Fates have smiled on us and he's going to leave, but his next words remind me why that kind of wishful thinking is so dangerous. "One more thing. Did you share this information with anyone else?"

My heart pounds violently against my chest. Despite the darkness, I can spot terror twisting Darrow's handsome features. His jaw is hard and his lips thin as he stares at the enemy before him. Silently, I reach for my blades and carefully remove two of them. Any moment now Darrow is going to give me up and reveal my presence.

"No, my lord." He shakes his head. "Only you."

Shock tears through me, but I don't have time to process it as the stranger tsks.

"What a pity," he says, taking a few steps back. "I had hoped to find further use for you, but I don't keep liars in my employ."

I don't need to see him to know what's coming next.

The shadows tighten again as Darrow's face twists into a horrific visage. His mouth hangs open silently trying to suck in air. His brown eyes are wide and bloodshot as they desperately search the room for some kind of help. I flinch each time his gaze passes over me, though it never lingers. He still can't see me.

Does he think I left, or does he somehow know I'm cowering in the corner while he dies right in front of me.

I try to block it out, taking deep breaths to remind myself I'm not the one being strangled. Phantom pressure grips my throat, but I force myself to stay in the present.

Don't think about it. Don't remember how it felt to be denied air.

Darrow may not be my friend, but he's also not quite my enemy. I wouldn't wish this kind of torture on him. I wouldn't have killed him this way; I would have done it swiftly, a knife to the throat. This is cruel. Only one person deserves this kind of death, and he is currently across the city, sleeping peacefully in his palace.

I've always been aware that there's an absence inside of me—a missing piece. Something that would have made me good and whole and right. A tug pulls at that empty space now, the ghost of an instinct that never grew.

Is this why I will always let people down when they need me the most?

Faces flash through my mind: some I killed, few I loved, *one* I made a promise to. An oath sworn at the graveside of a friend I'd mistaken for an enemy.

Forcing the air into my lungs, I remind myself that I am not owned. I am not controlled or caged.

I am not the *pet* they tamed.

I am the *beast* they let inside.

And I keep my promises.

Pulling my arm back, I send the blade flying toward the stranger, but just before it can make impact, a shadow strikes out, grabbing it midair. My eyes flare as he turns around, facing my corner. The noose around Darrow's throat must loosen because the sound of his gasps suddenly fill the room, yet I can't bring myself to drag my gaze away from the stranger as he steps forward, the ghost of a smile on his face.

"I was wondering how long you planned to stay hidden."

CHAPTER TWO

The stranger steps out of the shadows that have concealed his face. For the first time since he arrived, I'm able to get a clear glimpse of him.

He's beautiful.

So painfully beautiful that for a moment, I want to close my eyes, to look away before I have the chance to commit him to memory. All fae are attractive, but I've never seen someone who appears so carefully crafted, so cohesively made. Every feature fits perfectly into the complete image, is if he was designed by hand rather than by nature.

His skin has a slight golden hue to it, suggesting he spends time outside. Unruly dark hair is pushed back from his face, but a few wayward strands fall across his forehead. Sharp pointed ears tell me he's definitely high fae, but I doubt he's from the Seventh Isle. Almost all the upper-class residents here are clean shaven, and he has at least a week's worth of stubble hugging his sharp jawline, giving him an air of danger.

Everything about his appearance is immensely inviting to me.

His pale blue eyes are absolutely piercing as he stares in my direction. My gaze snags on his generous mouth, noticing the smirk forming there. For a moment, I wonder if I unintentionally dropped the illusion hiding me from his sight, but the faint whisper of power tickling my skin tells me it's still intact.

"Come now," he croons. "You were so brave just a moment ago. Such impressive aim."

His gaze never wavers from my corner. Despite the fact that I'm invisible, he seems to know exactly where I am. I recall the strange sensation I had as he approached the shop. I was immediately aware of his presence, like ice on the back of my neck. Can he sense me the same way I sense him? And if he's aware of my hiding spot, why haven't his shadow snakes slithered over here and forced me out?

My attention shifts to the black leather gloves covering his hands as he grabs a fistful of Darrow's long hair. "If you're not going to join us, I'll have to use your friend here to entertain myself."

For the past few minutes the enchanter has been completely silent, still on his knees with a shadow wrapped around his neck. He was probably hoping the stranger would forget about him so he could sneak out.

Summoning all my courage, I decide there's no point in staying silent

"If you want to play," I call out, my voice easily carrying over the quiet room, "I can think of a much more diverting game."

A self-satisfied gleam enters his eyes. "My lady, you speak at last. What sort of game do you suggest?"

Instead of answering, I send another blade flying toward his throat. Just like before, one of his shadows plucks it from the air before it can hit him.

"We could find out how many blades your shadows can handle at once?" I say, slowly edging in the direction of the door, keeping my back against the wall as I move.

His smirk turns predatory as his eyes track my invisible movements. "You know, I don't usually enjoy playing games."

"Because you're a sore loser?" I ask, sending another blade flying.

This time, it isn't one of his shadows that knocks it off course.

Without looking down, his hand catches the weapon less than an inch from his chest. My eyes widen at his speed. That's going to be a problem.

"Because I've never had a worthy opponent," he clarifies, tossing the knife aside with unnecessary force. It hits one of the display cases, causing me to wince as it shatters. We truly are making a mess of poor Darrow's shop tonight.

Several red dots stain the broken glass and I realize the blade must have cut his hand when he caught it. Unease festers in the pit of my stomach as the darkness ripples around us. All across the room, the shadow serpents writhe against the floor, hissing in a frenzy. As if they can smell the blood, they pounce on the droplets, lapping them up.

If my face were visible, it would be as pale as the moon. Bile rises in my throat, but I push it down. I've seen the depravity of mortals and fae, but this is something else. Every hair on my body stands up at the sight of this waking nightmare, vastly different from the familiar horrors I've spent my life learning to fight. A crazed laugh threatens to escape me as my thoughts twist morbidly. How do you battle a wisp of smoke? How can I strike a shadow that has gorged itself on blood?

The city of Solmare fears the invisible *wraith*; ironic that the *wraith* now fears a shadow.

My gaze darts back and forth between Darrow and the door. It's possible I could sneak out before the shadows stop me, but that would mean abandoning him. Breathing deeply, I try to calm my racing heart as I think through my options. I run my fingers over all four of my sheaths, hating that three are now empty. My only comfort is the knowledge that at least one of my blades drew blood.

"You know, it's sweet that you feed your shadows," I tell him, feigning levity I don't feel as I back around a display table that blocks my path. "It's like a momma cat nursing her baby kittens. Adorable really."

He barks out a laugh that sounds rusty, as if he hasn't made that sound in a while. "Yes, it will be truly *adorable* when they rip the flesh from your friend's bones."

My nose wrinkles. "Who says he's my friend?"

He tilts his head to the side. "The fact that you didn't abandon him suggests you might care a little."

"Maybe I need him for information, and I'm merely trying to spare myself some inconvenience," I argue.

"Well, I'd hate to put you out." His hard eyes bore into me, turning my blood to ice. "Give me your word that if I let him go, you will reveal yourself to me."

"I swear," I tell him, only half lying.

The second the stranger releases his hold, Darrow is on his feet running for the backdoor. He doesn't spare a glance in my direction, not that he can see me anyhow. Still, I roll my eyes at his lack of solidarity.

"Some friend," the shadow wielder scoffs, his gaze narrowing on Darrow's retreating form.

"Eh." I shrug. "We're not that close."

I spot a hint of amusement in his eyes, but it's gone in an instant. All his earlier attempts at charm evaporate.

"Now it's your turn," he announces, turning to face me again.

I swallow thickly. No two *Illusionists* are exactly alike, each of us having our own specialties. Some can shift their form, while others can alter what people see. But there's a reason we're often referred to as tricksters. Our talents are designed to mislead and deceive.

There's a little-known type of illusion called an *eidolon*: a living duplicate sometimes referred to as a shadow-self. It's a type of apparition, typically created in the image of the *Illusionist* casting it. As far as I know, I'm the only person currently alive with this ability.

Essentially, I can create a fully corporeal copy of myself. It moves and speaks exactly like me, relying on a mixture of commands and instincts. Creating one is both physically and mentally taxing, but they exist as long as I feed energy into them.

Apprehension pulses in my veins at the thought of how delicate this balance will be. I've never tried to create an *eidolon* while maintaining my invisibility, but right now I can't think of another way out of this situation. I just need to distract him long enough to slip past his shadows... Gritting my teeth, I force myself to stay silent as the familiar pain rips through me.

My body burns, my muscles twisting and stretching as if I'm splitting myself in half. As if my soul is being ripped apart. Warm blood tickles my upper lip, and I quickly wipe it on my sleeve, careful not to let any drops hit the ground where hungry shadows might be lurking. Unfortunately, nosebleeds always accompany this process.

The pressure in my head reaches its breaking point as the *eidolon* takes shape, forming directly in front of me, so I'm staring at the back of its head. Finally, the pain begins to ease. My jaw unclenches as I gently massage the aching joint. Fuck, that was brutal. But I got through it without losing my invisibility, which I'll count as a win.

I peer through my *eidolon's* eyes as she takes a few steps toward the stranger, giving me a closer view of him. At the sight of her, his brows momentarily raise, and his lips part slightly before his mask of cold indifference returns.

"Come closer," he demands.

She obeys him. I know I should be taking advantage of his distraction and continuing my escape, but I find myself strangely frozen. My fingers itch at my sides, desperate to trace the small constellation of freckles dotting his straight nose and sharp cheekbones. And those eyes... They're mesmerizing. His irises are such a pale shade of blue they almost appear translucent. But when I squint, I can make out silver flakes scattered throughout. As he inspects my apparition, I almost feel as if he's looking right through her.

"I confess myself disappointed," he says, startling me.

I blink. As his words register, I'm strangely insulted.

"I let your friend go in good faith because you promised to reveal yourself," he continues, reaching out to trail a gloved finger down her face. "But you cheated. That's no way to play the game, my lady."

Something about his tone sets off alarm bells in my mind, spurring me to action. I move backward again, unable to turn away as I blindly feel for the display cases. The *eidolon* gazes up at him, a confused expression on her face.

"As lovely as you are" —he whispers, leaning closer to her— "you're not real."

Before I can process his words, a scythe materializes in his other hand, and he hooks it into her gut. The echoes of her pain sear through me. My mouth opens, but no sound comes out as I hold back a gasp. I run my hands over my stomach, trying to convince my brain there's no injury there. Most sensations my *eidolon* experience are dulled, a whisper that never fully manifests in me. But with this kind of pain, there's no stopping it. It burns as if the blade has just sunk into my own stomach.

Holy Gods... Only one creature can summon a scythe, and they're meant to be extinct.

"Reaper," I whisper, the full weight of my situation hitting me.

The apathy on his face is chilling as he pulls the weapon out of her. He doesn't bother watching as she falls to the ground. Instead, he lifts his head in my direction.

I run.

Any illusion of control I had over the situation has been shattered. I'm strong, but even I can't fight a reaper. *A fucking soul collector from Death's Isle.* They aren't supposed to be here anymore.

Ten feet from the door, something cold slips around my ankle, causing me to tumble to the ground—hard. Thankfully, my training doesn't desert me. I'm able to land on my side and roll onto my back.

Searching for my attacker, I find one of the shadow snakes has wrapped itself around my leg. I don't bother to stop the scream rising in my throat as I struggle against its hold. It doesn't matter since the reaper has known exactly where I was since the second he got here.

Using my free leg, I try to kick at the snake, but its punishing grip only clings to me tighter. I dig my nails into the floor, pulling myself toward the door. I only make it a few inches before the snake drags me back, hissing at my attempted escape.

Ice drips down my neck as heavy footsteps make their way to me. I cling to my useless illusion, the only shield I have left.

"Reveal yourself," he demands from behind me.

"Bite me," I snarl, my broken fingernails still trying to find purchase in the grooves of the hardwood.

"The time for games is done."

The snake twists my leg painfully, forcing me to roll onto my back. The reaper stands over me, holding his scythe out toward my invisible form, it's tip only inches away from my nose. My gaze flits to his face, finding nothing but cold determination.

"And my patience is wearing thin," he warns.

I watch in disbelief as something moves underneath his heavy cloak. His shoulders roll as he shrugs it off, revealing two black feathered wings unfolding behind him. They're massive, at least six feet on both sides.

With the cloak gone, I get my first glimpse of the powerful man beneath it. He may be a demon, but he could rival any angel with his beauty. The strong lines of his body are wrapped in clothes similar to mine. Other than his face and neck, every part of him is hidden behind dark, durable materials that cling to his broad form like a second skin. His build reminds me of a panther, strong and lean, but undeniably graceful.

For a moment, I have the foolish instinct to reach out and touch his feathers, to find out if they are as soft as they appear. I squeeze my fists, quickly dispelling the wild notion.

"Reveal. Yourself. Now." His lips pull back as he bares his teeth, speaking each word like a curse.

At this point, I'm not sure I have any choice but to obey him. And since maintaining my illusion will only drain me, I release it. The whisper of magic fades from my skin as my body becomes visible.

As he takes me in, his full lips part on a silent gasp. His eyes are wide as they scan my features. I can't tell if the reaper is shocked or horrified by what he's seeing. He doesn't even seem to realize that he's lowered his scythe to his side.

A blush of roses stains my cheeks as they heat under the intensity of his gaze. In my mind, I imagine red petals falling from my face one by one, each marking another moment of this silence.

His wings start to curve inward briefly before he snaps them back, folding them to fit tight against his back. The movement is enough to pull me out of my daze. Capitalizing on his distraction, I snatch the last blade sheathed to my thigh and move to cut his shadow off me. He shouts as he reaches for my hand, but this time, I'm faster.

My blade strikes right through the shadow, as if there's nothing there, before sinking into my calf.

With the adrenaline coursing through me, there's no pain, only the cold jab of steel contrasting with the hot, thick blood dripping down my leg. Detachedness settles over me as I stare at the wound. This isn't my first time being stabbed. Sadly, this isn't even the first time it's happened by my own hand.

For a moment, everything goes completely still before the darkness shifts once more. Shadows loom closer, predators scenting their prey. An undercurrent of hisses and growls fill the room, reminding me of the jungles my brother and I used to read about when we were children.

The snake, still wrapped around my leg, goes rigid.

My eyes dart to the reaper's and I spot a trace of fear in his wintery gaze. His jaw clenches as the blood drains from his face. He holds himself absolutely still.

"Don't," he says, his voice clipped as my hand moves toward the blade.

I know the weapon wouldn't do me any good, but holding it would make me feel less helpless. Still, I listen to him. From the look on his face, I get the sense that even *he* doesn't have complete control over these shadows.

The snake slowly uncoils from around my leg until its dark head is pointed directly at my wound. The others are writhing on the floor, desperate to get a taste of my blood. Only a single pool of moonlight shines through the windows now, illuminating me like some sort of unholy offering. The reaper stands over me, his stance protective as he tries to hold them back. He stares intensely at the shadow, willing it to stop, but even his command can't compete with the lure of blood.

A whimper escapes me as the snake inches closer to the wound. I expect the sharp sting of its teeth, but instead I watch in frozen horror as its wispy tongue laps against my skin.

A deranged laugh bubbles up my throat at the strange sensation, but he silences me with a hard glare.

"It tickles," I explain.

The shadow pulls back, watching me with its red eyes for several seconds before moving to the wound again. Clenching my eyes shut, I hold my breath as I steel myself against the pain that is sure to follow. I've met death before, but this iteration is particularly gruesome. I don't relish being ripped apart in a feeding frenzy.

I wait for the agony to begin, but it never comes.

Opening my eyes, I find the shadow wrapping itself around the blade and pushing against the wound. I suck in a breath, wincing from the discomfort. The shadow isn't feeding, instead it looks as if it's... attempting to apply pressure?

It lays its head down on my thigh and nuzzles against me.

It's trying to comfort me?

I turn to the reaper for answers, but he appears just as stunned as I am. His eyes are comically round, and his mouth hangs open in confusion. Glancing around, I find that the other shadows have begun to calm down too, as if their blood frenzy has been sated.

"What are you?" he whispers, his tone a mix of awe and horror.

The question stirs an ugly feeling deep within my gut. Biting my lip against the searing pain, I pull the blade from my calf and toss it in his direction. The snake lifts its head to hiss at the disruption before returning to its task. The reaper doesn't even flinch as the weapon flies past him, only an inch from his head.

"You missed."

I almost laugh at the disappointment in his voice as the blade clatters to the ground somewhere behind him. Closing my eyes, I summon the last of my strength as I rub my temples. Blood drips from my nose and ears. Using so much power tonight has weakened me, but I force myself to push past the pain and dizziness. After several seconds, I look up and meet the reaper's gaze.

My grin resembles a grimace as my attention shifts behind him. "No, I didn't."

He turns around to find my *eidolon* crouched on the tips of her toes, baring her teeth at him. Her blood crusted fingers clutch my favorite dagger as she leaps. He dives out of the way as his shadows surge into action, trying to restrain her. Their distraction leaves me free to jump to my feet and run for the door.

Burning pain shoots up my calf every time I put weight on my right leg. Despite my exhaustion, I manage to summon an illusion and make myself invisible. I stumble slightly as my stomach lurches from the familiar sensation settling over my skin. Pushing past all of it, I tell myself the pain isn't real. It's merely another illusion, and I am its master.

Hidden from view, I race into the cool night air, quickly putting distance between myself and Darrow's shop. The streets of Highgrove are empty at this hour, but I still choose to cut down alleyways to stay far away from the glow of the streetlamps.

I glance over my shoulder several times, paranoid about the trail of blood I'm leaving behind. Every shadow that dances across the night has me nearly tripping in panic. My aching calf wants to give out, but I keep pushing forward. Luckily, Highgrove is the closest district to the palace.

Finally, the stone gates come into view. As always, there are two guards manning the side entrance. Their familiar faces feel out of place after everything that's happened tonight. As I slip past them, I pick up the end of a dirty joke followed by their muffled laughter.

Apprehension skates over my skin as I hasten through the palace grounds, limping with each step. My eyes scan the lush gardens, searching for the reaper. I tell myself it's all in my mind, merely the product of adrenaline lingering after the fight. But the tingling sensation on the back of my neck has me wishing for one of my blades.

Movement catches my eye, pulling my attention to the sloping roofs of the palace.

Gargoyles line the ledges, guardians peering down at us in silent judgment. As I scan their frozen faces, I notice something that has my blood turning to ice in my veins. The winged statues stand together in a row, but there's something different about one of them.

His giant wings aren't made of stone; they're made of feathers.

CHAPTER
THREE

A series of dull thuds has me shooting out of my chair, a blade in my hand as I land in a crouch on the floor. I groan as fiery pain shoots up my calf, a reminder of my self-inflicted stab wound. Slowly standing up, I stretch out the tightness in my leg, wincing as I flex and point my toes.

After spotting the winged reaper watching me from the rooftop last night, I took off running until I reached my room. Tending to the injury had been the last thing on my mind as I locked the doors and curled up on my settee. I planned to stay awake all night to ensure the soul collector didn't slip in through my balcony, but as the adrenaline faded, I passed out with a knife still in my hand.

Sheer ivory curtains do nothing to block the sun from forcing its way into my room and blanketing the soft colors of my decor in early morning light. As the incessant pounding continues, I realize the noise that woke me is coming from the other side of my door.

Ignoring the pain in my leg, I slip on a silk dressing gown in an effort to hide last night's conspicuous outfit. Keeping my blade behind my back, I make my way to the door and crack it open, scowling when I see who's woken me up so urgently.

Kaldar Burgess.

"Woof," he says, a smug smile gracing his face, clearly proud of the tired jab he's made hundreds of times before. Pet jokes are a favorite among the courtiers.

I shut the door, not giving him a chance to wedge his foot into the opening. I've only taken two steps toward my bed when the knocking resumes, and I'm forced to open it again.

"What do you want?" I demand.

He rolls his eyes. "If you hadn't slammed the door in my face, I might have been able to tell you."

I stare at him blankly as I wait for an answer to my question. He hates when I don't play along. Afterall, a good little pet lives to please.

"The king has requested your presence at his table this morning," he grinds out, frustration leaking through his pores.

As a second son from a wealthy family, he obviously thinks relaying this message is beneath him. Since his older brother inherited the title, lands, and their family's seat on the council, Kaldar went into politics. Despite not being blessed with any magic, he's made himself indispensable to the king, becoming his chief adviser. But unfortunately for Kaldar, Baylor often treats him like an errand boy instead.

A high fae forced into servitude—the horror.

Noticing movement behind him, I realize he's brought along my two lady's maids, Alva and Morwen. I open the door wider to let them in as Kaldar makes one of his typical quips.

"Be a good pet and don't take too long. You wouldn't want to keep your master waiting." He smirks, but I don't bother giving him a reaction before slamming the door in his face.

Alva and Morwen hurry to draw me a warm bath, adding scented oils to the water. I breathe deep, trying to allow the calming blend of rose and neroli to relax me. Neither of my lady's maids bat an eye at my suspicious bed clothes as they help me undress. After several years of being assigned to me, they've both come to expect a few oddities.

Morwen bends down, helping me remove my pants. Her straight dark hair is pulled into a braid, exposing the slightly pointed edges of her ears that mark her as a half fae. As she pulls the leather material down my legs, she catches sight of the still-healing wound on my calf, along with blue and purple bruises from where the shadow had wrapped around me. I wince as her hand brushes over the injury.

She looks up, arching a brow. "What's this?"

Dried blood is caked to my skin, making it appear worse than it is. At least it's scabbed over and should be fully healed within a few days. If the blade hadn't gone so deep, the only trace of the wound would be a faint pale line that would eventually fade back to its original color. One blessing of being high fae is that we heal quickly.

An image of the reaper flashes through my mind, sending a flare of heat up my neck as I'm suddenly filled with a strange sort of embarrassment.

"Nothing," I lie. "Just an accident."

Alva moves in closer, peering over Morwen's shoulder as her sweet face clouds with fear. "Are you doing it again? Did you want this to hap—"

"No," I cut her off, not letting my thoughts wander in that direction.

Both of them stare at me, waiting for an answer. I sigh, knowing they won't let this go.

"It was..." I search for a way to tell them what happened without mentioning Darrow or the reaper. "Complicated."

Alva's brows pinch together, but Morwen narrows her eyes, waiting for me to elaborate.

"It wasn't what you think." I shift uncomfortably. "I don't do *that* anymore."

Or at least, I haven't in the last few months. But sometimes I still crave the relief that would come after the pain. Without it, there's no end to the guilt that builds inside of me with each life Baylor forces me to take. Maybe it's wrong, but some misaligned sense of justice makes me associate suffering with atonement. It tells me the only way to pay for what I've done is to be punished. Only then can I finally be clean.

Which is why sometimes I used to stand still instead of dodging a hit. I'd even deliberately let an opponent reach for their weapon, knowing there was no way they'd be able to permanently wound me. Whatever minor injury they caused was nothing compared to what Baylor forced me to do to them. Still, it helped ease the worst of my shame.

"I promise," I instill as much sincerity into my voice as possible.

They drop the subject, but I can tell they don't believe me. And they shouldn't. I'm nothing if not a liar.

After I'm bathed, they dress me in a silk gown the color of sage. It hugs my chest, accentuating my curves in a way Baylor will appreciate. Gold metal adorns the shoulders of the sleeveless design, while the plunging neckline draws attention to my ruby collar. There are high slits on both sides of my legs, making it easier to access the blades I have strapped to my thighs.

I stare at my reflection as Alva brushes out my rich copper waves, taming them to soft perfection. Movement in the corner of my eye pulls my attention to Morwen. She meets my gaze in the mirror as she picks up the broken clock on my bookshelf and adjusts the time, pushing it ahead by over an hour.

I quickly glance back at Alva, but it's clear she didn't notice, her attention focused on the gold barrettes she's using to pin my hair out of my face. I make note of the time, knowing I'll be cutting it close. But if Morwen risked setting the meeting in front of Alva, it must be important.

Morwen returns to my vanity without a word and begins lining my eyes with brown coal, highlighting their slightly upturned shape. My brother used to say I had fox eyes. He'd claim it was because of their amber shade, but secretly, I think it had more to do with how mischievous I was.

To finish me off, they dust my face and body with a shimmery powder that makes my skin appear smooth and poreless. The king expects his pet to appear a certain way: deadly but beautiful.

He wants everyone to covet what only he has tasted.

The entire process takes less than half an hour, but by the time I thank my lady's maids and open my door, Kaldar is fuming. My teeth sink into my bottom lip, hiding the smirk forming there. The girls return to their other duties as Kaldar trails behind me through the halls.

"I don't need an escort," I remind him. "It's not as if I don't know the way."

"That's not for you to decide," he mumbles at my back.

The king always changes the rules, ensuring they can never be predicted. Some mornings, he wants to be by himself, and my presence is unwelcome. Other mornings, he demands I join him. Apparently, my ability to walk around unchaperoned is also subject to change without warning.

I glance over my shoulder, hating the sight of the advisors smug face. I comfort myself with the knowledge that I could gut him before he even has a chance to unsheathe the little dagger at his waist. Perhaps someday wishful thinking will lead to reality. Hope blossoms at the thought.

Kaldar's expression morphs into a scowl. "Stop looking at me like that."

I raise my eyebrows, my face becoming a mask of confused innocence. "Like what?"

He grunts, shifting his attention. I turn away from him once more, smiling to myself as I imagine the sounds he will make when he dies by my hand.

Men such as Kaldar are all the same. At first, they're overly confident in their inherit superiority, but once you have them unarmed and at your mercy, they beg. They cry and plead, so unused to being on their knees for anyone, so shocked to be facing real consequences for their actions.

After all, exceptions must be made for people of superior birth.

When we arrive at the king's breakfast chamber, I wait for his private guards, Doral and Huxley, to let me in. Even as his favored, who has been summoned to him, I am not permitted to walk inside unannounced. When the doors open and I'm ushered inside, I don't bother glancing back at Kaldar.

The king's breakfast room is lavish and bright. It's connected to his bedchamber, offering it an air of intimacy. Morning light gleams through the open balcony doors, giving us a view of the ocean below. Paintings of quaint country landscapes hang on the walls, and bouquets of fresh flowers sit on every surface. The cheerful yellow wallpaper mixed with the warmth of the wooden furniture paints an inviting picture. It's meant to draw you in, to make you feel safe and welcome. Make you feel at home.

But it's all a lie.

"Iverson."

Baylor rises from his seat at the head of the table, coming to greet me with a fond smile. I offer him a deep curtsy, silently hating how familiar my name sounds on his tongue, as if he's far too used to saying it.

His straight, pale blond hair hits right above his shoulders, barely brushing his gold dolman. Proud, pointed ears poke out between the strands, on display for everyone. And a gilded crown adorns his forehead, marking him as the king, in case anyone was unaware.

While he's never shared exactly how old he is, I know he's seen centuries come and go, yet his face shows no evidence of it. Based on his complexion, I'd guess he stopped aging somewhere around his late twenties. Like all fae, he has been blessed with the eternal beauty of youth. As a child, that beauty used to dazzle me. Now I struggle to find even a single thing to admire about him.

Baylor—the Beast of Battle, the King of the Seventh Isle, and my biggest regret.

He kisses me thoroughly, his tongue invading my mouth to taste what belongs to him. His possessive hand grips my arm, while the other paws my backside. I lean into him, forcing myself not to recoil from his touch. A soft hum rises in my throat, a noise that says I have craved this as much as him.

When he pulls back, there's a covetous gleam in his dark blue eyes as they settle on the low neckline of my gown. "I've missed you, pet."

"Me too," I lie, falling into my role effortlessly. It's an easy part to play, especially since it wasn't always an act.

"Damn these preparations for keeping us apart." He pulls me closer, his nose nuzzling my cheek. "I'm going mad without you."

I give him a patient smile, pretending I don't find his proximity nauseating. "I cannot always be your main concern."

I've relished his distraction these last few months as he's been working tirelessly to prepare for his twenty-fifth anniversary as king of the Seventh Isle. The rulers of the other Verran Isles have been invited to attend a ball in Baylor's honor, though it's doubtful that all of them will join us.

"Have you heard back from any of the other monarchs?" I ask, careful not to call them what they actually are.

Unlike Baylor, the other seven rulers are Gods. They didn't have to fight a bloody battle to conquer their thrones. They were chosen by the Fates, and their realms belong to them by birthright. A fact he is incredibly sensitive about.

Selim, the God of Accords, and Cassandra, the Goddess of Divination, have already confirmed their attendance. Selim rarely misses an opportunity to strengthen his bonds with the other realms. But Cassandra hasn't attended an event since Maebyn, the Goddess of Illusion and the former ruler of the Seventh Isle, disappeared a quarter of a century ago. Since the two were extremely close, her decision to attend Baylor's anniversary ball surprised everyone. Secretly, I wonder if perhaps one of her famous visions was responsible for her change of heart.

"Kerys, Alastair, and Atreus have declined," he complains. The Goddess of Love and Hate, the God of Chaos, and the God of War.

Not surprising since they would have to travel the furthest. "I'm still waiting to hear from Eyrkan and Killian."

"I'm sure they will reply to you soon," I lie.

Eyrkan, the God of Life, is the self-appointed leader of the Gods and likely thinks attending Baylor's party is beneath him. His refusal to respond is petty, but expected.

Killian is different, though. The God of Death is famous for turning down every invitation he receives. All the Gods are known for being secretive, but none so much as Death. Since ascending into Godhood ten years ago, he has remained incredibly private and little is known about him.

Baylor smiles, leaning in to give me another quick kiss before helping me into the cushioned chair to the right of his—a place of honor. These kinds of small gestures are well rehearsed, designed to make me feel special. Important. *Favored.*

Fresh berries, pastries, scrambled eggs, ham, and roasted potatoes make up our meal. The smell of garlic and rosemary brings my appetite to life, but it sours immediately when my gaze snags on the porcelain plate before me. A rim of cornflower blue hugs the inner edge with a sweet dusting of lilac flowers adorning it.

I'd recognize it anywhere.

The late queen was fond of her wedding porcelain, only bringing it out for special occasions. When I was a child, before our relationship soured, she'd use it during private lunches for the two of us. I once asked her what made it special, and she told me it was a gift, hand-painted by the person she loved most in the world.

For the past year, the king has been determined to erase every memory of her from these halls. Only small pieces of Leona have slipped past his notice—the last vestiges of his late wife.

Heat prickles behind my eyes as a lump forms in my throat. Guilt and shame war for dominance in my gut. I take a sip of water, forcing myself to choke down the unexpected emotion. Glancing at Baylor seated on my left, I find him staring at me, and I struggle not to flinch at the obvious lust in his gaze.

"It's decided." He shakes his head with determination. "My advisers can handle the preparations on their own. I want to spend the next few days holed up in my chambers with you."

"No," I say too quickly, still distracted by the stupid plate. His eyes sharpen, and I hurry to amend myself. "I wouldn't want to be the reason your celebration doesn't go as planned. It's such an important night for the whole realm."

Placing my hand on his, I let the emotion from before simmer in my eyes as I offer him a brave smile. I force all my best lies into the gesture. *I am being vulnerable with you. I put your needs first. You can trust me.*

I glance down as if this is difficult for me. As if these words are self-sacrificing and I am searching for the courage to speak them. "You deserve to enjoy it without having to worry about me."

I give him a brave smile that doesn't quite reach my eyes. He scrutinizes me for several moments before reaching out to cup my cheek, wiping a wayward tear with his thumb. As I gaze up at him with eyes full of love, something in my stomach burns, but I ignore it.

I feel nothing.

"Ah, my pet. You're always so sweet."

I send silent prayers to the Fates that his words are sincere as he returns his focus to the meal.

"Tell me, how was last night's outing?" he asks, nibbling at a strawberry. My eyes track a drop of juice that drips down his chin. "Were you successful?"

For a brief moment, I panic, thinking he's asking me about my time at Darrow's shop before I recall the unpleasant task he assigned me prior to that.

"It's done," I assure him. "Lord Ando Varish admitted to speaking treasonous lies against the crown." A falsehood he confessed to under extreme duress, and only to make the pain stop.

Last month, Lady Varish gave birth to the couple's first child, a baby girl with round ears. A mortal. This was extremely concerning, given the fact that both Lord and Lady Varish are high fae. Ando loudly proclaimed this was the result of Baylor's reign. Yet another punishment from the Fates for the Goddess's absence. He's not the first to make such a claim.

It started slowly. A few bad harvests, intense storms, lower birth rates. But in recent years, the crops have barely sustained us. Baylor has been attempting to make trade agreements with the other Isles, hoping to buy time. Building these alliances is part of why his anniversary ball is so important. Time is running out for him to find a solution.

The storms have become more violent too. Six months ago, a thirty-foot wave crashed into a village in the north, decimating their community. All over the Isle, sunny days now turn into hurricanes at only a moment's notice.

"Lord Varish admitted to cutting the child's ears himself to make them appear round," I tell him, the words tasting bitter on my tongue. "He wanted to destabilize your reign and gain power amongst your critics, but I executed Lord Varish, as you requested."

Requested is such a polite word. It implies choice, a kindness the king didn't give me. When Baylor places his hand on the collar, the enchantment upon it is activated. Any direct order he gives me must be obeyed, or the collar will be triggered.

But Baylor has grown complacent with me. He isn't careful with his word choice, leaving room for small acts of defiance. Like when I told Ando his pain would end if he admitted his claims were untrue, even if they weren't. Offering him the only gift I had the power to grant, I promised him I would protect his wife and child, making sure they weren't implicated in his treason.

"Lady Varish had no knowledge of the scheme," I assure the king sincerely. "She and her child were victims of his insanity."

Baylor nods thoughtfully. "Did he put up a fight?"

I shake my head.

"Then how do you explain this?" He gestures to my hand resting on the table, staring at my ruined nails, broken and jagged from digging into Darrow's hardwood floors.

My heart stutters, but I force myself not to react to the slip up. I've talked my way out of worse.

"He struggled a bit," I clarify, letting my gaze fall to my lap as if I'm embarrassed. "But it was nothing I couldn't handle."

He watches me silently for several moments as he weighs my words.

"You'll spend extra time training with Remard this week," he commands. "I won't see your skills grow rusty."

I nod, not wanting to fight him on this. Training is one of the few joys I have. "I'll let Remy know."

"Remy, is it now?" He wiggles his eyebrows at me. "And should I be jealous of how familiar you are with the captain of my guard?"

"You have no reason to worry about *Remard*." I use his full name, playfully rolling my eyes at the tired joke. Remy is an objectively handsome man. Tall and muscular with tan skin and close-cut chestnut hair. His warm honey-brown eyes are full of life, unlike Baylor's. But the king knows that Remy practically raised me, thereby making the idea of seeing him in a sexual light disgusting and absurd.

"I want no one but you." The lie sends a wave of nausea through my stomach.

Pale blue eyes and dark hair flash through my mind, reminding me of my strange reaction to the reaper. Physically, he's the most attractive man I've ever seen. But perhaps all reapers are beautiful. Maybe that was how they tempted the souls of the recently deceased to follow them to the afterlife?

Footsteps approach and I glance up to find Kaldar entering the room holding a stack of papers. His stringy black hair is tucked behind his ears as he dips his chin toward the king.

"My apologies, Your Majesty," he says. "But I have your morning report."

"Ah, business. The great bore of my life." Baylor sighs, waving

Kaldar forward. "What matters need tending to in my kingdom today?"

Kaldar hands him the stack, making sure to stand in-between us, cutting me out. I take a sip of my tea, rolling my eyes at his obvious tactics. As Baylor flips through the pages, I turn my attention to my breakfast, forcing myself to eat despite my uneasy stomach. Kaldar drones on about training schedules for new guards, a property dispute between two lords, and some issue with a vendor for Baylor's anniversary ball.

"And, Your Majesty" —Kaldar pauses, his gaze flitting my way to ensure I'm paying attention— "Lady Bridgid requested to meet with you today for a *tasting* to finalize the desserts."

Based on his tone, it's clear dessert isn't the only thing on the menu. Kaldar has been pushing his niece toward the king for some time. Enlisting Bridgid to help with the ball is merely another desperate attempt to capture Baylor's attention. Though judging by the self-satisfied smirk on the adviser's face, it might finally be working.

Baylor's eyes flash crimson as his gaze narrows on Kaldar, a small glimpse of the terrifying beast he hides within. Baylor isn't like me or Darrow. His type of illusion magic is called *vertere*. There are some *vertere* who can change their features, making themselves more beautiful or even stealing the face of someone they know. Others can take on the form of an animal, such as a bird or fox. But Baylor is different. He shifts into a monster... a beast.

Shivers trail down my spine, and a dull ache builds at my temples. I've only seen him fully transition into that form once, but it was enough to ensure I never want to see it again. Whenever he's truly angry, he'll give us a small peek behind the curtain at what hides inside of him. A terrifying reminder of what could rise to the surface at any moment.

"Anything else?" Baylor demands, his tone icy.

Kaldar shakes his head and the king's focus shifts to me. His blood-colored eyes scrutinize my face, searching for any sign that I understood the implication behind Kaldar's words. Ignoring them both, I pretend to be oblivious while I focus on my breakfast. If Baylor is having an affair, I need to be cautious in how I handle it.

There was a time when I would have been seething with jealousy at the mere thought of Baylor with another woman, but those feelings have long passed. When he first began pursuing me, he made a big show of getting rid of his other mistresses. Even before we became intimate, he made it clear to me I was the only one he wanted. It made me feel treasured and important, reinforcing that what we had was different.

Special.

"Yes, sire." Kaldar's voice takes on a nervous quality. "There is also the matter of the Angel of Mercy."

Baylor goes still. "You'd better be here to tell me we have him in custody."

For the past several months, a killer known as the Angel of Mercy has been carrying out their own vigilante justice all over the city. The victims have virtually nothing in common except for rumors of their abusive nature. Each one of them was suspected of harming their loved ones, but no proof was ever found.

"Unfortunately, not." Kaldar lowers his eyes. "There have been no updates on the murderer's whereabouts."

Pretending not to notice Baylor's rising temper, I reach for my table knife and scoop some strawberry jam from the dish in front of me, smearing it on my toast.

"You still don't have any leads on that?" I ask innocently before taking a bite.

"No." Kaldar's gaze flashes toward me, simmering with hatred. The way he clenches his fists makes it clear he'd rather be using them on me.

"Six murders and not a single witness or lead," the king seethes, pushing his plate aside. "It's ridiculous. I'm meant to be hosting a ball in two weeks, yet I'm having to take time out of my schedule to deal with these incompetent fools who can't even catch one random criminal."

"If it would make you feel better, I can look into it for you?" I offer. "That way you can focus on preparing for the celebration."

His eyes soften, shifting back to their usual deep blue as his temper wanes, and an indulgent smile curls his lips.

"That won't be necessary," Kaldar interjects, shaking his head forcefully. "I have this investigation perfectly under control, sire."

"I'll decide what's necessary." Baylor sends a warning glance to his adviser before returning his attention to me. "Thank you, pet. But this matter is far beneath you. A waste of your talents."

I beam up at him, preening from the compliment like a good little pet. As he leans in to kiss my hand, I catch Kaldar's fuming face turning red with a mix of humiliation and fury.

Without glancing at him, Baylor waves his hand dismissively. "Go do something useful with your time."

Kaldar's body is rigid as he storms out the door, sending me a dark glare before exiting. I pop a blueberry in my mouth to stop the amusement threating to show on my face.

"You know he resents when you reprimand him in front of me?" I remind the king, always trying to drive a wedge between the two of them. The Fates know Kaldar is trying to do the same to me.

"He has a propensity for arrogance," Baylor says, spearing a potato wedge on his fork and lifting it to his mouth. "He needs to be reminded of his place every now and then."

I raise a brow. "Not letting him get ideas above his station?"

"Exactly." Baylor throws me a conspiratorial glance.

"Vicious, my king."

"And you're not?" He leans across the table, getting closer to me. "Tell me, what would you do with this so-called angel if you found him? Would my *wraith* show mercy?"

"Never." I promise him, telling the truth for once. "For the guilty, I will deliver only death."

CHAPTER

FOUR

Foot traffic is heavy in the Midgarden district this morning, making it almost impossible to walk down the street as a *wraith*. After being bumped so many times I nearly fell into the path of an oncoming carriage, I was forced to become visible, relying on only a hooded cloak for disguise. Thankfully, my conspicuous attire won't attract much attention from the crowd. With dark clouds settling overhead, almost everyone is bundled up as we prepare for yet another dreary day.

"What's the rush, my lady?" a seductive voice croons as a pale hand reaches from my peripheral, attempting to grab my arm.

Before he can make contact, my own hand darts out, snagging his wrist in an iron grip. I push him backward, sending him stumbling into the brick wall of the shop behind him. Pedestrians scurry past us, only a few of them sneaking wary glances in our direction. No one intervenes. If Solmarian's excel at one thing, it's minding their own business.

The man raises his hands in a placating gesture, offering me a sheepish grin. He's attractive in an artistic way, with high cheekbones and a nose so thin and straight that I'm sure one sharp hit would shatter it completely. My fist curls in anticipation.

"I was simply going to invite you inside." He gestures to the building behind him. "Don't you wish to see whatever your heart desires?"

A frisson of unease unfurls within me as I notice the blacked out windows that reveal nothing about the business within. There's no sign hanging above the door, but based on what he asked me, it doesn't take a genius to guess what he's selling.

"Careful where you put your hands, *mendax*," I warn him.

Mendax are the most common type of *Illusionists*. While most of them are only capable of creating simple illusions, some have the ability to fabricate large-scale mirages that can leave you questioning reality. For a steep price, they'll let you spend an hour living out your wildest fantasies, all within the safety of your own mind.

It's bold of him to openly proposition people on the street. While it's not technically illegal for a *mendax* to sell their services, they are prohibited from soliciting. Given the controversial nature of their talents, their customers must seek them out of their own free will. If the city guards catch him trying to lure pedestrians into his shop, they won't hesitate to arrest him.

"Come now, lovely lady." His eyes gleam as they stare into mine, as if he's trying to peer inside my soul. "Surely you desire something…" He trails off, taking a step closer as his gaze turns heated. "Or *someone*?"

Before I can respond, a mortal man stumbles out of the shop, his face ashen. His horrified eyes settle on the *mendax* as he shuffles toward him.

"You have to send me back," he demands, pointing at the *Illusionist* beside me.

"Now, Mr. Saunders." The *mendax* tsks, forgetting about me as he prowls toward his victim. "I don't *have* to do anything."

The man's face crumbles as tears stream down his cheeks. He

doesn't even glance in my direction, as if the rest of the world is irrelevant to him now.

"Please," he begs, his voice full of anguish. "Send me back to my little girl. I was just with her, holding her in my arms again. She was healthy and *alive*." His voice cracks. "I have to go back to her."

The *mendax* wraps his arms around the man's shoulders, pulling him to his side.

"And you will, Mr. Saunders. First we need to settle the matter of payment. I gave you a discount the first time, but now I'm afraid you'll have to pay full price."

"I'll pay!" The man nods frantically as he digs into his pockets to pull out a few measly coins. "I'll give you anything you want if you'll send me back to my baby."

A sickening smile curls the *mendax's* lips. "That's what I love to hear."

He leads the man back through the door, glancing back at me once more before they disappear into the dim shop.

"Coming?" he asks, one brow arched.

Offering him a sneer, I take off down the street and ignore the slight temptation that blooms in my stomach. There's a reason *mendax* have a bad reputation. What they do can be addictive. Many of their customers waste away, spending every bit of coin they earn on another illusion.

Imagine escaping all your problems and living in a world where you have everything you've ever wanted. Your loved ones who've passed on are returned to you. Your biggest regrets are wiped away. Whatever you desire is yours for the taking. But then you wake up in the real world, and everything has gone back to the way it was before.

That crushing disappointment is exactly why I never partake in it. I know once I start, I'll never stop.

My calf aches as I push down the busy street. I would have preferred to let the wound fully heal before traipsing through the city, but unfortunately, this couldn't wait. I pull my cloak tighter, keeping my chin tucked as I pass two patrolling guards.

Suddenly, the contents of my satchel feel much heavier.

Distracted, I almost stumble into a group of people waiting outside Bryne's Bakery. The mouthwatering scent of their famous chocolate-filled pastries wafts through the air, bringing a smile to my face. Morwen's fiancé, Nolan, owns the bakery with his family. He often sends her to work with treats for me and Alva.

As much as I love their delicious creations, I've never actually been inside the bakery. There's only one reason I come to this part of town, and I try to remain unseen while I'm here. If any of their customers recognized me, they might be able to notice a pattern in the timing of my visits, sparking unwanted connections to certain illicit activities.

Slipping past the crowd, I duck into a narrow passage and hurry down the L shaped path. By happy coincidence, Bryne's Bakery shares a back alleyway with another business one block over.

MASQ, situated on the Midgarden side of Aogan's Cove, is one of the most successful clubs in Solmare. It's mostly empty this early in the day, but I still wouldn't risk entering through the front. Steel is cold against my fist as I deliver exactly six sharp knocks before slamming my open palm against the door. It's a simple code, but we've found it effective.

Only a few seconds pass before I hear muffled shuffling, followed by several dull thuds as someone unlatches various locks and deadbolts. When the door swings open, a stunning woman with warm brown skin stands on the other side.

"Come in," Della orders. "Quickly."

Her eyes scan the alley behind me as I slip past her into the large kitchen. Once she's sure I haven't been followed, she immediately closes the door behind me, her hands deftly moving over the locks to seal it shut. Releasing my illusion, I lower my hood and use my fingers to comb through my hair and smooth the wayward tresses. I don't bother to remove my cloak since I won't be staying long.

"I got your message."

"Obviously," she says, her tone blunt. "I didn't think you were stopping by for a chat. But you're late."

I roll my eyes, unbothered by her rudeness. Della has a right to her resentment.

"I was detained," I tell her.

Huffing at my vague explanation, she turns without another word and exits through a long hallway on the other side of the room. Used to this kind of behavior, I follow without complaint. She may be annoyed by my tardiness, but if I told her the real reason for it, she'd be furious. The mere mention of Baylor gets her hackles rising.

As she walks, her dark curls bounce against her lilac dress. For such a stern woman, her appearance is the complete opposite. Standing at only five feet and two inches, even with shoes on, she barely reaches my shoulder. Her big doe eyes radiate innocence, despite the fact that she's anything but.

Dellaphine Cardot is a walking contradiction.

"We need to make this quick," she tells me as we reach the door to her office. "I've got guests upstairs who will be waking soon, and it's best they don't see you."

Overnight guests aren't rare at MASQ. There are over a dozen guest rooms on the second and third floors, each available for a fee. While most guests pay by the hour, some prefer to spend the night.

"It must be important if Morwen risked giving me the signal in front of a witness," I probe, curious what this meeting is about. "Alva could have seen her."

My sweet mortal maid has no idea about any of this. And it needs to stay that way.

"It's time sensitive," Della says, offering no further explanation.

The front rooms at MASQ are styled in a sinful, dramatic aesthetic, but back here in Della's private quarters, the decor is soft and feminine. The warm glow of the fireplace casts an inviting warmth onto the cream settee. I notice that there's a fresh canvas on the easel next to the window and a few stained brushes laid out beside it.

Like always, my gaze is drawn to the painting that hangs behind her desk, featuring a dark-haired woman coyly glancing over her shoulder. Only half her face is visible, a sly smirk curling her lips while her eyes are cast down. There's something haunting about the image, something that makes you want to lift her chin and see her full visage for yourself.

But I don't need a portrait to remind me of what she looked like; her face is seared into my mind with perfect clarity.

I push those thoughts away as I settle on the sofa while Della heads for the desk in the corner. She lifts the silver key that hangs around her neck, using it to unlock one of the drawers. Thunder rumbles in the distance as she pulls out a piece of paper before relocking it.

"It's good to see you're alive," she says as she sits down next to me.

Six white candles burn on the candelabra before us, while a lonely maroon one sits in the center unlit. Della reaches for it, lighting it on one of the open flames. Instead of placing it back where it belongs, she holds it in her hand, letting the hot wax trickle down the sides and drip over her fingers like blood. If it burns her skin, she doesn't show any reaction.

"Was there cause for concern?" I ask.

She shrugs, but her eyes dance with secret knowledge. "One of our patrons thought so."

It's not hard to guess who she's referring to.

I recognize the candle she's holding as one of Darrow's creations. As long as the wick burns, anyone touching it can't be overheard. You could be shouting across a crowded room, yet no one would hear you except your intended audience.

This is where he ran off to last night?

"Do me a favor, let him go on thinking that." I grin at the thought of his distress.

"Always one for the dramatics." She rolls her eyes, handing me the note she took from her desk.

Unfolding the parchment, I quickly scan the first few lines to find the name of a familiar pub I frequent in the Dockside District. But as I read what's underneath, my blood begins to boil within my veins.

"I've got people working on the girl already," she tells me. "But I'm leaving the father to you."

"It will be handled before sunrise," I promise her.

I don't bother asking if she's double-checked the information. Della always authenticates her leads before giving them to me.

She nods, taking the paper and tossing it into the fire. She blows out the candle, signaling the conclusion of our business. A faint trail of smoke dissipates into the air while I work up the courage to give her what I brought.

Usually, I don't linger once she's relayed her information. The less time I spend here, the better. It would cause problems for me if our association got back to the king. Given the rumors that used to swirl through the city, he's always had a certain distaste for Della. I should already be on my way out the door, but today is different.

"I have something for you."

I barely hear my whispered confession over the sound of rain gently pattering against the window, such soft accompaniment to such a heavy scene.

Della narrows her eyes, appraising my strange behavior. Unable to bear her gaze, I pull the contraband from my satchel, desperate to rid myself of the terrible memories it carries. She takes it hesitantly, as if it will explode in her hands.

Her mouth falls open with a gasp as she unwraps the parcel, revealing the porcelain plates I stole from the palace earlier. Her body goes limp with shock, causing the plates to nearly tumble from her lap. I lean forward to help, but she pulls them close to her chest, shoulders curling inward in a protective stance.

"Don't," she whispers sharply.

My calf twinges as I rise from the sofa, but I relish the pain as I put space between us. Della gazes down at the plates reverently. Her fingers tremble as she softly brushes them against the painted lilacs, as if she can feel their petals against her skin. Is she remembering how much her lover treasured the gift?

"How?" Her voice is small, barely audible.

"Someone in the kitchens must have thought they belonged to the palace by mistake," I explain, my voice small. "They were on Baylor's breakfast table this morning. He didn't recognize them."

She looks up at me, her expression darkening the way it always does when someone mentions the king.

"But you did?" Pain and accusation are heavy in her tone.

She carefully sets the plates down on her desk before moving to the back wall and lifting the portrait with care, placing it on the desk. I notice her gaze lingering on the face of her lost lover before she tears herself away.

With the painting gone, a hidden safe has been revealed in its place. Taking a knife from her boot, she lightly pricks her finger and smears her own blood against the metal. There's a dull thud as it unlocks and swings open.

Inside is a teacup, the same pattern as the plates I've just given her, as well as a few pieces of jewelry, folded garments, drawings, letters, and a bottle of perfume.

All belonging to the late queen.

Della's hands shake as she places the plates inside. Taking a step back, she gazes upon her shrine to Leona. She makes no move to wipe the tears that run down her face, unashamed of this physical display of her pain.

Della's grief is a palpable presence, one she holds onto with both hands. Sometimes we curate our own hauntings, desperately crafting ghosts from faded memories as we beg our dear ones not to depart. As if our desperation alone could pull them back from the veil.

Deep within the dungeons of my mind, a ghostly scene slips through the cracks of its cell.

Would you do anything for me?

A shiver skates up my spine as I recall the way his lips brushed against my ear that night.

Of course, I would.

A foolish response from a foolish girl.

A flash of pain pulls me from my silent reverie. Uncurling my fists, I find my nails have left a row of crescent-shaped cuts marring my palms. I wipe them on my cloak, the wool roughly pulling at the torn skin. Grabbing my now empty satchel, I hug it against my chest, its weight somehow heavier than before.

"I'm sorry," I whisper.

Not bothering to wait for a response, I flee from the room, undoing the locks with haste. I don't stop sprinting until I reach the alley where I lean my head against the brick wall, gasping for air. Shame burns hot in my stomach as I throw the bag to the ground, along with my cloak. The skies open up, soaking my silk dress quickly and cooling my heated skin. My broken fingernails dig into the bricks as I frantically try not to slip away into the past again.

In the aftermath of Leona's death, I spent months caged within my own mind. Reliving the memories. Rewriting my perception of them. I don't have time to replay it all now.

Della gave me a name. A purpose, if only for a night.

Pressing my cheek harder against the wall, I rebuild the dungeon that houses the memories I can't face. I imagine myself filling the cracks, eliminating any chance of escape.

While Della and I are both the architects of our own hauntings, she welcomes her ghosts.

I imprison mine.

CHAPTER FIVE

As Lynal Skynner finishes his fourth ale of the night, I wonder if he has any idea that it will be his last. He isn't a particularly remarkable man. Dirty blond hair clings to his damp face, flushed red from the alcohol. Round ears mark him as mortal, but that's to be expected.

While the city isn't technically divided by species, it's generally known that high fae live in Highgrove, closest to the palace, while the half fae community has turned Midgarden into their artistic haven. Across the river in the Dockside District, commonly referred to as "the Lowers," mortals such as Lynal have carved out lives for themselves.

I recognize him as a regular, but I've never taken much notice of him before tonight. He was just another drunk making a fool of himself, not a unique signifier around here.

He's surrounded by a group of similarly useless men, all taking up one of the high-top tables near the bar. Lynal appears harmless enough, generous with his smiles and laughter. Tonight, he's being generous with his coin too, which is unusual for anyone around here.

"This should cover our tab tonight," he brags, making a big show of handing his silver coin to the waitress. "Drinks are on me tonight, lads."

He blushes as his friends pat him on the back, all cheering at their good luck. But around the room, covetous eyes watch the transaction closely. It's risky to show silver in a district where everyone pays with copper, but Lynal is no doubt feeling invincible after the deal he brokered this afternoon.

Looking at the man now, most people would never guess what he's capable of. But over the past year, I've learned that even the most innocent face can hide a myriad of sins.

And after all, Della is never wrong.

I've spent the last few hours cloaked in an illusion, sitting at an empty table in the back corner of the pub. In my line of work, there's a lot of waiting. The constant quiet before the brief storm.

But as the babble of the crowd washes over me tonight, I don't mind being patient. I enjoy coming to this pub for a reason. Sometimes the silence in my room at the palace eats away at me. The quiet burrows under my skin, stretching it tight until a single sound might snap me in half. But in a place like this, the noise never ends.

My corner is dark and far from the bar. It offers me privacy since most people prefer to remain near the action.

Except Calum.

The elderly gentleman comes here almost every night and always sits in the same spot, drinking the same ale. I've followed him home a few times to ensure he makes it there. He's gruff, and sometimes his mind strays from the present, but I appreciate how genuine he is.

Lynal and his companions throw their heads back in an uproar, laughing at a crude comment one of them made about the barmaid. Judging by the number of drinks he's consumed within the past hour, it shouldn't be much longer now until I can make my move.

"Keep it down, lads," Calum grumbles, the rich dialect of the northern villages decorating his words. "Yer not as funny as ya think ya are."

"Shut up, you old drunk," Lynal shouts from across the pub, spit permeating each word. "Before I make you."

"Just like yer humor, yer threats leave much to be desired," Calum calls back, shaking his head. "Nothing but empty words from an empty mind."

The men at Lynal's table freeze, all of them waiting to see how their ringleader will respond to the insult. The man to his right, whose name I'm pretty sure is Taron, leans closer.

"You're not going to let him speak to you that way, are you?" he asks, his brows raised.

Lynal's face hardens as he slams his ale down, causing several drops to splash onto the table as he stands up. "Not a chance."

My shoulders stiffen as Lynal makes his way to our corner of the bar. A few of the other patrons shoot apprehensive glances in Calum's direction, but none of them attempt to intervene.

"Why don't you piss off, you old drunk." Lynal glowers as he places his hands on Calum's table, looming over him in a domineering position. "Go back to talking to the wall like you usually do."

The sight of Calum's tan face flushing red has me reaching for one of my blades.

"Or you could do us all a favor and die already," Lynal continues, whispering so low I can barely hear him. "Save us the trouble of listening to you ramble?"

I grip the pommel of my sword tightly as he leans closer. If Lynal touches him I'll end his life here and now—damn the consequences.

The older mortal meet's Lynal's cool stare with one of his own.

"You first," Calum challenges.

Fury detonates across Lynal's face, and for a moment, I think he's truly going to try something, but just as quickly as it appeared, his rage is replaced by smug condescension.

"I doubt that will happen." He laughs as he turns around and rejoins his friends. "You've got one foot in the grave already, old man."

Taron, the one who spoke earlier, pats his friend on the back as he returns to their table. The others cheer, pushing drinks and compliments in Lynal's direction. Calum grumbles quietly, returning his attention to the foamy ale in front of him. Releasing my weapon, I drop my hands to my lap, wishing I could wrap them around Lynal's throat instead.

Patience, I remind myself. He'll get what's coming to him soon enough.

As the men continue laughing, a familiar sensation has the hairs on the back of my neck standing on end. There's a palpable shift in the room as the atmosphere becomes heavier. I glance around at the patrons, but they don't seem to notice. Is it because they've dulled their senses past the point of caution, or is there some other reason why only *I* can feel this?

My eyes shoot toward the door a moment before *he* enters.

Reaper.

His wings and shadows are nowhere to be seen, but he's no less menacing without them. Another thing that's missing is the stubble that hugged his cheeks. It seems he's shaved since I saw him last night. Silver flashes beneath his heavy cloak, drawing my attention to what is most likely a weapon. Though why he bothered to bring one, I can't say. Perhaps he's going for subtlety. Those shadows would surely spark hysteria if he whipped them out in here. But that would be nothing compared to what would happen if he summoned his scythe.

Before the Novian war, reapers would go around spearing souls on their scythes and ferrying them to their final resting place. But when the first Gods rose to power and created the veils, reapers became obsolete. Now, when a soul leaves its body, it feels an undeniable pull to the closest veil. Clara, my old governess, used to warn me to stay away from them.

Never pass through a lonely stone archway, love. For that way lies only death with no return.

It's commonly believed that no one has seen a reaper in nearly five thousand years. There are whispers that they still exist, living in seclusion deep within the mountains of Death's realm. After what I saw last night, I can now confirm that these rumors are at least partially true.

Now that he's entered the pub, the conversations dissolve into silence as everyone turns to behold the stranger.

Lynal and his friends stare at the reaper with varying degrees of awe and fear. Patrons who were standing near the door scurry in the opposite direction. The barkeep, Sam, glances up with a smile, ready to greet his new customer, but it slides right off his face as his mouth falls open in shock. An empty glass slips from his hand, crashing against the ground.

The sound seems to restart time, and everyone slowly begins to pick up their conversations again. Although they're far less boisterous than before. I doubt any of them can tell what the reaper is, but they sense something unsettling about him.

His dark hair is pushed back again, giving me a clear view of his narrowed eyes as they scan the room. Even in the dim light of this dingy pub, he's heartbreakingly beautiful. I spot a few women sneaking appreciative glances, no doubt debating the danger of approaching him.

The corners of his mouth curve as his gaze settles on my chair, and my heart gallops as he walks this way. Yet again, he has no trouble sensing me despite my invisibility. Him showing up at the same pub I've been staking out all night can't be a coincidence.

He's here for me.

The reaper ignores the rest of the patrons as he strolls past them and slides into the chair across from mine, arrogantly turning his back on everyone else. That's either bold or foolish. Alcohol tends to make men brave, giving them the courage to pick fights they have no business starting. My pulse spikes as I notice a few hostile stares gazing in our direction. I can't afford to get caught up in whatever game the reaper's playing tonight.

"Aren't you going to say hi?" He doesn't bother lowering his voice.

Calum glances up, turning to glare at the reaper with annoyance. "No, I had'na planned on it."

The reaper ignores him, keeping his gaze on me. "I'll sit here all night if that's what it takes."

The old man's head falls back as he releases a long sigh.

"Goddess spare me from the young," he grumbles before taking a long swig from his ale and twisting in his chair to face my new companion. "Hello, lad. How's yer evenin'?"

Foamy beer clings to his white mustache, causing me to bite down hard on the humor that threatens my foul mood. The reaper slowly turns his head toward the elderly mortal. His expression is cold, but I spot a flash of amusement in his eyes.

"Are ya happy with my greeting, since it apparently means so much to ya?" Calum demands.

"My apologies, sir," he responds evenly. "But I wasn't speaking to you."

Calum glances around our empty corner, his brows raised. "Who else would ya be talking to, lad?"

Without missing a beat, the reaper gestures in my direction. "Why, the beautiful woman across from me, of course."

I silently thank the Fates that no one can see the heat rising in my cheeks.

Calum eyes the seemingly empty seat before shrugging his shoulders with nonchalance. "Don't go thinking yer special, lad." He waves the reaper off before taking another gulp of ale. "She talks to me all the time."

His silvery blue gaze flickers in my direction as one corner of his mouth kicks up. "Does she now?"

Calum nods. "Always flirting with me, isn't she? I keep telling her it's no use. My heart will always belong to my Francie, Goddess rest her soul."

Leaning forward, I can't help myself from speaking up for the first time since I walked into the pub. "You can't blame a girl for chasing the most handsome man in the room."

His wrinkled cheeks blush instantly as a bashful smile plays at his lips.

"And that includes you, lad," Calum taunts the reaper. "She fancies me the most."

"So it would seem," my companion says, sitting back in his seat as he stretches an arm across the back of the booth beside him. His other hand pulls a few copper coins from his pocket and tosses them to elderly gentleman. "But I do need to speak with the lady privately, so why don't you go to the bar and get another round on me?"

Calum pockets the change. As if seeking my approval, he glances toward my side of the table, his rheumy gaze settling on a spot several inches to the left of my head.

"Go ahead." I keep my voice quiet, hoping not to draw any further attention.

Sparing one last glare in the reapers direction, he rises and makes his way to the bar. His steps are stable, but there's a frailty to his stature that betrays his age. Turning back to my companion, I find him staring at me with a strange expression. For someone who can't actually see me, he does a surprisingly good job of judging where my eyes are.

"What interesting friends you have." The hushed, intimate tone of his voice sends chills dancing across my arms. "I confess, I'm jealous. You've never commented on my good looks."

"Because you're hideous," I lie, crossing my arms as I lean back.

One hand moves to his chest in a scandalized fashion. "Is that any way to talk to an old friend?"

"We're not friends."

His pale eyes glimmer with suggestion. "I think last night makes us more than acquaintances."

My eyes narrow. "I threw a dagger at your face, and you decided to elevate me to friend instead of enemy?"

"Don't sell yourself short, my lady." A lazy grin pulls at his full lips. "You threw *four* daggers at my face."

"Pity none of them hit their target." My fingers move to the hilt of the sword I carry tonight, wondering how well he'd dodge a weapon of this size.

"You did draw blood, though." He leans forward, appearing genuinely impressed by this. "It's been years since anyone managed that. You should feel proud."

"And yet I feel patronized." I roll my eyes, catching sight of several other patrons who are watching the reaper with varying degrees of nervousness.

"Why are you following me?" I ask, taking charge of the conversation.

His head tilts. "Who says I am?"

"I'm not in the mood for games tonight."

"Good." He shrugs, sitting back again. "I don't play with cheaters."

"As your *friend*" —I instill every ounce of derision I can manage into the word— "I should probably point out that everyone in this room is staring at you. They think you're talking to an empty chair."

"How embarrassing," he says gravely. "Am I blushing?"

Frustration builds within me as my temper flares.

He rests his elbows on the table, leaning close enough for me to smell his bergamot scent as his voice turns soft, intimate. "If you're concerned about my reputation, you could always reveal yourself."

"You know, if you keep asking me to *reveal* myself," I whisper, "I'm going to take it the wrong way."

He bites his lip to stop a smile. "Then they'd really have a reason to stare."

The reaper's face is only inches away from mine, his breath floating against my cheek. I shoot back, realizing I'd leaned closer to him without meaning to. Swallowing thickly, I glance at the bar and freeze.

Lynal is gone.

CHAPTER SIX

My eyes frantically search the pub, but it's too late. Calf aching, I shoot up from the table, ignoring the reaper as I head for the back exit. Rushing through the narrow hallway, I squeeze past a couple who are locked in a passionate embrace against the wall.

Pushing the flimsy door open, I slip into a nearly pitch-black alleyway. The light from the streetlamps has flickered out, probably due to a lack of oil. It's not surprising since the king tends to skimp on those kinds of necessities in the Lowers. Tonight, the district must rely on only the glow of the moon to illuminate the darkness.

After spending the last several hours inside the stuffy pub, I welcome the brisk air despite the unpleasant smell. Lynal stands with his back to me, several feet away. He balances against the wall with one hand, leaning his head against the cool brick building. Based on the steady hissing sound of liquid hitting the ground, I can easily guess what he's doing.

The establishment has a lavatory, but there's something about alcohol that makes men long to empty their bladders outdoors. Lynal, like so many of his brethren before him, is partaking in this sacred male ritual. Not wanting to interrupt, I wait until he finishes and begins to lace up his breeches before I approach.

"Lynal," I whisper through the darkness.

"Who's there?" He whips around clumsily, impaired from the evening's activities.

Moving further down the dimly lit alley, I call his name again. "Lynal."

"Whoever's doing this, it's not funny," he slurs, his face turning red with anger.

His eyes widen as I release my illusion and step out of the shadows, into a pool of moonlight.

"Don't you want to play with me, Lynal?" I crook my finger, luring him deeper into the alley.

His gaze shifts over his shoulder, settling on the pub door that stands about ten feet behind him. For a moment, I worry he will do the smart thing and return inside. But when his head swings back to me and his lips pull into a slimy smile, I'm reminded that Lynal isn't very bright.

"Where did you come from?" he asks, swaying a few steps closer.

"I followed you. I've been watching you all evening," I confess, the shy tone of my voice at odds with the bold words. "Is that alright?"

"Depends on what you want, sugar." His gaze travels over my body. He can't see much underneath my cloak, but based on the way he's leering, I'm sure his imagination is filling in the gaps.

"I wanted to be alone with you."

It's not a lie—I prefer not to have witnesses. My fingers deftly remove my sword from its sheath, still keeping it hidden within the cloak. Because of its size and weight, it's not the most convenient weapon to carry around, but it's necessary for what I must do.

"It's my lucky night then." He rubs his palms together as he moves close enough for me to smell the stench of sweat and alcohol.

"No, Lynal." I shake my head. "I don't think it is."

As he reaches out to touch me, my sword cuts through the air, coming down on his wrist. His severed hand smacks against the ground with a wet thud, a pool of red forming around it. The metallic scent of his blood floats in the air, pushing me to make the final blow.

For a moment, there's silence. His eyes pinch in confusion as he stares at the bloody stump, his mind unable to process what's just happened. His gaze falls to the severed limb as understanding dawns, followed quickly by pain.

Lynal sinks to his knees, instinctively covering the gushing wound with his right hand to try to stop the bleeding. His mouth opens on a scream, but it fades into a shocked moan as I grab a fistful of his hair and force him to look at me.

"You will be dead in the next five minutes, Lynal." My sword rests against his throat. "If you try to scream again, I'll make them the most painful minutes of your life. Understand?"

He blinks rapidly as his mouth opens and closes, trying to form words.

"W-Why?" he manages to stutter.

Bending down, I rip free the coin purse tied around his belt, impressed by its weight.

"Heavy." I toss the bag up into the air and catch it. "But you should know better than to brag about silver in a place like this. It puts a target on your back."

"It's yours!" he offers, his eyes wide and pleading. "Take it!"

"I will, thank you." I smile at his generosity as I slip it into my pocket. "Tell me, Lynal, how did you acquire such a large sum?"

His gaze shifts back and forth, searching the alley for the right answer. "I found it."

"My, how lucky you are," I pause, bringing my free hand to my chin as my brow furrows. "Now, was that before or after you sold your daughter to a wealthy lord this afternoon?"

His eyes widen comically as he shakes his head back and forth. "No! No, I didn—"

"Don't lie to me, Lynal." The blade digs into his neck, nicking his flesh.

"Please, don't," he begs, his jaw quivering as he weeps.

"You might be interested to know that your daughter never made it to Lord Ruston's estate. Unfortunately, their carriage was intercepted by bandits," I tell him, leaving out the fact that those "bandits" work for Della. "You can't be too careful these days."

His face drains of what little color it has left.

"Mer-mercy," he pleads. "Please, have mercy."

My head tilts to the side, as I pat his ruddy cheek.

"This is mercy, Lynal. Just not for you."

A burst of fury blazes behind his eyes as he realizes I have no intention of letting him go.

"You filthy bitch!" he spits the words at me. "You whore! I will fucking kill—"

"Your five minutes are up," I say, cutting off his tirade as I swing my blade.

Twisting at the waist, I rely on the strength from my core to help me slice through his neck and tendons. His head tumbles across the ground, landing face up with his hateful eyes staring at the night sky. As always, I force myself to memorize his face. A small punishment for my crime. There's no use waiting for the guilt to overwhelm me. I know from experience that it won't.

Not that I don't have more than my fair share of remorse, I simply prefer to reserve it for my regrets.

Dipping a finger into the pool of warm blood, I drag it across the wall like paint. The swooping red letters create a haunting mural against the dark stone. Once I'm finished, I step back, admiring the message I've written.

One word.

Mercy.

"Impressive."

I jump as a deep voice cuts through the silence. Turning around, I raise my sword defensively, only to find the reaper watching me from the other end of the alley.

"Fuck off."

"I spoke too soon," he says blandly as he saunters toward me. "It seems your vocabulary is rudimentary at best."

Painting on a patient smile, I speak in my most saccharine tone. "Dearest Reaper, won't you please promptly vacate the vicinity? Or in other words, *fuck off.*"

"No, but thank you for asking so politely," he mimics my sweet tone, stopping only a few feet away.

I can hear my bones grinding against the pommel of my sword as I squeeze it in frustration. "Why won't you leave me alone?"

"It's dangerous to walk around this part of the city at night," he admonishes me.

I bring my sword up to his chest, letting the tip sit over his heart. Instead of stepping back, his gaze falls to the weapon with amusement.

"Is that why you continuously seek my company?" I ask. "Because you're afraid of the dark?"

His eyes widen innocently. "There's safety in numbers."

I arch a brow. "You just watched me kill a man."

"Eh." He shrugs, waving off my recent homicide. "Three's a crowd."

I apply slightly more pressure against his chest, causing a tiny bead of blood to appear on the tip of my blade. He catches it on his gloved finger before bringing it to his mouth and my lips part as I watch his tongue dart out, licking it away.

"Vicious," he chides.

"What do you want, Reaper?" I ask, my voice strangely breathless. "Why are you following me?" He opens his mouth to offer what will surely be another deflection, but I cut him off. "And don't say you aren't."

He sighs. "I need your help."

A laugh bursts from me at the simplicity of his answer. "I'm not interested."

"You know who would be interested?" Fire dances in his eyes, making him resemble a cat playing with its food. "King Baylor."

My amusement dies as I note the seriousness in his tone. Using two gloved fingers, he easily pushes my sword away from his chest and takes a few steps back.

"I bet he'd be extremely interested to learn about your activities tonight." His gaze flashes to Lynal's dead body before returning to me. "I imagine he doesn't know you're dismembering his citizens?"

I move one hand to my hip as I shrug my shoulders.

"What makes you think I'm not acting on his orders?" I bluff.

He gives me a flat look.

"You're saying this was a sanctioned kill?" He points to the messy crime scene. "See, I have a theory that the king's *wraith* has gone rogue. And I'd be willing to bet it's not the first time."

My breath catches at the implication in his words. "You have no proof."

"Charming little note you left behind." He gestures to the message I wrote on the wall. "Memorable. Should we go visit the king right now and ask him what he thinks of your penmanship?"

I scoff. He said that as if questioning a monarch is a simple matter. "You think you can simply walk into the palace and ask for an audience with the king?"

He nods. "I do, actually."

Taking off his right glove, he holds out his arm to show me a tattoo on his wrist. A single red rose engulfed in flames.

Death's sigil.

A triumphant gleam enters his eyes. "This tends to gain me entry to any court I wish."

Only those in the God of Death's most trusted circle bear the mark. Reaching for his hand, I try to get a closer glimpse at the intricate symbol, but he pulls away. I scowl at him as he puts his glove back on.

"I can't wait to see what the king does when he learns his trusted *wraith* is the infamous Angel of Mercy." He smiles wickedly.

The truth of his accusation is a gut punch. I know exactly what Baylor would do if he found out I was betraying him. Pushing those thoughts away, I search for something to turn the tide of this conversation.

"You're searching for the whisperer," I announce, wanting to shock him.

The smile slides off his face at the mention of the item he and Darrow were discussing.

"What do you know of it?" he demands.

Nothing, but I'm not telling him that. We stand in silence for several minutes before he releases a sigh, likely realizing I have no intention of answering him. His head cocks to the side as he observes me, the silence stretching on until he finally breaks it.

"I could use someone with your peculiar talents."

"Don't pretend you know anything about my talents, Reaper."

"I'd be interested in finding out." His eyes glimmer with challenge. "You appear to have a knack for remaining unseen."

"Is that what you're after?" I ask, putting the pieces together. "You want my help finding your weapon?"

He waves me off. "Weapon is such an ugly word."

"Then what would you call it?"

He rolls his lips, thinking for a moment before answering. "A unique object."

I laugh without humor. "I've had bad luck with men who abuse such objects."

He cocks his head, questions forming in his gaze as he studies me. "What if I swore to you that's not my intention?"

Discomfort blooms under his inspection, causing me to shift my weight back and forth. "In my experience, people only seek such objects for two reasons. To avenge an injustice. Or to commit one."

He takes a careful step closer. "And if I claimed the former?"

I lift my chin. "I'd remind you that no one is as honorable as they pretend to be."

"Including you?" he asks, his voice softer now as he snares my gaze with his own.

"Especially me," I admit.

His pupils dilate, the darkness nearly covering his blue irises completely. "What motivates you, then?"

"Guilt."

The word tumbles out before I can stop it. A far too honest answer to offer someone I don't trust.

I shake my head, retreating backwards. "It doesn't matter what you want with the object. I won't help you."

Disappointment flickers across his handsome features, and when he speaks again he sounds resigned. "Then I'll tell the king what you're up to."

"Do that and you ruin any chance of ever using my 'peculiar talents' to your advantage," I remind him.

"I guess we'll see." He nods. "Get home safe, my lady."

The reaper turns, his cloak billowing around him as he moves swiftly down the alley until the shadows swallow him whole. I stare after him for a moment, considering how likely he is to follow through on his threat. Did I make a powerful enemy tonight?

"What happened to your fear of the dark?" I mutter as I turn in the opposite direction.

"Your warm presence cured me of it." His gravelly voice drifts through the night, startling me.

I scowl into the darkness, considering what I've learned this evening as I let an illusion settle over my skin. The reaper works for the God of Death, and he's desperate enough for this whisperer to ask for my help stealing it. Whatever it is, it's important to the powers that be, which makes it something I'm now deeply interested in.

The sound of flapping wings follows me through the city as I make my way back to the palace. Just before I reach the gates, the reaper's amused voice reaches me once more.

"See you soon, *Angel*."

CHAPTER SEVEN

Darkness surrounds me.

"Fuck," I mutter.

My knee sinks into the soft training mat as I keel over from the pain in my abdomen. I anticipated the blow, but not where it would land.

"You could at least pull your punches." I wipe the sweat from my damp brow, careful not to disturb the strip of black fabric that sits over my eyes.

"And you could tell me why we're doing this," Remy's amused voice calls from somewhere on my right.

When I arrived at our sparring session today, I asked if Remy would teach me to fight while blindfolded. He found my request to be odd, especially when I wouldn't elaborate on why I wanted to start working on it immediately.

"But since you won't," Remy continues, "then neither will I."

My recent encounters with the reaper frightened me more than I'd care to admit. It's been one week since I last saw him, and in that time, I've admitted to myself that I most likely wouldn't have survived our first encounter without the help of my *eidolon*. Perhaps if I wasn't uncomfortable using her, I wouldn't have ended up running for my life with a self-inflicted stab wound.

Still, the idea of training with her has my palms sweating. I've kept this ability secret since it first appeared nearly a year ago. It's not as if I've never considered telling Remy, but every time I try, memories of the first time I summoned an *eidolon* keep me silent. Explaining those circumstances would be dangerous.

For both of us.

But it's becoming clear to me that I need to learn to use this skill during combat without draining myself. Or dying. While the *eidolon* does rely on a combination of my commands and instincts, there's also a mental tether connecting us that allows me to see through her eyes when I wish. But doing that is dangerous since it splits my focus and leaves my real body vulnerable. Training with a blindfold doesn't fully solve that problem, but it's the best I can do without revealing my true reasons.

Something hard smacks against my ribs, pulling my attention back to the fight. I lift the blindfold to find Remy holding a wooden sword in each hand.

"Really?" I rub the newly tender spot on my side.

"Be grateful they're not real." His bushy chestnut eyebrows pull together in admonishment as he dumps one of the weapons onto the mat in front of me. "Now get up."

Humiliation burns in my gut as I rise to my feet and grab the sword. My fingers brush over the knicks in the pale wood, tracing the familiar flower design in the pommel.

Is this the same set we used when Remy first began training me? I was terrified the day he tossed them aside and grabbed two steel blades from the weapons wall. At only eleven years old, it was the first time I'd ever touched a real sword. I walked away from that session with shallow slices all over my body, but the pride shining in Remy's eyes erased any pain I might have felt.

As one of the few half fae in a position of authority, he's worked tirelessly to rise to his rank as captain of the city guard. Despite not being blessed with magic, he's the greatest fighter I've ever met. I'm lucky that he took an interest in the strange little girl the king brought home one day. Without Remy, I doubt I'd have made it this far.

"I simply thought it might be fun to fight with my eyes closed," I tell him through gritted teeth. "It would even the odds a bit. Make things more exciting."

"Because fights to the death are usually so dull," he says dryly.

"It was just an idea."

"And the urgency with which you demanded to be taught?"

Pulling the blindfold back into place, I take up a defensive position. "I'm merely eager to correct the gaps in my education."

"As the person who educated you, I feel that statement was meant as an insult."

"Men and their tender feelings." I flick my wrist in his direction. "Take it how you will."

He lands another blow against my back, knocking the air out of me.

"Your problem is that you aren't listening," he says, his voice coming from my left.

"I've listened to every damn word you've said!" I seethe as my sword strikes out in his direction, but doesn't make contact. "Which, so far, hasn't been helpful."

His chuckle comes from my right now. "You always were a sore loser."

"I am not! Take that back, you cad." I swing blindly, my wooden sword waving through the air in what I'm sure is an amusing visual for him.

He knocks the weapon from my hand and grabs my wrists, pinning them behind me with embarrassing ease. I knock my head back, smiling when I catch him in the chin. His huff of pain has a slight improvement on my mood.

"*Listen*, Ivy." He lets me go and slips out of my reach. "Focus on my footsteps, the rustle of my clothes. Feel the air moving toward you before my strike lands."

Doing as he commanded, I empty my mind of the frustration and embarrassment that have taken hold of me. My encounters with the reaper haven't done much for my self-confidence.

At first, the room appears to be silent, but as I listen closer, I'm able to note several small sounds. A bird chirps outside the window, and distant laughter echoes from a passing guard somewhere down the hall. Suddenly, a slight breeze passes against my cheek a second before a fist connects with my skin. My free hand moves to my jaw, gingerly pressing against the tender joint. It wasn't a hard hit, but it still stung.

"Again," I tell him.

As we continue this strange exercise several more times, I begin to understand what Remy meant. While I don't successfully dodge any of his blows, I am getting better at anticipating them. I can now tell exactly where his strike is going to land a second before I feel it. In the back of my mind, I'm wondering how I'm going to apply this to my *eidolon*. When I'm staring through her eyes, will I be able to sense a fist coming toward me before it lands? And if I do, can I react fast enough to dodge it?

"Again," I repeat, wiping a spot of blood from my split lip.

"Let's take a break. We've been going at it for hours."

Lifting my blindfold, I note how the bright morning sun filters through the smudged windows. Considering the dawn had barely begun to rise when I got here, I'd say it's probably around nine now. As I stand still for a moment, all the aches I've been suppressing make themselves known.

"Ow." I hunch forward, rubbing my tender knee.

I haven't taken this many hits since my first lesson. I took to fighting quickly because I spent all of my free time either training or studying books on different techniques. When something doesn't come easily to me, I have a tendency to become obsessive about it.

Remy shakes his head. "I think we've done enough for today."

"One more time." I move the sword to my left hand, knowing I've been relying too much on my right today. "I almost had you in the last round."

"Ah, yes." He nods, tucking his hands behind his back. "You mean when you stood completely still as I punched you in the face?"

I shoot him a vicious glare—it's menacing effect only slightly dampened by my wince. "One more time, and then I promise I'll spend the whole day resting."

"Oh, really?" He cocks a brow.

"I swear. I'm planning a trip to the library."

"Well, that I believe," he laughs fondly. Since Baylor kept me isolated from other children growing up, when I wasn't with Remy or Leona, I spent the rest of my time in the company of books.

The humor falls away from Remy's face, leaving behind a hesitant expression. "I'll agree to one more round if you tell me what all of this is about."

"What do you mean?" I ask, feigning a casual tone as I bend down and fiddle with my boots. I pull one of the laces loose so I can retie it, giving myself an excuse to keep my head lowered.

"Just tell me what has you spooked." His patient tone grates against my nerves, making my skin feel too tight.

I stand up, meeting his gaze head on. "Why do you assume I'm spooked?"

Remy isn't supposed to ask me these things. He's always been my safe haven, the one person who doesn't push or pry. When I'm here in the training room, I'm free. Everything else fades into the background, and for a few hours, I simply get to exist.

"Ivy." His raspy voice practically swallows the nickname.

My gaze falls to the thin, pale scar on his neck. *An injury from my youth*, he called it when I asked years ago. It appears as if someone tried to slit his throat. A mortal wouldn't have survived such a wound. Being half fae saved his life. Supposedly, he was once a great singer with a rich and melodic voice, but after the injury, he was left with the warm, scratchy timbre that's so familiar to me.

"For the past few months, I've sensed you retreating further into yourself," Remy continues. "And now you come in here insisting I teach you to fight blindfolded? Has someone threatened you? Has—" He cuts himself off, taking a deep breath before continuing. "Has *he* threatened you?"

I take a step back on instinct.

Everything freezes as his words cut through all my lies, leaving me far too exposed. There's no doubt in my mind who he's referring to. The implication in his words is treasonous, and I know exactly what Baylor does to those he suspects of betraying him.

Would you do anything for me? Baylor's voice whispers again in my mind.

A sharp pain pulls my attention to my hand where I find a piece of wood has jabbed into my skin, drops of blood bubbling up around it. I must have been gripping the sword so tightly that I cracked the hilt. The weapon falls from my hand, hitting the mat between us.

"Shit," Remy mutters, stepping forward as he reaches for my injured hand. "Are you okay?"

"I'm fine," I insist, retreating backwards. "*It's nothing.*"

I meet his gaze, hoping he understands the message in my eyes.

"Ivy—"

"Captain!" a familiar male voice cuts him off. I turn to find Warrick, one of Remy's soldiers and Morwen's older brother, rushing toward us.

"Captain Remard, you're needed at once," he says urgently, his chest heaving.

Remy hurries to the weapons wall, replacing the wooden sword with his real one and grabbing a few small knives for good measure. Warrick startles as he notices me for the first time and bows his head.

"My lady," the half fae soldier says.

I nod back, forcing my face into a pleasant expression. Being interrupted before the conversation could get too dangerous might be divine intervention. Remy returns, his features stern as he reads each thought on my face. His eyes narrow as he pins me with a hard glare. He's in full captain mode now.

"This conversation isn't over."

He doesn't bother waiting for my agreement before exiting the training room.

CHAPTER EIGHT

The crackling of the fireplace is the only sound inside the library.

I sit in my usual chair, hidden in the back corner. Years ago, I purposefully reorganized a few of the shelves, strategically creating small open spaces between the books to give myself a perfect view of the door. Anyone walking into the room would believe it was empty, but I'd spot them immediately.

Flipping through the pages of an old tome, I multitask by trying to stretch out my calf muscles. Remy's always reminding me of the importance of working out any lingering stiffness that could prolong an injury. Thinking of the captain of the guard leaves a hollowness in my stomach. I know him well enough to know he meant what he said. He isn't going to let his suspicions go.

I push the thoughts away, returning my attention to the book in my hands.

Not knowing where to begin my search for information on the whisperer, I started by digging through the historical section. I'd read most of the texts before, but wedged behind several volumes, I found an old leather-bound book titled *History of the Verran Isles*.

After wiping away the dust, I brought it over to my chair and began reading.

The worn paper is rough against my fingers as I flip through the pages, my breath catching when I spot a familiar image. An illustration of a man with a hood pulled over his head, dark feathered wings stretched out behind him, and a silver scythe in his hand. My eyes dart to the caption.

The Fates have always been jealous of the beauty of those they called the Soul Collectors. When the Fates created their new children, the Gods, they found inspiration in the feathered wings of the reapers.

The image is hauntingly similar to my own reaper. *He's not mine*, I remind myself. Phantom tingles on the back of my neck tempt me to search the library for his pale blue gaze. *He's not here. It's just a picture.*

My fingers trail over the wings. No doubt the scratchy paper is a poor substitute for the real thing. Where do they go when he's not using them? How did they disappear so fully beneath his cloak? There wasn't even an outline... I know the Gods sometimes have wings, but I've never seen them in person. The divine are nothing if not secretive.

The reaper's threat flashes through my mind. From the inception of the Angel of Mercy, I've known the risks. Discovery was always a possibility. But Della and I have taken measures to ensure nothing can connect the two of us. When we started, it had been years since she and I had spoken publicly. My falling out with Leona and all of those connected with the late queen was well-known.

If I'm caught, at least it won't lead back to her.

I don't even believe Baylor will be upset about the actual murders. Instead, his anger will stem from being made a fool. His own *pet* betraying him in such a public way won't be something he can brush off.

I've been practicing my cover story since last night, in case the reaper follows through on his threats. But for some odd reason, I don't believe he will. From what I've seen, he could steal from Baylor without my help. However, I get the sense there's something else he wants from me. Whatever he's seeking, he won't get it by having me imprisoned.

I've allowed my mind to wander as I've flipped through the pages, but one fragment of a sentence catches my attention, making the hairs on my arms stand up.

"The whispers made me do it."

The fireplace crackles again, causing me to jump in my seat. Shivers worm their way down my spine as I trace my fingers over the words, wishing their meaning could be absorbed through touch alone.

Could this be referring to the same weapon Darrow and the reaper were discussing? My heart beats faster as I read the rest of the section.

Death of Claudius, the first God of Life.

Many have guessed at the motives behind why Philo, first God of Love, chose to slaughter Claudius, but none can say for certain. The murder shocked all residents of the Verran Isles. The Gods, our newly risen saviors, were seen as indestructible until Philo, the gentlest of them all, drove a sword through the heart of Claudius.

From that day on, Philo became known as the God of Love and Hate. Many have questioned how the seemingly ordinary sword was able to slay a God. Some have claimed it must have been enchanted, while others believed any blade in the hands of a God would become a God Slayer. It is unknown what happened to the weapon after Claudius died. All we know for certain is that when Philo was asked why he murdered Claudius, he claimed, "The whispers made me do it."

My eyes rove over the words again, positive I must have misread them. This can't be accurate. It's well-known that Claudius died in the war against the Novians five thousand years ago. Out of the countless historical texts I've read and the dozens of tutors I've studied with, none of them ever recounted a different version of events.

Until now.

My brows pinch together. Could the other texts have gotten it wrong? Or was this author simply mistaken? I flip back to the cover, realizing there's no indication of who wrote it. Eying the tome wearily, I begin to feel strangely uneasy about the idea of being found with it.

And what about the sword it mentioned? Is it merely another falsehood, or could it be the same weapon the reaper is searching for? If it is a God Slayer, there's only one reason to obtain it. He claimed he wanted to use it to avenge an injustice, which begs the question, which God does his master have a vendetta against?

A horrifying thought occurs to me.

Hypothetically, if Baylor was in possession of a God Slaying weapon, what are the chances it's only a coincidence that no one has seen the Goddess of Illusion since he rose to power?

When she disappeared, her husband Triston crowned himself king, but his brief reign was marked by ruthlessness and chaos. I was only a few months old when Baylor raised an army and marched on the palace, launching a brutal battle that ended with Triston dead.

In the following weeks, everyone waited for an Heir to step forward. Gods are notoriously secretive about every aspect of their lives, especially their Heirs. Most hide them away, letting them be raised by adoptive parents until they are old enough to defend themselves. But when no Heir appeared, Baylor took the crown for himself under the agreement that if the Goddess or her Heir ever came forward, he'd hand the throne over to our rightful ruler.

But in all these years, it's never happened. Everyone has always believed that if a God dies before producing an Heir, the Fates would choose one. That they haven't done so here has led many people to speculate that Maebyn is either still alive, or she must have given birth to an Heir before she died. We've been waiting to see which of those theories will prove true for more than two decades.

Nausea stirs in my gut as another sickening thought occurs to me. If Maebyn's Heir finally did come forward, there's no way Baylor would willingly give up his throne. He'd keep it through whatever means necessary.

Oh Gods... Did I make a mistake? Should I have agreed to help the reaper steal the sword? But is the reaper and the God he serves any more trustworthy than Baylor? I flip back to the page I'd been reading and my eyes catch on the same line once more.

The whispers made me do it.

My hands tremble as I push the book away from me. It tumbles to the floor, landing face up on the picture of the reaper, his silver scythe gleaming in the dim light.

Hugging my knees to my chest, I take deep breaths as I try to be rational. This book is just one historian's account. I don't even know if it's true. And I have no proof that the weapon they're describing is the same one the reaper is trying to steal from Baylor. All of this could be a coincidence.

It's fate, says a quiet voice in the back of my mind.

A shiver runs through me. I know the Fates work in mysterious ways. I can't help but wonder if I've felt their interference over the past week? Meeting the reaper. Finding this book. It all reeks of divine intervention. But why would they be pulling at the strings of *my* fate? I'm no one of importance...

Voices filter through the stacks as a small group enters the library. Peering through my peephole to the door, I spot Lady Bridgid, Kaldar's niece, standing with two of her friends. Her golden blonde ringlets bounce as she throws her head back, laughing at something one of her companions said.

My mouth twists into a grimace as I make myself invisible. The familiar prickling sensation covers every inch of my skin, setting my nerves on edge. The discomfort is worth it, though. These are the last people I want to be found by.

My foot lands on the book as I rise from my chair. Without giving myself time to think about the implications of my actions, I pick up the old volume and shove it into my satchel before continuing on my way. My feet silently pad over the plush carpet as I slip through the stacks, hoping to escape without drawing the attention of the courtiers. Unfortunately, instead of moving to one of the nearby tables, they continue to stand in the doorway, blocking the exit.

"He truly said that?" Lady Naomi asks as I try to find a way past them.

I'm not surprised to see her and Lord Darcus following Bridgid around. They're all children of council members and have frequently accompanied their parents to the palace over the years, always sticking close together. There was a time when I tried to nudge my way into their group, since we're all close in age, but they've never been welcoming toward me.

By calling me his pet, Baylor ensured I was alienated from the rest of the high fae, who are notoriously snobbish. A pet is not an equal. And the rumors about my questionable lineage certainly didn't help matters. While Lord Nigel Pomeroy has never publicly confirmed I'm not his child, it's been widely speculated that my mother was an adulteress. I've heard the insults the courtiers whisper behind my back.

Bastard.

Whore's daughter.

Bridgid looks gleeful as she nods excitedly to her companions. "Uncle Kaldar assured me that the king is going to announce his new bride at the anniversary ball."

I roll my eyes, doubting the validity of her claims. Kaldar has been pushing for a new queen since Leona died, but Baylor has never expressed a serious interest in the matter. It's barely been a year.

"Isn't it too soon?" Darcus asks, parroting my own thoughts.

"Is he supposed to mourn for the rest of his life?" Bridgid's nasally tone fills with petulance as they move further into the room, finally clearing out of the doorway and giving me an opening to escape. "He's ready to move on. Besides, it's not his fault she never gave him a child."

I grab hold of a nearby bookshelf, digging my nails into the wood to avoid accidentally reaching for her skull and cracking it against the stone fireplace. I need to get out of this room right now before I do something I'll regret. Slowly tiptoeing across the creaky floors, I try not to attract any attention as I head for the door.

"Do you seriously think he might choose you?" Naomi doesn't quite manage to hide the blatant envy in her tone as she joins Darcus on one of the plush couches.

Bridgid chuckles, leaning against the side table. "Let's just say we've been spending a lot of *intimate*, quality time together."

"You fucked him?" Darcus gasps, leaning forward as his eyes go wide.

My body freezes. I'm only two feet from the door now, but I can't force myself to move any further. My gaze is glued to Bridgid's face as she makes a show of looking around the room. The others lean forward, desperate for her answer.

Her expression turns smug. "Many times."

The trio descends into a fit of squeals and exclamations, but my own reaction is far different.

In the entire time we've been together, despite his many other crimes against me, Baylor has never strayed until now. Does he sense the distance I've put between us over the past year? Can he tell something is different?

I wait for my jealousy to ignite, but there isn't even a spark. The confirmation of his infidelity *should* devastate me. A few years ago, it would have. But there's no sinking sensation in my stomach, no catch in my throat.

Instead, I feel nothing.

A small flicker of hope flares in my chest at the realization. I never thought I'd be happy to not feel anything. A smile plays at the corner of my mouth, invisible yet genuine. Perhaps I'm finally done mourning a counterfeit love.

"What about the *wraith*?" Darcus asks, shuddering as he speaks the name. "We all know how attached he is to his precious pet."

"Shhh!" Naomi swats his arm as she glances around with fearful eyes. "The *wraith* could be anywhere. I don't want to end up on her kill list."

Bridgid bursts out laughing and Darcus chuckles, but his face pales slightly as he glances toward the door.

"Did you hear what she did to Lord Varish?" Darcus asks. Shame rises in my throat at his reference to the man Baylor had me slaughter.

"Don't speak that traitor's name," Bridgid warns. "He deserved what he got."

"Of course," they say in unison, both nodding fervently.

No doubt their strong reactions are due to fear of ending up like Varish. Even among friends, you can't be too careful with your words. It doesn't matter that he wasn't a traitor, or that he was telling the truth about his daughter. If Baylor decides someone has committed treason, no one can question him.

"But that's exactly why the *wraith* is no competition for me," Bridgid declares. "No one would put a violent bastard on the throne. Trust me, she's nothing. She can't even keep him satisfied anymore."

I guess that confirms that he *has* noticed the differences in our relationship recently. Still, something about Bridgid's demeanor today strikes me as odd...

The way she's dressed doesn't match her usual style. The gown she's wearing is dark burgundy, an unflattering color on her bright complexion and vastly different from what she usually wears. The courtiers tend to dress in pastels, like Lady Naomi's soft pink ensemble or Lord Darcus's yellow tunic.

But the color isn't the only thing strange about Bridgid's gown. The plunging neckline hangs awkwardly against her small chest and the thigh slit is far more daring than anything I've seen her in before. It actually reminds me of something I'd wear. Now that I think of it, it's shockingly similar to one of my own... Did she steal it?

That would explain why it doesn't fit her properly. Where my body is all shapely curves combined with lean muscle from countless hours of training, Bridgid is naturally willowy. She has that straight, waifish frame that's so popular among the upper-class.

I bite my lip, struggling to hold back a burst of laughter. Is this how she finally managed to capture Baylor's attention? By emulating me? I don't know whether to applaud her or feel sorry for her. Either way, I'm glad her efforts have paid off. Let her have Baylor as long as I can have my freedom.

Light footsteps hurry toward the room, bringing everyone's attention to the door. Morwen rushes inside, her cheeks flushed. She stops short when she sees the group of courtiers huddled together, her gaze immediately landing on the one person I know she hates interacting with.

Lady Naomi.

Morwen and Warrick were the product of an affair their mortal mother had with a wealthy high fae lord, who just so happens to be Naomi's father. Despite being half sisters, Naomi has never publicly acknowledged the relationship. In fact, she's taken every opportunity to destroy any hope of a familial bond between the siblings.

"My apologies for the interruption," Morwen murmurs, dipping into a curtsy and dropping her gaze respectfully. "Have you seen Lady Iverson? His Majesty needs her."

Bridgid's expression sours.

"Are you sure he didn't ask for me?" Her voice rises several octaves higher than before. "I'd be happy to go to him."

"No, my lady," Morwen answers politely. "He requested Lady Iverson."

Naomi scoffs. "Maybe you heard him wrong with your deformed ears."

A flush stains Morwen's cheeks as she adjusts her hair to hide her slightly pointed ears, the feature that marks her as half fae. Naomi's lips curve into a cruel smile as she openly delights in her sister's discomfort.

"Oh, you're terrible, Naomi." Bridgid playfully swats her friend's arm.

"She's not wrong, though," Darcus interjects. "Those ears are ghastly."

Deciding it's time to announce my presence, I release the illusion and appear right next to the small group.

For a moment, everyone stares at me in silence as the blood drains from their faces. Then Naomi leaps off the couch, pushing her friends out of the way as she runs for the door, her screams echoing through the halls. Meanwhile, Darcus dives toward the floor, using his hands to cover his head as he rocks back and forth.

"Holy Fates, protect me," his muffled voice whispers into the carpet.

Only Bridgid stands her ground. Her hard eyes meet mine as she lifts her chin in a show of bravery, but the pulsing vein at the base of her throat betrays her fear. I have to admit, in moments such as this, there's some sick part of me that enjoys the terror I inflict.

"Thank you, Morwen," I say, unable to stop the wicked smirk that curls my lips. "I'll join *Baylor* immediately."

Bridgid's fists clench as I say his name. The only people who have ever been permitted to use it were myself and Leona. To everyone else, he's "Your Majesty."

Morwen nods. "He's waiting for you in his study."

My mirth fades immediately.

When he calls me to his private chambers, he wants to use my body. But when he asks to see me in his office, he wants to stain my hands with blood.

After his most recent request, I didn't anticipate another this soon. Baylor has already given me four names this year. As his paranoia grows, so does his list of enemies.

Pushing those thoughts away, I offer a parting shot to Bridgid and Darcus. "Enjoy your reading. One always learns the most enlightening information in the library."

Her eyes go round as she realizes how indiscreet she's been.

Savoring the hatred blooming across her face, I follow Morwen out the door. I stopped yearning for the friendship of courtiers long ago. Instead, I delight in garnering their fear. It's much more useful.

"You shouldn't taunt them," Morwen warns.

"They deserved it." I shrug. "I'm sorry for what she said to you."

She shakes her head. "It's nothing."

I disagree, but it's not my place to correct her. I know from experience that brushing off those types of comments can be its own form of coping.

"The king is angry today," she continues. "I don't know what's wrong, but he's been this way all morning. Most of the servants are avoiding that wing."

I can relate to that. His bad moods are terrifying.

"Does it have anything to do with whatever Warrick pulled Remy away for earlier?" I ask.

"I'm not sure, but it's possible."

"Would you mind taking this to my room?" I ask, handing her my bag, which contains the book I stole.

As she takes it, the strangest urge bolts through me. For a moment, I want to rip the satchel from her hands and refuse to part with it. Brushing off the odd instinct, I release my grip on the bag, telling myself it would be madness to take such a conspicuous text into Baylor's study.

"Good luck," she says as we reach the stairwell that leads to the king's private floor.

"I'll need it," I whisper.

Taking a deep breath, I begin my ascent alone.

CHAPTER NINE

My lonely footsteps echo through the empty halls of the east wing. Glancing down at myself, I try to ascertain the state of my appearance. Since I meant to hide in the library all day, I never changed after my training session. I'm still wearing my fitted sleeveless tunic, now stained with several drops of blood. The fabric has torn in a few spots, leaving my skin visible underneath. Half the hair from my once sleek braid has come loose, curling around my face.

I would love to bathe and change into fresh clothes, but Baylor doesn't enjoy being kept waiting. Instead, I untie the ribbon that still holds a few of the strands together and use my fingers to comb through the thick, messy waves. I let it hang in front of my shoulders, hoping to distract from my attire. Unfortunately, this is the best I can do.

I arrive at the king's study and the guards usher me inside, not bothering to announce my presence. That lapse in protocol sends a shiver of apprehension down my spine.

I find Baylor pacing back and forth behind his desk, quietly muttering to himself. He keeps his eyes down, not acknowledging my presence as I enter the room. As odd as his behavior is, what concerns me most is his appearance. His jacket has been cast aside, leaving him in an untucked, wrinkly tunic. His usually smooth blond locks now fall into his face, tangled and stringy.

Alarms blare through my mind, signaling that something is wrong. He looks terrible... *He looks like someone capable of murdering a God.*

I shake my head, pushing the dark thought away.

"Baylor?" I ask tentatively.

At the sound of my voice, his head snaps up and his wild gaze connects with mine. For the first time since I've known him, the gift of eternal youth appears to have abandoned him. His usually brilliant skin is gray and haggard. Sweat peppers his brow, reminding me of what happens to mortals when they're struck by illness.

"What's wrong?" I ask, forcing myself to move closer while still keeping the desk between us as a buffer.

Lines appear around his mouth as he grimaces. "Someone has betrayed me, pet."

With Baylor, every betrayal ends the same way. I ball my fists, bracing for whatever name I am about to receive. My mouth turns dry as I run through my mental list of courtiers. I've suspected several lords of harboring negative sentiments toward the king, not that I'd ever share that with him. Whoever it is, their betrayal has affected him deeply.

You can do this, I tell myself as I force my spine to straighten. *You will be strong. You will endure.*

"You are no longer allowed to leave the palace," he announces.

The words echo through my mind, bouncing off my skull. Why would I not be allowed to leave? I thought we were discussing a betrayal...

My stomach sinks to the floor as a terrifying suspicion creeps into my mind.

"And I want a guard stationed by your door at all times," he continues.

Dread floods through my veins, poisoning my blood. It's only by the grace of the Fates that I manage to stay upright as the realization settles like a lightning strike straight to my gut.

The reaper did it.

I'd hoped I was calling his bluff, but clearly, he followed through on his threat to tell the king that I'm the Angel of Mercy. Underneath the shock is anger. I'm furious with myself for misjudging the situation. This is the kind of mistake I can't afford to be making. Why did I think he wouldn't actually do it? I'd gotten the impression there had been something he wanted from me, something other than my help stealing the *whisperer*. But apparently, I was wrong.

"Baylor, I can expl—" I cut myself off quickly as I remember my training. Liars try to fill the silence; honest people are more patient. Staying quiet, I mentally rehearse the cover story I was sure I wouldn't have to use.

Murdering Lynal Skynner was a tactic to lure out the true Angel of Mercy. I know you said this matter was beneath me, but I hated seeing you upset, my king. I seek only to please you.

A guard shouts from the hallway, snapping my attention to the double doors. Muffled voices rise with anger and I pull one of my blades free just as a familiar chill lifts the hairs on the back of my neck.

"What is the meaning of this?" Baylor demands behind me.

The doors burst open, revealing the last person I want to see.

The reaper glides into the room as if he has every right to be here. His dark hair is pushed back, but a few strands have fallen across his forehead. Dressed in his signature black, he's far more seductive than a soul collector should be. But what captures my attention the most is the fact that his wings are absent yet again.

"Your Majesty!" Huxley rushes into the room, appearing slightly worse for wear.

"Out!" Baylor orders the guard, his tone deadly. "I'll deal with you later."

"Oh, my apologies," the reaper says, not sounding sorry at all. "Was I supposed to wait outside?"

Baylor's temper becomes a palpable energy, sending ripples through the room. If the reaper isn't careful, he's going to push the king past his tipping point. I've seen what happens when he reaches that level. It isn't pretty.

If he already told Baylor my secret, what is he doing here? Has he come to watch my punishment? Annoyance sparks when the bastard doesn't even bother acknowledging my existence, his attention focused solely on the king.

"What are you doing here?" Baylor seethes.

The reaper's eyes widen innocently. "It almost sounds as if you're not happy to see me. Which is strange, given our new alliance."

My heart gives a heavy thud against my chest. Alliance? Questions pound through my mind as they continue speaking.

"You're mistaken," Baylor says. "I'm overjoyed by your unexpected arrival, Lord Thorne."

Thorne.

The name sits silently at the tip of my tongue as I suppress the urge to repeat it. To be honest, I'd forgotten I didn't know his name. Reaper suited him.

"Oh good," he says. "I'd hate to think I wasn't welcome."

My brows shoot up as Thorne helps himself to a plush chair near Baylor's desk. It's considered rude to sit before royalty unless they give you permission. From the hard glint in Baylor's eyes, I'd say he noticed the snub. The king reclaims his own seat, his rigid posture completely at odds with the easy facade Thorne displays.

"While I'm here," the reaper continues, his tone suspiciously light, "is there anything you want to tell me?"

Baylor shrugs, but the gesture comes off stilted. "Nothing comes to mind."

Thorne cocks his head to the side, his glacial eyes narrowing. "Think hard. What did you have yesterday that has suddenly disappeared today?"

A muscle twitches along Baylor's jaw as he tucks one of his blond strands behind his ear. "Whatever your spies have told you—"

"Don't lie to me," Thorne cuts him off, dropping any pretense of friendliness. "I don't need to remind you who I serve."

Tingles rush over my skin, warning me that this is about to turn ugly. Moving as slowly as possible, I start backing toward the door. There's no way I'm going to stay here and get caught in the cross hairs of their inevitable battle. Besides, it would appear the reaper has somehow made a deal with Baylor in exchange for the weapon he wanted. *The whisperer.* I've no idea what he's giving up in exchange for that, but it doesn't appear to be related to me. A small part of me wants to stay and get to the bottom of it, but my survival instincts are too strong.

Unfortunately, right as I'm about to make it to safety, a floorboard creaks under my foot. The king's head whips in my direction, his shock making it clear he'd forgotten I was here.

"Leave us," he growls.

I nod, already reaching for the door handle.

"She stays." Thorne's commanding voice stops me in my tracks.

My gaze snaps to his. Shivers skate over my skin as his attention shifts to me for the first time since he arrived.

"You overstep, Thorne. My pet doesn't take orders from you."

Distantly, I recognize that Baylor is speaking, but I can't bring myself to look away as Thorne rises from his chair and prowls across the room.

Mirth dances behind his eyes as they rake over me. "So, this is the infamous *wraith?*"

I bite my lip to keep from baring my teeth at him as he circles me, a predator searching for weaknesses.

"She's not involved in this," Baylor insists, pushing to his feet.

"Yet another failing on your part," the reaper murmurs, coming to a stop directly in front of me, leaving only an inch between us.

"Remember your place, *ambassador*," Baylor's words are like chips of ice.

"Remember yours, *King*," Thorne taunts. "Don't forget I speak on behalf of a *God*."

My eyes go round as my head whips toward Baylor. Heat crawls up his neck, staining his skin with the evidence of his fury. Whether Thorne knows it or not, he just pressed on Baylor's biggest insecurity. He's extremely sensitive to any reminders that out of all the rulers of the Verran Isles, he is the only one who isn't a God.

I take several steps back, putting space between myself and the ambassador. Baylor's hands grip the edge of his desk so tightly I'm surprised the wood doesn't snap in half. His temper is seconds away from lashing out at whoever's in his sight.

"You need this alliance more than we do," Thorne carries on, completely ignoring the danger as he turns away from me. "Don't forget that. Or do you no longer require our grain?"

That's what this trade is for? Grain in exchange for the *whisperer*?

Baylor stays silent as suspicion curls around the edges of my thoughts. While some rulers might endure humiliation to ensure their people are fed, Baylor wouldn't make this type of trade unless it was his own pantry that had gone bare. So, either the food shortages are much more dire than he's let on, or there's something else Baylor believes he will receive from this alliance.

Something worth the loss of such a powerful weapon.

"Killian is a benevolent God," Thorne says, moving toward the king once more. "He understands that none of this unfortunate business was your doing. He's agreed to make sure you receive our first shipment of grain by the end of the week."

"That's generous of him," Baylor begrudgingly admits.

"Remember, generosity only extends so far. If that blade is not recovered, there will be no more shipments." Thorne places his hands on the desk, leaning over it. "And there will be no more alliance."

Blade.

My mind reels. The weapon Thorne has been searching for, *the whisperer,* is a blade. Just like the weapon the book claimed was able to kill Claudius. Does this confirm my fears that they are one and the same? Has Baylor truly had such a powerful weapon in his possession all this time?

Baylor bristles under the reapers stare. "I assure you that everything is being done to find it. My men are currently searching the tunnels where the sword was last seen. If the thief left a trail, they will uncover it."

Tunnels? Didn't Darrow mention that the whisperer was kept in a tunnel deep underneath the palace? I believed I'd explored every inch of this place over the years, but evidently not. If there are guards searching down there, I'd imagine Remy is with them. That's probably what he got pulled away for this morning.

"Forgive me if I'm not overly confident," Thorne replies, turning his back on the king once more as he returns to the chair. "Wasn't it one of your own guards who stole the weapon in the first place?"

Well, that's unfortunate. It also explains what Baylor meant earlier when he said someone had betrayed him.

The king's eyes sharpen. "How did you know that?"

Thorne waves his hand as he sits down. "I truly don't have time to explain everything I know that you don't."

Baylor grinds his teeth so hard I'm sure they are going to crack, but thankfully, he doesn't rise to the reaper's bait.

"And just so you're aware," Thorne continues, "I plan to be involved in every step of this investigation. Starting right now."

Baylor nods his head. "Of course."

"And your *wraith* will act as my personal liaison, aiding me in the search however I see fit."

My brows shoot toward my hairline. Thorne's gaze momentarily flits toward me, a small smirk curving his lips. What game is he playing? He's enjoying riling up the king and giving him nothing in return. Does he have any idea how dangerous this is? For both of us?

The room is silent as Baylor stares at the reaper with restrained hatred. He despises being made to feel small, and that's exactly what Thorne has done.

"My pet and I will need to discuss your proposal privately," Baylor says coolly.

"Of course." Thorne rises from his chair, not bothering hiding his smile as he turns to face me. "I'm sure someone such as your *wraith* could truly accomplish anything if properly motivated. You are lucky to have such an *angel* by your side."

My breath catches. Does he mean what I think he means? Was that a threat? Either I convince Baylor to let me help, or Thorne reveals my secret. He can't be serious...

Victory flashes behind his pale eyes, and I know I'm right.

"I'll be in the hall," he says to Baylor, "eagerly awaiting your decision."

A surge of helplessness flows through me as I watch him exit the room. Does he realize the position he's put me in? Baylor's temper needs somewhere to strike, and I'm now the only target left in the room. *And* he wants me to somehow convince the king to let me join him in his search? Terror twists my insides as the door clicks shut. I turn to face my lover, my heart galloping in my chest. Baylor moves around the desk, coming to stand before me.

"I'm disappointed, Iverson."

My fingers twitch at the coldness in his tone, that same icy frost that has overtaken him many times before, making him unpredictable. The emptiness in his eyes makes my skin crawl. Even when I still believed he loved me, I was petrified when he'd get this way. He's dangerous at the best of times, but this type of fury almost always descends into violence.

"I told you to leave," he says softly. "You know better than to disobey me, pet."

Without warning, the collar activates, seizing my throat with enough force to snap my head back against the wall.

CHAPTER TEN

My vision blurs as I slide to the floor, pulling at the collar with useless fingers. My mouth opens wide as my lungs cry out, but there's too much pressure on my airway. I can't get a breath. Terror has pleading words rising to the tip of my tongue, but even if I could speak, I wouldn't voice them. I refuse to beg this monster for a life he has no right to take from me.

The vein in his forehead bulges wildly as he watches me struggle. Crimson swirls within his deep blue irises, reminding me of a shark attack I witnessed at the docks years ago. The sailor's blood staining the water had been an omen, warning everyone to stay away. I wish I'd heeded that lesson with the predator before me.

My back arches off the ground as I twist and struggle, desperate for just a single breath, but Baylor withholds it. I stare in horror as his *vertere* natures overtakes him, and the Beast of the Battle rages beneath his skin. His nails elongate into sharp claws that could slice me open with a single swipe, and those lips that profess to love me twist into a cruel smile. The monster he hides within is relishing my pain.

A few drops of blood trickle from his nose, a reminder that he isn't coming out of this unscathed. Using the collar is physically draining, always leaving him tired and sickly. His brow creases as blood drips into his mouth. A moment later, his head jerks back in surprise, his eyes blinking rapidly. The collar suddenly releases its iron grip and settles back into place against my skin, a killer lying in wait.

The entire episode lasted less than a minute, but it felt much longer.

"I'm sorry, pet," Baylor breathes as his eyes return to their normal shade and his claws disappear.

He wipes the blood from his face and hurries to my side, helping me stand as I hungrily swallow mouthfuls of air. He wraps me in his arms and pulls my head into the crook of his neck. The position is meant to provide comfort, but instead I'd compare it to being bound by iron chains. The urge to fight his hold is nearly overwhelming as his scent clogs my nostrils, making my stomach churn.

"Forgive me," he whispers, his warm breath tickling my ear. "I'm just upset."

"I know," I assure him, the raspy words scratching my throat as I force them out. "I understand."

But I don't.

I don't understand how anyone could do this to a person they claim to love. I close my eyes as tears threaten to fall. A burning rage simmers in my gut as his hand curves around my cheek, his thumb brushing away a falling tear.

"I'm under so much pressure," he says, repeating his usual excuse. His temper is never his fault. "But I'll do better. You'll see. Everything I'm doing is for us," he promises desperately, searching my eyes for forgiveness. "You believe me, don't you?"

I don't, but I nod anyway.

Exhaustion joins forces with gravity, threatening to pull to me to the floor as it weighs down my limbs. How much longer can I play this role? At some point, my performance will slip, and my lies will no longer be enough to convince him. What will he do to me then?

Something hot and oily coils in my stomach. The desire to hurt him burns through my veins, sending reckless thoughts to my brain. Whatever this whisperer truly is, it's powerful enough that Baylor doesn't want me anywhere near it. Which means that's exactly where I need to be.

"You should agree to his terms," I announce suddenly, ignoring the hoarseness in my voice.

I'll do what Thorne wants and convince Baylor to let me help in the search. But when I find the sword, I won't be giving it to either of them. Something that powerful doesn't belong in the hands of a king or a God. It shouldn't belong to anyone.

His arms fall away from me as he steps back, his features twisting with suspicion. "And why would I do that?"

"It's the smart move." I shrug, feigning indifference as I head for the pitcher of water sitting on a cabinet in the corner.

My fingers tremble as I pour myself a glass and swallow several large gulps. Thankfully, the cool liquid soothes my aching throat. Since the attack was short, hopefully any damage it caused was minimal. And with my fae heritage, it should heal quickly.

"Let him think he's won," I continue speaking. "Boost his ego a bit. Obviously, his plan is to drive a wedge between us in order to isolate you and get information out of me. So, we make him think it's working."

He watches me warily. "For what purpose?"

"To use his own plan against him. While he tries to gain my trust, I'll be spying on him and making sure he doesn't screw us over."

I don't mention that I'm planning to screw them both over.

Baylor is quiet, his expression betraying nothing as he deliberates on my proposal. Tremors threaten to give away my nervousness, but I force myself to appear calm despite knowing that his answer will determine my fate.

"I don't want you around the sword," he says finally. "That's nonnegotiable."

"Then I won't go near it," I lie.

He nods. "And you will report everything you learn to me."

"Of course."

And with that, it's settled. Baylor returns to his desk, riffling through his folders. My outward appearance is neutral, but inside I'm reeling. If I'm successful, this will be far beyond my usual acts of rebellion. The Angel of Mercy started as a small way to fight back against Baylor. It was intended to undermine the city's confidence in him while also helping those in need.

Taking the sword is different. I'll be destroying his alliance with the Fifth Isle, which will be a major blow to Baylor's reign. But there will be other consequences too. Without that grain, many people will go hungry. Can I live with that?

I don't need to search within myself for the answer. I already know it. No. I won't be able to live with that. Which means I'll need to find a way to ensure that grain is delivered with or without the sword.

I shove my worries away as Baylor returns. He hands me a sheet of paper, and I pray he doesn't notice the way my hands shake as I take it, finding a lifelike depiction of an antique sword.

"The sword's official name is the *almanova*," he explains. "But many have taken to calling it the whisperer."

Chills skate over my skin, but I ignore my unease as I examine the drawing. The blade is engraved with markings from an old language I don't recognize. There's something almost sinister about it. Glowing rubies adorn the faded white pommel, resembling drops of blood. My stomach twists as I realize the handle is actually made from bone.

I swallow. "It's certainly unique."

As I peer closer at the image, the hairs on my arms rise. My trembling fingers trace over the rubies embedded in the sword, noting the familiar shape and color. They appear almost identical to the ones clasped around my throat. Questions spark in the back of my mind but I stop them in their tracks. That's not possible.

"Very unique," Baylor agrees, pulling my attention away from the paper. "And very powerful. Which is why you must take great care. If you find the blade, promise me that you won't go near it."

I nod, still distracted by my suspicions.

He reaches out, gripping my chin as his eyes bore into mine. "Never let it touch your skin. This is extremely important, pet."

An icy shiver skates down my spine. "I promise."

I wait for him to offer further explanation for his strange warning, but he doesn't.

"Good," Baylor says, releasing me as he returns to his desk, writing out a quick message. He quickly folds the parchment before stamping it with his seal and handing it to me. "Give this to Kaldar. He's in the dungeon, guarding the entrance to the tunnels. He will allow you to pass through with our *guest*," he spits the word as he sits back down, effectively dismissing me.

I want to ask him about the similarities between the rubies, but I know better than to expect the truth from him. Instead, I head for the door, ready to escape this horrific encounter. My fingers have just brushed the brass handle when he speaks again.

"When you're down there, ignore any voices you may hear. The whispers cannot be trusted."

BAYLOR'S ominous words follow me into the hall, leaving me jittery and paranoid. I take deep breaths, praying no one notices the way my hands shake as I shove both papers into my back pocket.

Thorne stands outside the study, leaning against the wall with his arms crossed. His posture appears lazy, but the predatory glint in his eyes tells me he's anything but relaxed. Amusement plays at the corners of his lips as the king's guards glare at him.

His attention shifts to me, and the smug pretense momentarily drops. Concern flashes within those nearly translucent eyes, but it's gone as quickly as it appeared. His expression smooths over, becoming unreadable. Clearly, I'm not the only one who can don a mask when necessary. He opens his mouth to say something, but I hurry past him, keeping my chin tucked down as I make my way through the hall.

"Are you coming or not?" I call without glancing back.

His footsteps echo behind me as he jogs to catch up.

"Finally speaking to me?" he asks, his eyes drilling a hole into the side of my face.

I scoff. "Excuse me?"

"You didn't say a word the entire time I was in there."

"That's because you were speaking enough for both of us," I lie, surprised he even noticed. The truth is that I'm smart enough to choose my words carefully in Baylor's presence. The less I say, the better.

He tsks. "That was rude, but I'll forgive you since I'm guessing your king agreed to my terms?"

"I'd call them demands," I mutter. "And I wouldn't be here with you if he hadn't."

Both of his hands clutch his chest, right over his heart. "You wound me, Angel."

"Only your ego." I roll my eyes. "You shouldn't have pushed Baylor that way."

"Hazard of the job." He shrugs, but there's something about the action that rings false. Since my life is one big performance, it's easy to spot when someone else is putting on a show. Unfortunately, what he says next proves that recognition goes both ways.

"Have you been crying?"

My head whips in his direction. "No," I say too quickly.

"My mistake." His gaze lingers on my eyes, which are always bloodshot after Baylor uses the collar.

Does he suspect that Baylor took out his anger on me? As

Killian's ambassador, he's likely searching for intel to report back. Either way, I'm not going to confirm his suspicions.

"You know, you aren't acting very grateful," Thorne announces, pulling my focus back to him as I arch a brow. "Here I thought you'd be thanking me for not revealing your charming little hobby to your king."

"Thanking you?" I laugh. "I'd sooner throw another dagger at you."

His eyes turn heated. "I don't think that would have your intended effect, Angel."

"Fuck you." My pulse quickens as my voice turns breathy. Probably just a side effect of what happened earlier.

"There's that impressive vocabulary again." He cocks his head to the side. "You know, I'm sensing you might be *slightly* upset about my little threat back there."

I come to a dead stop in the middle of the hallway, my eyes narrowing into slits as I pin him with a glare. He takes a step back, lifting his hands in a placating gesture.

"But," he continues, "I'd like to point out that I could have done a lot more than make a few threats. Personally, I think I showed impressive restraint."

I take a step closer, eating up the distance between us as I lift my chin to hold his gaze. "You appear to be under the misguided impression that you have me at a disadvantage. You don't."

"Oh really?" One side of his mouth kicks up.

"I could have talked my way out of any tale you spun in there."

His gaze falls to my lips. "My, what a talented tongue you have."

"And even sharper teeth." I smile, giving him the full view of them. My voice is sounding better with each word as the pain in my throat begins to ease.

"Perhaps your bark is louder than your bite? Your beloved king does refer to you as his *pet*, after all. That implies domestication." His tone is light, but there's something disapproving underneath it. Does he not care for the nickname?

"Try me and find out," I challenge him. "Besides, it's you who should be worried, given this new alliance."

A wicked gleam enters his eyes. "Are you the one making threats now?"

I shrug. "Perhaps."

"Oh please, continue." His tongue darts across his bottom lip, drawing my gaze. "How would you ruin me, Angel?"

My heartbeat stutters as unwanted heat scalds my cheeks. I drag my attention away from him, ordering myself to stay focused. "Last week, you seemed more interested in thievery than politics. What a coincidence that the *almanova* was stolen so soon after you tried to blackmail me into stealing it for you."

He blinks innocently. "I don't believe I ever mentioned something called a—what did you say?" His head tilts to the side, his forehead creased with mock confusion. "*Almanova?*"

"Don't insult my intelligence," I snap. "The *almanova* and your *whisperer* are one and the same. Baylor confirmed it."

He rolls his lips to hide a smile. "I believe this is called mutually assured destruction. But it would be a shame to destroy someone so lovely."

"I wouldn't know." I shrug. "It's not something I have to worry about."

He clutches his heart once more. "Again, my lady? My ego can't take much more abuse."

"You'll survive," I mutter. "Unfortunately."

He crosses his arms. "And here I was about to offer you a truce."

"That would require me to trust you," I say, moving ahead of him as I lead us into a narrow stairwell. "Which, to be clear, I don't."

He follows behind me since it's too narrow to walk side by side, something I'm grateful for. I need a moment to refocus after the direction our conversation has taken. We walk in silence for several minutes, each lost in our thoughts until a footman comes upon us, carrying a large glass vase. We both move to the side, allowing him to pass through the tight quarters. Thorne's brows pinch together as he glances around, noticing where we are for the first time.

"Do you always take the servants' passages?" he asks.

"There are people I prefer to avoid." My mind turns to the courtiers from this morning.

"You mean whoever left those bruises?" he asks, a dark edge entering his voice.

My head whips around so fast I nearly trip on the steep steps. He reaches out, steadying me with his gloved hand before pulling it away.

"If you tell me his name, I'll make him regret ever laying a hand on you."

I blink. Seconds pass as I wait for him to smile or laugh, to signal in some way that he's joking. But he doesn't. His offer is completely serious.

"Why do you assume it was a man?" I ask. "It might have been a woman?"

His expression doesn't change. "Was it?"

I cross my arms. "Why do you care if someone hurts me? How does that impact you?"

Two lines appear in the center of his forehead. "I don't have to be personally impacted by something to care about it."

I suppose that's true. I care about the strangers I help as the Angel of Mercy, despite never actually meeting any of them. They only deal with Della and her spies, none of them ever learning who killed their abuser. But still, I care about their pain. Everyone, mortal and fae, deserves to live a life free of senseless violence. My eyes flit back to Thorne's, searching for the truth in his haunting gaze. Does he truly mean what he's saying, or is this another tactic to gain my trust? I shake my head, reminding myself that either way, it doesn't matter.

"Your imagination is concerning, Reaper." I turn around and continue down the stairs. "If you must know, the bruises were a gift from my sparring partner."

"Sparring?" He sounds shocked as he falls into step next to me, squeezing through the narrow passage.

I stiffen at his sudden closeness. "I trust you're familiar with the concept."

"That's what these bruises are from?" His attention flits from the cut on my lip to the bruise on my arm.

I nod.

"I see." He coughs into his fist, attempting to hide the flash of amusement in his eyes. "And are you usually this bad at it?"

I narrow my gaze at him. "I was learning a new technique."

"Mhmm." His lips twitch.

"With the intention of destroying you," I insist.

He cocks his head. "And how's that going for you?"

"Would you like to find out?" My temper flares dangerously.

I expect at least some semblance of the fearful reactions that typically accompany my threats, but instead, he appears delighted. A full smile lights up his face, chasing away the cold perfection of his features. The beauty of it is so striking that for a moment, I forget what we were talking about.

But then he opens his mouth to speak again, and my annoyance comes flooding back.

"I'm merely flattered you've gone to so much trouble on my behalf," he sighs.

I ball my fist, imaging how satisfying it would be to punch him in his perfect face. "You won't stand a chance, Reaper."

"Ah, how unfortunate for me." He gestures to my arms, lined with bruises from Remy's wooden sword. "Though judging by your appearance, I'd say my impending demise is still a long way off."

"I'm a fast learner," I promise him. "I give it a week."

"How generous of you to warn me." His demeanor turns grave. "I'll set my affairs in order immediately."

"Be sure to name me in your will," I tell him as we reach the bottom of the stairs, following a path that leads us into the dungeon. "I enjoy keeping trophies to remind me of my victims."

"Don't worry," he says, his voice as warm as melted honey. "I'll leave you something to remember me by."

"It's only fair." I hurry ahead, eager to put some space between us as he trails after me.

"You know, I think it's pretty trusting of me to follow my would-be murderer into an underground prison."

"I assure you, Lord Thorne," a dull voice cuts in, "you are perfectly safe."

CHAPTER ELEVEN

I find Kaldar in the last cell on the left, lying on a small bench. The rest of the dungeon is empty, as usual. If the king wants someone dead, he doesn't typically bother locking them up first. As the person who carries out most of those killings, I would know.

A yawning pit opens in my stomach as I realize how much of our conversation Kaldar might have overheard. Thanks to the warmth radiating across my cheeks, I know I'm still blushing. And based on the calculated gleam in the advisors eyes, he noticed.

Fuck.

"What about me?" I ask, attempting to distract him. "Am I perfectly safe?"

His eye twitches. "Unfortunately."

"I'm sure if that changes, you'll be the first to let me know."

"Happily." He makes a meal out of the word, relishing each syllable.

Thorne's gaze flits back and forth between us. I ignore the questions in his eyes, not wanting to give Kaldar anything else to use against me. Though I do notice his features appear colder now. He's once more wearing that mask of detached amusement he used with both Darrow and Baylor. I'm surprised to realize that every time I've spoken to him alone, his warmth felt genuine. Although I know better than anyone emotion can be faked.

"Interesting company you're keeping, Lady Iverson," Kaldar comments, a sly grin curling his thin lips. "I'd love to discuss what you and the ambassador were doing down here, but unfortunately, this area is off limits."

I blink innocently. "Then why are you here?"

"His Majesty trusts me more than you," he boasts.

"Are you sure?" I pull Baylor's note from my pocket. "Cause this little letter here says you're supposed to open some door for me."

Kaldar's eyes settle on the royal seal embossed in the wax. Darting forward, he snatches it from my hand and rips it open. His face contorts with anger as he reads the king's instructions.

"*You* are being assigned to search for the sword?" he demands as the color drains from his face.

I nod. "By order of His Majesty the King, who trusts me to hunt down the sword while you..." I trail off, making of a show of looking around the empty cell. "Guard a door."

He clenches his fists, crushing the letter. "His Highness relies on me for a reason. I have been given tremendously important responsibilities."

"By your mother, perhaps," I mutter.

He scowls. "No, that's—"

"You're right," I agree, waving him off. "I hear she prefers your brother anyway."

His hands shake, and for a moment, I think he's finally going to leap at me. Fates, I wish he would. My body braces, ready for an attack.

"As entertaining as this sparring match is," Thorne interrupts, his tone bored, "we should be going."

Rolling my eyes, I step back and give Kaldar room to do his job. He approaches the wall to our right and reaches into his pocket.

My spine straightens when he pulls out a small knife, but instead of directing it at me, he uses it to slice open his own palm. I grimace, but before I can ask what he's doing, Kaldar rubs his bloody hand over the wall. The red stain he leaves behind is quickly absorbed by the stones, as if it's some sort of sick offering. A moment, later a hiss of air escapes from the rocks and a large portion of the wall swings out, revealing the entrance to the tunnels.

I hang back as Thorne moves closer. His brow furrows as he inspects the hidden door. "A blood spell?"

"Yes." Kaldar lifts his chin proudly. "I am one of the few His Majesty trusts to be capable of accessing it."

I roll my eyes as I move closer, noting the gentle breeze that dances through the air, carrying an earthy scent with it. Inside I find a damp stairwell, lit by generously spaced out gas lamps, giving the corridor a haunted atmosphere. Lovely.

"Were you familiar with the guard who stole the weapon?" Thorne asks as he turns back to Kaldar.

"Grell Darby." He nods, tucking his hands behind his back. "I hired him."

"I wouldn't brag about that," I mutter under my breath.

Thorne's lips twitch momentarily before flattening out, erasing any hint of amusement.

"You two should be going," Kaldar says flatly. "It's a long way down."

I bite my lip to stop myself from needling him any further today. I've probably provoked him enough. Thorne crosses the threshold first, his large frame appearing disproportionate in the narrow tunnel.

"Don't mind the rodents." Kaldar steps up to my side, flashing me a dark glare. "They only come out when they're hungry."

"Does that mean if I feed you, you'll go away?" I ask as I step through the threshold, praying I make it out alive.

His only response is to slam the door behind us.

"Do you think he was lying about the rats?" I whisper, my gaze catching on the cobwebs that cling to the walls.

"Let's hope so," Thorne says grimly.

HALF AN HOUR PASSES as we silently navigate the steep stairs. They are narrow enough that I have to take calming breaths as I remind myself the walls aren't closing in on us. Thorne walks several feet ahead, leaving me with nowhere to look except the back of his head.

"I got the impression the king's adviser isn't your biggest fan," he says, breaking the silence.

"Trust me, the hatred is mutual."

"I can't imagine why," he says dryly. "He's such a charming man."

My lips twitch. "What about you, Reaper? Any enemies in Death's court?"

"No," he sighs. "I'm universally beloved."

I roll my eyes. "There's that imagination of yours again. Do you often lose touch with reality, or is this a new development?"

"I prefer to think of it as shaping my own reality."

He disappears from my view as he follows a bend in the stairwell. Maybe it's the eerie atmosphere, but this place has my anxiety spiking. There's a sinister energy to the air. It's palpable enough that when I turn the corner and catch up to Thorne a few seconds later, I'm strangely grateful for his company. This isn't somewhere I'd want to explore alone.

"Don't let the *Fates* hear you talking about shaping your own reality," I warn him with a teasing edge in my voice. "Those three sisters will think you're trying to steal their job."

"Perhaps they'll find it endearing? I hear they enjoy a little defiance."

"I certainly hope so," I murmur, thinking of how many times I've probably strayed from their plan.

We walk for a while longer until we reach a circular landing that is about ten feet wide. I spot an entrance to a dark tunnel on our right, but what lies beyond is a mystery. Every tiny hair on my body lifts, leaving me with the sense that we're being watched. As I scan the darkness, I almost expect to see beady eyes staring back at me.

The ceiling is low, only a few inches above Thorne's head. Drawing in a shallow breath, I silently will the walls to stop closing in on me. Old fears rise from the depths of my subconscious, clawing their way into the present.

I'm assaulted by images of rocks caving in, crushing us beneath their weight. My breath hitches as I remember choking on dirt fifteen years ago. How it filled my mouth when I tried to scream. The way it burned my eyes as I searched for a way out, clogging my nostrils with each desperate breath. It touched me everywhere, as if the ground had open up and swallowed me whole.

"Angel?"

I startle at the sound of his voice. Looking up, I find his wary gaze watching me, seeing far too much. Pushing my shoulders back, I take a deep breath, holding the air in my lungs for several seconds before releasing it.

"Are you—" His question is cut off by a high-pitched shriek coming from the tunnel. His attention shifts behind me as his eyes grow round with fear. "Get down!"

I don't need to be told twice. I dive to the ground, curling into a ball and using my arms to protect my head. Dozens of wings flap around us as we're swarmed by a colony of bats. Their wails stab my ears, louder than anything I've heard before. Eventually the noise dissipates, leaving only stark silence in its wake.

I sit up, finding Thorne a few feet away. A blanket of dust covers him, clinging to his clothes and hair. A laugh bubbles up my throat, halting when I realize I most likely look the same.

"At least they weren't rats," Thorne comments.

I scowl at him as I rise to my feet, both of us doing our best to wipe away the grime. "They're rats with wings. That's not better."

He chuckles, but I stiffen as a pressing question reoccurs to me.

"What happened to your wings?" I demand. "Where do they go when you're not using them?"

He shrugs, leaving me behind as he starts down the tunnel. "Maybe I'll show you someday."

I huff, following after him. "Do you practice being mysterious, or does it come naturally to all reapers?"

"I don't know," he calls back. "I haven't met many others."

I quickly catch up, grateful that the tunnel is wide enough for us to walk side by side. "Really?"

He nods. "Let me guess, you thought I came from some hidden colony in the mountains of Death's realm?"

Heat creeps up my neck at his words. That's exactly what I assumed.

He laughs, but there's an edge to it. "Yeah, that wasn't quite my situation."

"Are there other reapers?" I ask tentatively.

He lifts a shoulder noncommittally. "Speaking of which, I'm curious why you haven't told anyone what I am?"

I look ahead, avoiding his gaze. "Maybe I know no one would believe me."

He nods. "That's why I haven't told anyone about your *eidolon*."

I freeze, turning to face him slowly.

"Don't you recall introducing me to your pretty little friend?" he teases, running a hand through his messy hair.

"I didn't forget," I correct him, my cheeks now burning. "I simply didn't expect you to know what they were called."

"I read," he says, offering no other explanation.

My eyes narrow. I know damn well that topic isn't mentioned in many books. It's not information most people just stumble across.

"By my estimation," he continues, "you're the first *Illusionist* to be able to summon an *eidolon* in at least five centuries."

"Six," I correct him. "If we're counting."

The corner of his mouth kicks up in a crooked smile. "That,

combined with the fact that you're also a *wraith,* makes you truly rare indeed."

I toss a few copper strands over my shoulder. "The Fates must pick favorites. Try not to sound jealous."

"Formidable as you are"—his lighthearted tone disappears, leaving him sounding almost regretful— "you wouldn't stand a chance against me in a true fight."

"I guess we'll see," I murmur, not understanding his sudden shift in mood.

"I hope not," he says softly before changing the subject. "Are your parents as gifted as you?"

I shake my head. "My father has no magic, but my mother came from a strong line of *Illusionists*. Or so I'm told."

He raises a brow.

"She died when I was born," I explain.

Sympathy creeps into his eyes. "I'm sorry."

I nod, unsure of what to say next. We carry on in silence for a while until we reach a deviation in the tunnel, leaving us with two options. We could continue following our current path or diverge to a new one that leads up a flight of stairs.

On instinct, I step toward the new path. It feels right. Inevitable almost. But Thorne shakes his head, pointing the other way.

I start to follow him, but as if I'm being pushed by some unseeable force, I find myself turning back to the staircase again. As I take a step toward it, something unexpected happens.

My collar pulses.

A flash of heat radiates against my skin, fading quickly before repeating. I grab the necklace, my fingers frigid compared to its warmth. *What's happening to me?*

Something tugs at my arm, startling me. I glance down to find a gloved hand wrapped around my bicep.

"Iverson," Thorne whispers, his brows furrowed with worry. "Are you alright?"

I pull myself from his grasp, hating how strange I must seem right now.

"We need to go that way." He nods in the other direction. "*Listen.*"

It's only then I hear the faint voices in the distance. I frown. How did I not notice them before?

Touching my collar again, I find that the stones have cooled. Whatever was happening, it's over now. Shaking my head to clear my thoughts, I reluctantly follow him toward the original path. Still, I can't help myself from glancing back once more. Whatever is up there, something tells me the sword isn't the only thing Baylor hides down here.

CHAPTER TWELVE

After another half hour, we come upon a group of people. As we get closer, I realize they are passing large rocks to each other in an attempt to clear a collapsed portion of the tunnel. One of the men glances up, his face covered in dirt making him nearly unrecognizable. He squints, reaching for his weapon until his gaze settles on me.

"Ivy," the familiar voice breathes.

Remy breaks away from the others and rushes forward, pulling me into his arms with no thought of the dirt that covers us both.

"What are you doing down here?" he demands. His attention flits to Thorne, and he stiffens, appraising the larger man with wary suspicion. "Who is this?"

I glance at Thorne to gauge his reaction, noticing how his eyes are narrowed at the spot where Remy's hand lingers on my arm.

"Baylor sent us down here," I tell my mentor. "He wants us to help with the search."

"And this guy?" he presses again, shifting to stand between myself and the reaper.

"You could address me directly," Thorne interjects, clearly not planning to help me deescalate the tension.

The soldiers halt their efforts, all of them observing our exchange with interest. I notice several familiar faces in the group, including Morwen's brother Warrick. They each watch my companion with narrowed eyes.

"Thorne, this is Remard Durandus," I explain, my patience running thin. "The Captain of the City Guard. Remy," I give him a hard nudge with my elbow. He ignores me, continuing his staring contest with the reaper. "This is Lord Thorne, Death's ambassador."

Gasps sound off among the men as they gape at Thorne with open hostility. For all the obvious reasons, Death is no one's favorite God. Everyone from the Fifth Isle has the unfortunate luck of being tainted by that dislike.

Proving my claims, Thorne removes his glove and shows them his tattoo, allowing the burning rose to speak for itself. Death's sigil is well-known among all of the courts.

Remy crosses his arms over his chest. "His Majesty mentioned the alliance, but he didn't say anything about you taking part in the investigation."

Thorne shows no reaction to Remy's suspicious tone. "I'm afraid I insisted."

"We're grateful for your aid," The captain says, sounding completely the opposite. "Why don't you go help clear the tunnel while I have a word with lady Iverson."

Thorne's gaze flashes to me briefly before returning to Remy. "Always happy to be of assistance."

Without another word, he leaves us to join the others who are still watching him with a mix of fear and distrust.

"Back to work," Remy orders his soldiers. "I want that tunnel clear within the hour."

With their command given, they all return to the task at hand as Remy pulls me further away, giving us a bit more privacy. Thorne's pale eyes track our movement as he grabs a heavy rock from the pile and tosses it aside as if it weighs nothing.

"Explain," Remy demands, pulling my attention away from the reaper.

I fill him in as quickly as I can, leaving out a few key details, such as my theory about the sword, as well as the threats Thorne made. Remy isn't exactly aware of my illicit activities with Della.

His usually smooth forehead wrinkles with confusion. "Why would the king agree to this?"

I shrug. "I suppose he needs the grain Killian is offering. He seemed desperate."

That part isn't technically a lie. He did seem desperate, just not for grain. There's some other motive spurring his actions.

Remy jerks his chin in Thorne's direction. "What do you make of him?"

My gaze returns to the man in question, snagging on the way his tightly corded muscles tense underneath his shirt as carries the large stones.

"Ivy."

My face heats I drag my attention back to Remy. Clearing my throat, I meet his questioning gaze. "He's powerful. And he's willing to do whatever it takes to recover the sword. I think we should be wary of him until we know more."

He nods, his expression unreadable. "I agree. Keep a close eye on him."

Not too close, I remind myself.

Pointing to the tunnel, I ask the question that's been on my mind since I found him. "What happened over there?"

"That one." He points to a ginger-haired soldier at the back of the group. Even covered in grime, he appears younger than the others. His lanky arms shake with exertion each time someone hands him one of the larger rocks. The poor mortal can't be older than nineteen.

"He worked down here with Darby," the captain continues. "His name is Kipps."

He pulls a folded piece of paper from his pocket and hands it to me. My eyes widen as I open the parchment to reveal a map of the tunnels. "Where did you get this?"

"Kaldar gave it to me before sending us down here."

My lips purse. "Would have been nice if he'd given me one too instead of sending us down here blind."

Remy rolls his eyes and taps the paper in my hands. "What do you see?"

Huffing, I push aside my annoyance and focus on the task in front of me. Using the tip of my finger to trace over the page, I track the path Thorne and I took, briefly pausing when I reach the staircase. According to the map, the staircase leads to a dead end. I'm tempted to ask Remy if he went up there, but some strange instinct has me holding my tongue. Instead, I continue scanning the map and realize all the tunnels are connected by a circular path that leads back to the first chamber we entered.

"There's only one way in or out," I whisper as the skin on the back of my neck prickles.

"Exactly," Remy says, his hazel eyes watching me intensely. "And there were guards stationed at several points throughout the palace above us. Darby couldn't have gotten out that way without anyone noticing him."

Grell Darby could still be here.

A shiver coils up my spine. Did Baylor know that? If so, why wouldn't he warn me? We should have been told there was a possibility we'd meet a sword wielding thief down here.

"But here's where it gets interesting." Remy points to the spot on the map that's directly across from where we're standing. "According to what this shows, there isn't supposed to be anything there. So what is that?" He gestures toward the collapsed tunnel. "Funny that the only place we haven't searched yet was conveniently left off the map and blocked by a cave-in. So, it's possible Darby was crushed by the debris, or he could be hiding on the other side of it."

"Or the more frightening option," I murmur as a horrible

thought occurs to me. "There could be a second exit behind that collapse that no one knows about."

I've no doubt Remy established a perimeter around the city as soon as he learned the weapon had been stolen, which means that if Darby exited through the palace there's a good chance he's still in the Solmare. However, if there's a second exit we don't know about, it could release somewhere outside the city.

"Exactly." His hard eyes meet mine, both of us understanding the weight of that implication. If Darby escaped through another portion of the tunnel, then he could be anywhere.

"What did Kipps have to say about all this?" I ask, sneaking another glance at the ginger guard.

Remy huffs, crossing his arms over his chest. "He was pretty insistent that we do not try to remove the stones. He said the cave-in happened last year, and no one was in a big hurry to fix it."

I turn my attention to the partially blocked tunnel, noting how most of the broken stones have jagged edges. Squinting through the darkness, I make out a few cracks that appear fresh. "Kipps said this happened last year?"

He nods as the two of us share a meaningful glance, both understanding what the other is thinking. The rocks haven't settled yet, which means this cave-in was recent.

"Either Kipps is lying to protect his friend..." I trail off.

"Or he was involved," Remy finished my thought.

"Did you know about any of this?" I gesture to our current whereabouts. The idea of Baylor being able to hide such a large secret right under our noses is terrifying. But the thought of Remy knowing and keeping it from me is somehow worse.

"No." He shakes his head, sending a wave a relief through me. "I remember Darby from the wall, but I didn't get to know him well before Kaldar requested him for a special assignment." His features tighten. "I guess this was it."

"Strange that this has been down here all this time, and we never knew."

"Very strange," he agrees. I can tell he wants to say more, but he's holding himself back. Given my reaction to our dangerous conversation this morning, I can't exactly blame him.

"Captain!" Warrick shouts, pulling our attention. "We've cleared the path!"

As we join the group, the soldiers begin discussing strategies for entering the tunnel. Ignoring them, I squat in front of the opening and peer through the dark hole. It's completely black inside, like some kind of unholy void. My skin prickles at the thought of going in there. It's narrow, only a few feet wide. The height appears tall enough for us to crawl through on our hands and knees. Glancing at a few of the soldiers, I shudder as I realize how tight it's going to be for them.

Closing my eyes, I take a deep breath through my nose before releasing it from my mouth, repeating the action several times. After a few moments, my heartbeat begins to even out as I force myself to accept the inevitable. Swallowing thickly, I stand up and turn back to the group.

"I'll go first," I announce.

They all go silent, their expressions shocked as they glance back and forth between me and the tunnel.

"Ivy." Remy's hard voice makes his opinion clear. "It's too dangerous."

I tell myself not to take the statement personally, but I can't stop my eyes from narrowing at his implication. "I'm the smallest person here. It's already going to be a tight squeeze for your soldiers, and we have no idea how much worse it could become the deeper we go." He opens his mouth to argue, but I don't give him the chance as I continue speaking. "Out of all of us, I'm the least likely to get stuck. And I'll have the best chance of turning around if things get bad."

"She has a point, Captain," Warrick offers hesitantly.

"I said no." Remy turns his glare on his second in command.

I take a step closer, lowering my voice as I place my hand on his arm. "You know I'm right, Remy. This is the best way."

All the guards take a step back, their gazes shifting around the cave as they avoid glancing at the two of us. If any of them spoke to their captain the way I do, they'd be severely punished. But fortunately for Remy, I'm not under his command. My attention flickers to where Thorne stands away from the others, watching the scene play out with an unreadable expression.

Dragging my gaze back to Remy, I find him tense as he studies me. After what seems like hours, his eyes drift shut for a moment, and I know I've won.

"Fine," he sighs, begrudgingly conceding to my demands. "But you don't take any unnecessary risks. If it's too tight or gets unstable, you turn back immediately. None of this is worth your life."

I try to hold back my grin. "I will."

"Are we sure this is wise?" Kipps speaks up, his eyes wide as he nervously shifts back and forth.

"Is there some reason you don't want us going that way," I ask him pointedly as I step around Remy to get a closer look at the young mortal.

He swallows. "It's just... This whole section might be unstable."

My eyes narrow. "I guess we'll find out."

He nods, his gaze dropping to my collar. "Yes, *wraith*."

Clenching my jaw, I turn back to the others. They carry on with their preparations, passing around sunstone necklaces since it would be too difficult to try to carry a lantern while crawling on our hands and knees. As their name would suggest, the crystals gather their charge from the sun. Unfortunately they only give off enough light to illuminate a few feet ahead. Still, it's better than nothing.

As I make my way back to the entrance, Remy steps up beside me.

"Alright, I'll go in after—"

"I'll go second," Thorne announces, cutting him off as he speaks for the first time since joining the group.

Everyone goes still, watching the reaper with varying degrees of dislike.

"Excuse me?" Remy asks, his tone dangerous.

Thorne appears completely unfazed as he saunters closer. "As Death's representative, I go second. If you'd care to argue, you're welcome to ask your king what he thinks. But I'm afraid he'll side with me."

Remy balls his fists as a muscle twitches in his jaw.

"Fine," he grounds out between clenched teeth. "We'll do it your way." He takes a step toward the reaper,. "But remember that I'm going to be right behind you. And if anything happens to that girl" —he points at me— "I don't care which God you serve; you will answer to me. Understand?"

As Thorne watches the captain, a glimmer of respect flashes behind his eyes. Instead of offering another quip, he inclines his head. "I wouldn't have it any other way."

Not wanting to waste any more time, I lower myself onto my hands and knees at the entrance. Dark worries attack my mind, forcing me to conjure the worst possible scenarios. What if we get stuck down here? What if it collapses and thousands of rocks crush me to death? What if—

"Do you want me to go first?" Thorne's soft voice startles me as he kneels by my side.

I try to scoff, but it sounds more like a whimper.

"And get stuck behind you?" The bravado in my tone rings false, but thankfully, he doesn't call me on it. "No, thank you."

Remy hands me one of the sunstones, and I tie it around my neck. Bracing myself for whatever comes next, I crawl into the hole and pray I come out again.

Here, in this suffocating darkness, I begin to regret every decision I've ever made. Each one of them somehow led me to this tunnel. The dim light of the sunstone is barely enough to see my own hands in front of me. Everything past that is a mystery. Minutes feel like hours as dust clogs my throat, and the sharp rocks cut into my knees and palms.

My only comfort is knowing that everyone else's suffering must be far greater. If this tunnel is tight for me, I can only imagine how hard it is for them. Thorne grunts behind me as he claws his way through the enclosed space.

"How's it going up there?" Remy calls from behind him.

"Fine," I croak, choking on the little bits of dirt that hang in the air.

"Wonderful," Thorne grumbles.

My neck aches as I lift my head again, searching for any sort of progress marker in this never-ending shaft. Instead, what I find has me coming to a complete stop.

"What's wrong?" Thorne asks, a hint of exertion in his voice.

"Up ahead." I swallow, desperately wishing we'd thought to bring water. "It's going to get narrower."

"How bad?" Remy shouts.

I stare at tapered tunnel before me, trying to judge if we can squeeze through. "We'll have to lie flat on our stomachs, and even then, it's going to be tight."

"Do you need to turn back?" Remy asks, worry filling his tone.

Yes.

"No," I say instead. "But everyone needs to stay put for now. Once I'm on the other side, I'll call back, and the rest of you can make your way one by one. We can't risk anyone getting stuck."

"I don't like this," Remy says.

"Me either," I whisper as I lie flat on my stomach.

The light disappears completely. From this angle, there's no way to prevent the sunstone necklace from getting trapped under my body. Tears leak from my eyes as I use my forearms to pull myself into the narrow section. My fingers dig into the stones, trying to find purchase. Each breath comes out ragged as my heart rate rises. Even for me, a person who exercises my body every day, this is a vigorous work out.

My chest tightens as I tell myself the only way out is forward, through the dark abyss. A fearful voice in the back of my mind whispers that I'm trapped. Buried underground aga—

No.

I'm not going there.

I stow my fear, tucking it into that mental prison deep within my subconscious. But I'm sure it will soon find its way out, probably by slipping through the cracks and filtering into my dreams. I learned long ago that the horrors we hide within our minds are never destroyed—we merely save them for later. They always find their way to surface.

"You alright?" Thorne calls.

"I'm—" My voice cuts off as the dust gets caught in my throat again. It likely doesn't help that my trachea already took a beating this morning. Breathing in these particles is only further aggravating my poor throat.

"Iverson!" he calls out again, but this time, panic creeps into his tone.

"Here!" I force the words out. "I'm almost through."

As I push further, a strange noise begins to drown out their voices.

"I can hear something," I tell them as I move into a slanted section, the new angle putting me at a downward incline. "I think I'm—"

The words cut off as I slide forward, my body scraping over the rocks until I tumble through a dark hole. I hit the ground hard, landing on my back as the impact knocks the air out of me.

I guess I reached the end of the tunnel, I think to myself.

A damp smell hangs in the air, filling my nostrils with each ragged breath. Thankfully, my sunstone survived the fall. With it no longer trapped under my body, I survey my new surroundings. My neck aches as I turn my head, finding what appears to be an underground river about ten feet to my right. I must have landed on its rocky banks.

The sweat that covers my body cools as I stare at the water. In the absence of light, it appears almost black. A shiver passes through me. There's something unsettling about the rushing current. Before I can move closer, a loud voice shouts from within the tunnel, pulling my attention back to the others. My strained muscles protest as I push myself up to my aching knees, finding the hole I fell through a few feet above me.

"I'm here!"

"Ivy!" Remy shouts over the others. "Are you alright?"

"Fine. There's a river," I call back lamely.

"A what?"

"Stay where you are," Thorne orders.

I roll my eyes as I rise to my feet. Where exactly does he think I plan to go? For a swim?

"Captain," The reaper's muffled voice drifts through the tunnel, quieter this time. "You stay back as I go through."

Remy begins to protest, but Thorne cuts him off.

"I don't think this area is as stable as we hoped it would be. We need to do this one at a time. I'll call back to you when I'm on the other side."

Lifting my sunstone, I hold it up to the entrance in an effort to create a beacon for the others. If they see where the drop off is, hopefully they won't take the same tumble I did.

After a few minutes, Thorne's gloved hand reaches through the opening, followed swiftly by the rest of him. His exit is far more graceful than mine, but it still takes him several seconds to recover from the fall.

"Are you through?" Remy yells. "Is she alright?"

"Yes," the reaper calls back, wiping the dirt from his shoulders as he stands up. "I've got her."

I roll my eyes. "I told you I was fine."

"You can go ahead and start—" Thorne's words cut off abruptly as several rocks begin falling into the path we just exited.

Remy's voice grows muffled. "What's—"

"Turn back!" Thorne shouts urgently. "Go back now! It's collap—"

The rest of his words are eaten up by the sound of the world breaking in half. The cave exhales a cloud of dirt into our faces as Thorne pushes me aside. He follows, landing next to me right before a large stone hits the ground exactly where we just stood, the impact breaking it in half.

I cover my head with my arms as dust and rocks land around us. Once the debris settles, I shoot up and dart back to the tunnel. Only... it's gone. What was once a hole in the side of the wall is now completely caved in.

CHAPTER
THIRTEEN

Terror like I've never known races through me. Everything spins as I try to process what's happening.

"Remy!" I shout frantically. "Answer me!"

I pull at the rocks that fill the tunnel, trying to dislodge them.

"Stop." Thorne's gloved hands drag me away. "You can't touch those, or you risk it caving in even more."

I fight his hold. "I have to help him. Please, I can't leave him there."

"Ivy, look at me," he says gently and I realize it's the first time he's used my nickname. "If you start pulling at these, you don't know what that could do to the rest of the tunnel. A lot of these rocks are holding up the others. You pull them out, and the rest come crashing down."

My chest clenches at the thought of Remy being crushed. Helplessness weighs down my limbs as I squeeze my eyes shut.

"The area they were in was more stable," Thorne continues, his voice soft. "It's likely that section didn't collapse, and right now, they're going back the way they came."

I shake my head as hope threatens to bloom inside me. "You don't know that."

I open my eyes to find him rolling up his sleeve and exposing his forearm. My brow pinches in confusion. "What are you—"

The sight of his veins turning black cuts off whatever questions I was about to ask. Starting at the crook of his forearm, dark lines move underneath his skin toward his wrist. In some distant corner of my mind, I'm aware that this is the first time I've seen this much of him. He always keeps himself covered.

Right before my eyes, a small shadow snake appears in his hand, its red eyes gazing up at Thorne. He nods, and the snake darts toward the collapsed tunnel, disappearing as it slips in-between the cracks in the rocks.

He turns back to me. "If they're there, my shadow will find them."

"Thank you," I whisper, still vaguely unsettled by the sight of the strange snake.

Minutes pass as we silently wait for news.

"Will it need to return?" I ask quietly, unsure what kind of a connection he has to his beasts. "Or are you able to see through its eyes?"

He shakes his head. "She'll tell me what she finds."

My gaze widens. "She?"

He nods but doesn't elaborate.

"It's clear," he says finally. "There are no bodies in the tunnels, and she saw people at the other end."

"They made it." Air whooshes from my lungs, leaving me dizzy with relief as I fall to my knees, unbothered by the hard rocks beneath me. "Remy's alright."

Thorne nods, turning to check out our surroundings. "But we won't be if we don't keep moving."

Knowing he's right, I push the wave of emotions down and I force myself to stand up. The others will be alright, but right now I need to focus on getting out of this place. Stepping closer to the river,

I glance upstream as I try to get a sense for where we are geographically. "I suppose the water must flow in from the ocean that way. So, if we move downstream, we'd be going west?"

"The river could bend at some point," Thorne points out beside me. "No way to be sure."

"I guess we'll have to follow it and find out. Do you suppose Darby tried to swim?"

"No…" He says slowly as his gaze catches on something behind me. "No, I think I he paddled."

"What?" I ask, turning to follow his eyeline. Squinting through the darkness, I can make out the shape of wooden canoes sitting on the rocky shore about twenty feet away.

We hurry toward them, careful not to trip on the uneven surface. Apprehension stirs within me as I notice there are three of them. That number has always been considered important to those who worship the three sisters. This morning, I thought perhaps I'd felt the interference of the Fates. How fortuitous that these boats are here waiting for us in a tunnel that isn't even supposed to exist…

Is this a sign that I'm following the right path? A sinking sensation pulls in my gut. Given the things I've done, I can't imagine they're leading me anywhere good. Fate is never kind to someone like me.

"Do you think people used to use these tunnels often?" Thorne asks. "Before your king had them closed off?"

Cobwebs line the interior, sparking the terrifying question of how many spiders have lived in these boats over the years. I swipe my finger against the wood, leaving a dust trail behind. "Maybe, but they look like they've been down here for ages."

Thorne examines the canoes closely, poking certain spots as he searches for damage. "Lucky for us, the wood's not rotted."

Yes, I think. *How lucky.*

"Do you honestly believe Darby used one of these to get out?" I ask.

"I think that's exactly what happened." He points to impressions left in the dirt where something was clearly pushed toward the water. "I hope you're good with an oar."

Working together, we manage to get one of the boats into the river, where freezing water fills the soles of my boots. Thorne holds it steady as I climb in and take the back seat. After I'm settled, he hops into the front, letting the heavy current move us forward.

My tired arms protest as I drag the oar through the water, paddling in unison with Thorne. Unfortunately, it's much harder than the fisherman at the docks make it look. My body aches from the repeated movements, but I don't stop. I keep my gaze on Thorne, noting how his back and shoulder muscles flex as he rows. The movement is strangely mesmerizing.

Eventually, the water calms down enough for us to carry on a conversation. I can't stop myself from asking a question that's been on my mind since we started rowing.

"Why don't you just fly out?"

"And abandon you?" He tosses a grin over his shoulder.

When he turns back around, I briefly consider smacking him on the head with my oar. For a moment, I think he won't answer me, but then he speaks again.

"Look up." He points at the sharp rocks jutting out of the ceiling. The light from my sunstone catches the glare of beady eyes as they stare down at me. *Bats.* I quickly drop my gaze, hoping to avoid angering this group. I'd prefer *not* to be swarmed again.

"Those rocks combined with poor visibility don't make for good flying conditions," Thorne continues to explain. "It's not worth the risk."

"How do you conceal your wings?" I ask again.

"Magic."

As I roll my eyes at his nonanswer, something below the surface catches my attention. A flickering light darts past us beneath the dark waters.

My brows shoot up as I grab the side of the boat and peer over the edge. "Did you see that?"

"What?" he asks, twisting toward me.

Bursts of color move through the water: blue, purple, and green. Dozens of them swim in playful circles around our canoe.

"Well, I definitely saw that," he says, releasing his oar as he turns around.

Lights rise to the surface, coming close enough for us to make out their shape.

"Gormags," I murmur, mesmerized by the school of tiny fish.

Gormags are one of the most beautiful creatures in the world, despite their small size. Each of them emits a bioluminescent glow, creating a sea of color around us. They're usually only found at great depths, but somehow, a colony of them must have migrated to this underground river. I suppose it makes sense, since they avoid sunlight.

"I've never seen them in person before," Thorne muses next to me. "Only in paintings."

"Neither have I." I reach a hand into the water, utterly enthralled by their beauty. Several of the gormags come to investigate, sliding against my fingers with their slick scales.

Thorne's gaze flickers to me. "You and the captain seem familiar."

I twist my head toward him, surprised by the randomness of statement.

"He's the closest thing I've had to a father," I answer honestly as I continue dragging my hand through the water and letting the fish inspect me.

Thorne's brows pinch with confusion. "I thought Lord Pomeroy was still alive?"

I narrow my eyes at him. "Have you been checking up on me, Reaper?"

"Perhaps." He shrugs, not sounding sorry.

"Then I'm sure you can fill in the blanks about why my father and I aren't close," I say, turning my attention back to the fish. I laugh as one of them wraps its mouth around my pinky, nibbling at me with its gums.

Thorne chuckles, the sound rich and throaty. "Is it trying to eat you?"

I smile as the fish releases my finger. "Pretty difficult without teeth."

My amusement fades as the gormags suddenly scatter, disappearing back to the depths of the river and leaving us in darkness again.

"What happened?" My brows scrunch together.

"I think we should—" Thorne's words cut off as his gaze shifts behind me, his face twisting with horror.

I don't get a chance to ask him what's wrong before something wraps around my torso and drags me overboard. My eyes sting as I struggle to see anything through the dark water rushing around me. I make out a pale tentacle wrapped about my waist, pinning my arms to my sides. Thrashing against its hold, I fight to free myself as it pulls me to the bottom of the river.

The rope-like limb tightens against my stomach, squeezing the air out of me as I struggle to hold my breath. With my arms trapped at my sides, I use my limited mobility to stretch my fingers toward one of the blades strapped to my thigh. I manage to pull it from its sheath and twist my wrist, jabbing the creature. For a brief moment, it loosens, allowing me to free one arm before it tightens its hold again and slams me against the riverbed.

My head smacks off a large rock, sending a flash of hot pain through my skull. Momentarily disoriented, my eyes drift to the surface where light and dark dance above me. A vibrant red glow illuminates the water as inky shadows battle pale tentacles. I briefly wonder if the gormags have returned when I'm suddenly dragged across the muddy bed of the river.

Terror fills me as I realize it's pulling me toward a large hole about twenty feet away. Suddenly, a pale squid-like creature rises from its depths, opening its wide mouth to show me two large black teeth shaped like a bird's beak.

My heart hammers in my chest and panic sets in. A scream tries to claw out of my throat, but there's no air to give it voice. Thrashing around, I use my free arm to reach out, searching for anything to grab onto. My fingers cling to another large rock. I use all of my strength to curl myself around it as the long tentacle tries to pull me toward the monster's open mouth.

The creature yanks harder, squeezing me tight enough to crack a rib. I want to cry as the stone begins to loosen from the sand. There's no way it's going to hold much longer. My mind races as I search for a way out, but the only solution I can think of might just kill me.

A violent scream tears from my mouth as I roar at the monster. Water fills my throat as the familiar pain rips through me. My very core is being split in two. I'm sure my head is about to explode as the *eidolon* materializes in front of me. Her vacant eyes stare into the distance as I silently command her to swim toward me.

Obeying my orders, she grabs one of the knives strapped to my thigh, quickly using it to slice through the thick tentacle. Dark blood leaks into the water as its detached limb floats to the floor. A horrible, high-pitched shriek fills my ears as the creature leaps from its hole, gnashing its hideous black teeth at us as several more tentacles race forward.

My lungs burn as I use what little strength I have left to wrap myself in an illusion and push toward the surface, leaving my duplicate behind to distract the squid.

Kill it!

She obeys, swinging her blade at the monster while dodging its angry tentacles. I swim faster, knowing she won't last long on her own.

The lights above me are brighter now, but I don't have time to question their source. The pressure in my lungs is nearly overwhelming as my body urges me to breathe. Horrible screams come from the surface as a large creature crashes into the water. Another squid. Its body is blackened, *burned*. It's completely still as it sinks to the bottom.

A moment later Thorne dives into the water, his shadows following behind him. They move through the dark, searching for something. His eyes widen with fear as the water turns red around me.

A sharp pain slices through me, making my body jerk.

My *eidolon*.

Agony burns inside of me as I turn back, squinting through the crimson haze to find her floating in pieces. The image of my own likeness ripped apart in such a way has me gasping. The river fills my throat once more, the taste of it unlocking the secret prison within my mind. That fateful day so many years ago, I drowned in water just like this. Then, I felt as if I was being cradled in its embrace as it lulled me to sleep. This time is different. Brutal and unfair. I kick my legs harder as the strength begins to leave my body. My illusions dissolve, leaving me visible as my *eidolon* winks out of existence.

Thorne's gaze lands on me, and the last thing I see before my eyes drift shut are dark shadows speeding toward me.

CHAPTER FOURTEEN

"Open your eyes, Angel!" a rough voice shouts. "Come on. Open your eyes, Ivy!"

Something hard pounds against my chest, and my eyes shoot open. Wet coughs rack through me as water pours from my mouth. Rolling onto my side, I purge the river from my stomach until there's nothing left. My ribs protesting with each violent heave. Nausea still churns as I wipe my mouth and finally become aware of my surroundings.

I'm lying in the bottom of the canoe with Thorne sitting a few inches away. He watches me, his expression unreadable. Water drips from his soaking wet clothes, and I recall the horror on his face when my *eidolon* was killed. In the confusion of the battle, did he think she was me? The memory of his behavior is completely at odds with the indifference he displays now.

Tremors scurry over my skin like invisible spiders as my mind races to catch up. I scramble to my knees, ignoring the pain as I peer overboard. I should be thrilled by the absence of pale tentacles and large teeth, but instead I stare at the placid water with eerie suspicion. There's a certain type of paranoia that surges in the wake of violence. The shift from chaos to calm is too sudden to be trusted, leaving one with a pervasive sense that something is wrong. It *can't* be over just like that.

"They're gone," Thorne says as something dark swims out from beneath the boat. Barely a second passes before I've unsheathed a blade, my arm already cocking back to throw it.

"My shadows." He plucks the knife from my hand. "They are guarding us."

My brows pinch together as I lean further over the side to investigate. Several snakes circle the water beneath us, no doubt hoping for a snack. I nod as I sit back down. Forcing myself to meet his gaze, I speak the words I've been holding back.

"Thank you."

He shrugs as he hands me back my weapon. "I'd hate for you to lose more of your pretty knives."

"No." I shake my head as I sheath the blade. "For pulling me out of the water."

"Ah." He smirks, but it doesn't sit quite right on his face. There's something forced about the casual way he leans against the rail, reminding me of my own performances. "I imagine your death would put a damper on this alliance."

I suppose it would. A shiver skates over my chilled skin as I imagine what would have happened if he hadn't saved me. Despite the rumors people spread about me, I don't think I'd survive being eaten alive. Drowning, however, is a different matter entirely.

Choking and suffocating are much the same, both requiring the absence of air. But for some strange twist of fate, these familiar horrors should have cut my life short many years ago. Instead, they haunt me from grave to grave, unable to close the casket. No matter how many times I survive, each standoff with this enemy fills me with terror. My fingers move to my collar, wrapping around it as I recall the way my lungs burned.

"I drowned once," I whisper. "As a child."

That day marked the first time I escaped the clutches of death, but not the last. I'm not sure why I bring it up, but I can't take the words back now. Perhaps I longed to say something real. Something honest. Maybe I thought he might understand the urge to speak an ugly truth instead of a pretty lie.

Thorne's head tilts to the side, sending a strand of wet hair falling across his forehead. He makes no move to brush it away. Instead, his attention is focused on me, as if I'm some strange problem he can't solve. For a moment, I think he won't respond, but then he gestures to my necklace.

"You touch that a lot."

"Do I?" I drop my hands into my lap, balling them into fists to stop their shaking.

"I didn't think most highborn ladies wore the same jewels every day."

The unasked questions in his eyes demand answers, forcing me to look away before I do something crazy like give them to him.

"It was a gift," I murmur, staring at the shadows once more.

"From your lover?"

"From the king," I correct him, as if somehow that distinction matters.

"Is there a difference?"

Yes. I want to scream the word. I imagine my voice echoing off the walls of this cavern, bouncing all the way back to Baylor himself. But I hold my tongue, shifting to face Thorne with a practiced smile.

"No." I shake my head. "Not really."

We sit in silence for a few moments, swaying with the gentle swells of the river. He turns his head, gazing at the path before us. A bit of green clings to one of his dark locks, no doubt a piece of algae.

Without thinking, I move forward to brush it away, but a gloved hand darts out, snagging my wrist in a punishing grip. He drops it immediately, as if I burned him. He physically recoils from me as he moves to the other side of the canoe.

"Don't. Touch. Me." His eyes are feverish as he stares at me with disgust. "Ever."

My eyes widen as heat flames my face. "I'm sor—"

"Don't apologize," he cuts me off, his tone harsh. "Just tell me you understand."

Dropping my gaze, I nod as my stomach churns from the shame.

That's a boundary I can respect—should have respected from the start. I don't know why I reached out to touch him. We aren't friends. We're barely allies. Of course he doesn't want the king's whore anywhere near him. No one wants the dirty *pet* to get too close, even if it was innocent.

I scoot back, awkwardly settling into my seat at the opposite end of the boat. Picking up my oar, I avoid looking at Thorne.

"We should keep moving," I say, my voice steady.

"Ivy, I—"

I shake my head, cutting him off. "Those creatures are gone for now, but they could come back."

I don't glance in his direction again until he settles into his own seat, turning his back to me. Neither of us speaks as we begin to row again. The heavy atmosphere pushes in on me, but I ignore it.

Thinking back over my day, I realize it was designed to test me. All of my carefully concealed nightmares somehow followed me into my waking hours, accompanied by horrifying new monsters that will no doubt haunt me forever. Picturing the squid's sharp teeth, I wonder if Darby encountered them too. Did he even make it out of this cave, or did he meet his end underneath the waves? And if all of this was a test, what exactly are the Fates trying to prepare me for?

After another hour of rowing, we finally come upon a shoreline only a few yards from the mouth of the cave. A much-welcomed breeze floats over the water, carrying the scent of the lush forest on the other side. Moonlight peeks through the opening, casting an ethereal glow upon the lonely canoe banked in the mud.

"I guess this confirms Darby survived the squid," I mutter as we wade through the sludge, dragging our boat to shore.

"But he didn't escape unscathed." Thorne's voice is cold as he points to a bloody handprint on the side of the vessel.

My fingers move to my blades as I step closer. Peering inside, I find dark red stains marking the bottom of the canoe.

"Where would he go for aid if he were injured?" Thorne asks.

"I'm sure guards have been stationed at his home since this morning, and there's likely a perimeter around the city. But it's possible he went there before anyone knew the blade was missing."

He shakes his head. "I doubt he's stupid enough to stay at his own house, but we should at least interview his wife."

"I agree," I tell him. "But that conversation can wait until morning."

He gives me an incredulous glance. "We don't have time to waste."

I heave a frustrated sigh as I tuck a strand of wet hair behind my ear. "She's probably exhausted from the stress of her husband's crime. I doubt she will be in a talkative mood if we barge into her home and wake her children in the middle of the night."

He ponders this for a few moments before conceding. "I suppose your instincts may be better when it comes to women."

I roll my eyes. "Besides, do you even know where she lives?"

He pauses. "Fair point. I'm guessing you'll get those details?"

I nod as we step out of the cave. Tall pine trees surround us as we enter a forest. I'm guessing it's part of the woods that borders the Lowers. I nearly groan as my tired legs protest at the thought of the long walk back to the palace. Perhaps I will be able to pay someone for a ride, so I don't have to climb hilly streets for the next hour.

My mouth opens wide on a yawn as I stretch my arms above my head. "Meet me outside the pub around sunrise, and we can go speak to her together."

I start to make my way through the forest, hearing his steps behind me as I hop over a fallen log. We're heading for an opening in the trees when he tenses.

"The cavalry's coming." He points toward something in the distance.

I follow his gaze to find a dozen soldiers on horseback crossing over a hill about a mile out. They're likely scouring the entire city and its surrounding areas, searching for Darby. My heart squeezes as I pray to the Fates that Remy is in that group and he wasn't hurt when the tunnel collapsed.

I note their direction as they disappear behind a copse of trees. I should be able to cross paths with them and get a ride home. A strange ripping sound comes from behind me and I turn to find Thorne standing a few feet away with his wings fully extended. They stretch at least six feet on both sides, and I wonder once more how he manages to hide them.

My breath hitches at the sight of their beauty. The black feathers are just as lush and alluring as the first time I saw them. My fingers itch to feel their softness, but I ignore the impulse, remembering the anger on his face before.

He grins. "You said you wanted to see them again."

"That's not what I—"

"Until tomorrow, Angel," he cuts me off.

With a powerful flap of his wings, Thorne rises into the air and disappears into the night sky. Within seconds, he's nothing more than a speck among the stars.

"Fucking reaper," I mutter to myself as I begin my solitary walk to find the soldiers. I'll be glad when we've located Darby, and I never have to lay eyes on *Lord Thorne* ever again.

HIS HAND HOLDS my hair in a tight grip as he shoves my head underwater.

My *feet kick wildly as I try to push to the surface, but it hovers above me, another world just beyond my reach. My fingers claw and scratch at his hand, digging into his flesh with all my strength.*

He yanks me up by my hair, and I gasp, my mouth opening wide to take in as much air as possible.

My chest expands painfully as tears leak from my eyes, mixing with the dirty lake water that clings to my skin. Instinctively, I grab his wrist, trying to take some of the weight off my screaming scalp.

I want to call out for Bel and beg him to find me, but I can't catch my breath.

"You're an abomination," a rough voice whispers in my ear. "I should have done this the night your whore mother brought you into the world. Die, you wretched beast!"

The water swallows me whole as I'm plunged below the surface again. No. No. No!

Water floods my mouth as I release a scream of rage. In some distant corner of my mind, I recognize the voice. I understand the meaning behind his words.

I know exactly whose hand holds me under.

My legs still kick, but not as forcefully. Fatigue is settling into my aching muscles. I always believed water could extinguish any flame, but the heat in my lungs burns me from the inside out. My grip on the man above me slips right before my hand splashes back into the water. I want to reach for him again, but I can't think past the pressure in my head.

The temptation to fill my lungs is too great to be denied.

Tired of fighting, I give in to that deep, gnawing urge.

I breathe the water in, then out.

It's just like breathing air, only heavier somehow. My lips twitch with the ghost of a smile as the fire inside of me finally dies.

The hand that was holding me lets go, but instead of floating to the surface, I sink below the depths. The water welcomes me into its cold embrace, as if I belong here. Maybe I do? Now that I've stopped thrashing about, I see a few fish swimming in the distance. Their iridescent scales flicker pretty colors as the sun hits them.

My heavy lids fight to stay open, but sleep calls to me. If Clara finds out I'm napping, she'll be angry. She says ten is too old to still take naps every day. But Clara will never think to search for me down here. It's the perfect hiding spot.

Something large splashes at the surface, and a dark shape moves toward me. As it gets closer, I recognize my brother's face. The final image I *see before my eyes drift shut is Bel's hand reaching for me, but a dark voice whispers that he's too late.*

I'm already gone.

I shoot up in my bed, desperate for the air I'd been denied in my dream.

My original fear.

My first haunting.

I catch my dim reflection in the mirror across the room. My chest heaves against the white nightgown, and messy, unbound hair crowds my face. Staring into my amber eyes, I recite my familiar lies.

"It was just a nightmare."

It wasn't.

"The past cannot touch me here in the present."

Yes, it can.

"This will be the last time."

It never is.

CHAPTER
FIFTEEN

One good thing about the Lowers is its proximity to the water. A cool breeze moves through the district, carrying the briny scent of the fish market. The sun peeks its shy head over the horizon, sending orange and pink beams reflecting across the sea. They stretch toward the coast but never meet it.

The streets aren't crowded yet, relieving me of the need to become invisible. Leaning next to the front entrance of the pub, I feel strangely exposed. I think I've come to rely on my invisibility too much as of late, using it as a crutch. I've reveled in the comfort of anonymity to the point that being visible, even without an audience, sets my nerves on edge. Revealing myself right now is an exercise in control.

"This is healthy," I whisper as I push my toes into the ground to stop my knees from twitching.

"If you're talking about getting breakfast at the pub, I'd have to disagree," an amused voice says.

Pushing away from the wall, I find Thorne approaching. His dark hair is still slightly damp, curling around the ends. Is he staying nearby? For some reason, I can't imagine him renting a room. It's too mundane for someone like him. He's dressed in the same dark colors as always, though he's forgone the cloak today. He carries no sword, but I spot a dagger at his hip. Practical.

"Reaper."

"Angel."

"You didn't sneak up on me, you know," I tell him honestly. "I sensed you coming. You have a very distinct presence."

"It's too early for flattery." He examines my face, no doubt noticing the dark circles under my eyes. "How did you sleep?"

"Perfectly," I lie. "You?"

"I dreamed I was being eaten by a giant monster with tentacles."

"Condolences."

I ignore the amusement in his eyes as I begin walking in the direction of the Darby house, his footsteps following close behind me. Thankfully, one of the guards was able to give me the address after they found me wandering through the forest last night. They gave me a ride back to the palace where Remy was waiting for me. Fortunately, he only sustained minor cuts and bruises from our time in the tunnels.

I expected Thorne to be distant this morning, but he's still acting irreverent and amused. After the way he responded when I tried to touch him, I know he's not as unbothered as he appears to be. I peek over my shoulder, catching his eye.

He raises a brow. "Need something?"

"Just making sure you aren't falling behind," I tell him as I turn back around.

When he speaks again, he's much closer than before, his breath coasting over my ear.

"I wouldn't advise it," he warns.

I swallow. "What?"

"Underestimating me."

I speed up, quietly scolding myself. I'm not here to be his friend.

But Baylor expects me to get some sort of useful information out of my dear companion, and he won't be pleased if I come back empty-handed. Trying not to be too obvious, I settle for a safe conversation starter.

"Are you staying nearby?" I ask, giving him time to catch up.

His lazy gaze slides over to me. "I've made accommodations."

"Where?"

"Solmare."

"Which part?"

"One of the districts."

I sigh. Of course he would make this difficult. "Please, don't be so forthright. You have an air of mystery to uphold."

His lips twitch. "My apologies."

I shake my head. "Such an embarrassment."

"I hate disappointing my fans."

"In your dreams," I scoff.

"My lady, don't flatter yourself." He runs a hand through his hair. "My dreams are reserved for tentacled monsters."

I start to laugh, but it catches in my throat as I stop dead in my tracks.

The strangest sensation settles over me. It's as if some invisible cord is tugging me to the right. Hesitantly, I turn to find a dilapidated two-story house. The once white siding has been stained by time, fading into a muddy gray. A single blue shutter clings to the house, narrowly avoiding the fate of its fallen friends, who now rot in the damp soil of the overgrown garden.

It's no worse off than the other homes we've passed in the Lowers, but something about this one feels sinister, as if it's rotting from the inside out. Yet, it still calls to me. I take a step forward, noticing the collar pulse as it grows hot against my skin. It's the same thing that happened last night when we found the other path in the tunnels. The invisible tether tightens as I move closer, helpless against this instinct.

"Angel?"

Thorne's voice pulls me out of my haze, snapping the cord that was tugging me toward the house. I face the reaper, finding him staring at me with concern.

"Sorry," I mutter, blinking several times to clear my mind. "Just tired."

His eyes narrow. "I thought you said you slept perfectly?"

I give him a bland look. "I lied."

He gasps, pretending to be shocked.

"Get used to it," I tell him. "I do it all the time."

"For such a beautiful angel, your hobbies veer toward the demonic."

I shrug. "Even angels have their vices."

"Trust me, I'm aware," he murmurs, a faint note of sadness ringing in his tone.

Before I can ask what he means, he starts walking. I follow behind him, but I can't stop myself from glancing back at the house one last time. Movement in the upstairs window catches my attention.

The outline of a person stands on the other side of the glass, hidden by shadows. My skin tingles as a familiar awareness settles over me. They're watching us.

"Coming?" Thorne calls.

I drag my gaze away, finding him several feet ahead of me. "Yeah."

His eyes harden as he shifts his attention to the house. I glance back, stiffening when I notice the upstairs window is now empty.

Brushing off the paranoia, I force myself to keep walking. After a few minutes, we turn a corner, and the Darby house comes into view. It's small, but the contrast between this home and the previous one is striking. And when compared to the residences that line the outskirts of the Lowers, this is practically a mansion. It's not extravagant by any sense of the word, but you can tell those who live here take care of what's theirs.

Two soldiers stand guard outside the house. Recognizing me, they bow their heads and let us pass immediately. A few seconds after we knock on the door, it swings open to reveal a mortal woman.

Alice Darby appears to be in her early thirties. It's clear that she's usually quite pretty, but recent events have taken their toll. Her dirty blonde hair is tied back by a ribbon, though at least half of it has come loose. Based on the wrinkled state of her simple dress, I'd say she slept in it. Dark circles haunt her bloodshot eyes as they stare right through us. It's remarkable the impact heartbreak can have on the body after only one day.

In this moment, I hate Grell Darby for putting her through this.

"Hello, Mrs. Darby. I'm Iverson Pomeroy." I speak to her in a soothing tone, noting the spark of recognition when she hears my name. Even in the Lowers, people are aware of the king's *wraith*. "This is my associate, Thorne. We're here to speak with you about your husband."

"He's not home," she says harshly, trying to slam the door.

I catch it with my hand, using my strength to hold it open. "We were hoping to ask you some questions about him, if that's alright?"

She glares at me for a few more moments before her shoulders slump. Mrs. Darby steps away from the door, leaving it open for us to follow her.

The inside of their home is warm. The bottom floor is a single room, divided by a half wall separating the kitchen and seating area. I'd guess there are two bedrooms upstairs. The furnishings are dated but well-made. Bright yellow curtains hang in front of the windows, adding life to the room. On the floor, a handmade doll sits with her back to the wall, a tiny wooden tea cup knocked over by her feet.

I spot three oil lamps scattered through the room. With poverty rampant in this part of the city, many families are lucky to have a single candle to chase away the night. Clearly the Darby's are doing well for themselves.

Or they were.

"We're sorry to bother you this early, Mrs. Darby."

"Not sorry enough to leave," she mutters while gesturing for us to take a seat on the small couch.

We both ignore the loud screech as she slowly drags a chair over from the kitchen, positioning it across from us before plopping down in it. Thorne catches my eye, nodding toward the corner where two travel bags sit on the floor.

"Planning a trip?" he asks impassively.

She shakes her head. "I'm sending my children to stay with my parents, not that it's any of your business."

"It is my business, actually." He leans forward, resting an elbow on his knee. "Considering the item your husband stole was promised to the God of Death."

Mrs. Darby's eyes widen at that news.

"D-Death?" she stammers.

"Yes. And since I speak with his authority, you'd be wise to be forthcoming."

The room darkens as shadows creep along the walls and stretch over the floorboards. Mrs. Darby's face pales, her chin quivering as she glances toward the stairs, no doubt worried for her children. As the shadows continue spreading over the ground, getting closer to us, she lifts her feet onto her chair, hugging her knees to her chest with shaking hands.

"My lord?" I instill as much condescension as I can into the title.

Slowly, he turns his head toward me, his eyes colder than I've seen them.

I arch a single brow. "Are the dramatics necessary?"

"I'm merely ensuring she understands the gravity of the situation," he explains. "And who she'd be angering if she chooses to lie to us."

I nod toward Mrs. Darby, who's currently rocking back and forth in her seat while she whispers muffled prayers to the Fates.

"I'd say she gets it."

The reaper follows my gaze and shrugs. "Fair enough."

The shadows immediately recede, shrinking back into the corners like a predator in hibernation. The mortal woman releases a loud exhale, both hands covering her racing heart. I offer her a warm smile, hoping in vain to reassure her.

"Mrs. Darby, would you mind if my associate takes a look around while you and I talk?"

Thorne's head whips in my direction. "And why would I do that?"

I offer him a bright smile. "Because I asked you to."

He watches me for a few moments, annoyance battling with something else I don't recognize.

"Fair enough," he says, echoing his earlier words.

I turn back to Mrs. Darby. "Well?"

"You're giving me a choice?" she asks, shock evident in her voice.

I wonder if her thoughts are turning toward how she was treated yesterday morning, when soldiers busted through her door without asking. I remember the day soldiers stormed into my home and ripped my entire world apart. How helpless it made me feel to not be given a choice. Shame curls in my stomach. Putting on a mask of politeness doesn't make me better than them.

"No, ma'am," I whisper. "I'm not."

"Then I guess it's fine," she says, waving off the demand. I imagine she's reached the stage where she's tired of fighting useless battles.

Thorne rises from the couch and wanders into the kitchen. He disappears behind the half wall, creating the illusion that we're alone now. I appreciate him letting me take the lead on this interview, since his cold demeanor hasn't been much help here.

But he's not cold with you, my subconscious protests.

He was last night, I remind myself.

Shaking away the thought, I return my focus to the matter at hand. "Do you know where your husband is?"

She shakes her head.

"Have you noticed any odd behavior from him recently?"

Mrs. Darby shrugs, avoiding my eyes.

Sighing, I lean forward and rest my hands on my thighs. "I know this is difficult, but I need you to answer my questions honestly."

Her gaze drifts to the window, peering through the gap between the curtains. From the outside, little would be visible, but from here, we can see the early risers walking past.

"Not one of my neighbors has come to check on me." Her voice takes on a distant quality. "None of them have brought food or offered their support. They think we deserve this."

My brows scrunch together. "Why would they think that?"

"Because we reached too high," she says, a sad smile on her lips. "Even when Grell was stationed on the wall, he made a good living. More than most folks around here. But when he was reassigned six months ago, his salary tripled. That's when the whispers started."

I tense as my thoughts turn toward Baylor's warning. "Whispers?"

"About how we didn't deserve it. How we thought we were too good for them now."

My shoulders slump with relief. "You mean gossip."

She nods. "They thought they were being quiet, but I heard them. It never occurred to any of them that I'd give up the money if it meant my husband would go back to how he was before."

"What do you mean?"

"That job changed him." Her eyes drift in my direction, but it's as if she's staring right through me. "Ever since he got reassigned, he's been different." Her pretty features twist. "Distant. Mean."

"Did he have a temper?" I ask, afraid of where this story is going.

Her gaze drops to the floor. "He never hurt the children."

"But he's hurt you?" I ask softly.

She doesn't answer, but I know. I've heard similar stories from the women Della brings into MASQ. Most of the waitstaff came from similar situations.

"He's paranoid," she whispers. "One night last month, I could hear him from the other room. He was shouting at someone to leave him alone. I rushed in, thinking he was screaming at one of the children, but there was no one there. It was just him."

"Mama?" a small voice calls.

Turning toward the stairs, I spy a child dressed in a nightgown. Judging by her size, she can't be more than five years old. Her hair is the same dirty blonde shade as her mother's. Her big eyes are full of fear as they glance between us.

"Go help your sister get dressed, Bess," Mrs. Darby says, her voice brighter than before. If she didn't have her children to care for, I wonder if she'd still be trying at all. "We need to leave soon."

The little girl runs back up the stairs, and Mrs. Darby faces me once more, slumping forward with exhaustion.

"I understand how you're feeling," I tell her.

She snorts. "No offense, my lady, but I know who you are. What could someone like you possibly understand about my situation?"

It's a fair question. I know how my life looks from the outside. Growing up in the palace and becoming the king's favorite would be a dream for most people. But despite our differences, I relate to this woman more than any of the courtiers at the castle. Our lives are distorted versions of the same story.

"You used to feel lucky," I say softly. "Your life wasn't perfect, but it was better than most around here. Even though you didn't grow up with that kind of stability, you started to rely on it." My gaze moves back to the window, watching strangers through the curtains as they move about their lives. "You forgot how fragile it was, how tenuous. You gave him your love and trust... Your youth. And now you feel like a fool because, despite all his promises, he left you with nothing."

Her eyes are wide as I return my attention to her. It's clear she's shocked by my words.

"So now, you hate him," I tell her, forcing a deep breath into my lungs before I admit the next part. "But you also miss him, who you thought he was. And worst of all, you blame yourself because you should have known better. You should have remembered that good things aren't meant for you. Believe me, Alice, I understand that kind of disappointment very well."

Silence fills the room as my confession settles around us. After a few moments, a throat clears and we turn to find Thorne returning from the kitchen. My heart quickens, but I force it to slow down. A wave of self-disgust settles in my gut. I shouldn't have revealed that much. I'm meant to be spying on him, not sharing my deepest secrets.

The questions in his eyes confirm he heard our conversation. He looks me up and down, as if the emotional wounds I spoke of left physical marks on my body. The urge to squirm under his inspection is strong, but I sit still in my seat. I learned long ago that the best deceptions are external. Appearances lie better than words ever could.

He clears his throat, turning his attention to the woman across from me.

"Your husband was here the night before last," he says, the accusation dropping into the room like a bomb. "He was injured, and you helped him."

My gaze snaps back to her.

She jumps up, putting space between herself and Thorne. "How do you—"

"You did a good job cleaning the bloodstains on the floor," he tells her. "But you didn't throw out the rags you used to wipe it up."

"Please," she begs him. "I don't want trouble."

His face is cold. Not a single hint of compassion fills his ice-blue eyes as the room darkens again. "I told you there would be consequences for lying to me."

My pulse quickens. Is he actually going to hurt her? I thought he was bluffing, but the fury on his face can't be faked.

"Please," I implore her. Reaching out, I grab her freezing hand in mine and squeeze it tight. "I won't let anything happen to you, but you have to tell us the truth. Have you seen your husband?"

Her bottom lip trembles as her gaze flits back and forth between us.

"He was here." Her quiet voice is barely audible. "He showed up in the middle of the night, but he wasn't supposed to be done with his shift until morning. And his clothes were soaking wet." Her face pales. "And the blood... There was so much of it."

Sounds like he got dragged into the river too, only *he* wasn't as lucky.

"Did he have a weapon with him?" Thorne demands.

She shakes her head. "Not that I saw. I think something tried to take a bite out of his leg." Her mouth twists into a grimace. "I stitched him up as best I could, but I'm no healer."

"What else happened?" Thorne asks.

"He kept trying to get me to go with him. Kept telling me that he had something to show me, and I needed to follow him. I told him I couldn't leave the children, but that made him angry. That's when he grabbed me. Hard."

Her voice grows softer as her eyes become glassy. She rolls up her right sleeve, revealing the bracelet of bruises that decorate her wrist. "He was trying to drag me out the door, but I kept fighting him. Bess ran down the stairs. She was crying, and when he saw her, he dropped me. I expected him to apologize like he always does, but instead, he walked out. Grell left and he hasn't been back since."

She stares at the wall, tears streaming down her face. She appears so lost, and I'm filled with hatred again. I want to find Darby and paint the walls with his blood. Forcing myself to calm down, I place a hand on Mrs. Darby's shoulder.

"Thank you for telling us the truth. We'll go now."

She nods, not looking at either of us. I pull a folded piece of paper from my pocket. Grabbing her hand, I tuck it into her palm and close her fist around it as I capture her gaze with mine.

"If you need work, go to this address tomorrow. Ask to speak with Della and tell her Ivy sent you. She'll pay you enough to support yourself and your children."

Squeezing the paper in her hands, her eyes fill with tears again. "Thank you, my lady."

Uncomfortable with her gratitude, I head for the door where Thorne is waiting for me with curious eyes.

"Thank you for your time, Mrs. Darby," I say as I exit.

"Alice." Her quiet voice trails after us. "Please call me Alice."

CHAPTER
SIXTEEN

The air is sticky as we leave the Darby house and all of its hauntings behind. The two guards lean against the rail on the porch, straightening when they spot us.

"Get anything from the wife?" one of them asks.

I pin him with a cold glare, and his face pales as he takes a step back.

"She's more than just someone's wife," I remind him evenly. "Have some respect."

His throat bobs as he swallows, dropping his gaze to the floor. "Yes, *wraith*."

The name rankles, but I suppose it's better than being called pet. Still, the reminder of how everyone sees me stings. I'm not a person. *I'm a thing.* A dark, monstrous creature creeping through their nightmares.

Hurrying down the steps, I get some space from this cursed place. I breathe in through my nose and hold it for five seconds before releasing the air through my mouth. After a few minutes, my rapid heartbeat quiets, returning to its normal pace.

We spent barely half an hour in the house, but in that short amount of time, the weather has already changed. Dark clouds roll in from the sea, overtaking the bright morning sky. A series of loud thuds pull my attention to the neighbor's house, where I find a man and a boy nailing boards over their windows. It's smart. The incoming storm may appear minor to some, but this part of the city is prone to flooding.

Turning back toward the Darby house, I find Thorne speaking quietly with the guards, both of whom are glaring at him with a mix of fear and contempt. I cringe when I think about what he overheard inside. I used to be the perfect actress, never breaking character. Every performance was flawless. But lately, I keep screwing up and forgetting that I have a part to play. I break character and let little glimpses of my true self peek through. The worst part is I don't even know who that person is.

And I think I'm afraid to find out.

But searching for the *almanova* and keeping it out of Baylor's hands feels big. Important. For the first time in ages, I have a real purpose. More than an assignment from the king or a name from Della. I think I might actually be doing something good. And while I may have been pushed toward this path, I chose to follow it.

Now I just need to pull myself together and finish the job.

Thorne walks down the steps, coming to meet me near the street.

"What were you telling them?" I ask as one of the guards takes off running down the street while the other one heads around to the back of the house.

"I ordered that one to tell your captain what we learned." He points at the sprinting guard.

"Was it truly so urgent he needed to run?"

"That was all him." Thorne shrugs. "I got the impression he was frightened of me."

My lips twitch. "What gave you that idea?"

He ignores the question. "And I told the other guard to start boarding up the windows for Mrs. Darby."

"You did?" I ask as my brows shoot up. "But you were so angry with her?"

"I still am." He nods, shifting uncomfortably. "But I'm not heartless. Her situation isn't her fault."

I look away, trying to rationalize the various sides of his personality. I wouldn't have expected Thorne to be this thoughtful, especially after the way he frightened her inside. But people are complex beings. Perhaps it's impossible to ever truly know what another person is capable of. I'm sure Mrs. Darby never believed her husband could do the things he's done. I can't imagine how terrified she must have been when he showed up in the middle of the night covered in blood.

As her words replay through my mind, I realize something is bothering me about what she said.

It looked like something tried to take a bite out of his leg...

I stitched him up as best I could...

"Something's not right."

Thorne cocks a brow. "Care to elaborate?"

"Darby made it out of the tunnel with the sword," I say slowly, piecing my thoughts together. "But Mrs. Darby said he didn't have it with him when he came here last night."

Thorne nods. "So, if he didn't bring it with him, where was it?"

I glance around the street, taking in the run-down homes.

And the blood... Alice had said. *There was so much of it.*

"Darby's mortal," I murmur as everything suddenly connects in my mind.

"I'm aware," the reaper says flatly.

"No, you don't understand," I insist. My hand almost reaches out to grab his arm, but I pull it back midair. If he notices, he doesn't comment on the slip. "Darby's wound was still bleeding when he got here. For a mortal, that kind of injury would have slowed him down considerably. That much blood loss would put him on the verge of passing out."

I kick myself for not making the connection sooner, but as a high fae I don't usually have to worry about that kind of thing. It can be easy to forget that others do.

"And yet, he had time to stash the sword somewhere and still make it here for help." Thorne's eyes light up as he follows my thoughts.

"Wherever he left the sword must be nearby. Probably within a few minutes' walk."

He rolls up his sleeve, concentrating on his bare skin. Just like in the tunnels, dark lines move down his veins, and a snake appears in his palm before slithering to the ground between us.

"What are you doing?" I ask, urgently scanning the street to make sure no one is witnessing this.

"You said it yourself—Darby was bleeding when he got here. What do you bet he left a trail for us to follow?"

I nearly jump with joy as I recall how easily they sniffed out blood in Darrow's shop. "That's brilliant," I admit.

He shrugs. "It was mostly your idea."

The snake nudges my leg, and I peer down to find it gazing up at me. Its crimson eyes blink slowly, as if to say "hello." Unsure what to do, I find myself bending down to brush my fingers over its wispy scales. Part of me expects my hand to go right through it like my blade did, but instead, I find it corporeal. It nuzzles against my hand for a few moments before coiling around my leg.

"Your little friends aren't so vicious anymore," I tell Thorne as I straighten.

"Only with you…" He trails off, his brow furrowed as he watches the shadow cling to me.

When our gazes connect once more, a strange sensation flutters through my stomach. My lips are curling into a shy smile when a large raindrop splashes against my cheek. Our heads tilt back simultaneously as we take in the stormy sky above us. When our eyes meet again, the urgency I find in his mirrors my own.

"Quickly!" he commands the snake, who slithers into action.

Our feet pound against the cobblestone as we race behind it. Raindrops splatter around us, blurring out our surroundings as I try to keep track of the shadow roving the streets ahead of us. As we follow it around a corner, a prickle of unease stirs inside me.

I can't explain how, but I know exactly where we're going.

A few minutes later, the shadow snake comes to a stop in front of the gray home that captured my attention earlier. Something dark and oily settles in my gut, leaving me nauseous. No figures haunt the windows this time, but the house still radiates a sense of wrongness.

We shouldn't be here, my intuition whispers.

Unfortunately, I have to ignore the trusted voice that has kept me safe many times before. I offer a silent plea to the Fates, praying this isn't a fatal mistake. Thorne stands at my shoulder, his gaze drilling into the side of my face.

"Strange coincidence," he says as the snake at our feet dissolves, its shadows scattering with the wind.

I shrug, hoping the gesture doesn't look as stilted as it feels. "I guess my instincts are better than yours."

"That must be it," he agrees, but the doubt lingering in his eyes tells me he doesn't believe it. He's likely cataloging this strange coincidence in a mental folder with my name on it.

"Don't suppose we can just knock?" I change the subject.

"As much as I enjoy making an entrance, I'd suggest something more subtle."

"Perfect." I nod. "Breaking and entering it is."

Without waiting for his agreement, I disappear before Thorne's eyes.

The illusion stings as it settles over my skin, delivering tiny shocks to my nerves. But the prickles of pain are worth it as he takes a step back. His lips part as his eyes widen in surprise, and perhaps a tiny hint of awe.

"That truly is an incredible gift," he murmurs, sounding impressed.

Suddenly, I'm immensely grateful he can't see my blushing cheeks.

"We should split up. You can take the back," I say quickly, leaving him behind as I head toward the front door.

I eye the porch warily, noting how parts of the wood are broken and rotted. Choosing my steps carefully, I make it to the door without falling through. I try the rusted latch, finding it unlocked. I suppose there's nothing inside worth protecting. A creak echoes through the house as I push the door open. With one last glance at the empty street behind me, I call on my iron will and force myself to cross the threshold.

The first thing I notice is the smell. Something definitely died in here.

Perhaps multiple somethings, I think as I catch another whiff.

The lack of light is the next thing I notice. Whoever lives here has nailed moldy blankets over the windows. Paint is peeling off the walls in most places, revealing an array of black spots and gaping holes. Pieces of destroyed furniture are scattered around the room, dust and leaves littered on top of them. The only item that isn't broken is the couch, but judging by its threadbare appearance, I'd say it's probably mildewed.

Fuck Baylor.

It's his fault the mortals live in this kind of squalor. He has the power to clean up this district and provide aid to those who are struggling, but he does nothing. And whatever grain he brings in from his deal with Death, I doubt it will be used to feed the people of the Lowers. They'll continue to starve and live in filth while those in Highgrove have more than they could possibly need.

I take a deep breath, nearly choking on the foul air, as I attempt to quell my anger. It won't do anything to help me right now. I peer at the far corner, finding a narrow staircase that leads to the second level. The first step groans as I put my weight on it, the sound not inspiring confidence in its structural integrity. Holding my breath, I force myself to keep going. Whoever I saw here this morning must have used these stairs, so they can't be that bad.

Relief hits me as I reach the second level, but the feeling is short-lived. A faint sound comes from the last room. It takes a moment to identify it, but what I hear has me pulling a blade free.

Someone is in there.

The soft tones of their voice rise and fall as they hum quietly. The song sounds vaguely familiar, but I can't place it. I approach slowly, peeking into the other rooms as I go. They are all in a state of disrepair, but otherwise uninteresting.

Bracing myself, I push the final door open by a few inches and peer through the crack. A woman wearing a dirty shift sits on the floor. Gray hair hangs limply in her face, obscuring my view of her features.

With my illusion in place, she won't be able to see me, but she could still find it odd if the door opens on its own. It's better for me if I don't capture her attention at all. Very slowly, I crack the door slightly wider while keeping a close eye on the woman. If she notices the change, she doesn't show it as she continues to hum her song.

As quietly as possible, I slip through the gap.

The room is similar to the others. Though the paint in here has fared better than downstairs, someone has taken the liberty of drawing crude depictions all over the walls. I glance at the old woman skeptically. Is this her artistic work or do others live here too?

The sound of her low voice startles me as she begins to sing.

"The rats can run, but the rats can't hide."

Unease trickles through me, but I brush it aside. I need to finish my search and then get the fuck out of this place. Taking silent steps toward the window, I peer at the rain-soaked street below. Judging by the angle, this is where the person was standing earlier when they were watching us. It's hard to judge the woman's height while she's sitting down, but I don't think she's large enough to fit the outline I saw.

Someone else must have been here. Was it Darby?

"He's coming now, and he tells no lies."

The woman shifts restlessly, her nails digging against the floorboard. Judging by her agitated state, now is probably a good time to leave.

As I start for the door, her head snaps up. Her wrinkled skin is pale and sallow, as if she hasn't seen the sun in far too long. Wild eyes search the room before landing on my feet. Dread unfurls as my gaze drops, finding a shallow puddle collecting at my boots, the product of the rainwater dripping from my clothes and hair.

The woman's thin lips curve, revealing a black-toothed smile as her hand reaches behind her.

"He said all the rats will bleed and die, when all the stars fall from the sky."

A flash of silver catches my attention a second before the woman leaps from the ground, launching herself at me with surprising strength. Her body slams hard against mine, knocking me to the ground. The impact shocks me into dropping my illusion as a sharp pain stings my arm. Looking down, I find a dirty knife clutched in her hands as she slices into my skin.

Ignoring the pain, I grab her arm as she swings the weapon wide, digging my thumb into the tendons at her wrist. My own blade is still in my other hand, but I try to angle it away from the woman. Even though she's attacking me, killing someone so pathetic feels wrong. But getting her off me without doing serious damage is difficult, especially when she has no such qualms about hurting me.

She grits her teeth, hanging onto the knife as long as possible before finally dropping it. Her eyes track the blade as it lands somewhere near my head.

"You know what they say about hungry rats?" her scratchy voice asks.

The stench of her breath nearly chokes me as I finally get hold of her other wrist.

"They feed hungry mouths."

She snaps her teeth, her gaze trained on my arm as she leans forward to bite it.

I brace for the pain, but it never comes.

All at once, she's pulled off me. Her struggling form hits the wall with a loud bang before sliding to the ground.

Thorne stands over me, his vengeful gaze fixed on the woman. I can hear her coughing as she tries to pull air into her lungs, but I can't drag my attention away from the reaper. The tendons in his jaw clench as his eyes find mine.

"Are you alright?" he asks, his tone hard as flint.

I nod, finally pushing myself to my feet. My upper lip curls as I notice the fresh layer of grime coating my clothes. Honestly, I'm not sure if it came from the floor or the woman.

Probably both.

I attempt to brush it away, hissing as the movement pulls at the jagged cut on my arm. Thorne's eyes narrow on the wound before shifting to the knife lying a few feet away. The room darkens as he turns to face the old woman again.

"Who are you?" he demands.

A laugh bubbles out of her as she rolls onto her back. "It doesn't matter who I am. It only matters who *he* is."

My brows pinch. "Are you talking about Darby? Was he here?"

The woman's mouth opens wide as a horrible cackle comes out of her.

"Answer the question," Thorne growls.

Her attention flicks to him before settling on me, on my collar. Something flares behind her eyes, and her hands twitch.

"He's coming for you, little rat."

A shiver crawls over my skin. "Who?"

"*The rats can run, and the rats can hide,*" she sings, ignoring my question.

"Tell me!" I shout.

Her only response is to start humming again.

Thorne sighs. "Come on. We're not getting anything from her. We need to leave."

He moves toward the door, waiting for me to follow.

I can't shake the feeling that this woman knows something. If I could just get her to answer my questions, maybe it would give us a new lead. Some kind of clue as to where Darby is hiding.

But Thorne's right.

Whatever she knows, she lost the ability to share it with us a long time ago. The hard life she's lived has left her trapped in madness. Digging my hand into my pocket, I pull out a few coins and place them on the floor in front of me.

"Get some food," I tell her.

Her gaze meets mine once more, and the cruelty that flashes there makes me wonder if I'm going to regret not killing her when I had the chance.

Ignoring the morbid thought, I turn and follow Thorne from the room. The woman's voice echoes through the hall, louder now than it was before.

"He's coming now, and he tells no lies."

Neither of us speaks as we make our way down the stairs.

"He said all the rats will bleed and die, when all the stars fall from the sky."

Thorne shuts the front door behind us as we finally escape. I hurry over the rotted porch and into the street, desperate to put some distance between myself and this place. Closing my eyes, I lift my face to the rain and let it wash away the stench of the house. I take deep breaths, trying to dispel the strange sensation lingering in the pit of my stomach.

Heavy steps trudge through the puddles before coming to a stop a few feet away. I open my eyes to find Thorne watching me with that sharp gaze of his.

"Did you find anything?" I ask, praying my voice sounds steady.

He shakes his head as drops of water drip down his face. "Just some dried blood. If it belonged to Darby, he's already moved on."

I nod stiffly. "I guess it was a stupid idea."

"Just because it didn't work out doesn't mean it wasn't a good idea," Thorne offers.

I narrow my eyes. "Don't be nice."

"Why?" he asks, tilting his head.

I look away. "It doesn't suit you."

"My apologies." He hardens his voice dramatically. "It was the worst idea I've ever heard, and you're an idiot for suggesting it."

My lips twitch.

"Better?" he asks, softer this time.

"Much." My gaze drops to the rain splashing against the cobblestones. "What do we do now?"

"We should interview Darrow again," Thorne announces.

My brows lift. "Oh, is that what you called it the first time? An interview?"

He frowns, crossing his arms over his chest. "It was an exchange of information."

"More like a hostile extraction."

He rolls his eyes. "Either way, Darby was the guard who sold him information about the whisperer. They knew each other. If Darby needed help, it's possible he went to Darrow."

It's not a bad idea.

"Alright. You go reinterview Darrow at his shop, and I'll check with a few local healers around here."

His expression darkens. "You want to split up?"

I shrug. "We have a lot of ground to cover. We'll get through it all faster this way."

He scrutinizes my face for a few moments before relenting. "Fine. I'll check in with you tomorrow for a progress report."

I nod, turning to leave.

"Why did you try to help her?" Thorne calls after me.

I'm not sure if he means Mrs. Darby or the old woman, but either way, the answer is the same.

"Because I'm not heartless," I parrot his earlier words.

Leaving it at that, I make my way down the rain soaked streets. When I reach the end of the road, I turn around and find Thorne gone. Tilting my head back, I check the sky above me, exhaling with relief when I don't spot any wings.

Pulling up my hood, I continue on my way, checking again every few minutes. After several blocks, when I still don't sense him nearby, I wrap myself in an illusion and turn north, heading toward my true destination.

CHAPTER
SEVENTEEN

Darrow sleeps peacefully in his guestroom at MASQ. The furnishings here are as decadent as the rest of the establishment. Rich green paint stains the walls, contrasting nicely with the small gold chandelier. Darrow is tucked into a four-poster canopy bed, lying on his back with his hands resting over his middle. I've never been in the upstairs apartment in Darrow's shop, but I imagine its similar to this.

The lock on his door was surprisingly easy to pick. I expected more of a challenge from an *enchanter*. Perhaps a trap or some sort of alarm? But the entire process was disturbingly easy.

The silver gleam of my dagger flickers through the dark room as I rest the cool metal against his throat. The steady rhythm of his breathing changes slightly.

"What a strange dream I'm having," he murmurs.

"I'd prefer to be described as a nightmare."

His eyes blink open, connecting with mine instantly. "I'm honored to be threatened by you for a second time in as many weeks, but couldn't it have waited for a more reasonable hour?"

"Blame yourself." I shrug. "If you don't want people to break into your room, perhaps you should make it more difficult to pick the lock. I could have been a murderer."

He gives me a flat look. "If you meant me harm, you would have been electrocuted as you passed over the threshold. Never underestimate an *enchanter*, my dear *wraith*." He wiggles his eyebrows, and I have the sudden urge to dig the blade deeper into his skin. "But since you're perfectly fine, it would appear that this pet is all bark and no bite."

"Don't," I warn him as I slowly drag the blade across his neck, my pressure not quite hard enough to draw blood. "I didn't come here with violent intentions, but a girl can always change her mind."

His throat bobs as he takes in my sinister smile. Stepping back, I return the dagger to its sheath and make my way to the other side of the room.

"Noted." He grabs the robe from the end of his bed and wraps it around himself before sliding off the mattress. "So, why did you seek me out?"

"I require information," I say as I walk over to the armoire. Opening the top cabinet, I find it stuffed full of various suede jackets and satin shirts. What a curious amount of clothes to pack for what's supposed to be a short stay.

Rolling his eyes, he knocks my hands out of the way before shutting the cabinet. "I should start charging you."

"You owe me." I keep my tone light, but we both know there's truth under my words. "What do you know about the *almanova*?"

"The what?" he asks in an even tone as he slips his feet into silk slippers.

"Oh, my apologies. Would you prefer I call it the whisperer?"

His eyes widen slightly. "It appears you've been quite busy, Lady Iverson."

"I trust you've heard about Grell Darby?" I ask, helping myself to the cushy chair in the corner.

He nods, pursing his lips. "Have there been any updates?"

"He paid a visit to his wife after stealing the sword," I tell him. "She claimed he had a nasty injury on his leg." I lean back, watching his reactions closely. "You wouldn't know anything about that, would you?"

"No." His expression betrays nothing.

I narrow my eyes. "He didn't come to you seeking aid?"

"If he did, I wouldn't know. I haven't been at the shop since the last time I saw you," he reminds me.

"Mhmm." I cock my head. "That wouldn't that have anything to do with a certain dark-haired gentleman, would it?"

"I simply wanted to take a few days off." He folds his arms over his chest. "Do I need to explain my comings and goings to you?"

"I'd rather you explain how the *almanova* is connected to my collar."

He stiffens. "It's not."

"You have a bad habit of lying to me. Perhaps we should break you of it." I pull out a folded piece of paper from my coin purse and hold it up to Darrow. He glances impassively at the illustration of the sword. "Those stones look familiar, don't they?"

"One ruby is much like another." He shrugs. "What makes you think they're connected?"

I bite my lip, unsure how much I want to reveal. He's being cagey, and I'd rather not give up more than is completely necessary. Still, I need answers.

"There's something going on with my collar," I admit finally, twisting uncomfortably in my seat. "It's been... behaving oddly."

One of his blond eyebrows arches. "Care to elaborate?"

I take a deep breath, praying for the courage to be honest.

"It gets hot," I whisper, gesturing to the object in question. "And it pulses against my neck."

I tell him everything I can remember about both occurrences. My skin itches as I freely offer the information, but Darrow is the only person who might be able to explain what's happening. As wrong as this feels, I know this is a chance I have to take. As I speak, Darrow paces across the rug, his extravagant robe trailing behind him.

"Is it possible Darby was still in the tunnels when you felt it the first time?" he asks once I finish.

I shake my head. "According to our timeline, he had already been gone for hours by that point."

His nose scrunches. "Certainly makes one curious what else is being kept down there."

"My thoughts exactly." I swallow thickly.

"And you said the second time you approached the house, the collar didn't react at all?"

"No." I shake my head as I lean back. "And all we found there were some blood stains and a woman who was rambling about rats and falling stars."

He comes to a halt immediately. His gaze connects with mine, his eyes flaring. "She mentioned falling stars? You're sure?"

I nod as a frisson of apprehension curls around me. "Why?"

"Tell me everything she said," he demands, his tone more serious than I've ever heard it.

I lean forward. "She said 'he' was coming for me. I asked if she meant Darby, but she wouldn't respond."

His face pales as his gaze falls to the floor. "It's already starting."

"What are you talking about?"

Feeling too anxious to stay seated, I rise to my feet. My fingers fidget with one of the rubies on my collar and I desperately wish I'd never come here. Anything that could terrify Darrow this much is something I want to stay far away from.

The *enchanter* turns around, leaning both hands against the dark wooden dresser as he frowns at his own reflection. After a few moments, he sighs in disgust and closes his eyes, as if he can't bear to look at himself. It's a feeling I'm uncomfortably familiar with.

"How much do you know about the sword?" he asks softly.

"I know it was used to kill Claudius."

His eyes snap open as he spins around. "Where did you learn that?"

I cross my arms. "Doesn't matter."

He scowls, but I raise my brows defiantly. I've been forthcoming enough for one day. The book is my secret, and I'm not sharing it.

"Never mind." He waves me off. "Do you know why it's often referred to as 'the whisperer?'"

"I'd guess it has something to do with the voices Baylor warned me about."

He nods. "The *almanova* is more than just a sword."

"It's merely an enchanted object," I insist, despite my intuition telling me he's right.

"No." He shakes his head. "It's much more than that. The *almanova* is a living, sentient being. It has its own will, its own desires."

My mouth is suddenly dry as I try to swallow down my rising uneasiness. "If that's true, then what does it want?"

"Your guess is as good as mine," he mutters, not meeting my gaze. Cagey bastard.

"What happens when you touch it?" I ask, remembering Baylor's order.

"Never touch it!" His eyes flash as he nearly shouts the words. "Once you touch the sword, it owns you. Controls you."

"That's not possible," I whisper.

"I wish that were true," he says darkly. "Being in close proximity is all it takes to begin hearing the voices, but once you touch it, it's over. Very few would be able to fight against its will at that point."

My mind returns to the passage I read in my book.

"Is that what happened to Philo?" I ask, referring to the first God of Love and Hate.

He nods. "As a God, he probably would have been able to withstand its influence for a short time, but it would have taken all his strength. Eventually, he would have been too drained to keep fighting."

I always think of Gods as being indestructible, but they aren't. They were created by the Fates to unite our realms and rule over them, but they can still die. Even among the supposedly immortal, no one lives forever. While a high fae might live two or three thousand years if they're lucky, a God's lifespan is more than triple that. Like fae, Gods age slowly. Cassandra, the Goddess of Divination is the oldest among the current set, probably due to her ability to see threats in advance.

Claudius may have been the first God to die, but he wasn't the last. Many have been slaughtered by other Gods over the years. Though, I've never heard of one being felled by a mortal or fae.

"An Heir would succumb to the sword much faster," Darrow adds, referring to the children of the Gods. "They might be able to use it once, but even for someone with divine blood, it would be a risk."

A great rumble of thunder crashes outside, the force of it shaking the building. I move toward the window, wincing as lightning strikes nearby. These storms are getting out of hand.

"It's going to get worse," Darrow echoes my thoughts. "That tsunami that happened up north will be nothing compared to what the Fates will rain down on us."

He reaches for a decanter of brown liquid, pouring several fingers worth into a crystal tumbler. He holds the glass up to me, but I shake my head, politely refraining from commenting on the time of day or the generosity of his pour.

"You believe what they say about the storms?" I ask. "That it's Baylor's fault?"

He nods, taking a sip. "Him becoming king wasn't part of their plan."

Darrow is usually more careful than this. That small confession, offered so freely, was treasonous. While he may toe the line occasionally, he typically chooses his words more carefully. What's different today?

"Why are you telling me this, Darrow?"

He swirls the liquid in his cup, watching me with sad eyes. "Because I think you've finally seen Baylor for what he is."

My jaw clenches. "I don't know what you're talking about."

"My mistake," he murmurs, dropping his gaze.

"Is there any way to help those who've succumbed to the sword's influence?" I ask, changing the subject.

Thoughts of Alice's haunted face cloud my mind. Even if Grell Darby could break free of the sword's hold, the damage has been done. I don't know if she could ever see him the way she did before. Unfortunately, love is simultaneously the strongest force in the world, and the most fragile.

"Sometimes distance helps." Darrow knocks back the rest of his drink and sets the glass on his dresser before wiping his mouth on the back of his hand. "Sometimes it doesn't."

"Where did you learn all of this?"

He doesn't respond.

Strangely, his silence is a relief. As much as I want answers, his uncharacteristic forthrightness was worrying me. Whatever is truly going on with the sword, it's shaken him more than anything I've seen before.

"Is there anyone who would be immune to it?" I try another question.

"The Goddess of Illusion," he says, surprising me. "Or one of her descendants. But since she's missing, and the existence of her Heir has never been confirmed, no. There's no one who could wield it without consequence."

He moves to the window, peeking through the gap in the curtains. There's a faint tremor in his hands as he scans the streets below.

"Thorne isn't the only reason you've been avoiding your shop?" I ask tentatively.

Dropping the curtain, he turns back to me. The fear in his eyes is palpable. "It's dangerous, Iverson. More than you understand."

He moves closer, gripping my shoulders tightly. On instinct, I crane my neck back to put distance between us. I don't like anyone being this close to me.

That's not true. You liked being close to Thorne, my inner voice reminds me. *But he didn't like being close to you.*

"Do not trust anyone," Darrow orders. "Especially those who've come into contact with the sword. It doesn't matter how well you know them, or how close you are. Once the whisperer has them in its grasp, they are a stranger to you. Anyone can be corrupted by it. Anyone."

The hairs on the back of my neck stand up as shivers skate down my spine.

"The *almanova* digs its claws into the minds of its victims, making puppets out of them. It can see all their desires, whispering to them to take whatever they want. And no one can resist it for long. Never forget, the Forsaken are capable of anything."

My brow wrinkles. "Forsaken?"

"That's what they're called," he says. "Those who are under its influence."

Heaviness settles onto my shoulders as the full weight of his words sinks into me. The situation is precarious. It's as though this city is teetering on the edge of a cliff, waiting to see if the balance will hold. The sword is out there, corrupting who knows how many people. What are they capable of?

My gaze drifts back to the window, seeing faint outlines rushing down the avenue below. They scurry for cover as the streets soak with rain. How quickly will it turn to blood?

"That's why I'm going to remain here," Darrow says quietly, dragging a hand over his face. "In the comfort of Della's hospitality until this matter is resolved."

"Wait." I pull back, shaking my head. "You're not going to try to help at all?"

"No good deed goes unpunished, Iverson. While you hunt the sword, don't delude yourself into believing it's not hunting you too."

The thought makes me shudder. Despite everything I've heard today, some part of me still doesn't believe it's possible.

"You've spent all these years turning yourself into a predator," he continues. "But I know you still remember what it's like to be prey. You need to be careful."

"And what exactly should she be careful with?" a deep voice cuts in.

CHAPTER
EIGHTEEN

My head jerks toward the door, finding Thorne glaring at me from the other side of the threshold. He leans against the red wallpaper in what appears to be an easy manner, but I can spot the tension radiating through his lean body. He looks as if he's a moment away from pouncing on someone. Judging by the way his eyes harden as he takes in my proximity to Darrow, I guess that person is probably me.

"What a coincidence to find you both here," Thorne drawls. "Funny, this doesn't look like an apothecary in the Lowers."

"Well," Darrow drags out the word as he claps his hands together. "You two clearly have much to discuss. Won't you please come in and join us?"

"Thank you for the invitation," the reaper says sarcastically.

The *enchanter* watches with fevered eyes as Thorne lifts his foot, only seconds from crossing the threshold, when he suddenly stops.

A cruel gleam flickers in his eyes. "You didn't honestly think that would work, did you?"

"Worth a try?" Darrow's pitch rises as he offers the reaper a pained smile.

Thorne's gaze shifts to me, utterly unimpressed.

"I'll wait for you in the alley." His authoritative tone rankles. "And if I have to come back up here, I won't be stopping at the threshold."

Something tells me a little electrocution wouldn't be enough to take him down. With one last glare, he storms down the hall, his cloak billowing behind him.

"What are you waiting for?" Darrow exclaims as he begins shooing me from the room. "You heard the man!"

Grabbing my shoulders, he pushes me across the carpet and out into the hall.

"Darrow!" I spit his name. Pulling one of my blades free, I take a step toward him.

"Uh, uh, uh." He wags his finger before pointing to the enchanted doorway between us. "You look like you have a clear intention of harming me. But might I remind you, dear Iverson, that would be bad for your health."

"Bastard," I grumble under my breath.

"Takes one to know one, pet." He smirks, tossing one of his blond curls over his shoulder. "Now, please ask your new acquaintance not to murder me. I'm too beautiful to die."

"Coward."

"And proud of it!" He slams the door.

I roll my eyes as I trudge through the empty club. When I come here early in the day, I don't usually venture past Della's study. There's something eerie about seeing the front rooms empty. There's a wrongness to it, as if everyone suddenly disappeared in the middle of their revelry.

But, of course, MASQ isn't entirely empty. Della stands in the kitchen, her hands on her hips. The soft pink dress compliments her dark skin beautifully, but judging by her expression, the bright color is completely at odds with her mood.

"I do not appreciate uninvited men banging on my back door and traipsing through these halls this early in the day, Iverson," she says sternly.

"It won't happen again," I promise, raising my hands in a placating gesture.

Steel flashes in her brown eyes. "See that it doesn't."

I tuck my chin, staring at the tile floor as I head for the door. Getting scolded by Della takes me back to my childhood. I was constantly getting into trouble with her and Leona, always touching something I shouldn't. Even though she's genuinely angry with me right now, I have to bite my lip to stop a nostalgic smile from forming. For a moment, everything is exactly how it once was.

As soon as I step outside, the door slams shut behind me. Several clinks and thumps echo from the other side as she twists all of the locks into place. Her paranoia would be amusing if it weren't sad.

Thorne stands a few feet away, anger radiating off him as he holds himself slightly too still. If I had to describe him with one word, it would be restrained. Rain soaks through his clothes, molding them to his body.

"The *enchanter* didn't want to join us?" he asks, his tone far too soft.

I cross my arms over my chest. "His schedule was already booked."

"Yet again, he abandons you to save himself." Thorne takes a few steps closer. "Some friend."

I shuffle backward, hitting the brick wall behind me. "As I said before, we're not that close."

He moves forward, eating up the space I put between us. "You lied to me."

"You've lied to me many times." I lift my chin to meet his gaze, barely an inch separating us.

A muscle twitches at his jaw. "You two were pretty cozy up there."

My face heats at the insinuation. "Jealous?"

He barks out a laugh, and his breath coasts across my cheek. "Betrayed is more like it. I don't enjoy being given the runaround."

"And I don't enjoy how you expect me to share everything with you, while you share nothing with me," I tell him, shocked by how true the statement is. I'm tired of being kept in the dark by those who demand my unwavering loyalty.

"Too bad, my lady." One side of his mouth kicks up in a half smile. "That's the way this works. If you have a problem with it, take it up with your *lover*."

My hand moves through the air without my permission, halting a centimeter from his cheek as he catches my wrist. The leather from his gloves is soft where his fingers wrap around my skin, perfectly at odds with the anger simmering in his blue eyes. He looms over me, trapping my wrist against the wall above my head.

"What did I tell you, Angel?" Thorne demands, his voice deepening. "Don't ever touch me."

"Believe me," I tell him. "Touching you is the last thing I'd want."

His jaw clenches as his gaze flits to my mouth. My limbs turn heavy as an unwanted heat settles in my lower stomach. The sensation only increases as his thumb brushes back and forth over my wrist.

My attention catches on a raindrop carving a path down his face, slipping past the freckles on his cheeks before dripping off his chin. A shiver racks through me as my eyes find his again. The silver flecks that mingle within those pale-blue irises are maddening. It's not right for anyone to be this beautiful. Without meaning to, I find myself pushing onto my tiptoes and closing the distance between us further. We're both breathing harder now, our chest nearly brushing with each inhale. It would be so easy to lean forward and—

"Ivy?" a male voice calls, breaking the strange trance between us.

Thorne is gone in an instant.

As if I was being held up by his presence alone, I nearly slide to the ground. Thankfully, no one sees me catch myself at the last moment. I find the reaper with his back to me as he stares at the intruder, a predator sizing up his prey. Several feet past him, stands Nolan, Morwen's fiancé. His sandy brown hair is plastered to his forehead as the rain pounds against him. Instead of seeking shelter inside, he stands frozen by the back door of his bakery. His throat bobs as he takes in Thorne's aggressive stance. I don't miss the way Nolan straightens his posture and puffs out his chest in response.

"Everything alright, Lady Iverson?" Nolan asks, his voice sounding deeper than before.

"I'm fine," I assure him, keeping my gaze on Thorne as I edge a few feet in his direction. "Go back inside."

He must do as I asked because I hear the heavy door slam shut.

Hopefully, the reaper won't think too deeply about why a random man addressed me so informally. The last thing I need is for him to poke around and figure out Nolan's connection to my illicit activities. The sweet baker is the perfect go between to deliver messages from Della to Morwen, who then relays them to me. Thorne may know I'm the Angel of Mercy, but he has no idea who else is involved, and it needs to stay that way.

Thorne continues watching the door for a few more moments before turning back to me. Whatever existed between us a few moments ago is gone. There's no trace of warmth in his expression now, only cold suspicion.

"You must come here often to be familiar with the neighbors," he says, somehow managing to make the statement sound like an accusation.

Swallowing my disappointment over his abrupt change in demeanor, I force myself to be ambivalent. I slip into one of the easy roles I often play and shrug dismissively.

"I enjoy the ambiance."

His eyes narrow. "That all you enjoy?"

"Oh, Reaper." I offer him a flirtatious smile. "I'm fond of all manner of things."

Wisps of shadow curl around the edges of his eyes. "What did Darrow tell you?"

"Go ask him yourself if you think you'll get anything out of him."

His head tilts to the side as he examines me, no doubt trying to find a new angle to get what he wants.

"It doesn't have to be this way, Angel." His tone is softer now, more intimate. "We can share information."

"Alright," I agree. "You first."

He heaves an exasperated sigh, as if I'm the one being difficult. A hysterical laugh bubbles up as something inside of me snaps.

"How did you find me here today?" I demand, stepping forward. "How do you always know where I am, even when I'm invisible? And why can I sense when you're nearby? Right here." I pull up my hair, exposing the back of my neck. "I *feel* you. Why?"

I wait for a response that doesn't come. Instead, he remains unreadable, offering no explanations.

"Why did you keep my secrets?" I continue, unable to stop. "Why didn't you tell Baylor the truth? That would have been easier than manipulating me into convincing him to let me help you."

His face betrays nothing. Whatever he's thinking is hidden behind a mask of cold indifference. Or maybe there is no mask. Maybe he truly doesn't care. The thought severs whatever's left of my self-control.

"What do you want from me?" I scream.

Rain pounds against the ground around us, blurring our surroundings as it creates the illusion that we're completely alone.

"Why does Death need the sword?" I keep going. "Who does he plan to use it against? By helping you find it, am I complicit in someone's murder? Another God's perhaps?"

"Since when do you have a problem with killing?" Thorne steps forward, throwing the words at me like a weapon. "Isn't it the thing you're most known for?"

I step back, my shoulders curling inward as if I've been struck.

His words seep through my clothes, burning my skin with their truth. I am a killer. In fact, that's *all* I am. All I do. I kill and I lie. Guilt boils inside of me as that cell in my mind fractures once more, allowing all of my haunted memories to spill out.

Would you do anything for me?

The reminder of Baylor's words only fuels my anger more. That cursed night was when my whole world shifted on its axis for the second time.

"You keep your secrets but demand to know all of mine," I tell him, hating the emotion leaking into my voice. "This isn't a partnership. I don't owe you anything. Go back to wherever your *accommodations* are, and I'm sure someone will find you if you're needed."

He watches me with that all-seeing gaze, but I have no idea what he's thinking. Emotion flickers behind his eyes as he opens his mouth to speak. I hold my breath, desperate for whatever he's going to tell me. But a noise from behind me steals his attention, and the mask slides into place once more. For a moment, I think I spot a trace of regret in his eyes, but it's gone too quickly to be sure.

The sound of ripping fabric comes a second before his wings break free. A gasp slips out of me at the sight of the magnificent onyx feathers. Without another word, Thorne leaps into the air. Rain splashes into my eyes as I watch him disappear into the sky, wondering what he might have said if we hadn't been interrupted. Why were those unspoken words so important to me? Forcing myself to let it go, I turn to find Darrow peeking through the slightly cracked door.

Seeing he's been spotted, he yelps and quickly slams it shut.

I stomp across the wet ground, silently cursing the way my damp clothes awkwardly cling to my body. I only have to bang my fist against the hard steel once before the handle twists and Darrow cracks it open, peeping through the tiny gap with one eye.

"Enjoy the show?" I ask.

He frowns, having the nerve to look chastised.

"Ask me a question," he mutters.

"What?" I lean forward, sure that I've misheard him.

"Ask me one question," he clarifies. "And I *might* answer. If I can."

My mouth hangs open. Is this his way of apologizing?

"Quickly, Iverson. I don't have all day," he snaps.

Fates, even his apologies are petulant. I shake my head, trying to focus on what I want to ask. Half of my most pressing questions are things I'm sure he won't tell me. But there's one small thing that's been bothering me.

Meeting his gaze through the cracked door, I take a deep breath. "Why did you panic when I mentioned falling stars earlier?"

He bristles. "I didn't panic."

"Darrow," I say flatly.

"Fine." His eyes grow sad, and for a moment, I think he won't tell me.

Annoyance flares as I turn around, letting an illusion settle over my skin. I'm already walking away when he finally speaks.

"Do you know what *almanova* means in the old language?"

I turn around, shaking my head even though he can't see it.

"Soul of the star," he says softly. "It means '*soul of the star.*'"

With my back pressed against the hard marble of the clawfoot tub, I keep my head angled toward the door and a blade resting along the edge. When I returned from my outing, Alva thought a bath would help me to unwind from my stressful week. She always fills the water with scented oils and healing salts, telling me they are great for relaxation. Tonight she choose jasmine, hoping it would help me be more at ease.

Unfortunately, every time I try to close my eyes, they immediately snap open as phantom footsteps creep across the stone tiles. I do my best to ignore the imaginary hands brushing over my scalp, threatening to push my head under the water. Somehow, I am even more on edge than when I got in.

Three exhausting days have passed since I went to MASQ.

Each has been spent helping Remy in his search of the city. There's been no sign of Darby or the sword, but I've sensed the beginnings of the chaos Darrow predicted. There's a layer of hostility in the air, pushing everyone closer to their breaking point. I've seen customers snap at vendors over the most minor inconveniences.

Earlier today, I witnessed a man destroy a booth at the fish market because the owner was sold out of oysters. Remy's soldiers arrested him, but he was far from the only one behaving aggressively. And if Darrow was right, it will only get worse.

We've searched all of Darby's usual haunts and interviewed his known associates, but no one has seen him. And none of the healers admitted to aiding him with his wounds. Starting tomorrow, Baylor has given orders for every home and business in the city to be searched, even the ones in Highgrove and Midgarden. The king must truly be panicking if he's willing to risk angering the aristocracy.

Darrow's words from the other morning linger in the back of my mind. *Soul of the star.* Such a strange thing to name a sword. Could it be a coincidence that the old woman was singing about falling stars?

A knock on the door pulls me from my thoughts, sending a wave of dread sweeping through my veins. There's only one reason for someone to knock this late.

Water sluices down my flushed skin as I rise from the tub and wrap myself in a silk robe. My damp hair leaves a trail of droplets over the floor as I make my way to the door. I open it to find Huxley, one of the kings guards, standing across from me. His cheeks turn bright pink when he notices my lack of attire. Clearing his throat, he coughs several times before speaking.

"The king has requested your presence this evening, Lady Iverson," he says, the words sliding into my stomach like a knife.

The guards always say the same thing. Always frame it as a request, but the idea that I can say no is an illusion. No one denies a king. A useless scream rises in my throat, but I keep my mouth shut. Giving voice to my rage would accomplish nothing. Instead, I nod politely as I hold up a finger to signal I only need a moment.

The door clicks shut between us. Like the walls of a battle trench, the small barrier offers me only a moment's reprieve. I remind myself I need to be strong and emotionless. A perfect liar. But more than anything, I want to kill him. Kill all of them. I want to burn this entire city to ash and let the flames consume me too.

But instead, I sit down at my vanity and fix my face like a good actress.

Using a fluffy towel, I soak up some of the water from my hair before combing out the fiery waves. Next, I rub a soothing lotion over my body, making my skin smooth and supple. To add life back into my complexion, I lightly dab a berry tint onto my lips and cheeks, giving me a flushed appearance. My face is perfect, apart from the hollowness of my amber eyes, but he's never noticed that before.

It's almost funny that all of this soft beauty is required for such an ugly fate.

Hot tears threaten to spill, but I hold them back. If I let them fall tonight, they'll never stop. I'd hoped that with Bridgid as his new mistress, I'd have a reprieve from any late-night summons. Unfortunately, it seems the distraction she offers him is limited. I meet my own gaze in the mirror as my fingers dig into the wooden vanity. Could the weight of my rage be enough to crack it?

"You are so much more than this," I whisper to my reflection.

There was far more conviction in Leona's voice when she first spoke those words. Deserved or not, she truly believed them. Steely resolve settles over me at the reminder of the late queen. Clenching my eyes shut, I reach for that hidden spot deep within, the place where my power resides. Calling it forward, I let the pain rip through me. My mouth opens with a silent scream as the familiar agony cuts me in half. My nerves are strained to the brink, my cells shredded to bits.

The process feels endless, but in reality, it only takes a few seconds.

I gulp down heaving gasps of air as I lean against the vanity for support. Blood tickles my upper lip as it drips from my nose. I wipe it away with the back of my hand as I gaze into *eidolons* vacant eyes. She's an exact copy of me, even down to the berry tint on her full lips.

"You know what to do," I whisper, wincing from the pounding in my head.

Her silk robe trails behind her as she gracefully crosses to the door and disappears into the hall, taking my place like she does every time Baylor calls me to his chambers. I listen as Huxley greets her, completely unaware he's speaking to a fraud. When the sound of their footsteps retreat down the hall, I crawl into my bed and pull the covers over my head. The first part of this process is difficult, but what comes next is much worse.

The first time I created an *eidolon* was only one month after Leona died.

In the weeks following her death, Baylor gave me space. I don't think he expected me to be devastated by it, to need so much time to mourn. But when the first late-night knock came, I panicked. I told the guard I would be right out, but instead I curled into a ball on the floor and rocked back and forth with a dagger clutched in my hand.

I have no idea what I planned to do; I only knew I wouldn't let them take me to him. I couldn't let him touch me that way again after what he did. Even just the thought of it made me sick.

That night, it felt as if the world was being ripped apart. Something inside of me was breaking, shattering into tiny pieces that couldn't be put back together. The collar was so heavy around my neck, as though it was digging into my skin. I was convinced the weight of it was going to crush my bones. I still don't know how I kept myself from crying out, but eventually, something inside of me snapped.

As the minutes passed, everything calmed down. Sweat cooled against my skin, leaving me shivering. And when I opened my eyes, I was staring at an exact replica of myself.

I didn't tell a soul what had happened. If the king were to discover it, I've no doubt he'd find some way to use it to his advantage. But deep down, a small voice whispered that wasn't the only reason.

Shame curdles in my gut every time I think about what I use my *eidolon* for.

My duplicate doesn't have her own consciousness. She's more of a machine than a person. She relies on commands, along with my instincts and muscle memory that have been copied into her. She can experience physical sensations to a certain degree, but she has no thoughts or internal emotions.

Still, I hate myself for sending her in my place.

And yet, I'm unbelievably grateful.

Maintaining the illusion all night is incredibly taxing for me, but I'll gladly suffer the headaches and nosebleeds if it means I don't have to touch him. I can block out the link that connects us, ensuring I don't feel anything that's happening in his room.

Without my *eidolon*, I don't think I would have survived the past year.

I don't think I would have wanted to.

CHAPTER NINETEEN

My fists connect with the punching bag in rapid succession, hitting it harder every time an unpleasant thought flashes through my mind.

After Baylor fell asleep a little past midnight, my *eidolon* slipped out of his chambers, letting Huxley escort her back to my room, where I immediately dissolved her. Knowing sleep was an impossible goal, I came down here to the training facility to work through some of my frustration.

My knuckles ache as I pound them into the worn leather again and again, picturing Baylor's face as my target. I keep going until the rope keeping it suspended snaps and the bag lands at my feet. I should be exhausted by now, but my body is buzzing with unspent energy. My fingers twitch as I shake out my hands, unwilling to stay still. I have to keep moving, otherwise I won't be able to stop myself from dwelling on things I'd rather not think about.

Moving onto the row of training dummies, I toss my blades between their eyes, and occasionally straight into their groins. The soft thud of my weapons gliding into their bodies fills me with brutal satisfaction. But when I've thrown the last one, the restlessness returns.

Ugly thoughts claw their way out of the hole I tried to bury them in. Shame and hatred war for dominance as my breathing becomes unsteady. Anxiety seeps into my lungs, making each gasp feel ragged and hard-won. I force myself to pull air in through my nose and hold it.

One. Two. Three. Four. Five.

I breathe out through my mouth, repeating the process until my heartbeat begins to steady. This kind of thing never used to happen to me, but over the past year, I've found myself frequently struck by a strange sort of panic. The attacks always occur at the oddest times. There's no immediate danger in this room, yet my body is rigid with alarm and agitation.

Every day, I stand on the precipice of insanity, desperately trying not to tip over the edge. I constantly struggle to keep my emotions locked away and be a perfect unfeeling machine. To make myself into whatever is required of me.

To not care.

But I do. Far more than I should. And I don't know how much longer I can go on this way before I break.

As long as it takes, I remind myself. *Until I'm free. Until he pays.*

Forcing all these useless emotions back into their box, I decide to face my fears and summon the source of my shame. I welcome the pain, knowing I deserve every ounce of it. The metallic taste of blood fills my mouth as I bite my cheek, but I manage to stay upright the entire time. When the room stops spinning, the amber eyes of my *eidolon* stare back at me, lifeless as ever. There's something eerie about the blank perfection of her face as she stands before me now, waiting for a command.

I open my mouth to offer some meager apology when the hairs on the back of my neck suddenly rise.

A cool breeze kisses my left cheek as I turn toward the door. Half a second later, I'm slammed to the ground by a heavy force. Thankfully, I land on the soft mat, but strong hands pin my wrists above my head as a large body presses into mine. Familiar eyes gaze down at me, filled with amusement I don't share.

"Hello, Angel," Thorne croons, his self-satisfied smirk feeding my fury.

"Get off," I growl as I try to pull my arms free of his grasp.

My chest rubs against him as I twist and squirm, sending uncomfortable flutters racing through my stomach. Heat rises to my cheeks at my embarrassing reaction to his proximity.

"Was this the training you mentioned?" he asks, ignoring my demand. "You know, the one designed to destroy me? If so, I don't think it's working."

I clench my jaw as I drive my knee into his thigh, surprising him enough to wiggle one leg free. Hooking it around his hip, I use every ounce of strength in my core to flip us, reversing our positions. The move has me landing on top of Thorne, straddling his waist as I hold him down.

"I take it back." His voice fills with smoke. "I'm feeling thoroughly destroyed right now."

The silver flecks in his half-lidded eyes simmer, causing wild thoughts to course through me. I can feel Thorne against me. *Everywhere.* There's something wickedly dangerous about the fact that his warmth is seeping into me through our clothes, but not a single inch of our skin is touching. Technically, there's nothing wrong with me sparring with someone. Though I can't say my other training sessions ever inspired such reckless desires.

My core tightens, turning my breathing heavy. My focus drops to his sinful lips. Right now, they looks so soft and inviting, tempting me to taste the forbidden. Without conscious thought, my eyes begin to shut as I lean forward.

"You're bleeding," he whispers.

"What?" My eyes flutter open, finding the heat in his gaze has been replaced by horror.

"Did I do that?" he asks urgently, staring at me with disgust that cools my body instantly.

I sit up quickly, still straddling his waist as my fingers brush over my face, only to find a familiar wetness trailing from my nose.

Blood.

"No, that wasn't you," I mutter, wiping it on the back of my hand as I rise to my feet and put some space between us. "It happens every time I conjure her."

His eyes fill with concern as he pushes himself up. "Is it painful?"

"Extremely," I say, unable to stop the word from sounding bitter.

Turning away from him, I hurry to the dummies and remove the blades I'd left lodged in them. I slide them back into their sheaths, keeping hold of one just in case.

Thorne stands where I left him, watching me with an emotion I don't recognize.

"How did you get past the guards?" I demand.

His eyebrows shoot up as he makes a show of glancing around the room. "Oh, did you have security? Funny. I must have missed them."

I head for the door, planning to check on them, but Thorne moves faster than I've ever seen, appearing in front of me.

"They're fine." He rolls his eyes. "The one outside the barracks fell asleep on the job and I saw no reason to wake him."

My gaze flicks toward the window, and I'm shocked to find the sun rising outside. Orange rays pierce through the glass pane, stretching across the floor to create a chasm of light between us.

"Do you enjoy rising with the dawn?" I ask, wondering what could bring him here this early.

"I could ask you the same question," he points out as he saunters over to inspect the damaged punching bag.

"And I would evade answering, just like you." I trail after him, uncomfortable at the idea of him moving through my space so freely. "What are you doing here, Thorne?"

He shifts back and forth on his feet as his gloved hands slide into his pockets. Taking a deep breath, he meets my gaze straight on.

"I wanted to apologize," the reaper admits. "I was out of line the other day. I'm sorry."

Surprise nearly knocks me on my ass. I'm not sure anyone has ever truly apologized to me before. It's a novel experience.

"There's a lot of pressure to find the whisperer," he continues, his discomfort obvious. "I let it get the best of me and that wasn't fair to you."

I get the sense Thorne doesn't hand out many apologies. The fact that he's offering one to me is strangely flattering. It doesn't entirely make up for the fact that he's still keeping secrets, but the acknowledgment of his mistake means something.

I shrug my shoulders, trying to appear nonchalant about the situation. "I suppose Death must be a bit of a hard-ass."

His lips twitch. "That's certainly one way of describing Killian."

"Baylor's the same."

Silvery blue eyes flash to mine. "They're nothing alike."

The skin around his mouth is pulled tight, and there's tension in his body that he's trying very hard to hide. My comparison actually offended him.

"You don't like him, do you?" I ask.

Thorne doesn't look at me as he answers, nor does he pretend to question who I'm referring to. "He's careless with the things that belong to him. That's not a good quality in a leader."

I don't miss his implication that *I* am one of those things. I want to correct him, to tell him I don't belong to the king, but we both know it would be a lie. We stand in silence for a few moments, both of us considering each other's words.

"It's incredible," he whispers, his voice full of awe.

I glance up to find him watching my *eidolon* with rapt fascination as he moves closer to her. She stares blankly ahead, not acknowledging him.

"She truly is an exact replica of you," he marvels.

"I'm not sure that's a compliment, considering how disappointing you found her before." I want to bite my tongue as soon as the words slip out.

He cuts me an amused glare. "Did that comment sting, my lady?"

I shrug, ignoring his implication. I don't care what he thinks.

"If she's such a perfect replica, then how did you know it was me you were tackling?" I ask, changing the subject.

"Hmm?" He blinks innocently.

"You heard the question." I roll my eyes. "And while we're on the topic, how did you know she wasn't real the night we met?"

The mystery has been bothering me from the beginning.

"She's a convincing illusion," he says hesitantly. "And I'm sure she'd probably fool most people, but there was something about her eyes that gave it away. They were vacant. No thoughts behind them." He glances back at me. "Not like yours at all."

Heat flames my cheeks again as I cross my arms over my chest. "They're the exact same color."

"No," he insists, prowling closer as his gaze holds mine with shocking intensity. "Yours are far more captivating. Full of mischief and secrets. And there are times when the amber almost seems to burn..." He trails off before clearing his throat. "Anyway, I don't think I could ever mistake her for you."

Shock barrels through me. *Captivating?*

Thorne rolls his eyes. "Don't play coy now. You must be aware of how you look."

My mouth drops open as his meaning sets in. I suddenly recall the way he gaped at me when I revealed myself that first night. Was that truly because he found me attractive? It's not that I believe I'm hideous; I know that's not the case. But after everything with Baylor, niggling doubts and insecurities have wiggled their way into my mind.

Despite the embarrassment warming my body, I can't stop the shy smile that curves my lips. No one has ever spoken about me this way, not even Baylor. His compliments have never extended past the obligatory "you look nice this evening." And the only time he ever examines my eyes closely is when he's trying to spot a lie. The idea of him being captivated by any part of me is laughable.

A wicked gleam enters Thorne's gaze as he watches me process his words. I take a few steps back, positioning the *eidolon* between us, which only amuses him more.

"She's a fine illusion," he concedes. "But I prefer the original over the imitation."

My heart skips several beats inside my chest. As humiliating as it is to admit, I'm fairly certain that statement will haunt my mind for the rest of my days.

"Anyway, does she have a name?" he asks, as if he hasn't just fried all of the pathways in my brain.

I shake my head, unable to form words yet.

"Then how do you refer to her?"

"As my *eidolon*," I say obviously.

He raises a brow, clearly unsatisfied with my answer.

"I don't know if I want to give her a name," I admit softly, dropping my gaze to the mats as I try to put my complicated emotions into words. "She may be able to pretend, but she's not a person. Not really."

Thoughts of last night push against my mind. Giving her a name would make it much harder to send her in my place next time Baylor calls.

"She's not real, but she is an extension of you," Thorne reminds me.

A small voice in the back of my mind whispers that he's right. But I've never thought of her that way. I don't know if I could. It would force me to acknowledge things I'm not ready to face.

"You should call her something that's symbolic of that connection." He pauses, considering for a moment. "What's your middle name?"

"Rose," I say softly.

In an instant, the easy atmosphere between us dissolves. The temperature in the room plummets as shadows creep over the walls and windows, leaving us in near darkness.

"What's wrong?" I ask, searching for the source of this change.

He shakes his head, clenching his jaw as he takes a few steps back from me.

"Call her that then," he says, his tone icy.

My mind races, trying to follow the stark shift in his mood. What just happened? Was it the name that bothered him so much? *Rose?* My attention catches on his covered wrist, remembering the burning rose tattoo hidden beneath his gloves. The one every member of Killian's council bears. Death's sigil inked into their skin like a permanent brand. Does he not appreciate the reminder?

Before I have time to ponder this change in our conversation, Warrick rushes into the training room. He goes rigid when he notices I'm not alone, his hand moving to the sword at his side.

"The ambassador isn't a threat," I say impatiently. "What's going on?"

His attention shifts back to me, the lines of his face tense. "Darby's been spotted."

"Where?" Thorne and I ask at the same time, setting aside whatever strange tension was building between us.

Warrick pales and my body goes rigid, already anticipating that I won't be pleased with his answer.

"The docks."

CHAPTER
TWENTY

"Search the ships again," Remy orders his soldiers. "No one leaves this port until we find Darby."

The wooden boards of the docks creak under our feet as soldiers run back and forth. Unlike yesterday, the sky is cloudless, and the hot sun beats down on us as we scan the crowds. Vendors and pedestrians are scattered around the fish market, glaring at the guards who rummage through their stalls. The streets nearby have been closed off, meaning no one is free to leave the area.

Water splashes against the ships anchored behind us as soldiers check each one. Their crews, who were forced to disembark their vessels, stand nearby glaring at us.

"How much longer will this take?" one of the sailors demands, his cheeks red and weather-beaten from his years at sea.

I understand their frustration. We've been out here for two hours, and there's still no sign of Darby. When we arrived, Remy didn't appear happy about the fact that Thorne was with me. He immediately ordered the reaper to help search the ships. Technically, the captain doesn't have the authority to order him to do anything, but in a rare moment of civility, Thorne acquiesced without comment.

"Until we're done," Remy replies briskly, keeping his gaze on the crowd.

"My men and I have a schedule to keep," the sailor insists as his companions cheer him on. "Who's going to reimburse us if we miss our delivery window because of this?"

I head further down the dock while they continue arguing back and forth. Sweat dampens my brow as I scan the crowds, searching for someone who matches Darby's description. A seed of apprehension blossoms in the pit of my stomach. We should have found him by now.

The hairs on the back of my neck rise, and I turn to find Thorne approaching. His gloves and long sleeves are out of place among the exposed forearms of the sailors. How is he wearing all of that in this sweltering heat? Images flash through my mind of what it would be like to see him unclothed.

"Are you alright?" Thorne asks.

I swallow thickly. "Hmm?"

He tilts his head, examining me with concern. "Your cheeks are flushed. Is the heat getting to you?"

"The heat?" My face flames even hotter. "Yes, that's it. I'm fine, though."

"Alright," he says, clearly finding my behavior odd.

I use my hand to fan my face, trying to regain my composure. "Find anything on the ships?"

He shakes his head. "Just some mice."

A shudder rolls through me as we make our way further down the docks.

"I promise, they are more scared of you than you are of them."

"You underestimate my fear," I mutter.

"Only because I've seen how fearless you truly are," he counters.

I scowl. His words aren't helping me cool down. My attention snags on a light-haired man standing a few yards away. I stiffen.

From behind, his build matches Darby's description, but when he turns around a few moments later, I get a glimpse of his face and realize he's about two decades too old.

Instead of being relieved, my agitation only grows. Something isn't right about this situation. My feet come to a halt in the middle of the walkway. I'm distantly aware of a sailor shouting as he nearly barrels into me, but one look from Thorne silences him.

Everything about this feels wrong. If Darby were here, we would have found some trace of him by now, and yet we've come up with nothing. Not even a witness who remembers crossing paths with him today...

Following my instincts, I sprint back the way we came. Without checking, I know Thorne is right behind me. The thought pushes me forward.

I find Remy exactly where I left him, still arguing with the impatient sailors.

Not bothering to acknowledge them, I grab the captain's arm and spin him toward me.

"Who reported seeing Darby here?" I ask, my chest heaving.

His brows furrow at my strange behavior, but he answers without question. "Branson. Why?"

Letting Remy go, I scan the nearby area until I find the dark-haired guard exiting one of the ships behind us. Barely old enough to become a solider, the young mortal has only been on the job for a few months.

"Branson!" I shout.

His ears turn red at the sound of his name, and he immediately jogs over, his gaze flitting back and forth between me and Remy.

"You're the one who reported seeing Darby, correct?"

"Y-yes, *wraith*," he stutters, his gaze dropping as he shift back and forth on the balls of his feet.

My eyes narrow. "What exactly did you see?"

A bead of sweat drips down the side of his head, either from the heat or his nerves. His hand runs nervously through his dark curls.

"Well, I wasn't the one who actually saw him. Just the one who reported it."

"What are you saying, soldier?" Remy says, his tone hard as granite.

"Another guard was the one who saw him," Branson admits. "He told me, and I alerted everyone else."

The captain steps closer, crowding the man. "Who was the other guard?"

While Remy has always been gentle with me, those under his command know a different side of him. In these moments, he always appears larger than life. I can't imagine any of his men defying an order from their captain.

"I-I don't know his name." Branson shakes his head as his face pales. "He was wearing a uniform, but I'd never seen him before. Young guy. Mortal."

I turn back to the crowd, scanning the faces for someone who matches that vague description.

"Anything else you recall?" Remy presses him.

Strawberry-blond hair catches my attention as a young man moves through the mass of people. Only his back is visible as he pushes toward an alley that leads between two buildings, but something about his lanky frame pulls at a memory.

"He was a ginger," Branson announces right as the man turns his head, offering me a glimpse of his profile.

"Kipps," I whisper.

"What did you say?" Remy snaps in my direction.

His eyes meet mine through the crowd, holding my gaze for less than a second before he darts down the alley and disappears.

"It was Kipps!" I shout.

Wasting no time, I sprint after the guard from the tunnels. Thorne's boots pound against cobblestones behind me, followed closely by Remy and his soldiers. Pedestrians block my path, forcing me to push them aside to clear a way forward.

"Go around!" I shout to the others as I squeeze through a gap in the crowd. "We need to cut him off!"

With no time to glance back, I pray that they do as I ask. We can't afford to let Kipps get away, not when he's our only lead. Using my elbows to force people out of my way, I finally reach the mouth of the alley. Several yards ahead, I spot a flash of red hair darting around the back of the building. Pushing my legs as fast as they'll go, I race after him. I've never been so thankful to be high fae and blessed with speed mortals could only dream of.

Turning the corner, I spot Kipps only fifteen feet ahead of me. My determination blazes as I realize I'm gaining on him. I've almost closed the gap when I notice a woman step out the back door of one of the buildings ahead of us. She's carrying a broken milk jar toward a trash bin, completely oblivious to the danger she's in.

By the time her features twist with horror, it's too late. Kipps grabs her by the hair and brings a knife to her throat. I slam to a halt, my body nearly tipping forward before I right myself. Only a few feet separate us, but it might as well be a mile. With her back pressed against his chest, he uses her body as a shield.

"Mama?" a child's voice calls from inside the open door.

My heart aches as a small head peeks out, revealing a little girl who couldn't be more than five years old. Black ringlets tied together with colorful ribbons hang down her back. Without taking my eyes off Kipps, I grab the girl's shoulder and gently push her back inside before shutting the door. She doesn't need to see this.

"Please," the woman's desperate voice begs. "Don't hurt me."

"Shut up!" Kipps digs the blade harder against her throat, causing a small stream of blood to trail down her chest and stain the bust of her worn gown.

"Kipps. Look at me," I demand. "You don't have to do this. You can let her go, and we can just talk."

"I can't!" he shouts. "He won't let me!"

Footsteps race toward us from the other end of the alley, cutting off his only hope of escape. He starts to turn toward them, but I pull his attention back to me.

"Who won't let you?" I ask. "Is it Darby?"

"No!" he screams, his fevered eyes drilling into mine. "The voice! He whispers to me. He's always, always, always whispering." His free hand pounds against his head, emphasizing his words. "All the time. And I have to do what he says. I don't have a choice."

"Who is he, Kipps? Tell me his name."

His face crumples as he shakes his head.

"You don't understand. None of you have heard him yet." His gaze drops to my collar and stays there. "But you will."

A terrible scream fills the air as Kipps drags his blade across the woman's throat.

"No!" I cry, but it's too late.

Blood sprays from the wound, splattering across my face. I step forward, my arms outstretched on instinct as Kipps throws the woman toward me. Out of the corner of my eye, I see him lift the blade to his own throat right before another spray of blood washes over me. Soldiers swarm him, but all my attention is reserved for the woman dying in my arms.

Her panicked eyes find mine, the pupils so wide they've eaten up her green irises. Lowering her to the ground, I position her torso in my lap as I try to apply pressure to the wound. Her skin is slick, making it difficult to keep my hands from sliding. There's blood everywhere. In some distant corner of my brain, I know it's too much. Mortals are fragile, and their bodies can't replace it quickly enough.

"Just hold on," I whisper. "It will be okay."

Her gaze is unfocused now, staring blankly at the sky above us.

"A towel!" I shout at the soldiers. "I need something to stop the bleeding!"

No one moves. There's no longer any sound of a struggle, yet they all stand around watching us instead of helping.

"Save her!" I order them. "Do something!"

My hand slips again, and I adjust my grip, noticing the way her bleeding has slowed. Her skin is too cold now. Or maybe that's mine? I feel as though I've been covered in a blanket of ice. My brow furrows as I remember how warm it was earlier. Did the weather change already?

"Ivy."

I don't glance up to see who's speaking to me. It doesn't matter. I need to focus on the woman in front of me. She needs my—

Dead.

The word echoes through my mind as I stare into her lifeless eyes. Her chest is still, no longer moving up and down. Air hitches in my lungs as the world spins around me making the past and present blend together.

I run through the gardens as a wagon brings the body through the gate. I heard servants whisper it's the queen, but that's not possible. No. No, it's not her. It can't be. Leona isn't dead. The wagon hits a bump in the road, jostling the blanket that covers the body. It slips down, revealing a face I know too well. Frozen terror holds her eyes wide, but there's no life left in them. Her mouth is open, as if she died screaming and rigor mortis made her fear permanent. If only I had—

"Leona, no," I cry as I shake the woman in my lap. "Please! You can't leave me again."

A gloved hand settles on top of mine, startling me. I drag my gaze away from Leona to find Thorne staring down at me, his blue eyes full of sympathy.

"She's gone, Angel," he says softly. "It's time to let go."

"No, she's—" My words cut off as I glance back down, freezing when I see her face.

My chest deflates. This isn't Leona. The queen is long dead, and this is someone else. Some poor woman whose daughter is about to receive the worst news of her life.

My hands shake as he pulls them away from the woman and helps me to my feet. Embarrassment steals my breath as I notice the wary stares the soldiers send my way. Even Remy watches me with worried eyes.

"Get her out of here," he whispers to Thorne. "I'll handle this."

"Her daughter," I murmur. "Don't let the girl see her this way."

"We won't," Remy assures me.

Thorne's hand at my back guides me toward the street. I want to fight him, but I don't know what I'd be fighting for. Glancing over my shoulder, I catch one last glimpse of the green-eyed women before we turn the corner, and she's gone forever.

CHAPTER
TWENTY-ONE

Half an hour later, I find myself sitting on a rock by the shore.

I kept my head down as Thorne led me through the streets, my trembling fingers clasped in his gloved hand. I'm not sure how far we walked, but I can still hear the faint buzz of the marina in the distance. Thankfully, this cove appears to be deserted. The gentle waves carry a fresh citrus breeze. If I could have chosen a place to recover from the horrors of the morning, it would have been this one.

I should probably be worried about why he's brought me all the way out here, but I'm not. Strangely, I find that I trust him. The realization hits hard, nearly knocking me off the boulder.

I trust Thorne.

I don't know when it happened, but somewhere along the way, I began to think of him as an ally. We aren't friends exactly, but I trust him not to slide a dagger between my shoulder blades. And in my experience, that's rare.

He crouches by the water, dousing a faded white cloth into the waves. Before I can ask what he's doing, he returns to my side and kneels at my feet. His hand reaches for me, and I rear back on instinct.

"It's okay," he whispers, holding up the handkerchief in his hand to show me it's not a threat. "I won't hurt you."

I force myself to stay put as he leans forward again and wipes the blood from my cheeks, erasing the evidence of my failure. I try not to stare at his face while he works, but it proves impossible. It's only been a few days since we were this close, but already, I note small changes. A few more freckles have appeared on his nose, no doubt a gift from the unforgiving sun we've been under all morning. They soften him slightly, adding a hint of boyishness to his appearance.

"I thought you didn't want me touching you." The idiotic words tumble out of my mouth without permission.

"You're not touching me," he says. "I'm touching you."

We sit in silence for a few moments as he goes about his task. The cloth is soft against my skin. I spot a floral design embroidered into the corners of the material, and I can't help but wonder who gave it to him? Was it from a lover? My fingers dig into the rock beneath me.

"I'm sorry for the way I snapped at you that day," Thorne says, surprising me. "I just... I don't like being touched."

"You're handing out a lot of apologies today," I murmur.

"Only to you." One corner of his mouth kicks up in a half smile. "It seems I'm constantly on my worst behavior whenever you're around."

"I've been told I have that effect on people."

He chuckles, the sound rough and warm, but his humor fades quickly.

"What happened back there?" His cool eyes scan my face, searching for answers.

"Nothing." I shift my gaze, focusing on the waves meeting the shore in a cascade of white foam.

"You kept calling her Leona."

My eyes shut tight as the name echoes through my body. No one says it aloud anymore. Gone less than a year, and she's already been forgotten. But not by me. She haunts every step I take. Each time I lift my blade as the Angel of Mercy, in some delusional corner of my mind, it's her I'm saving. With each kill, I'm rewriting the story, reaching her before it's too late. But that's just another lie I tell myself.

No amount of pretending will change the fact that I *was* too late.

I *didn't* save her.

It was my fault she died, and that can never be undone.

"That was the queen's name, wasn't it?" Thorne presses, his voice painfully soft. "You two were close?"

My chin quivers as tears threaten to overflow. "She was like a mother to me."

"What happened?"

"I let her down," I whisper.

The words create another crack in that mental prison where I store my shame. A thousand memories leak from the fissure, each one ripping me apart from the inside out. The warmth of her voice. The smell of her perfume. The little sound she'd make in the back of her throat when she was focusing deeply on something. The gentle scratching of her fingernails against my scalp, soothing me after a nightmare.

Tears escape my eyes, freely falling down my cheeks as Thorne tries in vain to catch them all with his handkerchief.

If I could rip these memories from my mind and give them to Della, I would. She deserves them more than me. Let her treasure them. Let her find joy in remembrance rather than the shame I feel.

I don't know how long I sit there crying, but Thorne never leaves. He stays by my side, watching the tide until my tears finally abate. At some point, he put the handkerchief in my hand, allowing me to soak it in my grief.

"I was close to my mother," he say, barely above a whisper.

I turn my head to observe him, my mind catching on a single word. "*Was?*"

His throat bobs as he swallows thickly.

"She died. It was my fault," he admits.

"I'm sorry," I say honestly. It's a pain I know all too well, and I wouldn't wish that kind of guilt on my worst enemy. "What happened?"

"My father was very..." He trails off, running his fingers through his dark waves as he searches for the right words. "He was a difficult man. Paranoid. He kept my mother and me isolated from the rest of the world. He said it was to protect us, but I knew it was more about control."

Goosebumps travel over my arms as he speaks. Listening to him is like looking in a mirror and expecting to see my own reflection staring back at me, but instead, I find his. I already know where this story is heading, but I sit quietly and listen anyway.

"My father hired this *enchanter* to watch us." He spits the word, his fists clenching at his sides. "He was powerful, even more than your friend Darrow. My father ordered him to craft a tonic for my mother that would make her believe she was happy, that she was content to be a captive."

A wave of horror washes over me. What Baylor has done to me is vile, but I can't imagine being stripped of my own inner emotions. I know what it is to be controlled, but at least I've always been safe inside my mind. My thoughts are my own, even if my actions are not. My heart breaks for this woman and the suffering she endured.

The suffering her son was forced to witness.

"Seeing her with that complacent smile on her face and her pupils blown wide was terrible, but what happened when it would wear off was even worse." He winces. "You see, the effects of the tonic didn't last forever. It needed to be readministered whenever it wore off, and over time her body developed a resistance to it. What started as a monthly dose soon became weekly. And when that didn't work anymore, it was daily."

I remember Darrow warning of something similar when I asked him about binding spells. My fingers trail over the rubies at my throat as I imagine the fate that might have been mine if Baylor hadn't used the collar to control me. What other methods would he have employed?

"We'd know it was wearing off because she'd fly into a rage," Thorne continues, his body tense with years' worth of pain. "Or worse, slip into a sadness that nothing could pull her out of. It was as if that tonic stole her ability to regulate her emotions. It ate up all of her joy, and when it was gone, she was left with nothing but anger and sorrow. And then my father's guards would hold her down and pry open her mouth, forcing her to choke down that fucking poison again." He speaks the words through clenched teeth. "And a few minutes later, she'd be smiling as if she hadn't just been screaming and clawing for her life."

"I'm sorry, Thorne," I tell him honestly. "No one should experience what she went through. And those who were responsible deserve death."

His head jerks in a semblance of a nod before he clears his throat and continues, still staring at the sea.

"The guards used to clip my wings every night, so that I couldn't fly away. Not that I knew how. My mother and I were never allowed in the sky. But since we would always heal quickly, they didn't take any chances. One night, I wasn't cooperating. I was angry and lashing out at any of them who came close to me. I knew it was useless, but I couldn't stomach the thought of letting them slice into me again. I just couldn't do it."

His voice turns pleading, as if he's begging me to understand. And I do. Without thinking, I reach out for his gloved hand, taking it in mine. He goes still, but he doesn't rip it out of my grasp.

"They were holding me down and shredding my back with a whip. It was the worst pain I'd ever felt, but still, I refused to summon my wings for them." He pauses, taking a deep breath. "That's when they brought my mother in."

Ice slithers over my skin, as I realize what he's about to tell me.

"One of them was pointing a knife at her heart." His fists clench into tight balls. "I knew they wouldn't kill her, since doing that would guarantee their own death by my father's hands. But I had no idea how far they were willing to go, so I gave in. I stopped fighting them and summoned my wings..." He trails off, swallowing before he continues. "But what none of us knew was that my mother's tonic was wearing off. They had just begun to cut one of my wings when she started screaming like mad for them to let me go. They did what she said, but the guard continued to hold her. I'll never forget the look on her face."

His voice breaks off as he clears the emotion from his throat.

"She was resigned, but there was a spark of hope there that I hadn't seen in years. Her eyes met mine, and she whispered a single word. *Fly.* And then she grabbed hold of the man's hand and drove his knife through her chest."

I thought my eyes were done producing tears, but I realize I was wrong as one trails down my cheek. "It wasn't your fault. You have to know that, Thorne."

He doesn't answer, and I don't blame him. If he told me Leona's death wasn't my fault, I wouldn't believe him either.

"What did you do then?" I ask.

"Everything was silent for a moment as the reality of the situation set in. Then all of the guards began to panic. They knew my father would kill them all. I heard one of them shout to blame it on the kid, and next thing I knew, they were all swarming me. I felt something snap, like a power that had always been hiding beneath the surface was finally breaking free. My shadows were unleashed for the first time, and I slaughtered each and every one of them. The snakes ripped them to pieces."

"Good."

His eyes slide to mine. "So vindictive, Angel."

"What did you do after?" I ask, ignoring the shivers that race through me whenever he calls me that.

"I picked up my mother's body and took her to the cliff by our cottage. I figured either I'd learn to fly, or we'd sink into the sea together. It wasn't easy since I'd never been able to use my wings before, but somehow, I did it. It was painful, but I got us out of there. I couldn't leave my mother's body behind, trapped in that awful place. She deserved to be free."

"How old were you?"

"Eight."

I feel a sharp crack in my chest. "Fates... I'm so sorry, Thorne."

He nods.

"What happened to your father?" I ask. "And to the *enchanter*?"

He opens his mouth to speak but stops when a male voice calls his name.

We both stand as we spot a tall blond fae treading through the sand, dressed in dark trousers and a white tunic that is unbuttoned down to his chest. His features are stereotypically handsome. Straight nose and full lips. An angular jaw that's perfectly proportioned to his high cheekbones. As the newcomer's gaze switches from Thorne to me, a flirtatious smile breaks across his face.

"And who do we have here?" he asks, his voice low and seductive as he stops a few feet away.

"Griffen, this is Lady Iverson," Thorne replies, his tone suddenly turning cold.

"The *wraith*!" Griffen's eyes widen as his hand moves to his chest. "You are even more lovely than people say."

I bark out a laugh. "I imagine 'lovely' isn't the word they use when describing me."

"You're right," he agrees, a dangerous twinkle in his eye. "It's much too tame. If I were to describe you, I'd choose a far more sensual adjective."

Thorne steps forward, placing his body slightly between me and Griffen. "Watch yourself," he orders.

Griffen's forehead wrinkles as his gaze flicks back and forth between us before dropping to the soiled handkerchief in my hands. His eyes go wide as understanding dawns on his face. With his lips pulled into a wide, devilish grin, he leans around the reaper.

"My dear lady, how long have you known my friend here?" he asks, utterly beaming.

"I don't see how that concerns you," I say evenly, my eyes narrowing as I try to understand the dynamics at play here.

His brows shoot up as he nods approvingly. "Ah, a suspicious nature. I see you are well matched with my paranoid friend."

It's not lost on me that this is the second time he's referred to Thorne as his friend. The reaper doesn't correct him, so I suppose it must be true. My curiosity rises.

"And how long have you two known each other?" I ask.

"Too long," Thorne grumbles.

I bite down on a smile. "Strange you've never mentioned your dearest friend Griffen."

The newcomer gasps, stepping around Thorne to get closer to me. "Frankly, I'm hurt to hear that."

Thorne rolls his eyes. "You'll get over it."

Griffen grabs my hand in his. "Why don't you ditch him and have a drink with me, Lady Iverson? My broken heart needs mending."

"Griffen," Thorne growls, his shoulders tensing.

"Fine." He tosses me a conspiratorial glance, kissing my hand before he releases it. "Ruin my fun, why don't you?"

"What are you doing here?" Thorne demands, crossing his arms over his chest.

The humor drains from Griffen's face immediately as his tone becomes serious. "You're needed at home. I'm afraid it can't wait."

Thorne's jaw clenches as he turns his gaze to the ocean.

My mouth suddenly turns dry. "You're returning to the Fifth Isle?"

"It seems I must." He nods, his eyes full of regret as he turns to me. "I'm not sure when I'll be back."

Something heavy sinks into my gut as he turns to his friend.

"Make sure she gets home safe," Thorne orders, before leaning closer and lowering his voice. "And keep your fucking hands to yourself."

The newcomer scrunches his nose. "Hmm, sounds like quite a feat."

"Griffen."

"I'm only joking, old friend," he says, waving off the reaper's menacing stare. "I will be an absolute gentleman."

"Will I see you at the ball?" I ask, hating the question even though I'm desperate to hear the answer.

Thorne's gaze finds mine, full of some emotion I don't recognize. "I'll be there."

With that settled, he steps back and searches the area to ensure we're alone. A moment later, his wings rip through his shirt, shooting out around him in another jaw-dropping display. He's readying himself to fly away when something occurs to me.

"Wait." I say, hurrying to his side and awkwardly handing him the embroidered handkerchief he'd lent me. "I figured you wouldn't want to forget this."

He nods, and the tips of his gloved fingers brush against my palm as he takes it from me. He stares at the fabric for a few moments before stuffing it into his pocket. With one last glance at me, he leaps into the air. I try to track him, but within seconds, he's nothing more than a black dot on the horizon.

"So..." Griffen draws out the word, pulling my attention back to him. "You seem rather close to my friend?"

"Not really," I say casually.

His eyes narrow as the wind ruffles his blond hair. "That's how you're going to play it?"

My brows rise innocently. "I'm not playing anything."

"Fine," he grumbles. "Keep your secrets."

"I will." I smile. "And you should know, I don't need anyone to help me get home. I've got it covered."

He shakes his head, tucking his hands behind his back. "I'm afraid I must insist."

I grimace. "I'm afraid that will be difficult for you."

His brow furrows, not understanding my meaning until I disappear before his eyes. He jumps back, nearly falling on his ass before bursting out in laughter. Taking advantage of his distraction, I begin moving down the beach leaping from rock to rock to avoid leaving any footprints in the sand.

"No wonder he's taken with you," Griffen calls after me. "But please try to get home safely. If you don't, it will be my life on the line."

"No promises!" I shout back.

His laughter follows me all the way back to the docks.

CHAPTER
TWENTY-TWO

The ballroom is a sea of glittering gowns and sparkling jewels.

Hidden away in one of the alcoves, I observe the revelry from afar. The lords and ladies flit through the room, offering warm compliments before whispering ugly comments behind each other's backs. Bridgid stands in the center of the merriment, enjoying the fruits of her labor. She glides across the dance floor, wrapped in swathes of sparkly blue fabric that swooshes with each step she takes. Her blonde ringlets are piled high on her head and adorned with a decorative diamond comb that looks awfully similar to a tiara.

The bold choice only fuels the swirling rumors about her impending engagement to the king. Apparently, Darcus and Naomi took it upon themselves to share Bridgid's suspicions with the entire court. At this point, the guests are clamoring for her attention, behaving as if the announcement is already a foregone conclusion.

I hope they're right.

Several gentlemen, and even a few ladies, send admiring glances in my direction, but I can't say I blame them tonight. My lady's maids outdid themselves. They chose a rich burgundy gown that compliments my fair complexion beautifully. Tiny straps hold up the silk triangles that cup my full breasts, leaving nothing to the imagination. The dress is tight around my waist before flaring out slightly over my hips. A high slit allows for freedom of movement and gives me access to the blade I've brought, just in case.

In order to highlight my exposed back, Alva swept my deep copper waves into a messy chignon, with several loose pieces hanging down to frame my face. Meanwhile, Morwen applied her talents to my makeup, painting my lips the exact autumnal shade of my dress. As always, the only jewelry I'm wearing tonight is my collar, but I feel very pretty none the less.

I must admit, Bridgid did a marvelous job with the preparations. From the decorations to the refreshments, every lavish detail has been planned to perfection. Lord Darcus and Lady Naomi trail behind Bridgid, probably hoping some of the admiration being sent her way will trickle back to them. I roll my eyes, questioning why I ever sought their friendship in the first place. It likely had something to do with the fact that Bridgid is beautiful, charming, and adored by all the courtiers. Like her jealous companions, I was hoping some of that shine would rub off on me.

Speaking of courtiers, Kaldar and his brother, Lord Burgess, are currently surrounded by quite a few. By the way he's holding court, you'd think Bridgid's father is the one who's about to become royalty. Condescension radiates off him as lords and ladies clamor for his favor, searching for a connection to the future queen.

Unlike Kaldar, his brother, Lord Simon Burgess, is quite handsome. I can see why he's rumored to be their mothers favorite. His appearance is similar to his daughter's, both sharing the same angular features and sour expressions. His fine hair is a shockingly pale shade of blond that hangs down to his waist.

Tired of observing the party guests, I turn my attention to the decor. This room is usually closed off, since Baylor rarely hosts balls. However, I've snuck in here a few times over the years, strangely drawn to the haunting mural that adorns the ceiling. The centuries-old artwork depicts an ancient battle between Saint Vera and the Novians. A lone woman battling an army of pure light. Though she didn't survive that encounter, her bravery was remembered, and the Verran Isles were named in her honor.

There's a darkness to the painting that has always captivated me. When I squint my eyes, I can make out terrible faces within the brightness of the Novians. It's always bothered me that I can't tell if their expressions are twisted with horror or hatred. Humanoid in shape, their bodies were made of the purest light. Their victims were lured in by the creatures' otherworldly beauty, only to be devoured.

With my head tilted back and my focus enraptured in the magnificence of the mural, I'm too distracted to notice the approaching footsteps.

"Having fun?"

My lips part on a gasp at the faint note of familiarity in the masculine voice, one I haven't heard since that fateful night fifteen years ago. I turn and face him slowly, terrified to see how time has changed the sweet boy I once knew. My heart cracks as my gaze flicks over his features, so similar to my own. Though his hair is darker than mine, I spot a hint of auburn mixed with his brown strands, courtesy of our mother.

"Bellamy?" I whisper.

"It's me, Ivy." He steps forward, pulling me into his warm embrace.

Heat prickles behind my eyes as I breathe in his scent, awakening a rush of memories. Seven years my senior, Bel never fussed about being forced to chase me through the woods or attend tea parties with my dolls. He humored all my requests, happy to give me his time no matter the activity. Just like that horrible day I asked him to play hide and seek, only he wasn't the one to find me.

I pull back, meeting his hazel eyes. There are dozens of questions I want to ask him, but not a single one of them rises to the tip of my tongue. I'm frozen by the years that stand between us.

"How are you?" he asks.

I open my mouth to lie, but somehow the truth pours out instead.

"Terrible." Embarrassment fills me as his eyes widen, and my mouth feels suddenly dry. "And you?"

"About the same," he admits.

An inappropriate giggle bubbles out of me. I clasp my hand over my mouth, trying to keep it in. Bel's lips twitch and suddenly he's laughing too. I wipe a small tear from my eyes, noting the glassy sheen coating his own.

"Look at you, Ivy," he whispers, his voice full of something that sounds an awful lot like pride. "My baby sister, now a grown-up lady."

An involuntary smile lights up my face. "I'm not sure I'm much of a lady, but I did grow up. How long are you staying?"

"Just for the night. Father's insisting we leave tomorrow."

An invisible knife slides between my ribs, piercing my lungs as it knocks the air out of me. Fear that has lain dormant for a decade and a half reawakens, stretching itself into every corner of my being.

I lick my lips, my mouth suddenly dry. "He's here?"

There's compassion in his eyes as he nods. "Ivy, I—"

A dark shadow falls over us, cutting off Bellamy's words. Another ghost from my past appears, this one far less welcome.

"Daughter," Lord Pomeroy says the word like a joke. His cold eyes rake over me, no doubt finding a thousand flaws in my appearance.

"Father." I match his tone, making a mockery of the title we both know doesn't truly belong to him. Everyone is aware I'm not his child, but the great Lord Nigel Pomeroy will never publicly admit it, despite the rumors that circulate. He believes himself above such petty gossip.

"Have you been making yourself useful?" he asks. "I trust you're keeping the king happy?"

A muscle clenches in Bellamy's jaw at his father's implication.

"He's very pleased with me," I respond coolly.

"See to it he stays that way." A hard glint enters his green eyes.

"I've heard that little weasel Kaldar is trying to push his niece as a bride. You can't let that happen. The Burgess family has too much influence already."

"I won't," I lie, looking forward to his disappointment when the news is announced later tonight.

I'm sure he will be dripping with displeasure for the happy couple. Hopefully if Baylor announces Bridgid as his bride, he will stop calling me to his chambers at night. If that happens, I'll likely fall to her feet with gratitude. She can insult me as much as she wants, as long as she keeps him away.

"Father," Bel growls, his fists balled tightly at his side. "You haven't seen your daughter in years, and this is all you have to say?"

"Nothing else comes to mind." Lord Pomeroy paints a charming smile onto his face, probably for the benefit of the prying eyes that keep flicking in our direction.

I bite my lip to keep from laughing as a realization settles over me. I don't care what this vile man says. Any power he had to cause me pain died in that lake, along with my innocence. Now, he's nothing but a bitter memory.

"Apologies for the interruption, my lords." Remy's voice comes from behind me.

Turning around, I'm shocked by the sight of him in his formal uniform. Pride swells in my chest as I note the insignia and accommodations decorating the left side of his jacket. Despite being forced to serve a selfish king, Remy has always done his best to make the city of Solmare proud.

"I'm afraid His Majesty is asking for Lady Iverson," he continues, unable to hide the simmering hatred blazing in his eyes as he glares at Lord Pomeroy.

"Then you must not keep him waiting, daughter."

I ignore my father and turn to Bel. "I'll find you later."

He nods, regret shining in his brown eyes. After all these years, I'd hoped if I ever saw my brother again, we'd have more time together. I have so many questions. Why did he never reach out to me? Why didn't he come to visit? Does he blame me for the things that happened that night? I can only imagine how the memories of Clara's screams must haunt him.

I push aside the deep well of sadness that opens up every time I think about the young governess. Now is not the time to let such emotions consume me. With so many eyes watching me tonight, I need to play my part flawlessly. Courtiers whisper in every corner of the ballroom as Remy escorts me along the edges of the dancefloor. Couples move in sync with each other, their graceful bodies swaying with the music. There's a part of me that longs to join them, but Baylor would never allow it.

Glancing up at Remy, I can't help but notice the dark circles sitting beneath his tired eyes. Despite the time he's been spending outside, his skin has become pale and sickly, making the thin scar along his neck stand out more than usual. The search for Darby has worn him down, yet Baylor keeps pushing him harder. Remy is strong, but everyone needs to rest eventually.

"Any new developments?" I ask quietly, knowing he will understand I'm referring to the *almanova*.

He shakes his head, his gaze dropping to my collar momentarily before meeting my own. "The king is displeased."

"That's never good," I murmur distractedly as we dodge a group of lords arguing over some business matter. It appears the crowd is getting antsy as we wait for the Gods to arrive. I glance toward the staircase, searching for a specific face.

"He's not here," Remy says.

My gaze snaps to his. "Who?"

The warning in his hazel eyes has my spine straightening. "You need to be careful where you place your trust, Iverson."

My jaw clenches. "You don't know him."

"Do you?" he counters.

I ignore the words and the doubts they stir. My gaze shifts to Baylor, still standing on the dais at the far end of the room. His blond hair has been freshly cut, the color contrasting nicely against his navy-blue suit. His eyes are swimming with self-satisfaction as he collects praise from courtiers and nobles. Hopefully, the adoration of the crowd will quell the worst of the *displeasure* Remy mentioned. A frisson of apprehension skates down my spine. I can't imagine the kind of rage Baylor would unleash if tonight doesn't go according to his plans.

"Ah, my pet!" he exclaims as I approach.

The crowd around him parts wide enough for us to slip through. Lord Burgess, who has joined the group, sneers at me as I pass. Remy bows to the king before offering me a hand to step onto the platform. Baylor's focus dips to my leg, where the slit parts wide enough to reveal the sheathed blade at my thigh.

He arches a brow. "Expecting danger this evening, pet?"

I force my lips to part in a seductive grin. "I never expect it, but I'm always prepared for it."

He laughs, and the courtiers nearby follow his lead, pretending it's the funniest thing they've ever heard.

"She's so violent," he tells them, as if the thought of me using this blade is hilarious. As the crowd continues laughing, his attention shifts back to me. He pulls me close, letting his hands drift over my exposed back.

"Things are going to change tonight, Iverson," he whispers in my ear, his warm breath sending waves of revulsion through me. "But I promise you, everything I'm doing is for us."

The ominous words all but confirm he's going to announce his engagement to Bridgid. Hope sparks in my chest, and for once, the smile I give him is genuine. Taking a new wife means I might get a break from all this public touching.

"I know you will always do what's best for me," I force the lie to leave my tongue.

He smiles fondly, squeezing my hands in his.

A loud gong sounds through the ballroom, capturing everyone's attention. The crowd comes to a halt, turning to face the landing at the top of the stairwell. Everyone knows what that sound means.

The Gods are arriving.

I start to move from the platform, but Baylor keeps my hand in his, refusing to let go. "Stay," he commands.

With no choice but to obey, I wait by his side as muffled voices whisper to each other, speculating on which God is about to join us. Everyone faces the same direction, except for one person. Bridgid's hateful gaze remains on me, probably pissed that I'm by Baylor's side during this important moment. I swallow down a sigh, knowing that when she's crowned queen, she will make me pay for this. But whatever she throws my way, it will be worth it as long as she keeps Baylor's attention focused on her instead of me.

All thoughts of Bridgid are swept aside as the hairs on the back of my neck rise. I sense a presence approaching, similar to what I feel when I'm near Thorne, yet different in some undefinable way. My attention shifts to the landing, somehow knowing that's where the sensation is emanating from.

The double doors open, revealing a man and a woman. The crowd is utterly silent as the newcomers enter the room. The man's formal jacket is the exact burnt orange shade of his wings, complimenting his warm brown skin perfectly. Gold filigree lines his collar and sleeves, giving him an air of wealth. But unlike most of the upper class, there's a softness to his features that radiates kindness.

The woman next to him is several inches shorter, the top of her head only reaching his shoulder, yet her presence is far more commanding. Long raven braids fall to her waist, brushing against the mulberry silk of her gown. As she approaches the rail of the landing, she spreads her gilded wings wide. The feathers are breathtaking, but they are nothing compared to the rich swirling gold of her eyes. She holds her head high as her gaze drifts over the crowd, searching for someone.

My lips part on a gasp when her attention settles on me. Amusement plays at the corners of her mouth. It feels as though she's seeing right through me, as if every secret has been laid bare for her to peruse at her leisure. Instinct demands I take a step back, but somehow, I manage to stay still, holding her molten gaze as they begin their descent down the grand staircase.

"Selim, God of Accords," a booming voice announces as they near the bottom. "And Cassandra, Goddess of Divination."

As one, every person in the room drops to their knees and bows their heads. There's a palpable sense of nervousness in the air. For the last quarter of a century, we haven't had a single visit from any of the Gods. After Maebyn disappeared, the divine rulers of the Verran Isles refused every invitation.

Until now.

From the corner of my eye, I notice several young ladies shifting uncomfortably as they struggle to maintain the submissive pose in their heels and finery. At my side, Baylor stands proud, the only person in the room refusing to bend a knee.

"Welcome to the Seventh Isle," Baylor greets them as they reach the dais. "We are honored to have you here with us in the Realm of Illusion."

I'd kill to witness their reaction to his disrespect, but with my head down, all I can see is their shoes approaching us.

"King Baylor, it is an honor to be here in your beautiful realm," Selim's deep voice responds. "May everyone please rise and continue the merriment."

As if his proclamation has restarted time, the crowd follows his command. Music swells once more, and the conversations that previously halted continue, though at least half the eyes in the room are openly watching the Gods.

I push to my feet as I brush out the wrinkles in my gown. When I lift my gaze, I immediately lock eyes again with the Goddess of Divination once more. There's something strange about her presence, almost familiar. But in this moment, my mind is too jumbled to connect the fragments.

Her attention shifts to the man beside me as she addresses him in a honeyed tone. "Aren't you going to introduce us to your companion, King Baylor?"

It takes every ounce of my self-control not to squirm away from his touch as his hand settles on my hip, pulling me closer to his side. Instead of recoiling, I paste a vacant smile on my face.

"May I present Lady Iverson Pomeroy," he says.

"The famous *wraith*?" Her eyes dance with delight as they flit back to me. "A pleasure to meet you, Lady Iverson. Your reputation is quite impressive."

I bow my head politely. "The pleasure is all mine, Your Grace."

Sneaking a glance at Selim, I find him watching me warily. He opens his mouth to say something right as another man appears on the landing. Whatever strange awareness came over me at the arrival of the two Gods, it doesn't happen now.

The newcomer's chestnut brown hair is pushed back, putting his blue eyes on display. I can admit he's handsome, but there's something about the smug glint in his eyes that tells me he's too aware of that fact. It's as if he's ready to be adored by all who bear witness to his greatness.

Standing a few feet behind him is another man. Despite his smooth, unwrinkled skin, the way he carries himself makes him appear older than the other one, more mature. The sharp cut of his jaw combined with the coldness of his gaze gives him an air of ruthlessness. He's definitely not one to underestimate.

"Foley, Heir of Life." The announcer's booming voice cuts through the room. "And Leland, Adviser to the God of Life."

The crowd doesn't kneel again, since there isn't a God among their small party, but they do bow their heads as a sign of respect for the Heir.

"Welcome," Baylor says as they approach the dais, joining Selim and Cassandra. "We are pleased you could make the journey."

Foley sneers, crossing his arms over his chest as he searches the room for something more interesting. While most Heirs are hidden away from the public, the God of Life has kept his son by his side since the day he was born. Judging by Foley's attitude, I'd say being raised in a humbler environment would probably have done him some good. For a man slightly older than me, he somehow manages to carry himself with the petulance of a teenager.

"Thank you for inviting us," Leland responds for both of them.

I imagine Eyrkan sent his adviser along to smooth over any ruffled feathers his son may cause. Based on the not-so-covert nudge he gives the young Heir, Leland is used to such duties.

"Yes," Foley grumbles, rolling his eyes. "We're so very honored by your hospitality, King Baylor."

From the corner of my eye, I notice the vein at Baylor's temple is pulsing faster. The lack of respect is likely eating him alive, but somehow, he manages to refrain from commenting on it. Thank the Fates for small miracles.

"I see your manners haven't improved, boy," Cassandra interjects, having no need for restraint.

Foley turns to the Goddess and sketches an extravagant bow, the movement laced with insincerity. "How wonderful to see you again, Cassandra. Please entertain us all tonight with your little party trick."

"It's no trick." Her voice deepens unnaturally. "Speak to me with disrespect again, and I might tell you what I've seen in *your* future. And trust me, it's not for the faint of heart."

Foley scoffs, but judging by the way his face pales, her words had their intended effect. His eyes widen as he notices me standing next to Baylor for the first time. I don't miss the way his gaze rakes over my body with undisguised interest. Given his reputation as a notorious rake, the reaction isn't surprising.

Baylor's grip on my hip turns possessive. "I see you've noticed my pet."

"I imagine that's the reason you keep her around, is it not?" He reaches for my hand and brings it to his lips.

Biting down on my rising disgust, I keep my face impassive.

"You call her 'pet?'" he asks Baylor before turning his attention back to me. "I've never been fond of animals, my lady, but for you, I would make an exception."

"You're too kind." I smile, but my eyes are full of daggers. My blood boils within my veins as I rip my hand from his grip, unable to stop the words that tumble from my mouth. "Unfortunately, I don't make exceptions for sniveling brats."

Fury detonates across Foley's face, but before he can respond, Cassandra bursts out laughing.

"I like her," she announces, brushing one of her dark braids over her shoulder. "You've done well with this one, Baylor."

Gratitude swells in my chest. I catch her eye, hoping my small nod is enough to convey my thanks. Secrets twinkle in her golden eyes, and I can't help but wonder if she intervened because she *knew* what would happen if she didn't. Foley doesn't seem like the type to forgive any insult. Frankly, he reminds me of Kaldar—a little man, never content with what he has, always reaching for more. Still, I need to bite my tongue around him in the future. It would be foolish to make an enemy of a future God, no matter how odious he is.

"Perhaps we should all enjoy the festivities?" Selim interjects, his calming tone smoothing over the situation with an unnatural ease. I'd bet my life he's using his *gifts* to quell the heightened tension among our small group. As the God of Accord, he's blessed with the ability to soothe rising tempers. As much as I hate the idea of anyone toying with my emotions, I'm grateful for his interference right now.

"Please, make yourselves welcome," Baylor calls as they step into the crowd, leaving us alone on the dais.

I watch them go, noting the way Selim glances back at me, his gaze narrowing with something resembling concern. I don't have time to consider what that means before they are swallowed up by the crowd.

"That was careless," Baylor whispers, his tone deceptively soft.

"It was calculated," I counter, praying he buys my explanation. "Didn't you notice that Selim and Cassandra dislike him? Many alliances have been formed based on a shared enemy. And now the others know you won't stand for their disrespect."

He's silent for a moment as he considers my words. "Let's hope your gamble paid off. But in the future, leave the politics to me, pet."

"Of course." I dip my chin, lowering my eyes in a show of respect.

His finger taps nervously against my side. "Killian should have been here by now," he quietly seethes. "What is the point of this infuriating alliance if he's can't even uphold his end of the deal?"

I refrain from pointing out how generous the God of Death has been with us, considering Baylor is the one who hasn't made good on his promises. Still, I can't help but worry. Thorne said he would be here, but what if Killian changed his mind? A foolish pang of sadness settles in my chest at the thought of not seeing the reaper. I shove the emotion down, knowing there's no room for those kinds of sentiments tonight.

A second later, the double doors at the top of the stairs burst open, quickly followed by the clang of the gong sounding off for a third time. The signal can only mean one thing.

Death has come to the Seventh Isle.

Shadows spread throughout the room, devouring every ounce of light. Silence falls as three people step onto the landing. For a moment, I don't even notice the other two. My attention is stuck on the one in the center.

Thorne.

He's heartbreakingly beautiful in his dark apparel as he glides to the railing. He's so graceful, so *captivating*. Heat rises to my cheeks as I remember the way he used that word to describe me. He stands above us, silently judging the crowd with that ice-cold gaze. Something unexpected flashes in his eyes when they land on me, but he covers it quickly as his companions appear at his shoulders. My brows pinch as I try to understand the meaning behind that look.

My focus shifts to the familiar face on his right. Griffen is handsome in his maroon jacket. He appears far sterner than he did at the beach. The third member of their party is a woman I've never seen before. Her long inky black hair falls to her waist, contrasting beautifully against the midnight blue of her dress.

Something hot and vicious flares underneath my skin when she leans closer to Thorne, not close enough to touch him, but to whisper something for only him to hear. My eyes narrow at her proximity and a flash of amusement crosses his face, but it's gone a second later. He drags his gaze away from me, his features shifting back into the cold mask he wears so often.

Both Griffen and the woman flank Thorne, walking slightly behind him as they move to the staircase. Confusion blasts through me. Did Killian send ambassadors in his place? I glance at Baylor from the corner of my eye, finding his face pinched with tension. He won't respond to this insult kindly.

"K-Killian," the announcer stutters, his voice quieter than before. "God of Death."

Everyone else kneels, but I stand frozen, squinting at the open doors on the landing as I search for the God. Is he entering behind them? That would be odd. My attention flits back to the reaper, spotting a trace of shame swirling behind his eyes.

My blood turns to ice as my heart sinks into my stomach.

The announcer carries on, introducing Thorne's companions, but I don't hear him. The sounds of waves crash against my ears as the whole world narrows down to this single moment, this realization that's being forced upon me.

I hold my breath as Thorne raises his hands. Heat brushes against my face as a giant ring of fire appears over our heads, illuminating the ballroom. Gasps ring through the crowd. Many people cover their heads, fearing the blaze, but Thorne shows no reaction to their dramatics. He stands proud, his head high as he watches me. Only two people in this world have the ability to wield fire, the flames of creation and destruction. Life and Death.

Air catches in my lungs as my mind forces me to confront what's right before my eyes.

Thorne doesn't work for the God of Death.

Thorne is the God of Death.

CHAPTER
TWENTY-THREE

Denials rise to the tip of my tongue.

This can't be true. But when Thorne's eyes find mine again, I know it is. That mask I've seen him don many times is in full effect now. He carries himself with the power and authority of a God. Questions pound against my skull, one after another. How? Why? Was it obvious? Was he laughing behind my back at how easily I believed his lies? Was a single word out of his mouth true?

Baylor's anger radiates off him in waves, seeping into my skin and igniting my own bone-deep rage. Whimpers echo through the ballroom as courtiers cower in fear of the ring of fire swirling above our heads. Some duck into the alcoves, hoping to hide from the wrath of Death. Others push their noses deeper into the floor, as if they are trying to sink through it.

But I don't cower or hide or sink.

Instead, I hold my head high, my shoulders back as I watch him stride toward me.

I want *Death* to feel my disrespect.

The slight curve of his lips as he approaches tells me he knows exactly what I'm doing. It also makes me want to pull out my dagger and drive it straight into his gut. It wouldn't be enough to kill a God, but I could make it hurt. Whatever amusement simmered behind *Killian's* eyes fades quickly as his attention dips to Baylor's hand. Taking full advantage of my revealing gown, he's slipped his fingers beneath the seam of my low back-line, squeezing the bare flesh of my hip.

"I am pleased to welcome you to my kingdom, *Killian*," Baylor hisses.

"I assure you, King Baylor, the pleasure is all mine." Thorne's tone is deadly soft, raising the hairs on my arms. He lifts a gloved hand, gesturing to the two people behind him. "May I present my advisers, Griffen and Fia."

The king spares them a cursory glance, but my focus stays on the woman. *Fia.* The one who was so comfortable whispering in his ear earlier? Is she his lover? My fury intensifies as her dark eyes settle on me.

"What a delight to meet you," Baylor says dispassionately. "I trust you already know my pet, Lady Iverson."

I drag my gaze away from Fia to find Thorne still watching me. He's not even bothering to hide his anger.

"Of course." He flashes his teeth in a predatory smile. "But she won't be yours forever."

Baylor goes rigid. Something sharp skates over my hip, threatening to break the skin. *Claws.* The side of him I fear most is rising to the surface. The king has never been great at controlling his *vertere* nature. Instead, it seems to control him. I hold myself unnaturally still, not wanting to attract the attention of the Beast of the Battle.

The crowd, however, has no such survival instincts. Not a single one of them understands how precarious this situation is. Several guests audibly gasp at Thorne—*at Killian's*—open disrespect. Many even lift their heads from the floor to watch this dangerous scene play out.

Thorne carries on as if he's completely oblivious to the room's reaction as he deigns to glance at Baylor for the first time since he arrived.

"Soon, what you believe is yours will be *mine*," he promises.

Barely a second passes before the tips of Baylor's claws pierce the skin beneath my dress. Despite the pain, I don't react outwardly. I know better than that.

"After all," Thorne continues, "every soul belongs to Death, eventually."

The room is silent as we all wait for Baylor's response. He takes his time, his simmering stare focused solely on the God before him. "As you say, Your Excellency. I hope you and your companions enjoy—"

"I would love to dance with your charming *wraith*," Thorne cuts him off.

"No," I say quickly as Baylor's claws threaten to dig deeper into my side. "I'm sure that's not necessary."

If Thorne keeps this up, he's going to push the king too far. Baylor is going to quickly forget all the reasons he cannot fight a God.

"Come now, Lady Iverson," Thorne croons. "We are *allies*, are we not?" I narrow my eyes at the way his velvet-soft tone makes the word sound much more intimate than it is. "Why not prove to everyone here how close our two realms are? Consider it a stipulation of our alliance."

Baylor's face twists into some semblance of a smile, but it appears painful and forced. In this moment, I'm sure he regrets ever making a deal with Death.

"My pet would be honored to dance with you," he says between clenched teeth. "But don't forget, while her soul may be yours eventually, *she* is mine."

A dangerous glint enters Thorne's eyes, but he doesn't respond. I bite the inside of my cheek as Baylor pulls his claws from my skin. Hopefully whatever pinched expression may have momentarily crossed my face will be written off as unease over being so close to

Death. A scream of frustration rises in my throat, but I swallow it down as I force myself to take Thorne's gloved hand.

He gazes over the crowd, finally acknowledging their existence. "Rise."

All at once, the swirling fire above us disappears and the shadows recede. The room returns to its former glory, though it takes a few moments for the revelry to recommence. The low tones of a cello swell through the room as the band returns to their instruments. My lips curve down as I recognize the haunting melody.

The Ballad of Death.

I cut a glare at Thorne as he leads me onto the dancefloor. "Interesting song choice."

His lips twitch. "A coincidence, I'm sure."

Every eye in the room is trained on us as we stop in the center of the dancers. I ignore them, focusing all my attention on the God whose arm slips around my waist. His gloved thumb brushes over my bare skin, sending a shiver skating through me. His nearness is dizzying as he sweeps us into a sensual dance.

"You almost look as if you're unhappy to see me," he whispers, only loud enough for me to hear.

"Because I am." I force my lips into a pleasant smile, keeping up appearances for our audience. I catch sight of my brother standing near one of the alcoves, glaring at my dance partner. Bel raises a brow as his attention shifts to me, but I subtly shake my head, hoping that's enough to dissuade him from doing anything foolish. "Do you have such limited entertainment in the Fifth Isle that you must come here and play pretend, *Killian?*"

Lines appear around his mouth, the only sign of his discomfort. "Don't call me that."

"It's your name," I remind him. "Or are you saying you'd prefer me to call you 'Your Majesty?'"

He rolls his eyes. "That won't be necessary. Although, I'm honored to know you find me majestic."

I give him a bland look. We're both silent for a few moments as he spins me with one arm before drawing me close again. While Baylor's hand on my waist was a chain, Thorne's is a brand. Hot and scalding. Leaving an indelible mark I'll never be able to wash away.

"I needed information," he admits.

I nod, keeping my eyes down. For some reason, his confession stings. I knew he was working an angle, but hearing it confirmed hurts more than it should.

"What possessed you to come here yourself?" I ask, praying my voice sounds even. "You could have just sent an emissary."

"I prefer a hands-on approach." His tone implies something else as he pulls me even closer.

The soft leather of his glove brushes against my back again, sparking a connection in my mind. I recall that night in the caves when I tried to wipe a piece of algae from his hair, and he reared back as if he'd been disgusted by me.

Don't. Touch. Me... Ever.

He apologized later, claiming he simply doesn't like to be touched, but it's deeper than that. Now I know it wasn't just Thorne I would have been touching, it was Death.

Beware the touch of Death...

An old memory stirs, words uttered by my former history tutor years ago. He claimed that to be close to the God of Death is to die yourself.

My body goes rigid as I play back every interaction, allowing them to take on new meaning. His gloves. The ones he's always wearing. How he never lets me close enough to actually touch his skin. His reaction that day when I reached for him. Everything shifts as the truth sets in. A deranged laugh bubbles up in my throat as I consider his last words.

"Really? A hands-on approach?" I ask slowly, glancing meaningfully at the half inch that separates our bodies. "I was under the impression you have to keep your hands off."

A muscle in his jaw jumps as his eyes darken with shadows.

"Or perhaps the rumors have it wrong? Is Death's touch not as lethal as they say?" I lift my hand from his shoulder and reach for his face.

His own hand snaps out, gripping mine tightly before spinning me around and pulling my back against his chest. Other dancers glance over at us, but I can't bring myself to care as he pulls me close, his hand splayed across my stomach. My breath hitches as something tightens in my core.

"Don't," he whispers against my hair.

"That's why you never take off your gloves?"

He doesn't respond.

"Why you panicked when I—"

"You don't need to worry about it," he cuts me off. "I'll never touch you."

My shoulders curve inward as his words hit me like a gut punch. It's foolish to be hurt. He should mean nothing to me. Knowing what I do, I'd have to be out of my mind to wish for his touch.

"Good," I tell him, pretending the brightness in my tone isn't ringing false.

Several moments pass in silence. I twist my neck to find him glaring at something across from us. I try to search for whatever has angered him, but he spins me to face him once more.

I narrow my eyes. "What was that?"

"Nothing," he mutters, glancing away.

Anger swells inside me. "I wouldn't believe the word of a liar anyway."

His sculpted lips curve upward as his voice fills with smoke. "Takes one to know one, Angel."

Heat sparks in my belly at the endearment. I hate the fact that him calling me that still affects me. It shouldn't, but I can't deny that it does.

"I saw a familiar face," he admits, surprising me. "One I'm not fond of."

I open my mouth to ask who, but he spins us again. Before I can speak, I spot the Heir of Life standing next to the dance floor, scowling at us as he snatches a goblet of wine from a passing tray.

I arch a brow. "You don't get along with Foley?"

"That's one way of putting it," he says.

The man in question guzzles down his wine, sparing one more sneer in our direction before delving back into the crowd, probably in search of another drink. "Well, it appears the feeling is mutual." My nose scrunches as I lift my shoulders sheepishly. "Although, it's possible his withering glare was directed at me."

Amusement flickers in Thorne's eyes. "And why would that be?"

I shrug. "I may have implied he was a sniveling brat."

He barks out a loud laugh, catching the attention of several people around us. He ignores them all, keeping his warm gaze on me. "How?"

My cheeks heat. Probably from the wine I had earlier. "By calling him a sniveling brat straight to his face."

A true smile stretches wide across his face, leaving me strangely breathless. "I would have paid good money to see that."

We continue dancing, our eyes never straying from each other's faces. I don't even realize the dance has ended until I hear the crowd clapping. Startled, I step back and put a few feet between us. Thornes grip on me falls away as something flashes in his eyes, there one second and gone the next. The desire to understand it is strong, but we've already drawn too much attention tonight. Lingering any longer would be unwise.

"Excuse me," I say, turning to flee.

I only make it a few steps before someone blocks my path.

"I would have been a better partner," Foley slurs. It's clear he's been enjoying the libations a bit too much. "At least I can touch you without killing you."

His hand moves toward my face, but before it can connect with my skin, Thorne is standing between us.

"I don't believe the lady invited your touch." His voice is low and gravelly.

Foley's expression sours. "I'm sure I could persuade her."

"You can't," Thorne growls.

Watching the two of them, I get the sense I'm only catching a small glimpse of their history. There's animosity here that stems from more than just me.

"And let you have all the fun?" Foley says. "I've never known you to take an interest in anyone before, Killian. I must say, I'm curious how you became so close with Baylor's pet." His eyes drift back to me, lazily trailing over my exposed skin. "I never considered an alliance with him before, but if this is the kind of *benefit* that comes along with it, I might change my mind."

Thorne closes the distance between him and Foley, staring down at him with barely restrained rage. For a moment, I'm truly concerned for the young Heir.

"You don't have the authority to make an alliance," Cassandra's voice cuts in as she joins our group.

I glance around, noticing that we're drawing a small crowd of spectators. Bridgid's pretty features are pinched furiously as she watches us. She's likely pissed that our little scene has stolen attention away from her big night. My gaze flicks to the dais where Baylor stands. He appears calm as he smiles at something Selim has said, but when his eyes briefly shifts to me, I can sense the anger simmering there.

"You are neither God nor king," Cassandra continues, her purple gown trailing behind her as she moves to stand directly between the two men. "An Heir should remember their place."

"I will be a God someday," Foley grumbles petulantly.

"Are you sure about that, Son of Eyrkan?" Her golden eyes simmer and swirl, as if she's seeing beyond this room. When she speaks again, her voice is eerily soft. "The future is rarely set in stone."

"At least my father's realm is peaceful," the Heir snaps. "From what I hear, the Fifth Isle is a sea of unrest." He steps around the

Goddess to address Thorne. "Losing support in your own kingdom, Killian? That why you're cozying up to Baylor's little pet?"

Thorne's fists clench at his sides as he takes a step toward the Heir, who visibly blanches at their new proximity. His gaze drops to Thornes gloved hands, as if he's suddenly remembering what those hands can do.

"Call her '*pet*' one more time, and it will be the last word you ever speak," Thorne warns, his voice barely above a whisper.

A muscle twitches along Foley's jaw. With one more seething glare in my direction, he storms away, stomping like a child. An unlucky waiter has the misfortune of crossing his path and ends up pushed aside. His tray crashes against the marble floor in a heap of broken glass and spilled wine. I can't help but think it resembles blood. Unease skates over my skin. Someone as irresponsible as Foley shouldn't be inheriting any throne. He already abuses what little authority he has. I can't imagine what kind of atrocities he'd commit with actual power.

"Thank you for your assistance," Thorne says to the Goddess of Divination.

"You're welcome." She turns her golden gaze on him, her voice low. "But I have warned you before, Killian, while some futures are not set in stone, others are inevitable. You seek to alter a fate which cannot be changed."

He bows his head, his face hard with determination. "I thank you for your council."

"But you will not heed it." Her resigned tone suggests this is a topic they've discussed before.

I think she's going to leave, but instead she turns that unsettling stare on me. Similar to what happened earlier, I'm filled with the uncomfortable sense that she's seeing all the dark secrets I hide within me.

"*You are so much more than this,*" she says softly.

I take a step back, blood draining from my face. Those words that Leona said to me all those years ago. The ones I say to myself on the nights Baylor summons me. The ones I keep repeating, even though I know they aren't true.

"When you're ready," she continues, "you already know where to search for the answers you seek. I only hope that you'll be willing to embrace them. The truth cannot be fought, child. Only accepted."

She takes a step back, her silk dress swaying from the movement. Her painted lips curve into a smile, but there's something melancholy about it. "Enjoy your evening. I'm sure it will be a memorable one."

I quickly lose sight of her as she disappears into the crowd. The desire to flee from the ballroom is strong, but unfortunately, my legs are frozen to the spot.

"Iverson," Thorne begins. "I—"

His words are drowned out by the sound of a trumpet blaring through the room, demanding our attention.

Kaldar steps onto the now empty dais, soaking in the applause of the crowd. From the corner of my eye, I spot Bridgid and her father shoving people out of their way as they move closer to the platform. So, the moment has finally arrived? A spark of nervous energy ignites inside me as I wait for the announcement that will change my life.

"Ladies and gentlemen," Kaldar speaks over the crowd. "Honored guests, it is my great privilege to introduce our illustrious ruler. I give you King Baylor, the Beast of the Battle!"

The man of the hour steps onto the stage amid a sea of applause. After a few minutes, the room quiets down enough for him to speak.

"I want to thank you all for joining me this evening to celebrate my twenty-fifth anniversary as king of the Seventh Isle," he says, scanning the faces before him. "I am honored that you have trusted me with this position for so many years. I hope I have made you proud."

Everyone claps. I want to roll my eyes at his humble tone, noting how it sounds slightly too rehearsed. He doesn't care at all about making anyone proud. He'd kill anyone in this room if it meant he could hang on to power a little longer. Glancing to my right, I realize I've lost Thorne as the crowd has pushed in.

"Tonight, I can't help but think about someone who is not with us." Baylor's tone turns somber as his gaze falls. "My late wife, Leona."

My spine goes rigid at the sound of her name. I don't think he's spoken it since she died.

"This kingdom misses her greatly," Baylor continues. "Over the past year, I've realized how much my queen did for us. How special she was to our kingdom."

Many people in the crowd nod with sympathy, despite the fact that not a single one of them mourned her. Naomi dabs a nonexistent tear from her cheek as Darcus comforts her.

"This is why I believe the time is right for me to take a new wife," Baylor's voice grows louder with excitement. "You shall have a new queen!"

Everyone cheers. The ladies of court size each other up with daggers in their eyes, all prepared to fight to the death for the position. Bridgid ignores them all as she smooths out her dress and fusses with her curls. A bright smile lights up her face in anticipation of her name being called. I guess she was right, after all.

"I'd like to announce my engagement to a beautiful and talented young woman in our midst tonight," he says. "A woman I believe you will all grow to love as much as I do."

Everyone leans forward, desperate for his next words.

"Please congratulate my fiancée, Lady Iverson Pomeroy."

Shock radiates through me, and I'm sure I must have heard him wrong.

A few people clap, but the room is mostly silent. Kaldar stands at the edge of the dais, his mouth hanging open. Bridgid's head snaps in my direction as her cheeks turn red with a mixture of anger and embarrassment. A few people send nasty glances my way, but most are too shocked to do anything other than gape.

I shake my head. Surely Baylor made a mistake and said the wrong name. This can't be right.

My father appears by my side, gripping my arm painfully.

"Pull yourself together," he whispers as the king steps down from the stage.

The crowd parts, creating an open path leading directly to me. Baylor sweeps me into his arms and presses his lips against mine, but I'm too shocked to respond.

"I told you I would make a future for us," he whispers in my ear.

No.

It wasn't supposed to be me. I was supposed to be free. As his wife I will be even more trapped. There will be no escape. No freedom. My throat constricts as I struggle to pull air into my lungs. The weight of the collar around my neck increases, pushing my shoulders down. It's too heavy, too tight.

"Cheer for your future queen!" he shouts.

The crowd erupts with applause. People come from all sides to congratulate us. Some distant part of my brain tells me I should thank them, but I can't form words. I can't even breathe. Baylor's hand around my waist is an anchor pulling me underwater.

Air. I need air. *It's too much.* The room shrinks as the walls move closer. Sweat drips down my forehead as the crowd pushes in on us further. Too many people. Not enough air. I'm suffocating, but they keep smiling at me and speaking as if I'm not dying right in front of them.

It's too much. *It's all too much.*

I scan the room, desperate for an escape. I lock eyes with my brother. His face is pale as he shakes his head, mouthing a single word. *'No.'*

"This offense cannot be accepted!" one voice rings out above the rest, pulling everyone's attention.

His words mean nothing to me as I take a ragged breath. Finally, the endless swell of well-wishers fall back as they search for the source of the complaint. My head falls against my shoulder as the room spins. Baylor's hand around my waist is the only thing keeping me upright as my legs threaten to give out. My chest heaves as I pull air into my lungs in labored gasps.

The owner of the voice steps forward, his face red and twisted with rage.

Lord Burgess.

The crowd parts into a circle around us. Their eyes are fevered as they shift back and forth between their king and his challenger, nothing but ravenous vultures, delighting in their entertainment.

"It was supposed to be my daughter!" he insists. Based on the way he stumbles and slurs his words, I'd guess he started celebrating early. "But instead, he chooses her? After everything my family has given him! The support! The money!"

Kaldar steps forward, his eye wide as he lifts his hands in a placating gesture. "Brother, now is not the time."

"Now is the time!" the lord insists.

"Listen to your brother, Simon," Baylor commands, his eyes shifting blood red as his control over the *vertere* part of himself wanes.

"How about you listen to me?" Burgess shouts as he pushes strands of blond hair out of his face. "I helped you take that throne when Maebyn disappeared. I loaned you my armies to defeat Triston. And *this* is how you thank me?"

Baylor's lip curls, but he makes no move to approach the drunk lord. "Guards."

On cue, Remy appears behind Lord Burgess and seizes the man in a tight hold. The lord struggles, continuing his tirade.

"No! You're insane if you think anyone would bow to her!" he seethes as his gaze lands on me. "No one in their right mind would put a crown on a bastard-born whore."

Gasps erupt around us. I push myself away from Baylor as he shakes with fury, and his claws extend once again. He's about to shift into his other form, when suddenly, Thorne steps out of the crowd.

"Release him," he orders Remy as he removes one of his gloves.

His voice is calm, but there's something underneath it that sends warning bells ringing through my mind.

The captain's gaze moves to Baylor, waiting for instructions. The king nods and Remy steps back, allowing Burgess to fall to the floor before the God of Death.

Thorne tsks as he shakes his head, staring down at the drunk lord. "Pity you never learned to hold your tongue."

He reaches out, splaying his bare hand across the man's face.

The screams are instant. Burgess jerks back as he tries to escape the pain, but Thorne is faster. Grabbing a fistful of his long hair, he twists it mercilessly to hold the man in place. The crowd is utterly silent as the lord waves his arms, searching for help.

"Stop him!" Bridgid rushes forward. "He's killing my father!"

No one moves, not even Naomi or Darcus.

"Please!" She turns her pleading eyes on Baylor. "Stop this!"

He doesn't spare her a glance, instead signaling one of the guards to pull her away. Less than a minute passes before Thorne releases the lord, allowing his limp body to fall forward.

Silence hangs in the air for several seconds before he turns and faces the crowd.

"Thank you for a wonderful evening, King Baylor."

With those parting words, he makes his way to the stairs without even sparing me a glance. His companions follow after him. Griffen is the only one who looks back at me, a hint of sadness in his eyes as he trails after his God, and they disappear the way they came.

It takes several seconds before time restarts. Baylor is pulled away to handle the aftermath. With no one to stop me, I head toward the stairs, desperate to flee, but a hand snags my arm and pulls me to a stop. Glancing up, I find my father's furious face staring down at me.

"Do not screw this up, daughter," he orders. "You have a duty to your family."

I bare my teeth. "What do you know of family?"

His grip tightens as his face contorts in rage. For a moment, I think he's going to hit me. Gods, I wish he'd try.

"Let her go." My brother appears by my side, glaring at the man who sired him. "I've warned you what would happen if you laid hands on her again. Do not test me, old man."

Lord Pomeroy blanches, releasing my arm. I know I should thank Bellamy, but my brain isn't working properly right now. My only thought is escaping this nightmare. Without wasting another second, I summon an illusion and disappear from sight. Not a single person notices as I sprint from the ballroom.

CHAPTER
TWENTY-FOUR

I sense him the moment I step into my room.

Thorne doesn't acknowledge me as I enter. Instead, he lies on my bed, his hands tucked under his head as he leans against the headboard. His position is casual, but the tension in his body betrays his anger.

"So, you're going to be a queen?" he asks, his voice low.

My jaw tightens. "Apparently."

"I wonder if your king will still refer to you as his *pet* after you become his wife?"

I shrug off his words, pretending they don't sting.

"I would think you'd be too busy running your own kingdom to have time for such frivolous thoughts," I say as I move toward the vanity. "Perhaps that's why the Heir of Life was hinting at trouble in your court? I thought Death was the great equalizer, but I suppose dissenting voices must be heard everywhere?"

"What a quick tongue you have, *pet*."

"Don't call me that," I snap, turning to face him.

"I thought you liked it." He shoots off the bed, standing before me in an instant. "You don't tell Baylor not to call you that."

He's close enough that I have to lift my chin to meet his gaze.

"He is my king and my betrothed." My stomach turns at the thought. "You are not."

A muscle ticks along his jaw. "I wouldn't want to be either."

I bark out a laugh. "Doesn't sound like it."

His eyes blaze brighter than the inferno he created above our heads earlier. "You are nothing to me."

I step forward into his space, crowding him despite the danger. He tries to move back, but I follow him. Our chests are brushing, yet our skin doesn't connect anywhere. His breathing is heavy as his gaze falls to my lips and shivers of anticipation dance through me.

Lifting a single finger, I drag it up the long sleeve of his shirt from wrist to shoulder, and his entire body shudders under my touch.

"Tell me again how indifferent you are," I say softly, keeping my gaze locked with his.

The last of his restraint snaps.

Thorne grabs my arms with his gloved hands and pushes me back into the wall. His body traps mine, making it abundantly clear just how much he wants me. Less than an inch separates our faces, his warm breath coasting over my cheek as he speaks.

"Is it true what they say about kings making poor lovers?"

"You tell me," I reply. "Had any complaints recently?"

"Oh, my sweet, poisonous Ivy," he whispers. My breath catches as the tip of his leather-clad finger trails over my collarbone, stopping just above my heavy breasts. "A king merely rules, but a God dominates."

Something tickles my arms, and I glance down to find his shadows wrapping around my wrists, lifting them up and pinning them to the wall above my head. I bite my lip as his entire hand rests right over my heart. Does he feel it racing? We hold each other's stares, unable to look away.

"I can feel the heat of your skin through the leather," he whispers, his voice rough. "Do you always burn hotter than the fires of Life and Death?"

His other hand trembles as it caresses my face and gently traces my lips.

"Tell me, Angel, if I keep touching you, will you ignite in my arms?"

I pull against my restraints, desperate to touch him too. "I'd burn you alive."

"Perhaps?" His hand on my chest moves lower, cupping my breast and making me moan aloud. His eyes darken at the sound. Shadows swirl in his irises, eating up any trace of blue and silver. "But I am a creature of fire, remember? I can take a little heat."

"Can you?" A smile pulls at my lips as I hook my leg behind his back and roll my hips against him.

He groans through clenched teeth. "Fuck, Ivy."

His hands fall to my waist, and my other leg wraps around him too. Thorne pushes me harder into the wall as we move against each other. I gasp as his hands slip under the slits of my gown to cup my ass, his fingers kneading the flesh there. My eyes are locked on his as something tightens deliciously in my core. He's not even truly touching me, and already I'm about to explode.

"Ivy," he whispers my name over and over.

I gasp. "Don't stop."

"Wasn't planning on it."

"Tell me again that I'm nothing to you," I demand, my voice breathless. I'm so close now.

"You're—" A loud knock cuts him off.

Thorne's head swings to the door, his teeth bared in a snarl as his hips still trap mine. A low warning growl rises in his throat.

"Quiet," I order, slapping his shoulder. He turns his dark gaze on me, eyes narrowed into slits as he shakes his head.

The knock comes again.

"Lady Iverson?" Huxley's voice calls from the hallway.

I'm truly fond of the shy guard, but in this moment, I could kill him.

"My lady? Are you awake?"

I scream internally, knowing from experience that he won't go away if I ignore him. "Yes?"

"My lady, are you alright?" Huxley asks. "You sound out of breath?"

Smugness pulls at the corners of Thorne's mouth.

"Fuck you," I whisper to him, making his eyes widen innocently.

"What was that, my lady?" the guard calls.

"Nothing! I'm just..." I search for a suitable excuse, my mind still hazy from Thorne's close proximity. "Drunk?"

The smirk turns into a full-blown smile as the God tries to stop himself from laughing.

"That's nice," Huxley says lamely.

I roll my eyes, ready to murder the young guard.

"Was there a reason for your interruption?" I ask, my voice taking a shrill tone.

"Oh, right," he says, as if he truly forgot why he knocked in the first place. "The king has requested you join him in his chamber tonight."

Thorne goes rigid against me.

Bile rises in my throat at the thought of going to Baylor right now. All of the heat that had been building in me disappears at once, leaving nothing but ice behind. Pale eyes bore into mine, daring me to speak. His hands grip me tighter, but nowhere near painful. I've never felt more trapped by my circumstances than I do in this moment.

"I'll be right out." My voice sounds hollow even to my own ears.

Thorne goes cold as the mask slips over his face. He pulls my legs away from his hips, lowering them to the ground before stepping back. My arms fall limp at my sides as the shadows disappear from my wrists. Without saying another word to me, he turns and walks to the balcony, opening the doors and stepping out into the brisk night. A second later, the sound of wings flapping against the wind carries him away.

My hands shake as I adjust the fallen straps on my gown and

smooth out the wrinkled silk. I try to focus on my breathing exercises, but it doesn't help. I glance toward the door where Huxley waits on the other side to escort me to Baylor. Right now I should be brushing out my hair or touching up my face.

I should be conjuring my *eidolon*.

Rose.

Something cracks in my chest. A tiny fracture that splinters, piercing my heart. I should be calling forth Rose. But I'm not. I can't.

Abomination.

Whore's daughter.

Killer.

I know the names I've been called, most of them accurate. I don't deny what I am. But right here, in this moment, I can't be the person who sends Rose to him. I don't want to look too closely at why giving her a name, *that name*, has changed things so much. I don't want to acknowledge the connection it created in my mind because she's not real.

But are you?

That hateful voice in the back of my mind rears its ugly head.

You are nothing but a deceiver. You lie, even to yourself. You're just as fake as her.

But what I experienced tonight was real. The way Thorne touched me was the realest thing I've ever felt, despite the fact that he's just as much of a liar as I am. Is that why we're drawn to each other?

"Lady Iverson?" Huxley's voice calls again.

I have no idea how long I've stood here trying to pull myself together. The only thing I know is, come what may, no part of me is stepping foot outside of this room tonight.

"I'm unwell," I shout through the door. "The wine has made me sick."

"Should I fetch a healer?" His voice fills with concern.

"No," I say quickly. "I just need to sleep it off. Please send the king my apologies."

"Alright, my lady."

His footsteps fade as he disappears down the hallway. I try not to imagine the reaction he will receive when he relays my message. I've never once denied Baylor before. And doing so tonight, after his announcement and Thorne's behavior, is extremely risky. But smoothing over his bruised ego is a problem for tomorrow.

I don't glance at my reflection in the mirror as I quickly rinse my face. I'm not ready to acknowledge the changes I might see there. As I crawl into bed, the events of tonight hit me all at once. Bellamy. My father. Baylor. The Gods. Thorne.

As I close my eyes, only the latter remains. And when I drift away, it's his touch I feel against my lips.

CHAPTER
TWENTY-FIVE

Guards chase me through the halls.

My bare feet pound against the cold marble floors, leaving a trail of muddy footprints in my wake. The once white gown is now stained and ripped, the length of it getting caught in my legs as I run. Usually, I beat Bel in every race, but these guards are gaining on me. They are close enough that a hand brushes my shoulder when one of them reaches for me.

A familiar voice echoes from the dining hall. I use the last of my strength to charge toward it, praying to the Fates I make it before these guards catch me. My tiny hands push against the grand oak doors, spreading them wide and revealing a small group of people seated at the large table. Every eye in the room immediately turns toward me.

My father sits in his usual spot at the head of the table. The shock on his face is quickly replaced by rage. An unfamiliar man sits across from him at the other end of the table, watching me curiously. In one of the middle chairs, a pretty lady clutches her chest as her worried eyes scan my dirty frame. Relief nearly knocks me over as I spot the person sitting next to her.

Bellamy.

My brother is frozen, staring at me with a mixture of joy and horror. I peer down, taking in my mud-soaked dress. No doubt my face looks the same as his. I open my mouth to say something right as a firm hand grips me from behind and lifts me into the air.

"Release her!" Bel shouts, rising from his seat. "Release my sister!"

With his free hand, the guard reaches for his weapon.

"Doral," the other man at the table says, the one I don't recognize.

His dark blue eyes watch me intensely as the guard, Doral, sets me down. I don't have a moment to ask what's going on before I'm swept into Bellamy's arms.

"Ivy!" he cries, clutching me to his chest.

I lean into the warmth of his body, suddenly realizing how cold I am. Shivers rack my small frame as he runs his hands over my arms.

"How?" he asks, his tone full of wonder. "How are you—"

The sound of a scuffle cuts him off. A moment later Clara sprints into the room, her blonde ringlets in disarray. She ignores my father and his guests completely, the first lapse in decorum I've ever seen from my young governess. Tears stream down her pretty face as her gaze lands on me. I throw myself at her, and she wraps me in her warm embrace.

"My girl," she whispers as her hands run over my limbs, searching for injuries. "My sweet girl."

In this moment, all I want is for her to carry me upstairs and tuck me safely into my bed. I won't even complain when she recites her morbid bedtime tale. She always repeats the same story, insisting the stars that shine the brightest actually died a long time ago. She says their light is nothing but the last remnants of their souls desperately clinging to life, racing through the galaxy as they try to outrun Death. And once that light goes out, their memory is erased from the night sky and they are forgotten. As if they never existed at all. But not if we remember them in our dreams and carry their light in our hearts during the waking hours. Then it's as if they never left us. And that's true immortality, she always whispers as she ends the odd story.

Bel kneels next to us as he and Clara exchange a meaningful glance, something they do often. They always think I don't notice.

A chair scrapes against the hardwood as someone rises from the table. The man. The one Doral obeyed.

"What do we have here?" he asks, moving closer as he continues to study me. His pale blond hair touches his shoulders, framing his handsome features.

"Your Majesty," my father interrupts, speaking for the first time since I crashed into the room. "This is merely some little village chit. An impostor."

I push myself deeper into Clara's embrace as his words at the lake echo through my mind. "You're an abomination," *he'd said.* "I should have done this the night your whore mother brought you into the world. Die, you wretched beast!"

My lip quivers. I can't remember what happened after I sunk to the bottom of the lake. I thought I saw my brother swimming toward me as I closed my eyes, but when I woke up, I was alone. I was trapped somewhere new. Dirt was everywhere, filling my mouth and choking me.

An awful sound bursts out of me as tears slip down my cheeks, prompting Bellamy to lean closer. He wraps his arms around me and Clara, as if he can shield us from whatever comes.

"Silence," the man commands my father before kneeling in front of me, bringing us eye level. He ignores Clara and Bel, keeping his focus solely on me.

"Do you know who I am?" he asks.

I shake my head.

"My name is Baylor." He smiles as my eyes turn round. "I see you've heard of me? Your father kindly allowed my wife and me to stay here while traveling home from the north."

My gaze quickly flashes to the pretty dark-haired woman at the table. Her eyes are sad as she watches us, and I want to ask her why, but the king keeps speaking.

"We were sorry to hear of your accident at the lake, Lady Iverson."

"It wasn't an accident." *My hands cover my mouth as the words slip free. My eyes flash to my father, finding him glaring at me with a red face.*

"What is she talking about?" Bellamy demands, moving away from us to confront our father.

"She's letting her imagination run away with her, as usual," Lord Pomeroy spares his son a withering glare.

"Enough." The king's stern voice brings silence to the room.

He turns his cold stare on Clara until she finally releases me, taking a few steps back. Without her arms around me, the room becomes much colder.

"What happened to you, Iverson?" he asks.

I tremble under his gaze. "I went to sleep in the pond, but when I woke up, I was in a wooden box underground," I whisper, too scared to tell him how my father held me under the water. I keep my eyes down, focusing on the dirt caked under my fingernails. "I had to dig my way out."

"Blessed Fates," the queen murmurs as her face pales.

The king says something to my father, but I'm too distracted by the queen to hear him. When he turns back to me, there's a strange expression on his face. Everyone else in the room is either shocked or horrified, but not him. He almost appears... gleeful. As if I'm the answer to a problem I didn't even know existed. Something about the gleam in his eyes has me taking a step back.

"Clara." I reach for her, and she returns to my side in an instant, hugging me close again as Bel steps up beside us.

"My sister needs rest," he announces. "If you'll excuse us."

We head for the door, but as if they are acting on a silent signal, the guards move as one to block our path.

"Get out of our way," Bellamy demands, his voice colder than I've ever heard it.

Something pulls my attention back to the king, where I find him addressing my father.

"The girl is coming with me, Nigel," he says, making my heart drop into my stomach. "And I think it would be best if there were no witnesses. Obviously, you and your boy are spared from that. So long as you comply."

I look to my father, not understanding what the king means. Witnesses for what? Bellamy moves to stand in front of me, blocking my view of the others.

"Baylor, please—" The queen's voice reaches my ears.

"This doesn't concern you, woman," her husband answers. "Guards."

Soldiers move toward us, ripping Bel and Clara away from me. My back presses into the wall, where I try to make myself as small as possible.

"Let go of her!" Bel screams as Clara pushes back against the guards.

"Shut up, boy!" my father shouts. "You will only make this harder on yourself."

As the struggle continues, my gaze connects with the queen's again. She's frozen in her chair, eyes wide as she watches the horror unfold. A soldier stands next to her, his hand on her shoulder, as if to keep her in her seat. A tear leaks from one of her eyes, dripping down her pale cheek.

"No!" Clara's shout pulls my attention from the queen as one of the soldiers bashes the hilt of his sword over Bel's head. My brother's eyes roll back in his head, and he falls to the floor, unmoving.

Clara's fearful gaze finds mine as the guards drag her from the room. "Run! Ivy, run!"

I start toward the door, but the king is in front of me again.

"Shh." He reaches out, brushing away the tears that stream down my face. "Don't be frightened, child."

I nod, wanting to make him happy, but I am terrified. A hiccup rises in my throat, and I accidentally disappear. My face squinches from the pain of the illusion settling over my skin like thousands of tiny needles pricking me all at once. I only developed my abilities a few months ago, and Bel always teases me for having no control over them.

"A wraith," the king whispers, his eyes wide as a genuine smile lights up his face. "Even more unique than I realized."

I try to hold on to the illusion, but it slips away, leaving me vulnerable. I turn toward my father, my desperate eyes begging him to intervene, but he does nothing. A scream tears from my throat as the king reaches out, lifting me into his arms with ease.

"It's alright, child." He rubs his hand against my back, trying to soothe me. "I mean you no harm."

I squeeze my eyes shut, leaning into the crook of his neck as tears stream down my cheeks. Chairs scratch against the floor as people rise from the table, but I don't look up as we exit the room and make our way through the halls.

"You are going to come live with me for a while," the king murmurs into my ear, his soft voice hypnotizing. "Doesn't that sound nice? Living in a palace like a princess?"

"I don't want to go," I protest, my voice trembling. "I want to stay with Bel and Clara."

He ignores my request as he continues to whisper calming words. Despite my fear, I find my eyes drifting shut. I don't want to leave, but I'm so tired. It's as if I'm back in the lake, giving up once again. It's hard to keep fighting when everyone is stronger than me.

We're passing through the front doors when the screaming starts.

I lift my head, searching for the source of the frantic cries, but the king keeps walking and the guards around us don't react. I find the queen's gaze again, seeing anger warring with her heartbreak.

Whatever's happening in there sounds horrific, yet no one is doing anything. I don't understand any of this as we continue out front to find a carriage waiting. The king loads us inside, positioning me in his lap while the queen sits across from us. As soon as the doors are shut, the carriage takes off. I wobble as the movement jostles me. Twisting my neck, I peek out the window and get my final glimpse of the only home I've ever known.

The screams follow us all the way down the drive, so loud I'm sure I will never stop hearing them.

~

My eyes shoot open as the dream fades.

I find myself in my bed at the palace, lying on my side facing the window. Morning light sneaks past the gaps in the curtains, not quite reaching me. It's been a while since I dreamed about that night. Over the years, the truth of it became buried in my mind as I convinced myself it was more nightmare than memory. Nothing but the dramatic imaginings of a lonely child.

At the time, I didn't understand most of what happened. I was weak and tired, barely staying upright on my own. And after all, Baylor was kind to me. He spoke softly, treating me like something precious. Somewhere in my subconscious, I think I knew I couldn't afford to hate him. So, I hid the truth, lying to myself the way I do with everyone else.

It wasn't until recently that I realized that Clara and the other servants had fled for their lives like the desperate stars she talked about. But death gave chase in the form of soldiers, creeping ever closer until their lights were snuffed out. Forgotten.

Their lives were erased just as easily as the events of that night.

But the rumors lived on. I'm not sure where they started, but someone began telling tales of the little *wraith* who clawed out of her own grave. When asked, most brush it off, claiming they don't believe the story. But their lies are as evident as the fear on their faces when I glance in their direction.

I close my eyes, wanting to relive the dream again and punish myself a bit more with painful memories. Just as the stars were cursed to die, I'm cursed to be the only one who remembers the way they once shined.

I've just begun to slip away when the bed dips behind me. My hand skates over the silk sheets, slipping under the pillow where my dagger hides.

"Careful, pet," a familiar voice admonishes me.

My eyes snap open as his hand presses against my stomach, pulling me into his hard chest. His face nuzzles my neck as he nips at my ear with his sharp teeth.

"Good morning, *fiancée*."

CHAPTER
TWENTY-SIX

F*iancée.* He relishes the word, drawing it out in a way that is meant to be seductive. My stomach churns. I never thought I'd hate an endearment more than *pet*, but this is somehow worse.

"I missed you last night," he continues, his fingers playing with a strand of my hair.

"I was unwell," I mumble, trying to slow my racing heart. My mind spins as I try to process the situation. I can feel him everywhere. His arm around my stomach is a chain trapping me against him. I try to focus on my breathing again—in through my nose and out through my mouth—as he trails kisses down my neck. "How did you get in my room?"

His body goes still. "Are you not happy to have me here?"

"No!" I say quickly, inwardly cursing my own stupidity. But I can't think with him this close. It's too much. Especially after last night. Being close to Thorne was overwhelming is the most incredible way, but this is completely the opposite. The wrongness of it makes me feel sick.

"I'm just confused," I offer. "My mind is struggling to catch up."

His hand goes to my shoulder, pressing me flat on my back as he hovers over me. His face is utterly blank, but there's a coldness in his eyes that is terrifying. I've fucked up. Denying him last night was the wrong decision. If I'd sent my *eidolon* to him like I always do, this wouldn't be happening.

But was it really the wrong choice? Why should you have to do any of this?

I push those thoughts away, knowing they won't help me right now.

"Did your sudden illness last night have anything to do with Killian?"

My eyes widen as I shake my head. "No, I—"

His hand moves to the center of my chest, less than an inch from the collar. "You two seemed very close last night, before he ruined my ball."

I swallow, begging my heart to maintain a steady rhythm. "I was following our plan, trying to get information out of him."

His eyes harden as he leans closer. "And how's that working out for you, pet? Because you missed a pretty big piece of *information*."

I lower my gaze. "You're right. I'm sorry I let you down."

He sighs as his hand moves to my chin, lifting it so that I'm forced to look at him. "Were you upset about my announcement? Is that why you didn't come to my chambers?"

"No. I want to be with you." The words taste awful on my tongue as I search for a way to explain my strange behavior. "I was just overwhelmed. Surprised."

"Surprised?" His head tilts back in shock.

"Elated," I clarify, hoping the word appeases him. "It was a happy surprise, but I didn't expect it." I drop my gaze again, hoping to emulate the insecurity he loves to see in me. "I know Kaldar was pushing for Bridgid to be your bride. I thought maybe... you were going to pick her."

He barks out a laugh. "You couldn't have thought I was actually entertaining that idea?"

His gaze trails over my face, moving down my neck and settling on my chest where the sheer fabric of my nightgown hides nothing.

"As if it could have been anyone else," he murmurs, his hand shifting to rest on my stomach again. "Only you could be my wife... The mother of my children."

My whole body recoils. "*Children?*"

"Not right now, pet." He offers me a conspiratorial smile as his earlier anger is replaced by something far more dangerous. "Though we could practice making them?"

He leans in to kiss me, but I turn my head, forcing his lips to land on my cheek instead.

"I should probably bathe first," I try to excuse myself as I lightly push against his shoulder. "I'm sure I smell."

"After," he whispers against my cheek. "We'll bathe together."

His hand moves to the buttons of my nightgown as he presses open-mouthed kisses into my neck. His scent is everywhere. Bile rises in my throat, mixing with the taste of blood as I bite my cheek to keep from screaming. He hasn't actually touched *me* this way since before Leona's death. Every instinct in my body screams at me to stop this. To push him away. But I can't. He'll use the collar. He'll choke me. Or worse...

He'll *make* me do it. He'll use the collar to command me to comply.

Hot fury boils underneath my skin, burning the blood in my veins. Some dark beast inside of me thrashes against its cage, desperate to be free. It yearns to feast, to destroy. Sweat seeps from my pores as all my buried rage bubbles over.

Baylor lifts his head, brow furrowed as he searches my face. "You're so warm—"

A knock on the door cuts him off.

He turns his head slowly toward the source of the interruption, his jaw clenching.

"What?" he barks.

"My King," Huxley's nervous voice filters through the door, a much more welcome sound than last night. "There is an emergency with one of the guests. You are needed at once, sire."

For a moment, I think he's going to ignore the guard, but then he releases me. He groans as he rolls off the bed, gazing down at me with unrestrained need.

"Sometimes being king is a terrible burden, pet," he complains. "We'll have to finish this later."

He leans in to give me a quick peck, but again, I turn my head. I know I shouldn't. As evidenced this morning, Baylor loathes being denied. It's completely opposite from the usual strategy I employ against him, but right now, I can't bring myself to play the game. If I'm being honest, I'm not acting off any plan right now. There's nothing calculated in my choice to snub him.

I simply cannot bear his touch.

He pulls back, searching my face for answers. I force my lips to curve into some semblance of a smile. It will have to be enough because I'm not capable of more right now. The gesture must mitigate the rejection slightly because with one last goodbye, he leaves.

The moment the door shuts behind him, I leap from the bed, unable to stay there now that his scent is all over the sheets. *All over me.*

He's gone, but I can still feel his touch lingering on my skin. His phantom fingers send another wave of nausea through me, and this time, I don't bother to choke it down as I empty my stomach onto the hardwood floor. When there's nothing left to expel, I grab a pillow from the bed and shove my face into it. A ragged scream tears out of me, leaving my throat raw and scratchy. My sharp nails pierce the plush fabric, causing a sea of white feathers to explode through the room as I rip it in half. They float around me, covering everything in a blanket of softness that only infuriates me further.

I wrap my fingers around my collar, pulling at it with all my strength. The metal digs into my skin, but the clasp refuses to break. I desperately scratch and claw at my neck, ignoring the pain as I pray to the Fates to help me.

"Please," I beg, my voice nothing but a mangled rasp. "Take it off. Take it off!"

Blood drips down my chest, staining the white lace of my nightgown. My legs give out and I sink to the floor beside my bed, rocking back and forth as I keep pulling at the collar.

"I'm begging you," I cry. "I'll do anything. Anything!"

I don't know how long I sit there, soaking in my own rage and terror as I send wretched prayers into the void. Eventually, another sound reaches my ears, clashing with my pathetic murmurings. A door creaks open, followed by the thud of heavy boots stepping into the room.

I lift my head, the weight of it almost too much for my ruined neck. My brow furrows as I find my bedroom door shut. Confusion prickles my dull senses until I hear the sound again. It's coming from behind me.

The balcony.

Somewhere in the back of my mind, I know I should probably care about this. I should be reaching for the dagger still lying somewhere on the bed. At the very least, I should stand up and prepare to fight. But I stay where I am. If the worst has already happened, what do I have left to fear? Whoever is coming for me now can't compare to the man who just left.

"I'm here to apologize."

Thorne.

No, I remind myself. *I'm supposed to call him Killian now.*

His voice registers, even though his words are meaningless. If my mind was in better shape, I'd probably have sensed him coming the way I always do. Whatever strange connection lies between us would have alerted me to his presence.

"I was out of line." The words sound painful, as if they're being pulled from the God of Death against his will. "What happened last night will never happen again."

I know what he's saying should mean something to me, but it doesn't. Even his voice sounds distant, as if he's calling out to me from the other side of the veil. Have I died? And if so, do I care? Warning bells sound in the back of my mind, trying to alert me to the dangerous direction of my thoughts.

"Are you hiding from me now?"

Boots appear in front of me. Slowly, I drag my gaze up his rigid body, moving over his legs and torso until I find his face. He sounded annoyed when he spoke, but now a different kind of fire blazes behind his eyes. One that I recognize.

Fury.

Muscles clench along his jaw as his eyes rake over my bloodstained nightgown, and the scratches along my throat and face. He's completely still as he watches me, his fists clenched tight at his sides.

"Who did this to you?" he grinds out the words.

The authority in his voice compels me to speak, but when I open my mouth, nothing comes out. He takes a step closer, lifting his gloved hand toward my aching neck.

I flinch.

His eyes flare and his hand quickly retreats, flexing at his side. I wish my brain was working better right now. I tilt my head, grimacing as the movement pulls at my wounds. But I need to get a better look at him. I need to understand why the most fearsome person I know appears helpless before me. Is it my fault? Did I cause this?

"I'm sorry," I whisper, not knowing what else to do.

Apparently, it was the wrong thing to say. His gaze moves to the bed behind me, and a second later, he's lunging forward. I lift my arms to shield myself, but all he does is rip the sheet from the bed and lift it to his nose. His eyes darken at whatever he scents, causing the tiny hairs on my arms to rise.

"I'll fucking kill him," he spits the words.

Baylor, I realize. He's going to kill Baylor. And he could do it. He could actually destroy that heartless bastard. Fear charges through my foggy thoughts, reminding me why that's a terrible idea.

"Don't!"

He stares down at me, his eyes wide with disbelief. "You beg for his life? Even now? After this?"

The implication in his words causes another sharp crack in my chest. "You don't understand," I offer lamely. "You don't know what he's done."

The God of Death drops to his knees before me.

"Then tell me!" he begs, reaching forward slowly, giving me a chance to pull away before he takes my fingers in his. "Tell me what he's done?"

I shake my head, unable to force myself to explain the truth of the collar.

"Please," I beg him softly, my voice catching on the words. "Please, just get me out of here."

Tears flood down my face unrestrained. His mouth falls open and his gaze flits around the room, as if he's searching for a way to fix this. He rises to his feet, pacing back and forth as he runs a hand through his dark hair, already messy from the wind. When he turns back to me, his face is hard with resolve.

"Okay," he agrees, taking deep breaths to steady himself. "I can do that. But I need you to be careful not to touch my skin."

I nod.

Thorne disappears behind me for a moment, and I can hear him riffling through my armoire. When he returns, he's holding my thick cloak and a pair of gloves I haven't worn in ages. He gently wraps me in the soft garment, buttoning it all the way up to my throat before finagling my hands into the gloves.

As if I weigh nothing at all, Thorne lifts me in his arms and cradles me against his chest. Doing as he asked, I make sure not to touch any part of his skin as I lean my head against his shoulder and close my eyes. Immediately, a strange sensation settles over me. One I've never truly felt before.

Safety.

"Will anyone see us?" I whisper, enjoying the cool air that kisses my cheeks as we step onto the balcony.

"No," he promises, his voice sounding strained. "I'm rather good at staying out of sight."

The smallest smile appears on my face as he leaps into the sky, carrying me away from all my troubles.

"Me too," I murmur.

CHAPTER
TWENTY-SEVEN

The waves rush toward me, swallowing my feet and part of my calves before retreating to the ocean. I sit on the shoreline, the sand hot beneath me as the sun shines above us, unimpeded by any clouds. I removed the cloak and gloves as soon as we got here, wanting to feel the bright rays on my skin.

Movement nearby catches my attention. An orange crab scuttles toward me, freezing when it notices me watching. After a few seconds, it scoots forward another inch. I arch a brow, waiting to see what it will do. Making a wise decision, the crustacean quickly turns around and scampers off, sending a flash of amusement flickering through me. Was it my frightening appearance that scared the creature away?

When Thorne landed here in this secluded cove, I immediately began washing off the blood that stained my neck and chest. The saltwater stung the unhealed cuts, but I refused to stop. Maybe I thought if I could wash away the evidence of the morning, it would be as if it never happened at all. I was able to clear the worst of it from my skin, but the nightgown is beyond repair.

"You might as well come enjoy the water," I call to Thorne, who's been pacing through the sand since we arrived. Even with all of his layers, there's no sweat on his brow. He doesn't appear to be fazed by the heat at all.

He comes to a halt at the sound of my voice. A second later, he's kneeling into the sand a few feet away, his eyes intense as he watches me.

"Are you alright?" I ask.

"Me?" His head cocks back incredulously. "Are *you* alright?"

I open my mouth, but no words come out. For the first time in ages, I can't bring myself to tell a lie. What's wrong with me lately? Why can't I pull myself together and do what has to be done?

"I'll have to go back soon," I mutter.

"Back?" He shakes his head, eyes blinking rapidly. "Why would you go back?"

My eyebrows pull together as I tilt my head to the side. "Because I have to."

"Fuck that," he growls.

I clench my jaw, getting really tired of his attitude. "You don't understand."

"On that, we can agree," he mumbles under his breath.

We sit in silence for several minutes, both of us stewing as we watch the waves.

"Are you actually a reaper?" I ask one of the many questions that has been bothering me since I learned his true identity last night.

He raises a brow. "That was random."

"It's a fair question, given your propensity for lying about who you are."

He rolls his eyes. "My mother was a reaper, which means I am too."

"Oh." I want to ask more questions about her, but I know it's a sensitive subject for him.

"Can all reapers make shadows?" I ask instead.

"All reapers can *wield* shadows," he says, staring out at the waves. "And we can all take a life with only our touch. But both of those abilities manifested differently in me. More vicious. Less controlled," he admits. "I don't know if that's because of how I was raised or because of who my father was."

I suppose being the child of a God would have an impact on your magic. Everything Thorne told me about his father fills me with hatred for the God I never met. All the stories I've heard about Desmond, the former God of Death, lead me to believe he was a beloved leader. Is that how the history books will remember Baylor too?

Pushing those thoughts away, I return to my other pressing questions. "Why did you choose to go by Thorne?"

"Because it's my name," he says flatly.

My eyebrows pinch together. "Your name is *Killian*."

"Killian Blackthorne," he corrects me. "My father chose to name me Killian, but Blackthorne was my mother's last name. Those I'm closest to have always called me Thorne."

An inkling of warmth blossoms in my stomach at the knowledge that not everything was a lie.

"How old are you?" I ask after clearing my throat. "A thousand?"

He barks out a deep laugh, shaking his head. "Not that old. Not nearly."

My eyes narrow. "You're evading the question."

"Do you truly want to know?" He glances at me from the corner of his eye and I spot hesitance in his gaze. "I fear the answer might disappoint you."

"Just tell me," I insist.

"I'm a little over two years into my third decade of life."

Shock has me nearly tipping over into the sand. "You're only seven years older than me."

He shrugs. "If you say so."

"But—But you're a God," I stammer.

His shoulders shake as he chuckles, rich and deep. "I'm afraid being centuries old isn't a prerequisite. There's only one requirement for the job."

It's what every Heir who ascends into Godhood has in common. Their parent, who held the title before them, must die.

"I'm sorry," I say, unsure how to approach the subject of his father.

He waves his hand. "Don't be."

"The things you've told me about your father make him sound horrible."

"He was."

"I'm sorry," I tell him sincerely.

He glances sideways at me. "You said that already."

"I know." I dig my fingers into the sand, wishing one of the waves that splashes against my legs would drag me away. "I just... I really mean it. I understand what it's like to hate your father."

He's silent for a few moments. "I suppose you do."

"I saw mine last night for the first time in fifteen years."

"How did that go?" he asks hesitantly.

"Surprisingly well." Relief washes through me as I marvel at the truth of my confession. "I realized I truly don't care what he thinks of me anymore. It was empowering."

"Then I'm glad you had that experience," he says, his tone earnest. "Still, I think if I ever meet him, I'll likely do to him what I did to that man at the ball."

"Lord Burgess?" I smile at the thought. "That was fun."

His eyes widen, and I force a somber expression onto my features.

"Disturbing," I correct myself quickly. "I meant that was disturbing. Personally, I didn't enjoy it at all."

"I'll bet it was just terrible for you," he murmurs, amusement filling his tone.

We sit in silence for a few moments, both of us staring at the water as the waves stretch toward us.

"Are you ready to talk about what happened this morning?" he asks finally.

Something ugly twists in my gut. "I don't know."

He swallows, and I can tell he's gearing up to ask one of his pressing questions. "Has that sort of thing happened before?"

"Sometimes," I admit in a small voice.

His jaw clenches, and his hands dig into the sand. It's obvious he's trying very hard to restrain himself.

"Does he—" He cuts himself off, taking a few deep breaths before finishing his question. "Does he force himself on you?"

I shake my head.

"It's not me," I whisper. "Not really."

A puzzled expression crosses his face before his eyes go wide with understanding. "The *eidolon*."

I stay quiet, unable to do anything as he uncovers my greatest shame.

"That's why you refuse to believe it's a part of you?" he presses, twisting in the sand to face me. "Because of him. And that's why you've kept your ability a secret. So Baylor won't find out."

I nod.

"Come to the Fifth Isle," he begs, leaning forward. "I'll hide you from him."

The request sends a wave of shock radiating through me. I turn to face him fully, crossing my legs beneath me.

"Why would you do that?" I ask.

He shifts uncomfortably but doesn't answer.

"Never mind." I shake my head. "It doesn't matter anyway. I can't leave."

"You can!" He grabs my shoulders with his gloved hands, and the contact startles me. "Let me help you. Why won't you just leave?"

"Because of this!" I pull at the collar, wincing as the movement reopens a few of my cuts. "It's not that I *won't* leave. I *can't!*"

I know I'm saying more than I should, but I can't stop myself as the confessions keep pouring out of me.

"No matter how much I hate him, no matter how much I want to be rid of him forever, this fucking noose around my neck keeps me tethered to his side."

His mouth gapes open as his gaze furiously flits back and forth between the collar and my eyes.

"That's why you never take it off?" he murmurs softly, almost as if he's speaking to himself instead of me.

My chin dips as I glance down at my hands twisting in my lap. "He's the only one who can remove it."

"Fine," he says a moment later, his tone resolved. "Then we'll get rid of the problem."

My heart flutters at the way he says "we," as if him helping me is a foregone conclusion. But I push those useless thoughts away, trying to focus on the important part of his sentence. "I told you, he's the only one who can rem—"

"I'm not talking about the collar," he interrupts. "I'm talking about Baylor."

My head tilts. "What are you saying?"

"I'm saying I'll kill the king."

Air catches in my lungs. I pull my knees up to my chest, wrapping my arms around them as I shake my head. "You can't do that. Promise me you won't kill him."

"Why?" he demands, pushing himself to his feet. "Give me one good reason I can't kill that bastard."

"Because the enchantment won't fade with his death," I whisper. "If he dies before the collar is removed, it will be activated."

"What happens then?"

I meet his gaze. "It tightens around my throat, cutting off my air so I can't breathe. And if he's dead, it won't stop like it usually does. It will keep going until..."

His eyes widen with horror. "Until you suffocate."

Unable to respond, I turn my head away from him, leaning forward to rest my cheek against my knee. A tear leaks from my eye, tickling me as it trails down my face.

"*Like it usually does?*" he asks slowly. "That's what you said."

I don't respond.

"He's done this to you before," he says, a statement of fact rather than a question.

A moment later, the beach is covered in darkness as shadows press in on us from every angle. His snakes slither over the sand, circling me as they hiss at every nearby crustation.

I push myself up, my legs coated in sand. He stands a few feet away, his wings outstretched behind him. In this moment, he's every bit the menacing God of Death. His eyes are solid black as he watches me with a hard expression.

"That day in his office?" he asks. "When you came out to the hallway, you looked as if you'd been crying, and your face was so pale. I thought perhaps you were just..." he trails off as he clenches his jaw. "He was doing it then, right? He was using the collar against you?"

I nod.

Rage radiates through him at my admission, causing his body to tremble. Shadows press closer as the snakes hiss and snap at invisible threats.

"Tell me how to fix this," he commands, his body vibrating.

"There's nothing you can do," I answer honestly.

"I don't believe that!" His fingers grip clumps of his hair, pulling at them furiously. "How are you so calm about this?"

My head snaps back. "What makes you think I'm calm?"

"Oh, I don't know." He throws his hands up. "How about the fact that you're standing here so fucking calmly?"

Anger stirs in my gut as I eat up the distance between us. "Do you think I don't hate this? I do! I'd give anything to be free! But until that happens, I have to be smart! I have to give him whatever he wants and pretend to be his good little pet!"

His eyes darken. "Don't call yourself that!"

"Why not?" I demand. "You did."

"And I hate myself for it!" he shouts back at me, taking a step closer. Our chests are nearly touching now. "I should never have thrown that in your face."

"It's fine." I brush it off, uncomfortable with his apology. "Everyone does."

"That doesn't make it okay," he says, his tone softer than before.

He's right. It doesn't make it okay. But just like when Naomi hurls hurtful comments at Morwen, it's easier to pretend it doesn't sting than to admit the truth. Apathy is the only weapon I have against their attacks. Somehow, I know it would be a thousand times worse if I let them all see how much they've broken me.

"I didn't know at first," I find myself confessing.

I shuffle back, putting space between us. The shadows have receded somewhat, but the snakes still guard our perimeter.

"Go on," he says, nodding at me encouragingly.

His wings fold against his back as he forces himself to sit on a large stone. I appreciate the effort he's exerting to keep his temper in check. I know it's not easy for him right now.

"When he put it on me, I was only ten years old," I continue, keeping my gaze on the shore instead of facing at him. It's easier to divulge shameful truths when I'm not looking at anyone.

"I believed him when he said it was going to protect me." A dark chuckle claws up my throat. "I was actually excited to have something so nice since my father never let me have beautiful things."

"Because he's worthless too," Thorne grumbles.

"Do you remember down in the tunnels, when I told you that I'd drowned once before?" I ask him in a small voice. "What I didn't tell you was that it was my father who held me under the water. He—" I cut myself off as I clear the emotion in my throat. "Afterward, he thought I was dead, but I wasn't. I'd only passed out. And when I woke up, I was in a coffin six feet under."

Thorne's fingers dig into the rock beneath him. "Tell me I'm *allowed* to kill your father."

I bite my lip against an inappropriate smile and continue without answering him. "That was the chain of events that started all of this. That night, after I crawled out of my own grave and walked home, Baylor was there. He took me away, and I haven't been home since."

I squeeze my eyes shut as images flash through my mind of Clara fighting against the guards.

"I'm so sorry."

I wince. "Don't apologize to me. I'm not innocent."

He leans forward, his blue eyes intent on me. "Tell me why you think that? Where does all this guilt stem from?"

I lower my gaze, not wanting to see the expression of disgust on his face when I admit the next part. "There was a time when I believed that I loved Baylor. When I let myself forget everything he'd done. I wasn't like your mother." My voice breaks. "I was a willing captive."

"Look at me," he demands.

I shake my head. I hear him rise from the rock and stomp through the sand until he's right in front of me, but still I refuse to do as he asked.

"Look at me, Angel," he says again, softer this time.

Taking a deep breath, I force myself to lift my chin and meet his gaze. What I find shocks me. Not a single ounce of judgment or disgust clouds his features. There's no revulsion. Instead, his eyes are full of understanding.

"You have nothing to be ashamed of," he says, cupping my face in his hands. "We all do what we must in order to survive. No one understands that more than me."

"I should have been stronger," I argue.

He shakes his head, using his thumbs to wipe the wayward tears from my cheeks. "You were a child. That kind of strength should never have been required of you."

His words penetrate some dark corner of my mind. Would I feel the same way if this had happened to someone else? Would I blame any of the women I've helped Della rescue? Call them weak because they succumbed to manipulation or abuse? Would I feel the same disgust for Lynal Skinner's daughter that I do for myself?

Logically, I know I wouldn't. I'd tell them it wasn't their fault. But for some reason, it's so much harder to offer that same grace to myself. There's too much residual shame built up inside of me. Every time I try to wash it away, I find more hidden deep within the crevices of my mind. To truly cleanse myself of this guilt, I'd have to open up the vault and face every single monster I locked away inside my mental prison.

And I'm honestly not sure I'd survive that.

"What did the queen think?" Thorne's voice pulls me from my worries.

"Leona?" My eyes widen. "She was... disapproving." The word feel painfully inadequate. "Baylor convinced me it was jealousy. That she saw me as a threat. She kept insisting that I was too young for him, and I took that as an insult. I spent all of my time with adults and I'd had too many experiences that no kid should ever have to face. So, when she called me a child, it made me even more desperate to prove to her that I wasn't, that I could handle a relationship with a grown man."

I go quiet for a moment, searching for the strength to speak my next words. "That's the thing I'm most ashamed of. That in the last years of her life, we were so at odds. And it was all my fault."

"What about Remard?" Thorne asks. "Why didn't he intervene?"

I stiffen. "Remy was different. He never really commented on it."

His eyes darken as he balls his fists. "Coward."

I shake my head, hating that anyone would associate that word with Remy. "No, I think he saw how I pushed Leona away and choose to keep his concerns to himself so I'd still have one person in my life I could trust. One person who genuinely wanted the best for me. It's only now that I'm older that I've begun to realize how difficult that must have been for him."

Feeling tired, I sit back down by the water and let the waves wash over my legs again.

"When did things change?" Thorne asks as he comes to sit beside me. "When did you realize the truth about Baylor?"

"When he asked me to kill Leona," I confess. His eyes widen, but I don't stop. "By that point, he'd already begun using the collar to force me to kill people."

His brow furrows. "What do you mean '*force?*'"

I swallow, not wanting to admit this part.

"When he places his hand on the collar, any order he gives must be obeyed," I whisper. "It's as if he takes control of my body, making it impossible for me to disobey."

He goes still at my words, but I keep speaking.

"I hated killing those people," I insist, my eyes bulging as I plead with him to understand. "But I believed him when he told me they'd plotted treason against him. He'd done so much for me, and I told myself I was being ungrateful for not wanting to protect him. Then one night, he said he had an important assignment for me."

Would you do anything for me?

Of course.

I shudder at the memory. "He said there was someone who was standing in the way of us being together, that this person was trying to separate us. He told me the only option was for me to kill them. I didn't even think about it. I just immediately agreed."

Revulsion roils in my stomach as I recall the smile that crossed his face as he asked me to murder his wife.

"I remember being shocked after he said it was Leona. I couldn't even speak. I just kept waiting for him to tell me he was joking or something…" I trail off, remembering the way my heart fractured in my chest the moment I realized he was serious. "When I didn't respond, he got nervous. He started reaching for my collar, and I knew he was going to order me to do it. So, without thinking I just—I slapped his hand."

The shock on his face in that moment was staggering. Neither of us knew what to do until I shot up and ran from the room. Thankfully, he didn't follow me.

"That's when I realized I'd been wrong about everything," I tell Thorne. "I'd been unbelievably stupid. The next morning, I went to tell Leona everything, but it was too late. She was gone." My voice cracks as tears stream down my cheeks. "They said she did it to herself, that she went to the veil in the forest to take her own life, but I knew that wasn't true. Baylor killed her. And it was all my fault." I squeeze my fists, my body shaking as the guilt overwhelms me. "I should have gone to her immediately. I shouldn't have waited until morning."

A gloved hand reaches for mine, forcing my fingers to uncurl as he takes them in his strong hold. "It wasn't your fault, Ivy."

My face crumbles. "Then why am I so ashamed?"

The fractured pieces of my soul snap apart as a horrible noise rises in my throat. In this moment, with all of my defenses shattered, I can admit to myself that I want Thorne to have a good opinion of me. But I won't lie and present myself as something I'm not. I don't want to lie anymore, not to him.

His arm comes around me, pulling me close without letting our skin touch.

"More often than not, our shame isn't deserved. It worms its way into our minds, infecting us with guilt for things that were never our fault." His brows pull together as his eyes search mine. "Do you truly believe Leona would want you to blame yourself this way?"

I shake my head. Deep down I know he's right, but this kind of pain doesn't release its hold on a person easily. Some hurts don't get better with time; instead, they burrow so deep it feels impossible to root them out.

Something tickles my leg, and I glance down to find one of Thorne's snakes curling around me, laying its shadowy head against my calf. The barest hint of a smile pulls at my lips as I realize it's trying to comfort me.

My face aches, my eyes raw and strained. I'm sure in this moment I look hideous, but there's no judgment in Thorne's eyes as he wipes my tears away and tucks a strand of copper hair behind my ear. Maybe it's good to break sometimes. Perhaps I've shattered myself so fully that the only option left is to begin to heal? And for once, I don't push the emotion back. I don't try to lock it behind some mental prison.

I let it out.

∼

THORNE OFFERED to fly me back to my room, but I didn't want to risk us being caught together. Instead, I had him drop me off near the edge of the forest line, only a short walk to the north entrance of the palace gates. Before he left, he looked like he wanted to say something, but instead, he turned and shot back into the sky. I've noticed it's becoming a habit of his.

Twigs crunch under my bare feet as I make my way through the woods. The trees are thick enough to block out most of the light, creating an eerie atmosphere. If I turned and walked in the opposite direction, I'd soon find myself standing before the veil. The idea of souls being pulled through this forest, unable to deny the call of the lonely stone archway, leaves me cold.

I can't help but feel sorry for them. Not being given a choice of whether to pass on or not seems terrible...

I'm unsure if I'm happy about sharing so much with Thorne. I'm not foolish enough to believe he's trustworthy. He's a God. And he lied to me from the moment we met. I'd be stupid to ignore the fact that it benefits him to create instability in Baylor's court. I believe he truly cares for me, but we both know it can't go beyond that. Neither of us are in a position to choose our own fate.

Still, it felt good to unburden myself a bit. To be open and honest is a rare gift.

Unease sparks as I near the Palace gates. There's a strange energy buzzing through the air, something that makes my senses go on alert. Up ahead, a man sprints toward me. I tense for a moment, my hand reaching for a blade that isn't there, before I realize it's

Bellamy. Pulling my cloak tighter, I try to conceal the bloodstained nightgown underneath it. I'm sure my dirty feet are already conspicuous enough.

I expect him to slow down as he gets closer, but instead, he slams into me. His arms wrap around me immediately, holding me tightly to his chest.

"I was so worried," he breathes.

"Bel?" I ask, unsure of what's gotten into him.

He pulls back, his gaze catching on my puffy eyes, red from the tears I've shed.

His face falls. "So, you've already heard?"

My brows pinch as I shake my head. "Heard what?"

"About father," he says, as though it should be obvious.

I push against his hold, taking a few steps back as I try to understand what I'm missing. "What about father?"

"You didn't—" Realization dawns on his face. He drops his gaze, his hand running through his hair as if he's uncomfortable. "I just assumed. You looked like you'd been crying."

"Iverson!" Baylor shouts as he runs up to me, pulling me into his arms. "You're safe! When we couldn't find you, I was terrified that bastard had gotten you too."

My skin crawls at his proximity, but I manage not to stiffen too much. When he lets me go, I glance back and forth between them, a sinking sensation settling in my gut. The urge to turn and run back into the forest is nearly overwhelming, but I force myself to meet Bellamy's gaze instead.

"What's going on?" I ask hesitantly.

"It's father," my brother answers. "He was found in his room this morning."

"Okay?" I drag out the word, not understanding what he's getting at.

"His throat had been slit," Baylor announces.

My brain accepts this information without protest. There's no denial or despair. Only a deep well of nothingness. They both watch me, searching for signs of shock. I do my best to appear appropriately distressed.

"Do we know who did it?" I try to make my tone sound somber.

"That bastard left a message," Baylor fumes. "The word 'mercy' written in your father's blood."

Everything spins as I try to follow his meaning.

"The Angel of Mercy killed your father."

CHAPTER
TWENTY-EIGHT

Della startles as I storm into her office. She jumps up from the sofa, releasing a high-pitched squeak as her hand flies to her throat. Chest heaving, she scowls at me as her shock melts into anger.

"What do you think you're doing, Iverson?" she demands.

My hands shake as I shut the door behind me. "Have you heard?"

Her head tilts to the side as she eyes my disheveled appearance. "How did you get in here? The back door is locked."

"Through the front," I explain, frustrated that she's wasting time with inane questions. "That doesn't matter. Did you—"

"The front?" she exclaims, her brown eyes wide. "Someone could have seen you!"

"But no one did!" I snap. "I'm not an idiot. Obviously, I used an illusion." I force myself to take a deep breath as I push a piece of hair out of my face. "Did you hear what happened?"

"Your engagement? I'm sure everyone's heard by now." She rolls her eyes as she grabs a glass of brown liquid from the side table and raises it in my direction before knocking it back. "Congratulations. You're finally getting everything you ever wanted."

Nausea stirs at the mention of my betrothal, but I can't think about that. It's too much. Too overwhelming.

I shake my head. "No. About my father's murder."

A sentence like that should be full of emotion. Sorrow, grief, or at the very least, anger. But I speak the words blandly. His death means nothing to me. I'm only bothered by the method his killer employed. I don't know what that says about me, but right now, I don't think I care.

"What?" she gasps, her eyes bulging. "When?"

"Last night. Someone slit his throat after the party."

She sits back down, observing me in a way I don't appreciate. "Do they know who was responsible?"

"The killer wrote 'mercy' on the wall in his blood."

"Iverson..." She drags out my name, accusation heavy in her tone.

I bark out a humorless laugh. "It wasn't me."

"You sure about that?"

"If I'd killed him, it wouldn't have been a quick death. His pain would have lasted for hours."

Her brows shoot up, and I realize perhaps that was one of those thoughts that shouldn't be spoken aloud. Feeling uncomfortable, I drop my gaze to the floor as I cross my arms over my chest. "Anyway, I didn't kill him."

There's silence for a few moments before she clears her throat. "Then who did?"

"I don't know." I deflate, falling into the chair across from her. "Every lord has enemies, but I can't think of any who would have done that."

"Is it possible it was a coincidence?" Della asks. "Maybe his killer panicked and tried to cover up their crime by blaming the Angel of Mercy?"

"Maybe," I say, even though we both know that's not true. This was personal. Someone is sending me a message. Which means that someone knows our secret.

Della watches me again, suspicion radiating off her. She has every right to distrust me, but still... It rankles.

"How did you get out of the palace tonight?" she asks. "After an attack like that, Baylor will have guards everywhere. And I'm sure the ones stationed outside of your room would have known to be on the lookout for doors mysteriously opening on their own."

I stay quiet.

Her doe eyes narrow into slits as she leans forward. "How did you get out, Ivy?"

I flinch at the sound of my nickname. She hasn't called me that in years. Not since I implemented the distance between us.

"Answ—"

"I climbed," I snap.

She goes completely still. "From the third floor?"

I shrug. "It's not as if the fall would've killed me."

"But it would have hurt," she insists, anger twisting her doll-like features. "A lot."

"Then it's just more of the same," I mutter as I wave off her concern.

Pity clouds her eyes, and I regret choosing today of all days to give up lying. I should have made something up.

"You're being reckless," she says. "Sloppy."

Tension tightens my muscles, making my body rigid. I roll my shoulders, trying to ease the anger pulsing through my veins. "You're making too big of a deal about this, Della. No one saw me."

"But they could have," she points out, her fingers picking at her dark curls, pulling the larger strands apart.

Leona loved those curls. For years she pestered Della to paint a self-portrait, telling her that such perfection needed to be preserved for posterity. Della would always brush off the comments, but I used to catch her smiling to herself in the mirror as she took extra time styling her hair.

The memory only spurs my anger.

"Why are we even talking about this?" I shoot to my feet. "It doesn't matter! Whoever killed my father did it to send me a message. They know who I am!"

"You can't know that for sure," she insists, but I can tell she doesn't believe it.

I pace back and forth across the rug, taking deep breaths as I try to steady my racing thoughts. I didn't come here for pointless arguments.

"We need a lead," I say calmly, clasping my hands together. "Reach out to your contacts around the city and see if they know anything. And talk with the girls who work on the floor. Drunk men are always chatty when they're trying to impress a woman. One of them might have mentioned something useful."

"I'm not going to do that."

I halt my pacing and slowly turn my head toward her. "Why the fuck not?"

"Because it doesn't matter," she responds evenly. I open my mouth to argue, but she cuts me off. "Baylor is probably going to put a high bounty on the Angel of Mercy. That will spark the interest of every desperate person in this city. Right now, we need to lie low. Asking questions and calling in favors isn't how we do that. And if you were thinking clearly, you'd see that."

"How long?"

Her forehead wrinkles. "Excuse me?"

"How long do you suggest we lie low?" I demand, my body shaking.

She cocks her head to one side, observing me with some emotion I don't have the energy to puzzle out. "Until it's safe."

I bark out a harsh laugh. "So, in the meantime we stick our heads in the sand and ignore anyone who needs our help?"

"We can't help others if we can't even help ourselves," she says in a patient tone that sets my skin on fire.

"Coward."

Della goes still. "Excuse me."

"You're quitting!" Somewhere in the back of my mind, I know these words are unfair, but that rational, reasonable part of me has been locked away, chained by some reckless monster wearing my face.

She rises from the couch, coming to stand before me. I can tell from her restrained movements that she's barely holding onto her own temper, but it doesn't matter. I can't stop.

"Just until it's safe," she promises.

"It was never safe!" I shout, pounding my fist against my chest. "It will never be safe! Not for me!"

"Then maybe we should stop forever!"

The ground wobbles beneath me. Or at least I think it does. I'm not sure.

"No." I shake my head, trying to stop the heat building behind my eyes. "I won't."

"You will." The hard set of her jaw tells me I've lost her.

"You don't control me. No one controls me." The words catch in my throat, sounding wet and muffled.

Her expression fills with pity. "We both know that's not true, Iverson."

My head snaps back as if she's slapped me.

"If you keep going, you'll be caught," she continues, her voice softening. "And I'll be caught with you. All the good that we're doing will end."

My bottom lip quivers. "Aren't you trying to end it right now?"

"There's a difference between stopping permanently versus staying quiet for a few months," she explains. "And with your engagement, you need to be careful. There will be more eyes on you than ever before. You shouldn't even be here right now."

The rational part of my mind insists that her words make sense, but I refuse to accept them. I can't lose the only thing I'm good at. The only thing I'm good *for*. Without this, who am I? Just the *wraith*?

Baylor's pet? His fiancée? The Angel of Mercy was the role *I* chose. Without it, only counterfeit versions of me exist. I'm nothing.

Worthless.

"Della, please." My voice cracks.

She drops her gaze, shifting back and forth on her feet.

"I have to protect them," I whisper, unable to hide the tears sliding down my cheeks.

"Why?" she asks, a strange expression haunting her lovely face. "Why is this so important to you?"

"Because I didn't protect her!" I shout as something cracks inside of me.

My hands cover my mouth instantly, but it's too late. Shame burns in my gut as my eyes dart back and forth between the woman in front of me and the portrait on the wall.

"Ivy—"

"Don't," I cut her off as I stumble backwards, unable to hear anything over the roaring in my ears. "I'm sorry. I'm so sorry."

I don't know which of them I'm speaking to, Leona or Della.

Without saying another word, I flee. My head spins as I race through the halls and into one of the front rooms. The club is structured into sections, all of which cater to different sorts of clientele. This one is essentially a casino.

Tables are spread throughout the room, each of them set up for a different game of chance. Tonight, most of the onlookers are gathered around one of the craps tables where a high roller is entertaining the masses. He should know better than to tempt the Fates by risking his fortune on the roll of the dice. It's not in their nature to show restraint.

Smoke wafts through the air, clogging my throat. Heavy music pounds against the wall, coming from the room next door where drunk patrons grind their sweaty bodies against each other. They'll be dancing until the sun rises. Many of them will likely end up in the upstairs rooms after that, along with some of the gamblers in here.

Instead of heading for the exit as I know I should, I find myself at the bar. Without asking, the bartender slides me a glass with a generous pour. I swallow the whole shot in one gulp, grimacing at the unpleasant taste. He chuckles at my reaction as he refills the glass and leaves me alone to go check on his other customers. It's unwise to sit here in the open, but I'm past the point of caring. Perhaps I long for danger...

I roll my eyes as someone slides into the seat next to mine.

"Am I expected to call you 'Your Highness' now?" Darrow asks in an amused voice, sitting backward on the stool as he leans his elbows on the bar.

"Go away." I sip my drink, letting it burn my throat on the way down.

"Is that any way to speak to your future subject?" he asks, his tone haughty.

"You won't have a future at all if you keep talking to me," I warn. "Go play foolish games with the rest of the degenerates."

"Speculation isn't my thing." He signals the bartender for a drink. "Too many variables."

"Didn't you tell me recently that sometimes the risk is worth the reward?" My voice turns icy.

His gaze drops to the floor as he shifts uncomfortably.

"I heard about what happened," he says carefully. "I'm sorry."

I huff out a laugh. "Why?"

We fall silent as the bartender returns with Darrow's drink and he downs it quickly before wiping his mouth on the back of his hand.

"I know what it is to hate your father," he whispers.

It's the shared fate of all bastards. I glance down at my own drink, wondering if finishing it would make me feel better or worse. Honestly, I don't know which one of those outcomes I'd prefer.

"I guess you do," I say as I push off my stool and prepare to leave.

My gaze slides to Darrow. For the first time since he sat down, I take a real look at him. Dressed in maroon velvet trousers and a billowing white shirt that's unbuttoned down to his navel, his outfit is utterly ridiculous. A gold medallion sits at his neck while a matching hoop hangs from one ear.

"You look like a pirate."

He waggles his eyebrows as the side of his mouth kicks up in a crooked grin.

"A very *wealthy* pirate, lass," he corrects me.

Rolling my eyes, I start to make my way to the door when suddenly a familiar face blocks my path.

Alice Darby appears even worse than before. Her bloodshot eyes are too big against her hollow face. The outfit she's wearing appears to be the same one she had on before, only now it has several more stains. Based on the smell radiating from her, I have to wonder if she's been wearing it since then. Her gaze shifts nervously between me and Darrow as she clutches a piece of paper in her hands.

"I see you took my suggestion."

It would appear Della hired the young mortal woman. I'd meant to let her know Alice might be stopping by, but with everything going on, it slipped my mind.

"Yes." Mrs. Darby smiles, but it doesn't reach her eyes. "Thank you, my lady. They've been good to me here."

"I'm glad," I tell her honestly, my gaze flitting to the door momentarily. "Did you need something?"

She holds out the paper, gesturing for me to take it. "Miss Della told me to give this to you."

I inspect the folded cream parchment, finding no seal or address. Ripping it open, I quickly scan its contents.

I changed my mind.
Tonight. 8p.m. The Lowers.
Mortal male, late thirties. Red cloak. Blond hair.
-D

Ignoring the thoughts racing through my mind, I shove the paper in my pocket and return my attention to the woman in front of me.

Alice watches me expectantly, her gaze flickering back and forth between my collar and my face.

"Thank you." I nod. "Please let Della know I'll handle it."

"Of course." She lowers herself into a curtsy before leaving us.

My eyes follow her as she makes her way through the crowd, keeping her head down until she disappears into a dark hallway.

"What was that?" Darrow asks, coming to stand beside me.

"A new development." I reach into my coin purse and toss a few copper pieces onto the bar, but as I turn to go, Darrow snares my wrist.

"You should know that you were right." Lines appear around his mouth, as if it's physically painful to force the words out. "I lied to you when I said I didn't have a way to remove the collar."

My blood turns cold as I rip my arm out of his grip. "Why are you telling me this?"

"Because I heard about the king's announcement last night." Darrow's chin dips, and I spot a trace of shame in his gaze. "And I'm sorry for my part in what's happened to you." He takes a deep breath, his eyes darting around the room before returning to me as he lowers his voice. "The *almanova* can remove your collar."

I grab onto the bar to keep from falling as my legs threaten to give out. Darrow continues speaking, but I barely hear him. My entire being has been chiseled down to one single sentence.

The almanova can remove your collar.

The words reverberate through my mind, bouncing against my skull as I try to understand them. For weeks, I've suspected the sword was connected to my collar, but I couldn't let myself truly believe it. I couldn't bear to carry the weight of my disappointed hopes if I was wrong.

"But you need to listen to me, Iverson." Darrow grabs my shoulders, shaking me until my eyes focus on him again. "It's not that simple. I know how much your freedom means to you, but it will come at a price."

"I'll pay it," I mutter as I push him away and force myself toward the door.

He trails after me, his voice quietly urgent. "If you touch that sword, you'll be trading one master for another."

I keep walking, ignoring his warning. One way or another, I'm removing this collar.

Tonight.

CHAPTER
TWENTY-NINE

My feet scamper silently over the broken cobblestones of the Lowers. There's a sinister energy hanging in the air tonight. The streets are practically empty, which is unusual for the typically boisterous Dockside District. I noticed several businesses locking their doors early.

The only place that appears to be open is the pub. I peered through a window as I passed by and found a few scattered patrons silently sipping their ale, Calum, among them. Somewhere in the back of my mind, I register relief at his presence, but the feeling dissipates before I have a chance to dwell on it. Right now, I don't have room for anything but determination.

Whatever price I have to pay, whatever I have to risk, I don't care. The sword is mine. And the collar is coming off.

Tonight.

Streetlamps flicker overhead as they run low on the precious oil that fuels their flames, creating a pulsing darkness that beats in time with my pounding heart. Even with my heightened vision, the thick haze of fog permeating the air is making it difficult for me to navigate my path. I have to give it to Alice Darby, she picked a good night to lure someone into a trap.

The moment she gave me that note, I knew it was fake. Della's paranoia may be annoying, but it also means she's predictable. She'd never stray from our established methods and entrust someone she'd just met to deliver an incriminating letter to me. The only way for Alice to even know about the letters is if she's been watching me.

Anger burns under my skin. I bet she was even listening outside the office door tonight. Since I'd surprised Della earlier, she didn't have time to light the candle that usually keeps our voices from being overheard. I silently curse myself for the stupid mistake. I wasn't behaving rationally.

Like right now?

I brush off the unhelpful thought, choosing instead to latch onto my anger. I tried to help Alice... I was sorry for her circumstances, for what was done to her. But it doesn't matter. Without her betrayal, I wouldn't have any chance of finding the sword tonight, so I suppose she did me a favor. Perhaps it's irresponsible to knowingly walk into a trap, but I'm past the point of caring.

Alice clearly hasn't mastered the art of moving silently. I've heard her shuffling steps trailing me since we left MASQ. Although, technically, I'm not the one she's following. My *eidolon... Rose...* walks ahead of my invisible form. The name rankles, feeling awkward and uncomfortable, but Thorne was right. It does make me feel more connected to her. The problem is I'm not sure I want that.

I tuck my hair behind my ear for the tenth time tonight, scowling at the wind for constantly blowing the copper strands into my face. If I hadn't been in such a hurry to sneak out of the palace earlier, I might have remembered to bring a ribbon to secure my braid. Instead, the thick waves hang freely down my back, eager to dance with the wind at a moment's notice.

I constantly tell Alva and Morwen that I'm going to chop it all off, but I know I'll never go through with it. Secretly, my hair is one of the few things I love about myself. When I was a child, Bellamy always told me it looked just like our mother's.

A flash of red catches my eye, drawing my focus to a figure leaning against the wall of a building up ahead. As if they've noticed my attention, they dart into an alleyway, their blood-colored cloak billowing behind them. Wanting to get a closer peek, I hasten ahead of Rose and scurry after the mysterious figure.

My shoulder hugs the wall as I turn into the alley and scan the area for threats. The cloaked person has their back to me, pausing where the path extends behind the building. Warning senses tingle along my spine. No doubt there are more people around the corner, waiting to ambush me. I note the closed doors along the brick walls. I'd guess that once Rose reaches the curve in the alley, enemies will rush out of those doors. They'll block the exit, leaving her trapped on both sides with her back against the wall.

I have to admit, it's a good plan. Too bad I won't be the one they have trapped.

Rose enters behind me and the cloaked figure turns their head at the sound of her footsteps, giving me a glimpse at the sharp chin that peeks out from the edges of the scarlet hood.

A second later, the figure disappears around the bend. Knowing it's risky, I dart forward and tuck myself into the corner, so I have a view of both sides of the alley. Over a dozen mortals are crowded into the cramped space. Most of them hold crude weapons—rocks and bits of rusted pipe. Only a few carry actual blades, and from the looks of them, I doubt they know how to use them.

Like the old woman from the empty house, most of these people have seen better days. Pity sparks in the back of my mind as I scan their haggard faces, but it dries up immediately when I land on the man in the red cloak. The only familiar face in the bunch.

His name comes to me quickly. Taron. The one who sat with Lynal that night at the pub and encouraged him to threaten Calum. My lips curl in a sickening smile. I'm going to make his death hurt.

Rose reaches the curve, setting the rest of their plan into motion.

Just as I predicted, more people rush out behind her, roughly doubling their numbers. Alice is among the newcomers and the crowd parts for her, telling me she's in charge of this little group.

Interesting.

As she glances in Rose's direction, something ugly and ancient flashes in her eyes. Something that wasn't there when I visited her home. Alice Darby is a killer now. Brutal and unfeeling. Every trace of that sweet, overwhelmed young woman I met before has disappeared. An ugly thought occurs to me, sparking a trace of fear in my gut.

Will I have to end her life?

I'm assaulted by images of the frightened little girl who stood on the staircase that morning. Will I be the reason her mother never comes home? I've killed parents before, but this time it wouldn't be the collar forcing my hand. It would be my choice. Sweat dampens my palms, making my blades slippery. I grip them tighter, forcing myself to focus.

"All these people just to capture little old me?" Rose says, following my command. I need to gain control of this situation before I let my emotions ruin everything. "I must admit I'm flattered."

"Perhaps we overestimated your skill," Alice replies in a patronizing tone. "You did fall for a rather obvious trap."

Rose shrugs. "I guess I trusted the wrong person. Kind of like you."

I position myself slightly behind Rose, using her as a shield in case any of these idiots decide to take matters into their own hands and toss one of their rocks at me. Though they'd be trying to hit Rose, I don't trust their aim.

Alice laughs. "You still think you know me?" She shakes her head, giving Rose a pitying glance. "You think you understand me, *pet*, but you don't. Only *he* understands. Only *he* knows what's truly in our hearts."

"Are you talking about your husband? Cause last I heard, he was a deadbeat."

I need to keep her talking. If I give in too easily, they'll be suspicious. Rose has to stall until they attack. Then I'll follow behind as they lead her away, hopefully to wherever the sword is hidden. The plan has plenty of risks, but as long as I find the sword I don't care what else happens.

She laughs again. "You really don't know anything, do you? Just like the other *rats*."

My mind zeros in on the word, the same one the old woman used. I rack my brain, trying to remember anything else she said that day.

"Now, now," a new voice cuts in. "No need for name calling."

A soft breeze tickles my cheek as a body drops from the rooftop and lands right next to me. Griffen appears perfectly comfortable as he steps forward, positioning himself shoulder to shoulder with Rose.

"Miss me?" Griffen asks my *eidolon*, amusement shining in his eyes as if this precarious situation is of no concern to him.

My jaw drops open, and I'm grateful no one else can see the shocked expression on my face. What is he doing here? How did he find me? A new realization sets in, bringing a fiery anger with it. Did Thorne order him to watch me? Has he been following me this entire time?

"What are you doing here?" Rose whispers.

"Saving you, of course." Griffen winks.

My eyes nearly roll back into my skull at that response.

"I don't need your help," Rose says, her voice clipped. "Leave. Now."

"I'm afraid that's not possible, my lady," he responds. "Bosses orders."

I want to scream at the confirmation of Thorne's interference. Who does he think he is? Just because he's a God doesn't give him the right to intervene in my life. I'm not one of his subjects. He has no authority here.

"Aren't you going to introduce your friend?" Alice asks, pulling my attention back to our current situation.

Griffen thankfully follows my lead and stays silent.

"Well then," Alice sighs when we don't answer. "He can wait with us."

My brows scrunch.

"Wait for what?" Rose asks.

A bright smile breaks across her face. "You'll see."

Fuck.

Griffen being here changes things. Continuing with my original plan means I'm no longer risking only my own life, I'm risking his too. And unlike me, Griffen doesn't have an *eidolon* to take his place. Frustration tightens my muscles until they burn. This was my one chance at freedom.

But is your freedom worth more than his life?

My gaze flits toward Griffen, noticing the way he's shifted his body slightly in front of Rose. We don't know each other very well, but he jumped into a fight where he is severely outnumbered in order to help me. I steel myself as determination settles into my veins. I know what I have to do.

Moving to stand directly behind Griffen, I balance on my tiptoes to bring my mouth closer to his ear. If anyone else hears me, our chance at survival will be over before it begins.

"Don't say anything," I whisper, only loud enough for him to hear.

His body tenses, and his mouth opens to speak.

"I said to be quiet," I remind him. "This is going to sound insane, but the person next to you isn't me."

"How?" he asks, barely moving his mouth.

"You remember my special trick?" I ask, referencing the time I disappeared before his eyes. "Let's just say I have a few more of those." Hopefully, he doesn't ask for more details. "Listen, I'm going to provoke the one in red. As soon as he makes his move, I need you to take out the two big guys on the left. The ones holding the knives. See them?"

He nods subtly.

"After that, we make a run for that first door and try to lose the rest of them inside the buildings. Sound good?"

He dips his chin once more, pretending to glance at his feet. Taking a deep breath, I move around Rose and crouch down, ready to strike.

"Taron, isn't it?" Rose breaks the silence.

His eyes snap to her, crinkling with confusion. "Do I know you?"

She shakes her head.

"Don't engage," Alice reminds him.

"How do you know my name?" he asks, ignoring her orders.

A sweet smile blooms across my *eidolon's* face. "Because I killed your friend Lynal."

Taron's eyes go wide as he shuffles back a few steps.

"You remember, don't you? You were in the pub getting drunk and flirting with barmaids while I was out back slaughtering your friend."

"Stop talking!" Alice orders Rose as she steps forward, getting between the two of them. She focuses on the man in red, holding up a placating hand. "Don't let her get to you. Remember *his* orders. He chose you for a reason, Taron. He saw something in you."

"Did you know that Lynal peed his pants after I cut his hand off?" Rose announces. "It was actually kind of funny."

Fury breaks across Taron's face, turning his cheeks as red as his cloak. "I'm going to kill you, bitch."

He lifts his blade, taking a step toward her.

"Taron, stop!" Alice cries, but it's too late. The large man barrels forward, pushing her out of the way as he raises his knife toward my duplicate.

Alice's head hits the wall with a startling crack right as my blade slices across the back of Taron's calf, causing him to tumble to the ground. Glancing up, I find that Griffen has already slit the throat of one of his targets and is about the drive his blade into the other.

I'm moving to finish Taron off when Alice lifts her head, blood trailing down her smiling face. "He's here."

A sickening wave of nausea churns in my stomach as my collar grows warmer against my skin. In some unholy imitation of a God's arrival, everyone in the alley drops to one knee and bows their heads. The only people left on their feet are Rose and Griffen, who stand back-to-back in the center of the group. Through the fog, a newcomer enters the alley. His face is familiar, despite the fact that I've never seen him in person. His likeness has been circulated constantly for the last few weeks, branding itself into my brain.

Grell Darby.

He's different than I imagined. Calmer. More refined. The way he carries himself speaks of power and dominance I wouldn't expect to find in someone like him. Darby's features are cold, his gaze shrewd as he makes his way to Rose.

All at once, a scalding heat pulses against my neck, stronger than it was outside of the dilapidated house. I grit my teeth against the pain as I tuck myself into the corner.

"This is the infamous *wraith*?" Darby asks, observing Rose with indifference. "I expected more."

Ivy, a new voice whispers into my mind.

I close my eyes, trying to clear my head as Rose replies to Darby. "I could say the same."

"Charming," he says before turning his gaze on Griffen, who glares at the former guard. "And the spare?"

Listen to me, Ivy, the voice speaks again, tickling my brain with its seductive tone.

"Nothing to worry about," Alice speaks up, still kneeling a few feet away.

"I find that to be offensive," Griffen mutters under his breath.

I've seen the desires of your heart.

I pull against the collar as the world tilts on its axis, becoming blurry and unfocused.

I've seen the shame you seek to hide.

"It's unfortunate things have to end this way," Darby says to Rose. "But I'm afraid you've got something that doesn't belong to you. Something that needs to be returned to *him*."

Those intrinsic instincts I've learned to rely on are screaming at me to run, to fight, to do something.

Your shame can be erased. You need only give into me.

I try to push to my feet, but the pain turns searing. The heat from the collar is scorching as it burns my skin.

Let me in, Ivy. You know you're nothing on your own. So weak. So unworthy.

The words echo inside my skull, reverberating against my bones. The voice is everywhere. It's unescapable.

Let me in.

I cover my mouth with my hands, desperate to stop the screams rising in my throat. Blood drips from my nose and ears. My entire body convulses as I struggle to hold on to my illusions.

Let me in.

I no longer sense my *eidolon*, nor the prickle of invisibility against my skin. I can't even feel my own body. Like some sort of ghostly figure, I'm floating on the wind, untethered to anything but that all-consuming voice.

LET ME IN.

Through the haze, something silver flashes above me. It gleams brightly as it cuts through the air, heading straight for my—

The ground shakes as a large presence lands right in front of me, the force pulling my mind back from the ether. For a moment, I'm sure it must be a meteor, some righteous fury raining down on us from the stars.

But then I spot the wings.

Black feathered wings fully extended, shielding my view of the rest of the alley. Somewhere in the back of my mind, I recognize the curved blade peeking out from beneath those feathers. A scythe.

"Kill them all," a dark voice growls.

Barely a second later, bloodcurdling screams fill the air as shadows descend upon the alley, blocking out any trace of moonlight.

Flee, the voice pounds through my mind again, louder than before. *Run, you fools!*

A flurry of footsteps race past me as our attackers try to escape the avenging angel of death who's come to claim them. The wings disappear from my sight right before a sickening crunch comes from my left, telling me someone's just had their bones broken.

"You thought you could hurt what's mine?" Thorne's voice tugs at the dark recesses of my mind, pushing me to fight through the fog clouding my thoughts. "You thought you could touch *her*?"

The screaming continues all around me as the alley descends into utter chaos. I slowly become aware of the rest of my body, noting how my cheek presses against the bloodstained cobblestone. I push myself onto my forearms, but before I can rise to my feet, something heavy lands on my back, shoving me down again.

"You fucking bitch!" Taron shouts in my ear. "You're going to pay for this."

His hands grip my hair tight, tugging my head back before smashing it against the hard ground. Pain shoots through my skull, radiating down my spine. Moving on instinct, I reach for his wrist and drive my thumb into the tendon there, causing his grip to loosen. Before he can react, I pull his hand to my mouth and dig my teeth into one of his fingers, biting down until I hear that horrible snap.

New screams join the horrific symphony of cries filling the alley. Blood spews into my mouth, but I don't give myself time to let the disgust set in. Instead, I use his distraction to my advantage and flip myself over.

"You've ruined everything!" Taron screams from above me as he pulls his bloody fist back.

Those words hit me harder than the blow that lands against the side of my face. They're the same words I've forced myself to hold back again and again. Every time I see Baylor's face, I want to scream and rage at how he's destroyed everything that my life could have been. Whenever I see him, I'm forced to mask that same searing hatred that's burning in Taron's eyes right now.

Have I become the very thing I despise?

Another punch lands on my cheek, the impact making my body jolt. But still, I don't block it. This pain is different from what came before—sharp and focused. Seductive. An indulgence I haven't allowed myself to enjoy in far too long. I swore to Alva and Morwen that I would stop doing this, but what's one more broken promise? One more failed oath. If I ruin everything I touch, let this pain be my punishment.

A cleansing.

Taron's fist flies toward me once more, but it never connects. Instead, his body is suddenly thrown off mine, and he hits the wall with a force that likely snaps several bones. Before I can even blink, a new face is in front of mine. Blacked-out eyes search my features, cataloging every bruise and scrape. I do the same, noticing the drops of blood scattered across his face. Without asking, I already know it's not his.

"Angel," he breathes.

Shivers trail over my skin, mingling with pain and exhaustion. A reminder that I'm undeserving of the nickname. I'm not something good or pure.

"I'm fine," the muffled words end on a wince as I force myself to sit up.

"You're not." His fists clench at his sides, as if he's physically restraining himself from forcing me to lie back down. I bristle at his concern, hating the way it makes my skin feel too tight.

So weak, the voice whispered before.

Gathering all my strength, I push myself to my feet and try to take inventory of the damage. My head aches as if it's cracked in half. A trail of fresh blood drips from my hairline, telling me a skull fracture might not be that far off. Using the edge of my sleeve, I wipe the evidence from my face as best I can, wincing every time I brush against a fresh bruise.

As I scan the alley, I find bodies everywhere. Some are piled on top of each other while others lie in pieces. Shame curdles in my stomach. Darrow tried to warn me, and I didn't listen. He told me I wouldn't be able to fight the sword, and he was right.

So unworthy.

Whatever the *almanova* truly is, it was able to see me more clearly than anyone else. It knew me, straight to my core, as if it weighed me in the balance and found me wanting.

"Leave those be," Thorne says as I gently prod at the burns marring my throat.

Ignoring him, I continue tracing the edges as I try to see how far it extends.

"You're going to make it worse if you keep—"

"Just stop!" I snap. "Stop saving me. Stop trying to make things better."

The words pour out of me, bubbling over before I can stop them.

"This?" I toss my arm out, gesturing to the massacre surrounding us. "I caused this. All of this suffering was my fault. Whatever pain I'm feeling right now is the least of what I deserve."

His eyes rake over my face, shrewdly observing me. "You let him hit you."

I open my mouth to respond, but movement at the other end of the alley catches my attention. Thorne stiffens, his body shifting to block mine once more. It's moments such as these when I remember just how large he is. With his giant shoulder blocking my view, I'm cut off from the entire alley.

"Easy," Griffen's voice reaches us. "It's only me."

Thorne's rigid posture softens as he scoots over, giving me a glimpse of the golden-haired fae. He appears slightly worse for wear, but overall, he fared well.

"Darby and his wife got away," Griffen says. "And they took the sword with them."

My head swings around, sending a shooting pain through my skull and neck as I search the nearby bodies for confirmation.

"See if you can catch their trail," Thorne orders.

Griffen nods, darting back toward the mouth of the alley and leaving me alone with the God of Death. Not wanting to let him steer the conversation back to our previous discussion, I go on the offensive.

"You were having me followed," I accuse him.

Thorne's eyes flash to mine. "It's a good thing I was."

I scoff. "I could have handled this on my own. I had a plan."

"Oh, I'm sure this is going to be good." He rubs his hands together. "Please, enlighten me. What was your plan exactly?"

Anger builds in my veins, sending a fresh wave of adrenaline to dull the pain. "I was going to let them capture my *eidolon* and then follow them to their hideout."

"And how would you avoid being seen while you followed them?"

I roll my eyes. "I'd be invisible."

"See, you say that like it should be obvious, but when I arrived here, you weren't invisible at all." He shakes his head. "Instead, you were collapsed on the ground, pretty fucking visible."

I bristle. "That wasn't part of the plan."

"Plans change," he says, his tone flat.

"I would have come up with something."

"Really?" he asks. "Or would you have lain there and let them beat you to death like you were doing earlier?"

Heat flames my cheeks. "I wasn't—"

The words cut off as something catches my eye. Moonlight glistens off a blade heading straight for me, but before it can reach its target, Thorne shifts his body. Hot blood splatters against my cheek as he hits the ground next to me.

Male screams erupt as the shadow snakes descend on the culprit, the sound of ripping flesh and hungry growls filling the air. Somewhere in the back of my mind, I recognize that it's Taron screaming. He may have survived the injuries Thorne inflicted, but that certainly won't be the case once the shadows are finished with him.

My hands shake as I roll Thorne onto his back, his body limp. Every bit of fire in my blood turns to ice the moment I see his neck. Blood spurts from the jagged slice along his throat, already soaking his shirt.

"No," I gasp as everything in my mind comes to a screeching halt. I'm frozen with fear, unable to move or think.

Weak. Worthless.

No. No, I can help him. I have to help him.

"Pressure." I nod my head as my trembling hands move to his neck. "I need to apply pressure to the wound."

His skin is slippery under my fingers. There's so much blood. How much can a person lose? I used to know that information, but it's gone now. Everything's gone.

"Please," I beg the Fates. "Don't let him die. Save him."

As if my prayers have been answered, Thorne's eyes drift open, finding mine instantly. His lips curve in a soft, content smile. He almost looks peaceful... At least until his gaze flits down, filling with horror as he spots my hands on his neck.

"What?" I ask, scanning the alley for a new threat. "What's wrong?"

"Get away from me," he insists, putting all his strength into the words. "Now!"

Hurt flares through me, potent and crushing, but it subsides quickly as a shocking realization sinks in. I stare at my hands, pressed firmly against his bare neck.

I'm touching Thorne.

I'm touching the God of Death.

CHAPTER THIRTY

I snatch my fingers away from his skin as if he's burned me.

"I'm sorry! I wasn't thinking!" The words rush out of me in a single breath.

"Are you alright?" Thorne sits up. His gloved hand reaches for me on instinct, before he pulls it back, cursing under his breath.

I stare at my own hands, waiting for them to catch fire or something equally horrifying. My brain is moving far too quickly to form rational thoughts. Am I going to die? The memory of Lord Burgess screaming in agony sends a fresh bolt of terror through my veins.

"How bad was it? I'm sorry, Ivy." His fingers run helplessly through his hair, pulling at the inky black strands as his pleading eyes beg me to be alright. "Fuck! I'm so sorry."

My heart pounds against my chest, the force of it jolting me into action. I need to calm down. I take a deep breath through my nose and hold it for five seconds before releasing it through my mouth. I do this several more times, my eyes glued to the slash on Thorne's neck. The blood has slowed, telling me it's already clotting. As my pulse steadies, the realization that he was never truly in danger sinks in. The wound, while terrifying, wasn't enough to kill a God. Somehow, that knowledge had been overshadowed by the sight of his blood staining my hands.

Relief melts my bones, leaving me weightless. Thorne will survive.

But will I?

I squeeze my eyes shut, waiting to be struck by the terrible pain of Death's touch. Helplessness paralyzes me as the seconds pass, spreading into minutes. And yet... nothing happens.

"Ivy!" Thorne begs, his tone sparking a suspicion that he's been speaking to me for quite some time. "Please look at me, Angel."

Doing as he asked, I peek one eye open. Evidence of the night's horrors is smeared across Thorne's cheek, the blood stark against the unusual paleness of his skin. His fists are clenched at his sides, his body rigid with restraint. When my gaze connects with his, the terror I find there is staggering. There's no evidence of the smug confidence he always carries. Instead, it's been replaced with fear.

For me, I realize. He's terrified for me. Warmth flutters in my chest, but I push it aside, choosing to focus on the other emotion hiding in his eyes. One I recognize quite well.

Self-disgust.

Each time he ordered me not to touch him replays in my mind. This has to be a nightmare come true for him. I want to assure him I'm going to be alright, but I have no idea if that's a lie. Is it possible that the attack is delayed? When he touched Lord Burgess, it happened immediately. But when I placed my hands on him, I felt nothing.

Well, that's not exactly true. I was a mess of emotions. Urgency, desperation, terror.... I felt all of those. But physical pain? That never struck me.

"I... I'm fine?" The statement comes out as a question. How is it possible that touching him didn't hurt me at all? He's the God of Death. His touch is lethal.

"What?" he breathes.

"I'm not hurt."

He shakes his head as his brows pinch together. "That's not possible. You touched my skin, Ivy. I felt you."

"I know." I rack my brain, searching for answers and coming up blank. "I don't understand how, but you didn't hurt me."

His mouth opens only to quickly close again. Those blue eyes shift wildly, searching for answers that aren't there. His broad shoulders curl inward, as if he's trying to protect himself from something.

"You're in shock." He shakes his head again. "It hasn't hit you yet."

My brows pinch. "Has it ever been delayed this way?"

His silence speaks for itself.

"Exactly." I lean forward and Thorne jumps back, immediately rising and putting more space between us. He stumbles, nearly tripping over one of the bodies littering the ground before righting himself. I follow him, unwilling to let him pull away now. I'm surprisingly steady on my feet after everything that's happened tonight.

He holds his gloved hands in front of him as he continues to retreat. "Angel, it's not safe—"

"You didn't hurt me!" I insist. "You touched me, and nothing happened."

His eyes go round with fear as his back hits the wall, giving me the opportunity to close the space between us.

"Give me your hand."

"You don't know what will happen," he pleads.

I take a deep breath, ignoring the truth in his words. "Do you trust me?"

His brow furrows as he tilts his head. "That's not the problem."

"Then what is?"

His beautiful lips twist into a grimace as his gaze drops. "I don't trust myself. If I hurt you... I think it would destroy me."

My foolish heart stutters at the admission. I can't think about what it means. I can't think about anything except this moment right now.

I hold out my hand, willing it not to tremble as I wait for him to give me his. "Then let it destroy us both."

His eyes connect with mine instantly. I can see the hesitation there, but underneath it, I also spot a faint spark of hope. He wants this too—he's simply afraid to let himself believe it will work.

Slowly, he lifts his gloved hand and places it in mine, palm facing the sky. The black leather is soft against my skin, but it's not what I want. Pinching the material between my fingers, I begin pulling it off. I move slowly, giving him time to pull away if he wishes. I don't think he breathes the entire time. Maybe I don't either.

Once the glove is gone, his bare hand is cradled in mine, skin to skin. He's warmer than I expected. For some reason, I always believed Death would be cold. Seconds tick by as we wait to see if this will be a mistake or a triumph.

"Am I hurting you?" he whispers.

I shake my head, my heart pounding against my chest. Can he hear it?

His jaw is clenched so tight I'm sure it's going to crack. Tension radiates through him as he speaks again. "I need you to say it out loud, Angel. Am I causing you pain?"

For the first time in my life, there isn't an ounce of ugliness in the truth.

"No," I promise him.

Guided by instincts I don't bother to question, I lift his hand and bring it to my face. A guttural noise rises in his throat, but I ignore it. Shivers coast over every inch of my skin as I nuzzle my cheek against him, marveling at how soft he is.

"Don't," I beg as Thorne tries to pull away.

Watching him closely, I keep my eyes locked on his as I slowly release my grip and force my arms to my sides. I need him to choose this too. Completely frozen, he holds himself rigid as if he believes one wrong move will ruin everything.

"Touch me," I whisper.

His mouth falls open in a gasp. He hesitates only a moment

longer before his fingers begin their soft exploration over my cheekbone, leaving tingles in their wake. He wipes away something wet, and it's only then that I realize I'm crying. His progress halts as questions fill his eyes.

"Continue." I nod. "Please. It's perfect."

Spurred by my assurances, his touch becomes more confident. His fingers move to my mouth, tracing the bow shaped lines of my upper lip. His eyes are focused, as if he's utterly entranced in his task. Tingles erupt over my skin, and I can't stop the shudder that racks through me.

His gaze finds mine again, full of fire now. An instant later, he's reversed our positions, his body now pushing mine into the wall. What started as pure becomes wicked, turning from want to need as desire burns in my core. Restless and desperate, I pull him closer, reveling in the feeling of his hard length pressing against my stomach. He brings our foreheads together, and his eyes blaze into mine with a swirling mix of hunger and awe. His hand finds my leg, hooking it around his waist to bring us closer together.

As he presses featherlight kisses over my cheeks, something inside of me cracks into a thousand pieces. The move is so tender that I want to cry again. His lips continue moving over my skin until suddenly they hover right above my own. We stay that way for several seconds, nose to nose, as we breathe each other's air.

"I don't want to let go," he admits, his voice rough. "What if this was just a dream?"

"Do you dream of me often?"

"Every night."

The earnestness in his eyes gives me the strength to speak my next words.

"Don't stop," I whisper, causing him to go completely still against me. "You don't have to stop."

Without hesitating a second longer, he closes the gap between our mouths. His lips move against mine gently as he gives me the sweetest kiss I've ever known, but I'm so desperate for him that I need more. I bite his bottom lip before running my tongue against the seam, begging for entrance.

His response is immediate. His tongue is in my mouth, tasting all of me as he pushes us harder against the wall. The kiss turns hungry and desperate. The ache deep in my stomach increases as my other leg comes up around his hip and he grinds into me.

His hands are everywhere, cupping my ass, squeezing my breasts, feeling all of me. I do the same, greedily trying to touch every inch of his body. My fingers brush against his feathered wings, finding them softer than anything I could've imagined. I moan and squirm, wanting more. I know we should stop, but I can't. His skin on mine is an addiction I've only just begun to indulge.

My hands move to the laces on the front of my tunic, needing to remove every barrier between us. He pulls at the material until it comes down, exposing my heavy breasts to the night air. His eyes are hungry and focused as he stares at me, utterly enraptured. One hand glides up my stomach and cups my flesh in his palm. Taking my nipple between his fingers, he squeezes it gently before increasing the pressure. I inhale on a breathy gasp as a bolt of pleasure shoots through me. A satisfied smile plays at the corners of his mouth as he immediately repeats the action, eliciting the same response.

His gaze finds mine, a thousand emotions swirling there. "You're the most beautiful thing I've ever seen."

With the way he's looking at me and touching me so reverently, I believe him. His lips trail over my shoulder, sucking on my skin as I grind against him. One of his hands moves to cup my core, and I groan into his neck. *I need him.*

"Please, Ivy," he begs. "Please let me taste you."

"Yes," I gasp, unable to deny him anything right now.

Setting my feet back on the ground, he quickly kneels before me. His fingers immediately get to work undoing the laces of my breeches, and he pulls them down, exposing me. There's no time for embarrassment because his mouth is on me in an instant. His tongue pushes through my slit, gliding from my entrance up to that pulsing bundle of nerves.

A startled moan falls from my lips as sparks shoot through me.

"You taste even better than I imagined," he murmurs, licking his lip to savor the flavor before returning to his task.

His tongue teases my clit mercilessly, moving against me with unrestrained enthusiasm. I had believed he hadn't done this before, but I must have been wrong because the skill he's displaying is astounding. Our gazes connect again as he sucks me into his mouth.

"Thorne," I gasp as I writhe against his face.

His eyes light up with smug satisfaction as my movements become more sporadic. Liquid heat builds in my core as I cry his name again and again. He slips two fingers inside me, pushing them in and out at a tantalizing pace.

"Please," I beg.

His fingers curl, pressing against that sensitive spot that makes my vision go black as everything explodes.

"Thorne," I shout, unable to stop myself as I combust in his arms.

Before I know it, he's rising to his feet and bringing his lips to mine in a feverish kiss. His fingers still pump in and out, letting me ride out the last waves of pleasure. I moan at the sinful taste of myself on his tongue.

"Please, Ivy," he whispers against my skin as the high finally ends. "Let me do it again."

"Hmm?" I murmur as my hazy mind tries to follow his request.

"You said I didn't have to stop," he says, his tone completely serious. "Does that still apply?"

I'm about to say yes when footsteps echo from the other end of the alley. Griffen stands there, his features twisted into absolute shock as he stares at the two of us, pressed together. Heat flames my face as I remember how much of my body is currently exposed. My hands drop to my laces, my fingers shaking as I quickly tie them. Immediately, Thorne's wings expand to shield what's left of my dignity, blocking off my view of his friend.

"I—" the confused fae begins.

"Leave," Thorne cuts him off, his voice low and menacing.

"How are you able—"

"Now!"

Footsteps retreat in the opposite direction, telling me Griffen is gone, but his interruption has created room for sober thoughts to overtake my lustful haze. Nausea rises in my gut as I spot one of the bodies lying dead on the cobblestone. Oh gods. This was wrong. We shouldn't have done this here. We shouldn't have done this at all.

Questions swirl through my mind, one after another. What if Thorne doesn't truly want me the way I want him? What if he was only interested in me tonight because he realized he could touch me without harm? I wouldn't blame him for that. It'd be normal to seek that opportunity with whoever you could. But the thought makes me strangely ill.

"Stop that." Thorne's voice pulls me from my spiral.

Glancing up, I find him watching me with narrowed eyes. "What?"

He moves to stand directly in front of me. "Whatever you're thinking."

I raise my chin. "You don't know what I'm thinking."

"I know it's not good."

Despite his orders, the poisonous thoughts spread. Tonight was reckless. We're lucky it was Griffen who interrupted us and not someone else. Anyone could have seen us out here in the open. And with news of my engagement sweeping the city... I don't even want to imagine what Baylor would do if he found out. Della was right. I am being reckless.

If we were discovered, there would be no more chances at freedom, no more glimpses of a better life. I risked all of that for what? A few minutes of pleasure with someone who's done nothing but lie to me.

That's not true, an annoying voice in the back of my mind reminds me. *He cares for you.*

I shake my head. Whatever this was, I need to sort through my emotions away from Thorne. Because the harsh reality is that even if he does care for me, he'll still be gone as soon as he gets what he came here for. And I'll be left behind, trapped with Baylor for eternity. The thought leaves me cold and unsteady.

"This was a mistake," I whisper as I move past him.

His bare hand grabs my wrist, pulling me to a stop as the feeling of his skin against mine sends another wave of shivers through me. "You don't mean that."

"I do," I insist, refusing to look at him. "If word got back to Baylor—"

He grabs my chin, forcing me to meet his gaze. "I'd protect you. You don't need to—"

"You can't protect me," I cut him off as I rip myself out of his hold. "As long as this collar sits around my neck, no one can."

His eyes blaze with determination, but we both know I'm right.

"I need to get back."

He nods, slowly moving backward and putting space between us. His palms close into fists, as if he's having to physically restrain himself from touching me. If I'm honest, I'm fighting those same instincts. Every nerve in my body is screaming at me to reach out and kiss him again.

One side of Thorne's mouth kicks up at my hesitation. "I thought you needed to go?"

"I do." My brows pinch together as I realize I've been standing here staring at him for longer than I intended.

"Then you should probably do that." He prowls closer, a predator scenting blood in the water. "Unless you changed your mind?"

I shake my head, my thoughts turning fuzzy again.

"Are you sure?" he whispers as he reaches out to tuck a strand of hair behind my ear. "I'd be happy to prove to you why leaving is the wrong choice."

I lick my lips as my mouth turns dry. Knowing I need to escape before I sink back into his addictive touch, I call on the last of my strength to wrap myself in an illusion. The sensation of needles pricking my skin helps to steady me.

Thorne doesn't move as I make my way to the edge of the alley, his eyes on me the entire time. He still hasn't revealed how he always knows exactly where I am, even when he can't see me. Frustration builds, making it easier to leave.

"Goodnight, Reaper," I grumble.

His warm laugh echoes through the dark, and when he speaks, I can hear the smile in his voice. "Goodnight, Angel."

Shaking my head, I rush out of the alley and make my way back to the Palace. The sound of wings follows me the whole way home.

CHAPTER
THIRTY-ONE

"Nigel Pomeroy was one of the best men I've ever known," Baylor declares from behind a podium made of solid gold. He's immaculate as ever in his black dolman, not a single blond strand out of place. "And one of the most loyal."

Hushed cries echo through the room as the crowd pretends to be overcome with grief. Thankfully, the veil Alva placed on my head this morning hides a myriad of sins, such as my dry eyes and expressionless face. There's no performance today. No need to manufacture sadness for all the courtiers and nobles nodding along with Baylor's every word. I can simply exist.

The funeral took two days to prepare. It's costing the treasury a small fortune, but Baylor insisted it be held in the royal temple, a place even the elite are lucky to enter. The main room is a sea of glittering gold. Every inch of it decorated with priceless art. Gilded statues of the Fates stare down at us from the back of the stage, the three sisters depicted as terrifying warriors. The sculptures are frighteningly realistic, giving one the sense that at any moment, they could lift their weapons and attack. Honestly, that doesn't sound half bad.

My father would have been pleased with the turnout. The temple is packed with dozens of simpering lords and ladies who are eager to mourn with their king. I spot Lady Naomi and Lord Darcus a few rows behind me, dabbing invisible tears with their handkerchiefs. I expect they are trying to distance themselves from Bridgid's taint after her father's unfortunate fall from grace. I doubt anyone in this room will truly grieve for Nigel Pomeroy. Most will have forgotten his name by the end of the day.

"When Nigel realized my dear pet was a *wraith*," Baylor gestures toward my spot in the front row. "He sent his only daughter to serve me and the kingdom, despite how devastated he was to be parted from her."

Oh, so we're just completely revising history now? Great.

"That was true loyalty to our great isle." His voice rises as it echoes through the temple. "May we all be more like Nigel Pomeroy."

I shift in my seat, arching my back. You'd think with the amount of money they've invested in this place, they could have at least provided some cushions. But no, the wooden bench is hard and unforgiving, just like my late father. At least Bellamy and I don't have to share our row with anyone else since the front is reserved for family only.

Ignoring Baylor's monologue, I observe my brother next to me. Strangely stoic, he hasn't shed a single tear today. As a child, I never quite understood their relationship. I knew it was different from the one I had with my father, but Lord Pomeroy wasn't a warm or loving man. Not even with his true born heir. And yet Bellamy has stayed with him all these years. He appears to have been a dutiful son, and yet he appears completely unaffected by his father's death.

As if he can sense my stare, Bel subtly turns his head, one brow arched in question.

"Are you alright?" I whisper, not knowing what else to say.

His gaze drops and lines appear around his mouth. "I'm feeling too many things to put into words."

"That's okay." I reach for his hand and take it in mine. "You don't have to."

As much as I hated the man, if Bel did care for him, then he deserves to grieve however he wishes. It's not my place to judge.

"Maybe we could have dinner together?" I ask. "Just the two of us?"

His eyes meet mine again, this time full of regret. "I'm leaving as soon as the funeral's over."

For the first time all morning, true sadness pierces my heart. I let go of Bel's hand, pulling mine back into my lap. "Oh. Of course."

"I wish I could stay longer," he says, his voice so soft I can barely hear him over Baylor's prattling.

I tuck my chin, not wanting him to spot my disappointment through the veil. "I understand."

"The king ordered me to return home and set father's affairs in order."

My head swings back toward him as anger stirs within me. I should have seen it coming. Of course, Baylor would try to isolate me from the one family member I have left. He's always kept me away from Bellamy. I'm sure he never forgot the way my brother tried to fight for me that night, the way he begged them not to take me. That kind of bond is dangerous to Baylor. He knows it might teach me the difference between genuine love and Baylor's cheap imitation.

"I can try to talk to him," I offer, knowing it's probably useless.

Bel shakes his head.

"No. It won't do any good. Besides," he says, his tone conflicted, "there's a reason I need to be elsewhere right now."

My eyebrows pinch together. I want to ask what he means, but the crowd erupts in applause as Baylor finishes his speech and steps to the side, signaling the choir to begin their performance. The crowd rises to their feet as the melodic tones swell through the room. Voices join in all around us, creating a symphony of echoes.

Desperation blooms as I sense my time with Bellamy coming to an end. Will we see each other again? That uncertainty fans the flames of my anxiety, pushing me to do something reckless. My gaze flits to the crowd behind us, ensuring no one is close enough to overhear before I grab Bel's arm, squeezing it hard. His head snaps in my direction, concern clouding his eyes.

"Listen to me carefully," I whisper, my voice barely audible above the singing. "As soon as you get home, you need to create an exit plan."

"Ivy—" he starts, but I cut him off.

"Find somewhere safe, a place no one else knows about that you can get to quickly. You'll need enough funds and supplies to get you through several months, maybe more."

He grabs my hand in both of his. "Why are you saying this?"

I wish I could tell him the truth, but there's no time. And even if there was, it would be too risky to bring him into everything. This is my mess to sort, not his.

"There may come a time soon when things..." I trail off, searching for the right word to explain. "Change."

"Change how?"

"I can't say. But when it happens, everything is going to move very quickly. If I—" I cut myself off, taking a deep breath before I say something I'll regret. "I need you to be ready to leave the moment things turn bad."

"What about you?"

"Don't worry about me." I shake my head, letting the lies roll smoothly off my tongue for old time's sake. "I have a plan in place."

His eyes narrow, and I'm reminded of how he always used to be able to tell when I wasn't being truthful.

"How will I find you after?" he asks, not calling me on my dishonesty. The question surprises me, but it shouldn't.

"Contact Dellaphine Cardot," I say without hesitation. No matter how strained things are between us, I know I can trust Della with my brother's life.

His eyebrows nearly reach his hairline. "The club owner?"

I nod, knowing he's likely dying to ask how I'm acquainted with the infamous woman who was rumored to be the late queen's lover. "She'll know where I am. You can trust her."

He watches me for a few moments, squeezing my hands between his own. "I hate leaving you."

"I know." And strangely, I do. I know that if Bel could stay and help me, he would.

The song comes to an end, and we take our seats once more. I expect one of the temple priests to lead us in a closing prayer, but instead, Baylor returns to the podium, causing whispers to circulate through the room.

"Before we conclude the service," Baylor begins, his jaw hard as his gaze moves over the crowd. "I want to make an announcement."

A frisson of apprehension has me straightening my spine. The last announcement Baylor made didn't end well for me.

"What happened to Nigel Pomeroy was an unspeakable tragedy." Anger contorts his features, sending a spark of fear through me.

My hands lie in my lap, my fingers twisting together. Warnings blare through my mind, urging me to flee. The room is completely silent, everyone sensing the shift in his demeanor. Whatever is about to happen isn't going to be good.

"It was a crime only the most monstrous and cowardly soul would commit," he continues. "It's for this reason that I have placed a bounty on the Angel of Mercy."

Gasps erupt from the crowd as my stomach drops.

"Anyone who comes forward with information that leads to the capture of this vile individual will be awarded fifty-thousand gold coins. Together, we will catch this villain!" Baylor shouts as the crowd cheers. "Together, we will destroy the Angel of Mercy!"

CHAPTER
THIRTY-TWO

Wine coats my tongue before it settles in my stomach, warming my body from the inside out. The one thing I will compliment Baylor on is his taste in alcohol. He spares no expense on his indulgences.

"Your Majesty," Kaldar's dull voice says. He hasn't stopped talking since dinner began. "You need not rely on vigilantes and opportunists to capture the Angel of Mercy. And given the food shortages in the north, I'm not sure such a large sum should have been promised."

My eyes roll back in my skull as he carries on with his protests. Unfortunately, saying no wasn't an option when Baylor ordered me to join them for dinner tonight. The scent of butter and herbs wafts through his private dining chamber, but I have no appetite. Instead, I'm choosing to consume a liquid meal this evening. But if they don't start eating faster, I'm going to pass out before dinner's over. They've barely made it past the first course, and I'm already finishing my second glass.

Resentment brews over the topic of conversation, making the alcohol sour in my stomach. It appears Della was right about the bounty. Everyone in the city is going to be hunting me now. Memories of the way I spoke to her that night poison my already terrible mood. I should never have said those things to her.

The list of people who know my identity is small, only those we trust, but fifty thousand gold coins is enough to make people do things they swore they never would.... like turn on a friend.

"If you would only give me another chance, I'll prove to you that I'm more than capable of catching this bastard," the adviser insists, his dark eyes beseeching the king.

"Then why have you not succeeded already?" Baylor snaps, evidently just as annoyed as I am.

A flush blossoms under Kaldar's pale skin and he tucks his chin, hiding his embarrassment behind the stringy black hair that falls into his face. "I will not fail you again."

Baylor sits back, taking a sip from his goblet. "I should hope not."

I hide my smirk behind my own glass, my gaze snagging on the way Baylor checks his pocket watch for the third time since dinner started. His lips thin as his attention flickers to the door. Are we expecting an addition to our party? When I sat down, I noticed the table was set for more guests, but I assumed it was an oversight.

I lean forward, setting down my wine. "Is someone else joining us?"

The words have barely left my mouth when the door swings open.

Doral enters, bowing at the waist. "Your guests, my king."

My heart constricts as the last person I expected to see strides into the room.

"Sorry we're late," Thorne says, a wicked grin curving his lips.

Memories of those lips on my skin send a flash of heat straight to my core. I shift in my seat, willing myself to calm down. If I don't get my reactions under control, everyone will know what happened between us the other night.

"No matter," Baylor responds coolly. "We started without you."

"I'd expect nothing less."

Behind Thorne, two others file into the dining room. Griffen catches my eye and I cringe when I recall the way he caught us in that alley. I can't imagine what his thoughts were when he stumbled upon me and Thorne doing... whatever it was we were doing. Steering my thoughts away from that topic, my attention settles on their other companion, recognizing her instantly.

Fia.

The woman who accompanied them to the ball. Her dark hair is pulled back into a simple, yet elegant chignon. I catch the slightly rounded points of her ears poking out, marking her as half fae. Dark coal lines her eyes, complimenting the depth of her brown irises. She's extremely lovely, and yet the sight of her next to Thorne makes my stomach twist.

I expect Thorne to take the seat at the end, directly opposite from Baylor. But instead, he pulls out the chair next to mine, sliding into it despite the questioning glances thrown his way. Griffen helps himself to the seat across from Thorne, accepting the unfortunate task of sitting next to Kaldar. Which leaves Fia stuck at the other end of the rectangular table, across from the king.

Thorne's eyes burn into the side of my face, but I refuse to glance in his direction.

"*Wraith*," he drawls.

It takes immense effort to suppress the shiver that threatens to overwhelm me. How he makes such a simple word sound sinful, I'll never know.

"Killian," I instill as much disrespect as I can into the name.

The room goes silent. I can feel everyone staring at me. Perhaps addressing a God by his first name and in that tone was a bit too far? I blame the wine as I guzzle down the rest of my glass.

Griffen snorts, breaking the silence. "You are as charming as ever, Lady Iverson."

I find his warm gaze, latching onto it like a lifeline. "How nice to see you again, Lord Griffen."

Strangely, I find that I actually mean that. Apparently, the charming fae has worked his way under my skin. My attention shifts to the woman sitting to his right. "I don't believe I've been properly introduced to your other companion."

"May I present Lady Fia," Griffen gestures to the female fae. "A valued member of Death's advisory council."

"A pleasure to meet you, Lady Fia." I nod politely.

Her gaze flits between me and Thorne, a knowing smile on her lips.

"Trust me, the pleasure is all mine. I've heard many interesting things about you." The words are spoken with such warmth that I automatically believe her. The ugly feeling in my stomach eases slightly. "And please, no need for formalities. Just call me Fia."

"Now that we've all been introduced," Baylor chimes in, a hint of petulance in his tone. "Perhaps we can move ahead with our meal."

Servants enter, carrying plates of food that they deposit in front of the newcomers and topping off our glasses. Finished with their tasks, they file out, leaving us alone once more. Griffen immediately digs in, but Thorne holds back.

"I must say, Lady Iverson," he drawls. "I greatly enjoyed our time together the other night."

I sputter as wine catches in my throat, choking me.

"When we danced together," he explains after I catch my breath, his thick brows raising innocently. "Surely you remember. You were a wonderful partner. So pliant."

I consider stabbing him with a dinner knife. If I was fast enough, I might be able to do it without anyone noticing.

"Yes, my pet is an excellent dancer," Baylor agrees evenly, his lips pursed as he watches the God at my side.

"And flexible too," Thorne purrs.

Griffen coughs, his face turning red as he covers his hand over his mouth. "Apologies," he croaks.

"Personally," Kaldar interjects, "I found the dance to be inappropriate and unbecoming of a future queen."

"No one cares what you think," I grumble.

"Please excuse my pet." Baylor glares at me. "She's had a trying day. Her father's funeral was this morning."

Kaldar nods. "Yes. Very tragic."

My gaze narrows on the bastard. "Really? I don't recall seeing you there."

"I was in the back," he says, his tone clipped.

I roll my eyes. "My, how the mighty have fallen."

Muffled laughter comes from the other end of the table as Griffen and Fia attempt to camouflage their amusement as indigestion.

"Iverson," Baylor's tone turns dangerous. "Behave yourself, pet."

I cast my eyes down in a submissive gesture. The conversation carries on as Kaldar claims the king's attention, regaling him with gossip about some lord whose wife is having an affair. Thorne takes full advantage of their distraction, shifting his chair closer to mine.

"I expected to see your brother here," he whispers.

The mention of Bel sends a sharp stab of sadness through my heart. "He left. It's for the best."

I nearly jump when something warm touches me under the table. Peering down, I subtly lift the tablecloth that covers my lap to find Thorne's bare hand slipping underneath the slit in my gown. His thumb rubs tiny circles against my thigh, causing my core to clench.

I glare at him, but he doesn't acknowledge me as he chuckles at something Griffen says. With his other hand he brings his glass to his mouth and takes a sip of his wine. My breath hitches as his tongue darts out to catch a wayward drop clinging to his upper lip.

"Mmm, delicious," he murmurs.

Everyone in the room carries on with their meal, completely unaware of the inappropriate behavior happening beneath the veil of the white tablecloth. I squirm in my seat as I cross my legs in an attempt to dislodge him. Thorne's grip tightens, stilling my movements. He keeps his focus on the others, but I spot the faint curve of his lips. He knows exactly what he's doing to me. My breasts feel heavier as my nipples harden into points. Clearly my body remembers how much it enjoyed his touch.

"There's a matter we need to discuss," Baylor announces loudly.

The gentle scraping of silverware against porcelain comes to a halt as everyone turns to the king, but his attention is reserved solely for the God next to me.

"I have a proposal."

"I'm flattered," Thorne replies, one brow arching. "But I believe you're already engaged."

A cold chuckle forces its way out of Baylor's mouth, but his eyes are unamused. He keeps his gaze on Thorne as he snags my hand and brings it to his lips. "True," he whispers against my skin, sending a wave of revulsion through me. "I couldn't be more thrilled that Iverson will soon be my wife."

Thorne's fingers curl into my flesh, possessive but not painful. Tingles skate over my skin, making me shiver.

Baylor lifts a brow. "Cold, pet?"

I nod, not trusting myself to speak. Finally, the king releases my hand, and his attention returns to Thorne. "My proposal for you is of a different nature."

There's no warmth in the God of Death's voice when he responds, "I'm listening."

"We expect to find the *almanova* any day now," Baylor explains, leaning back in his chair. "The city is closed off, and my soldiers are going door to door. It will be returned to us shortly."

"I believe we've heard that line before," Fia speaks up, her gaze narrowing on the king. "Didn't you assure Killian that the sword would be found weeks ago?"

A muscle ticks along Baylor's jaw. "The task has proven more difficult than we originally anticipated. But we're confident that will be changing soon."

"For the sake of your pantries, I hope that's true," she warns, referring to the second shipment of grain that will be withheld if we can't follow through on our end of the bargain.

"Once the sword is in your possession," Baylor carries on, ignoring Fia as he addresses Thorne. "I want you to do something with it. You see, I've got a prisoner who has proved rather difficult to kill, but I believe the *almanova* could take care of that."

"Forgive me," Griffen chimes in, "but wasn't the blade in your possession for many years? Why didn't you take care of this problem before?"

His upper lip curls. "Circumstances prevented me."

Baylor doesn't elaborate any further, raising several questions in my mind.

"So, you want me to use the sword to kill your prisoner?" Thorne asks directly.

"I do."

The God's eyes turn hard. "And what do I get in return?"

Baylor crosses his arms, his lips twisting into a thin smile. "I'm assuming my gratitude wouldn't be enough?"

Thorne shakes his head. "But there is something of yours I'd be interested in."

Baylor's eyes flash red as they dart to me, narrowing into slits. "Do tell."

"I'll kill your prisoner," Thorne agrees, surprising me, "*if* you remove Lady Iverson's collar."

My mouth drops open as my head swings in his direction. Even his advisers throw him curious glances, wondering if he's lost his damn mind.

"You've grown rather fond of my pet, haven't you?" Baylor asks, his tone deceptively soft.

My nails dig into Thorne's hand, still resting on my thigh, as fear worms its way through my body. Baylor is going to make me pay for this later.

Thorne shrugs. "Perhaps I'm impressed by her talents, and I want to use them for myself."

"And why should the collar stand in the way of that?" the king asks innocently. "Surely she could perform whatever tasks you need done while wearing it?"

"Come now." Thorne gives Baylor a patronizing stare. "There are rumors about what that collar does. If I have any hope of using her services for myself, I'll need it gone." He leans back in his chair, appearing completely at ease. "And besides, it would still be her choice. Even without the collar, she could always refuse me. So, I guess it comes down to how much you trust your fiancée."

Baylor is silent for a few moments, his unwavering stare glued to the God at my side.

"It's something we can discuss, but you'll understand if I need time to consider it," he responds finally. "She is to be my queen, after all."

"Of course." Thorne's hand disappears, leaving me suddenly cold. For a moment, I have the wild urge to pull it back.

He rises to leave, and his companions follow suit. When they reach the door, he turns back, sparing me a brief glance.

"My lady." He inclines his head in my direction, ignoring the others.

Once they've all departed, leaving me alone with Kaldar and Baylor, the room grows silent. No one moves as I keep my gaze down, avoiding eye contact with either of them. Whether Thorne knows it or not, he's left me in a precarious position. This wasn't his mess to solve.

Kaldar is the first to speak, using his words to strike a blow at me. "Iverson appears awfully comfortable with the God of Death. Too comfortable, I think."

Baylor stays silent, watching me with interest.

"Forgive me for suggesting this, Your Majesty," Kaldar carries on, "but is it possible our dear Iverson has been compromised? For him to ask for such a thing, she must have given him reason to believe she would be open to his advances. For all we know, she could have already spread her legs for him. Infidelity does run in her blood."

Barely a second passes before I lunge across the table, driving my dinner knife into the space between his fingers. The metal cuts clean through the tablecloth, digging into the wood below. For a moment, everyone is silent as the blade wobbles back and forth.

"You little bitch!" he shouts, leaning forward to retaliate.

"Leave," Baylor orders, his tone cold. "Now."

Kaldar sputters as he rises from his seat, storming out of the room. I move to follow him, but the sound of Baylor's voice stops me in my tracks.

"Not you," he snarls. "Sit back down."

Doing as he demanded, I return to my seat and stare straight ahead.

"Is it true, pet? Have you been compromised?"

I shake my head.

He leans forward, his finger trailing over my arm. "Have you betrayed me?"

"No, my love." My heart gallops, but I keep my voice even. "He's only trying to drive a wedge between us."

"Perhaps," he murmurs, his tone deadly soft. "I was under the impression it was impossible for him to be close to another in that way, but maybe I've been misled. Have you allowed him to touch what belongs to me?"

A truly reckless plan forms in my mind. The risks are exponential, and even if it's successful, it would change our relationship forever. But still, I can't think of another way to throw off his suspicions.

"I'm loyal," I insist, pausing to take a deep breath as I prepare to drop a bomb that could annihilate me too. I turn to face him now, my eyes brimming with accusation. "Unlike you."

His head snaps back, and his hands slam against the table as claws sprout from his nails. "What's that supposed to mean?"

I lean forward, my voice low. "What do you think it means?"

"Is he the reason you've been distant lately?" he presses, his lip curling with disgust. "The reason you haven't been coming to my bed when I call?"

I scoff. "Don't pretend you've been lonely."

Fury detonates behind his eyes as the meaning of my words sinks in.

"What happened with Bridgid meant nothing!" he snarls, rising from his chair. "And you can't blame me for seeking comfort elsewhere when you've been distant for months! Your body may be here, but your mind is somewhere else. It's not the same as before."

"And whose fault is that?" I scream, unable to hold myself back as I unleash far more than I intended.

His eyes widen as he takes a step back.

The accusation seeps into the air between us, making it thick and cloying. Neither of us has ever acknowledged what he did to Leona. The silence pushes against my nerves, making my body rigid. I never meant to say that last part. It revealed too much of my hatred. I glance around, desperate for a way to reverse time and take back my words.

"Please," I beg him, my voice small. "I buried my father today. Can we discuss this tomorrow?"

He watches me in silence, a million thoughts racing behind his eyes.

"Of course, pet," he agrees finally. "We'll talk tomorrow."

CHAPTER
THIRTY-THREE

My hands shake as I slam the door to my room. Panic seeps into my bones, making them brittle. I play back the end of our conversation, trying to puzzle out his expression just before I left.

It appears while I was gone, either Alva or Morwen turned down my bed and left an oil lamp burning. The orange glow creates a romantic atmosphere in the room, but it's wasted on me now. Stomping over to the vanity, I sit down and remove the pins from my hair with excessive force.

Just as I'm reaching for my brush, a familiar sensation tells me I'm not alone. I spin around, searching for the source of the sensation. A bolt of lightning flashes outside, illuminating a dark figure on the balcony. Only a second passes before I'm throwing open the double doors and pulling the bastard inside.

"How dare you?" I accuse him, my fingers digging into the soft material of his shirt. Dampness coats my hands from the rain that soaks him. It drips to the floor, creating a puddle at our feet.

Thorne's expression is cold as he stares down at me. "I was trying to help you."

The excuse only fuels my outrage. "I didn't ask for your help."

He says nothing as I push him away and begin pacing across the rug. Thunder booms outside, mirroring the rage rising within me.

"Is this all some game to you?" I demand. "Did you think I'd become part of your trade? As if you could buy me from him?"

His eyes narrow at the accusation. "You know that's not what I was doing. If you would calm down, you'd see that I don't want to *own* you. I'm trying to *free* you."

"I can free myself!" I scream.

My face blanches as my hands cover my mouth. I glance toward the door, my eyes round as I wait to see if any of the patrolling guards heard my outburst. Nothing but silence comes from the hallway, telling me I'm safe for now. I ball my fists, willing my anger to cool.

"All you did was make things worse," I whisper.

His eyes harden as he crosses his arms over his chest. "At least I did something."

I take a step back. "You think I haven't?"

"I think deep down you don't want to be free," he accuses. "You'd rather stay here and punish yourself for something that wasn't your fault."

His words are an invisible knife slicing across my middle, leaving me wounded and exposed. "You don't know me."

He laughs darkly. "I know you, Angel."

"Clearly not if you think I want to stay here."

"Then why didn't you fight back when that man was hitting you?" he demands as he takes a step closer.

Seeking shelter, I turn around and ignore his question as I return to my vanity. Some small voice in the back of my mind warns not to read too closely into his insinuation, afraid of what I'll find.

I pick up my hairbrush, resuming my earlier task as if he's not here.

"Obviously, what happened between us was a mistake if you think it entitled you to any say over my life." My gaze meets his through the mirror as he leans against the balcony door. "You didn't care about any of this before."

His arms fold over his chest as he cocks his head to the side. "We both know that's not the truth."

"It is!" I yank the brush through my fiery waves, wincing as it catches on a tangle. "You only care now because you realized I'm the one person on this planet who can actually bear your touch!"

Genuine hurt splashes across his face, causing something ugly to twist in my gut. I instantly wish I could pull the words back into my mouth and never let them out.

I drop the hair brush as I spin around. "Thorne, I—"

"In case it wasn't abundantly clear," he cuts me off, his voice low and even, "I've wanted you from the moment I saw you." My eyes widen at his admission, but he keeps going. "No, before that. Since you tossed that first dagger at my head. So, you don't get to call what happened between us a mistake." He shakes his head. "Not when we both know you've been craving it just as long as I have."

I want to deny his claim, but I can't bring myself to lie in the face of his honesty.

"And before you try to purposefully misunderstand me, I've never wanted anyone the way I want *you*. Before we met, I thought my..." he trails off, searching for the right word. "*Condition* was a gift. Fates" —he chuckles darkly— "I even thought it made me better than other people because it prevented me from getting distracted by petty dalliances. I never saw it as a hinderance until you. But despite all of that, I'd trade the ability to touch you ever again if it meant you would be free."

Wetness pulls behind my eyes. No one has ever spoken to me this way, not even Baylor. I try to latch onto my fading anger from before, but it slips through my fingers.

"I'm not some weak creature you need to save."

"Weak is never a word I'd use to describe you," he says, his tone gentle. "But everyone needs help sometimes."

That tiny voice in the back of my mind whispers that he might be right. Wouldn't it be nice to have someone to watch out for me the way I do for others? To find *me* in the darkness and be *my* shield. Someone I could count on. Believe in. Trust.

It would be nice.

But experience has taught me that niceties are synonymous with lies. If I let myself truly believe he cares for me, I know it would only be a matter of time before he revealed it was all fake.

I close my eyes, unable to bear the weight of his pleading gaze.

"Leave," I beg softly.

There's silence for a few moments before his gravelly voice reaches me. "Alright. But this isn't the end, Angel."

A moment later, I know he's gone. Even without looking, I sense his absence.

I did the right thing, I tell myself as my cheeks dampen. *It was for the best.*

But if that's true, why do I feel so empty?

CHAPTER
THIRTY-FOUR

Hours after Thorne leaves, I find myself doing something both reckless and stupid. I clutch the handle of my oil lamp, praying the flame won't extinguish. Maybe it's because I'm down here in the middle of the night, but the tunnels are far creepier than before. At least I haven't seen any bats.

Yet.

You'd think it wouldn't matter what time it is since we're underground, but there's a sinister edge to the air tonight. Or perhaps it's simply the fact that I'm down here alone. I exhale a sigh. If I hadn't pushed Thorne away, I could have asked him to come with me.

Perhaps this is something I'm meant to do alone. A few weeks ago, when all of this started, I questioned whether the Fates were intervening in my life. Now I'm almost positive they are. Far too many coincidences have piled up. Meeting Thorne when I did and somehow being the only person who can touch him without harm? And then it turns out the missing weapon I was tasked to find just so happens to be the only thing that can remove my collar and free me from Baylor?

But if I'm right and they are interfering, why? What makes me worthy of their interest? And worst of all, I can't help but wonder if perhaps it's not a good thing to attract the attention of the Fates.

These were the worries that plagued me as I tried to fall asleep after Thorne left. Eventually, I gave up trying, deciding instead that I would put my theory to the test. If I return to the spot where I had the odd feeling and find nothing, then I can rest easy knowing it was all in my head. But on the other hand, if I do find something...

I stop those thoughts in their tracks, not ready to face them yet.

My impulsive plan was almost ruined before it even began when I remembered the way Kaldar had cut his hand open to unlock the door. Knowing I needed the blood of someone who'd been authorized to come and go from the tunnels, I dug through my closet searching for the ruined tunic I'd been wearing the day I got soaked in Kipps's blood. Thankfully, when I smeared it over the stones in the dungeon, the door swung open.

A startled yelp escapes me as something scampers over my foot. Before I can unleash one of my blades upon the crawling menace, it darts into a tiny hole in the cave wall and disappears. My heart gallops as I jump back, scanning the area to make sure none of its little friends are waiting to ambush me. *Fucking rodents.* If this entire thing is one big joke the Fates are having at my expense, I'm going to find a way to kill those three sisters.

My palms dampen as I continue down the path, making it difficult to keep hold of my lamp. Not that it's doing me much good since the damn thing only gives off enough light to cover a few feet ahead of me. The journey feels endless, but eventually, I come upon the fork in the tunnel where the lonely staircase waits for me.

The moment of truth passes swiftly.

Just like before, the collar's reaction is immediate. The rubies warm against my skin, the heat pulsing in waves. Steeling my spine, I don't give myself time to reconsider my reckless plan as I force my feet up the stairs. With each step I climb, the collar burns hotter. By the time I reach the top, my upper lip is damp with sweat and my breathing turns heavy.

Holding the lamp higher, I realize I'm standing in a small alcove. My forehead creases as I take in the cushioned chair that sits in the corner. Next to it is a small table stocked with a leather bound book, a bottle of spirits, and a single empty glass. While I find these items odd, it's what's across from them that turns my blood to ice. Even the heat coming off the collar is no match for the cold spreading through my veins at the sight of iron bars separating the other side of the room, blocking off whatever lies beyond it. Revulsion rises in my throat as my stomach threatens to expel the wine I drank at dinner. The truth of what this place is reverberates through my bones.

A prison.

Based on the angle of the chair and the lack of dust on the items left behind, it's clear Baylor visits frequently. At least, I assume he's the one who placed these things here. None of the guards would be that bold.

A flash of movement within the cell startles me, sending my lamp crashing to my feet. The flame flickers wildly, but thankfully, it doesn't extinguish.

"Careful with that," a feminine voice calls from within the darkness. "You don't want to start a fire down here."

Grabbing the handle of my lamp, I lift it toward the cell and try to make out anything about the space.

"I wondered if you'd come back," the woman speaks again, her melodic voice closer this time.

My brow furrows at her words. "Back?"

The outline of a woman materializes through the darkness. It's hard to know for sure, but she appears to be around my height, though her build is much slimmer. Almost frail.

"I sensed you a few weeks ago," she says, her tone becoming unsure as she sighs. "Or maybe it's been longer than that? Time has little meaning to me now."

Her silhouette disappears, followed by the sound of shuffling as she rummages around for something. A few seconds later, another lamp flares to life, illuminating the cell. It's much larger than I anticipated, and well furnished. Every inch of the floor is covered in rugs and a four-poster bed stands in the corner, covered in thick fur blankets. There's also a seating area complete with comfortable looking couches and artwork hanging along the walls. I even spy a few bookshelves. Everything about the space feels lived in, as if someone has made this their home for quite some time. But that makes sense given how long she's been down here.

The moment my eyes settle on the woman before me, I know exactly who she is. After all, I've seen her portrait many times.

Maebyn, the Goddess of Illusion.

Hair the color of moonlight hangs past her waist, the shade blending with her nearly translucent skin. Her lips are pale and chapped, and the cheekbones that were once her best feature have become gaunt and jarring, protruding too far from her hollow cheeks. The nightgown she wears is cleaner than I would expect, but it hangs awkwardly from her sunken frame.

Despite all of this, she's still heartbreakingly beautiful.

Yet the most shocking thing about her appearance isn't any of that. Instead I'm struck speechless by the sight of the ruby collar that hangs around her throat, an exact replica of my own.

Her indigo eyes watch me process this information, hungrily cataloging every expression that flashes across my face as she studies me the way I have her. Her lips part as emotion ripples across her face, but I'm too lost in my own racing thoughts to translate it.

How is this possible? The Goddess who's been missing for twenty-five years is right here, caged beneath the palace that was once her home. Despite the questions racing through my brain, there's one I don't bother seeking an answer to. The moment I saw the ruby collar around her neck, it was obvious who's responsible for all of it.

Baylor.

Just thinking his name is enough to send a wave of fury racing through my veins, burning away the shock and fear that had left me frozen. I bend one knee as I start to kneel, a show of respect for the Goddess before me.

"There's no need for that, little one." She waves her hand. "No one has bowed to me in years. Stand up, please."

I rise, not wanting to offend her.

She watches me closely, almost warily. "When you came before, you were searching for the *almanova*, correct?"

My head snaps back, eyes widening at the mention of the sword. "How do you know about that?"

The barest hint of a smirk pulls at her cracked lips.

"I know many things," she says vaguely. "I could always hear it talking to the guards, egging them on. It's grown louder these past few months. More insistent... You've heard it too, haven't you? It spoke to you a few nights ago?"

"How do you know that?"

Her gaze drops to my collar. "Call it intuition. Was that the only time you've heard the whispers?"

I nod.

"That will change." Her voice takes on a sad quality as her eyes glass over, turning distant. "It won't let either of us go. What was shattered into pieces longs to be whole once more."

I open my mouth to ask what she means, but she changes the subject before I get the chance.

"He asked me about you, you know," she announces.

My head jerks back. "Who?"

She ignores my question, rambling on in that strange way of hers. "He wanted to know who you came from."

"What are you talking about?" I ask.

Was Maebyn always this way or have her years of isolation addled her mind?

"You see, he was afraid he'd have to kill you," she continues. "At the time, I didn't have the answers he was seeking." She moves closer as her hands grip the bars in front of me, her fevered gaze boring into mine. "But now that I've seen you, it's obvious. Those amber eyes could never be a mystery to me, not when they still haunt me every night in my dreams." Her forehead creases as confusion splashes across her face. "But lately, when I see them, they're full of anger." She tilts her head, eyeing me warily. "Will yours turn on me too, I wonder?"

"Who are you talking about? Whose eyes do I have?"

She blinks. "Your father's, of course. Who else?"

I stand there frozen, absolutely speechless. She knew my father? Since Nigel's eyes were nothing like mine, I can only assume she's speaking of my true father, the one whose identity has always been a mystery to me.

"If the other one asks me again, I'll tell him I don't know where you came from," she promises earnestly, shifting the conversation once more. "But if he were smart, he'd have killed you the moment he laid eyes on you."

A shiver coils down my spine. I glance over my shoulder at the path that brought me here, wondering if I should be running for my life.

Glancing back at the chair that faces her cell, I register that she's talking about Baylor. He's the one who asked about me, who wanted to know where I came from. My fists clench at my sides as I realize she's right. He *should* have killed me.

"Do you want to know a secret, little one?" she whispers.

I turn to find her clutching the bars, pressing the center of her face between them.

"We Gods are so secretive." She rolls her eyes. "Always hating for anyone to know our weaknesses. But I remember when the Gods were new, when we believed we were immune to weakness. That all changed the day Claudius was murdered."

My eyes widen. "You were there?"

She nods. "I'd never seen my father that furious. Of course, this was back before we began sending our children away to be raised in secret. Before we knew that would become necessary. We hadn't learned yet just how vulnerable an Heir was before they were fully ascended." Her knowing eyes cut to me conspiratorially. "But that's a different secret for a different day." She shakes her head. "When Philo killed Claudius, everything changed. My father had warned him not to touch the *almanova*. But Philo was always optimistic in those early days, never believing anything truly bad would happen. He was wrong."

"You mean when Philo used the sword to kill Claudius?" I ask. "The book was right..."

Her eyes brighten, a genuine smile warming her face. "Oh, you found my history book? Was it still hidden in the library after all this time?"

My eyebrows pull together. "*Your* history book?"

"Of course." She shrugs. "Who else could have written it? I left it so there might be some small record of the truth hidden among all the lies."

I want to ask her what other lies she's referring to, but she moves on too quickly.

"Back to my secret, little one," she continues. "The *almanova* is dangerous in the hands of both mortals and fae. It whispers to them, warps their minds and bends their will. But did you know that in the hands of God, it becomes divinely lethal?"

Chills race over my skin. "What are you saying?"

"In the hands of God, the *almanova* becomes a God Slayer."

Her words echo what was written in the book.

"That's why Baylor wants Thorne to use the sword for him," I whisper to myself. "He plans to kill you."

She nods.

"But why?" I ask. "What would he gain from that if you're already trapped down here?"

Sadness creeps into her eyes. "Once I'm gone, my Heir will ascend."

"And he plans to kill them next?"

Her gaze falls. "You'd have to ask him about his plans. They stopped making sense to me a long time ago."

"Did you know Baylor?" I ask. "Before all of this?"

She shakes her head, her eyes turning distant. "I knew *of* him, but I hadn't seen him since he was a boy. His mother once served in my court, a very long time ago."

Baylor has never mentioned his parents. I tried to ask once, but he shut me down. "What happened to her?"

"I expect he ended her life shortly after taking the throne."

"Why?" I gasp. I knew Baylor was capable of anything, but killing his own mother is a new level of evil.

"Because in this world, those who love us the most are usually the ones who destroy us. I pray he at least gave her a swift end," she says. "Not the slow death he's giving me."

"You aren't going to die," I promise. "I'll find a way to get you out of here."

"You should worry about getting yourself out." Her eyes harden. "I'm far too wise to lie to myself. I will die here in this cell. It's only a matter of when."

I yank at the bars, but they won't budge. I pull again and again until my arms are shaking and sweat is dripping from my brow.

"It won't work. I've tried many times. Only the *almanova* can cut through these bars.. Ironic that the weapon that brings my freedom also brings my death."

"No," I argue. "I can't leave you here."

"There's strength in acceptance, little one." A wistful smile pulls at her lips. "I welcome the next world. May it bring me the peace I never found in this one."

Her words echo something the Goddess of Divination said to me at the ball. *The truth cannot be fought, child. Only accepted.*

I shake my head. "No. I won't accept this." Memories flood my mind, haunting images of Leona's pale face, frozen in death. "He doesn't get to do this. Not again."

Her gaze falls to the collar around my throat. "How long have you been chained?"

"Fifteen years," I admit. "Since I was a child."

"Terrible things happen to those who meddle with fate." She reaches her frail arm through the bars. The sight of her bony wrist makes my eyes burn. Her fingers are cold as they brush across my cheek, wiping away an escaped tear. "But remember, fate can only be delayed, never changed."

Her eyes are sharper now than they were before. For a moment, I catch a glimpse of the cunning *Illusionist* she once was.

"Some Heirs were fated to rise, others to fall. But your destiny, is yours to claim, Iverson."

I open my mouth to ask her what that means, but she pulls her hand back.

"It's time for you to go now. It's dangerous to linger." Worry creeps into her eyes as she glances at the darkness behind me. "Find the sword and break the chains that bind you. Go now. And don't come back, lest you find yourself trapped down here too."

I meet her gaze, finding a hint of shame hiding there.

"Go," she says again.

Picking up her light, she prepares to extinguish it but pauses, taking one last look at me.

"You truly are very beautiful." Dampness coats her eyes as they rake over my face, scanning each small feature. "So like your father."

The flame flickers out, and her cell is cast in darkness once more. I try to think of a way to set her free. It feels important, as if that's why I was led here. But it's useless. The bars are enchanted, just like my collar. The only way to free her is to find the sword.

It's not only about my own freedom anymore.

With one last look, I turn and walk back through the cave, promising myself that I will find the *almanova* and free us both.

CHAPTER
THIRTY-FIVE

Leaves crunch beneath my feet as I make my way through the thick forest. The rust-colored silk of my gown catches on every twig and thorn, shredding the hemline to ribbons. It's not a practical outfit to wear for a stroll through the woods, but I wanted to look my best today.

For Leona.

I carry a bouquet of lilacs with me. Her favorite flowers. The same kind that Della painted for her. I thought about going to MASQ to spend the anniversary with her, but I wasn't sure I'd be welcome. Besides, she would probably prefer to suffer her grief alone. I loved Leona greatly, but it wasn't the same as how Della felt about her.

Coming out here seemed like a good way to honor the late queen. This forest is one of the few places that is evenly split between the living and the dead. The temperature is always cool here. Most of us assume that has something to do with the spirits who are pulled through these woods on their way to the veil.

But life has its place here too. A fox races across the forest floor, leaping over a tree root as he disappears into a bush. And in a nest above my head, curious eyes peer down at me over their tiny beaks as a group of baby birds wait for their mother to return with breakfast. Death may make its home in these woods, but life has not abandoned this place.

My mouth opens on a wide yawn. For the past five days, I've barely slept. I've been out at all hours, searching for the blade all over Solmare. I caught glimpses of Remy here and there. By the state of his appearance, I'd guess he's even more exhausted than I am. Between holding the perimeter and sweeping the city, the soldiers are spread razor-thin. If we don't find Darby and the blade soon, I fear the city will descend into chaos.

Baylor has given me my space all week, which has been a welcomed reprieve. I haven't seen Thorne in that time either.

It's for the best, I tell myself. *This is what I wanted.*

But is it?

I lock those thoughts away within my mental prison; unfortunately, those walls have developed several cracks of late.

But today isn't the time for any of those worries.

I come upon a small clearing in the trees, finally reaching my destination. The stone archway sits about six feet off the forest floor with a wide staircase leading up to it. However, the other side, is just a steep drop-off. Anyone who passes through this veil has no need to worry about getting hurt on the way down. Their soul will have departed their body before it even hits the ground.

The veil is a place of mystery. Vines reach from the earth and wrap around it—another example of life mingling with death. Several fractures run along the stones, betraying the age of the structure. Five thousand years ago, when the Fates first created the Gods, in order to end the Novian war, they erected these veils throughout each of the eight isles. Now every time a soul leaves its body, it's pulled through this archway and welcomed into the afterlife.

Shame fills me as I stare at the spot where Leona died exactly one year ago. Moving toward the base of the stairs, I sink to my knees and place my flowers on one of the steps. Tears slide freely down my cheeks and I make no move to wipe them away.

"You didn't deserve any of this," I whisper, praying my words are able to pass through the veil and find her soul on the other side. "I should have listened to you from the beginning, Leona. But I'm going to make him pay for what he did to you. I promise you that. Baylor will suffer for—"

My words break off as a sharp hit strikes my back, knocking the air out of me. My body tips forward and my hands shoot out to catch myself before I hit the hard staircase. I try to turn around to search for whatever struck me, but the movement causes a horrible burning sensation in my abdomen.

Looking down, I find the pointed tip of a blade protruding from my stomach. My mind tries to process what I'm seeing, but it doesn't make sense. The pain worsens as my skin begins to burn. Biting my lip against the agony, I twist my head over my shoulder and find the hilt of a dagger lodged in my lower back.

What's wrong with me? I wonder as fire spreads through my veins. *I've been stabbed before, and it's never felt like this.*

A moment later, a hard body slams into me. My head bounces against the side of the stone steps, causing the world to spin. I try to roll over, but someone grabs a fistful of my hair and pulls my head back. I scream as the awkward angle sends a shooting pain down my spine. A second later, they smash my head into the stone once more.

Pain radiates through every inch of my body. I try to move, but it's as if my limbs are being weighed down by something stronger than gravity. They no longer respond to my commands. A dark shape stands over me, and I squint, trying to make out their blurry face.

"You have no idea how long I've dreamed of this moment," a familiar voice says.

He leans down, his face finally close enough for me to make out his features.

Kaldar.

True fear sinks into me as I catch a glimpse of his murderous expression. He's going to kill me. As if he's heard my thoughts, his fingers dig into my bicep as he drags me up the stairs. My shoulder joint cries out in pain from the cruel angle.

"I always knew you were nothing but a traitorous whore," he gloats as my head bounces off each step. "Just like your mother."

My leg strikes out awkwardly as I try to kick him, but he dodges the blow with embarrassing ease.

"I knew I'd never beat you in a fair fight," he continues as the pain eats away at my sanity. "But my skill set is much different from yours. You may be strong, but you're also reckless. Which is why I was smart enough to lace the dagger."

My gaze settles on Kaldar as his words penetrate the haze. *Poison.*

"That's right, Iverson." He smiles down at me. "I'm not the fumbling idiot you think I am. I can admit my weaknesses and learn from my mistakes. I knew I'd need to plan ahead after things almost went wrong last time. I didn't expect Leona to put up such a fight. Who knew she had it in her?"

Everything goes still as his words bounce around my skull. My eyes bulge as I stare up at the man who murdered my friend.

He chuckles. "You should see your face. I keep telling you, pet, the king has trusted me with all manners of things. Even the murder of his queen."

We reach the top of the stairs, and he grabs my shoulders, pulling me to my feet. My back presses into the side of the arch, my gaze flashing toward the edge. Hot blood drips into my eyes, clouding my vision with a red tint.

"He'll kill you for this," I whisper, the words sounding slurred.

His thin lips pull into an ugly smile. "What Baylor doesn't know won't hurt him."

He raises his hands to push me over the edge, but I'm faster.

Calling on the rage building within me, I summon the last of my strength. Reaching around, I pull the dagger from my back as a scream tears from somewhere deep within. Fire burns me from the inside out as I plunge the blade straight into Kaldar's chest.

His eyes widen as he stares down at the protruding hilt.

"You—" he sputters, blood staining his lips.

The edge of the stone digs into my back as I desperately try to keep my balance. I glance at the edge again as the world continues spinning. It's in that moment that Clara's words from years ago drift back to me.

Never pass through a lonely stone archway, love. For that way lies only death with no return.

But it's too late to heed her advice.

Kaldar begins to tip forward, his body knocking into mine. I try to twist, but the ground disappears from under my feet. Suddenly, we're both tumbling toward the veil.

Toward death.

CHAPTER
THIRTY-SIX

The sun has long since set by the time I return to the palace. I bite my lip against the lingering pain in my abdomen as I hurry past the servants and guards. They're the only people left walking the halls at this hour, and I do my best to avoid bumping into any of them. They'd likely be confused if they got knocked to the ground by someone they couldn't see.

My fingers tremble as I push open the door to the back stairwell that leads to my floor. I've done a plethora of foolish things in my life. Yet, killing the king's chief adviser and hiding his body inside of a hollowed-out tree probably qualifies as the most idiotic. Despite that, I can't bring myself to regret my actions. Not after what he did to Leona.

My mind swirls with too many emotions to name as I think about how many times he'd crossed my path in the last year. Every day I was forced to interact with him, all the while having no idea he was the one who murdered the woman I loved like a mother. Baylor may have given the order, but it was Kaldar who carried it out. It was his face that she saw in her final moments.

Whatever comes from my actions today, I'll never regret ending his life. I only regret not dragging out his death and making it as painful as possible.

Finally, I reach my room and shut the door behind me, latching the lock to be sure no one else can enter before I drop my illusion.

"I've been waiting for hours."

I spin around, my hand over my heart as I spot the intruder standing in the corner. His arms are crossed over his chest as he leans against the wall next to the balcony. Despite the chill in the air, he wears no cloak tonight. Its absence provides me with a tantalizing view of the way the fabric of his shirt stretches tightly over his muscular form. It's only now that I become aware of the familiar sensation on the back of my neck, the one that always accompanies his presence.

Despite the uneasy way we left things, I can't seem to stop myself from drinking in the sight of Thorne. Here. In my room... Memories of his other visits send a wave of heat creeping up my neck. It's been a week since I've seen him, and I hate how relieved I am to find him here. Dark hair falls across his forehead, obscuring his eyes and giving him an air of danger. Several days' worth of stubble covers his cheeks, which hasn't happened since the night we met. What's kept him too busy to shave?

His full lips curve into a grin when he notices me staring. Suddenly, every candle in my room flares to life, their flames illuminating the dark chamber as they highlight the smug gleam in Thorne's eyes. I latch onto my new annoyance, preferring it to the longing I was feeling before.

I scowl. "Stop doing that."

"Doing what?" Thorne asks.

"Showing off. It's impolite."

"I noticed you were squinting, and I thought I'd make it easier for you to ogle me," he says innocently. "I believe thoughtfulness is the opposite of impolite."

My hands move to my hips as my voice rises several octaves. "I wasn't *ogling* you."

"There's that lying tongue I adore so much," he says wistfully, his lips curving at the edges.

I glare at him. "While you're at it, stop sneaking up on me too."

His eyes narrow as they rake over the cloak hiding my body from his view. "I believe you're the one who's been sneaking. What have you been up to, Angel?"

I open my mouth to tell him it's not his business, but for some reason, that's not at all what comes out.

"I killed Kaldar," I announce, my eyes bulging at my own admission.

Thorne's expression remains unchanged as he continues to lean against the wall, completely unaffected by my confession.

"In the woods," I add, as if that somehow makes it better.

He shrugs. "Okay."

"He tried to kill me first."

"You don't need to explain." He waves a hand, pushing himself away from the wall as he meanders over to my bookshelf. "If you killed him, you had a reason."

My head tilts to the side. "You're processing this information in a very calm manner. You do understand I just admitted to murdering the king's adviser, don't you?"

He picks up one of the romance novels from my shelf and flips through the pages. "The second time we met, you were hacking a man into pieces while he was trying to take a piss behind a bar."

Indignation flares through me. "I waited till after he'd finished, thank you very much."

"And then," he continues, a smirk kicking up one side of his mouth, "you used his blood to do some finger painting on the wall."

I shrug. That was the least of my crimes. "Your point?"

He turns to face me again, his expression earnest. "I'm not frightened of the violence inside of you. There's no crime you could commit that would turn me away."

My pulse stutters as my heart trips over itself at his words. The heat at my neck races to my cheeks, staining them to match my hair. No one has ever made such a vow to me...

My body is rigid as I try to hide the puzzling emotions swirling through me. I put one hand on my hip and narrow my gaze, hoping the gesture doesn't look as awkward as it feels. "Not even if I did something truly heinous?"

"No." He shakes his head, still watching me with that all seeing gaze. "But you would never do something like that. You're too good."

My nose wrinkles as genuine surprise overtakes everything else. "Me?"

He arches a brow. "Do you see anyone else here?"

"Really?" I ask, ignoring his quip. "You think I'm *good*?"

"I know you are."

My head tilts to the side. "How?"

"Because I'm not," he says as he helps himself to the chair in the corner near my bed. His tone is matter-of-fact, but there's a hint of sadness there that tells me he genuinely believes what he's saying. "The lines I'm willing to cross would shock you."

"Name one thing that would shock me," I demand, positive he won't be able to.

The sadness on his face fades, replaced with something wicked and predatory as he leans forward. "Sneaking into an innocent angel's room, hoping to get a peek at her in a nightgown."

I offer him a bland look as I pretend to be unaffected by his words. "How's that working out for you?"

His eyes fill with mirth as his lips pull into a wide smile. He leans back in the chair, making himself comfortable as he props his hands behind his head. "Yet to be seen."

Biting my lip to stop my own smile, I turn around and make for my vanity to begin cleaning myself up. I cringe at the mud staining my cloak as I slip it off and toss it onto the nearby settee.

A swift intake of breath comes from behind me, and a moment later, Thorne is standing before me. His eyes cloud with shadows as he stares at the giant bloodstain marking my dress.

"You're hurt." Every ounce of humor has vanished from his tone as his body goes rigid.

I shake my head, moving to step around him. "It's nothing."

He blocks my path, his fingers bunching into fists within his gloves. "Was it Kaldar?"

I nod, dropping my gaze to my feet.

"Let me see it," he demands, his voice unnaturally deep.

"No," I whisper. "I'd have to remove my dress to show it to you."

"I've seen your body before, Ivy. The image is seared into my brain."

My cheeks darken as my pulse skitters once more. "This is different."

Unperturbed by my refusal, he grabs hold of the soiled material and rips the silk with his bare hands. Given the circumstances, it shouldn't be attractive, but I can't deny the fact that my breath is coming faster after witnessing that.

My hands fly to my chest, ensuring the rest of my gown doesn't receive the same treatment. The fabric that once covered my stomach now hangs in tatters, exposing my entire abdomen to the night air. Shivers dance over my skin, and I tell myself it's merely from the chill.

If he notices my reaction, he doesn't show it. His gaze is locked on the ugly wound. "How long ago did this happen?"

"This morning," I tell him honestly.

His eyes darken even more as they connect with mine again. "Then why is it still bleeding?"

"Kaldar poisoned the blade," I explain. "Whatever he laced it with slowed my healing."

"Fucking bastard," he swears through gritted teeth. "It goes all the way through?"

I nod. "He snuck up on me while I was taking flowers to the veil for Leona."

His eyes widen with understanding, and perhaps a bit of sympathy. "Today is the one-year anniversary? I'm sorry, Ivy."

My mouth opens to tell him I don't deserve any apologies, but I snap it shut when I realize that's exactly the kind of behavior he recently accused me of. *Maybe he was right*, I think as Thorne disappears into the bathing chamber. *Maybe I do have a tendency to punish myself?*

He returns a minute later, carrying a small basin of water and a clean rag. He places them on the vanity before taking a seat on the stool. His hands land on my hips as he positions me in front of him to get a better view of the injury on my stomach.

"This needs to be cleaned," he explains.

Despite the gloves he wears, his hands are a brand against my skin.

"I can do this myself," I mutter, feeling like a helpless child.

"Let me." His gaze lifts, connecting with mine. "I want to do this for you."

Several moments pass as we stare at each other, both of us affected by our close proximity. Unable to do anything else, I agree to his request.

"You can take those off," I say softly, nodding to his gloves. "If you want to."

A thousand emotions pass over his face as he watches me. His throat bobs, and he swallows thickly as he removes the gloves and sets them on the vanity.

My head falls back as his bare fingers brush over my stomach, sending a thousand tiny shockwaves through each nerve in my body. His eyes are hooded as he grabs the rag and gets to work. Despite how gentle he's being, I still wince as he dabs the wet rag against my wound.

He opens his mouth to apologize as he snatches the cloth away, but I cut him off.

"It's fine," I whisper between gritted teeth. "I can take it."

With one hand, he resumes his task, while the other sits on my hip, his thumb softly brushing back and forth over my bare skin. The movement elicits more of those shockwaves, distracting me from the pain.

"You're so strong, Ivy." His breath coasts over my stomach, the heat of it sparking goosebumps. "You take so much, and yet none of it breaks you."

My chest clenches. "Some of it breaks me," I admit in a small voice.

"No, Angel." He shakes his head. "You may get knocked down sometimes, but if you were broken, you wouldn't keep trying the way you do. You wouldn't be doing everything you can to help others."

My breathing turns heavy as I process his words. The way he sees me is... staggering. The fact that he views me as something worthy of respect, even admiration. Has anyone else ever done that before? Maybe Leona and Remy. Possibly my brother too. But this is different, heavier, somehow.

After a few minutes, he finishes with my stomach and turns me to face the opposite direction as he begins the same process on the other side.

"If any of the poison is lingering on your skin, it will only delay your healing more." His voice is rougher than I've heard it before.

"I know."

"Some of these bruises are pretty bad," he says as his fingers brush softly over my back, eliciting a mix of desire and pain.

"I fell."

"Through the veil?" he exclaims, turning me again to get a glimpse of my face.

"I'd be dead if that were the case," I remind him. "Kaldar tried to drag me through with him, but I twisted and went over the side instead. I ended up laying on the forest floor for most of the day, completely paralyzed from the poison."

I don't mention how the wound burned for hours before the pain finally began to fade. I doubt he'd take kindly to that knowledge.

"Gods," he breathes, squeezing his eyes shut. "You're going to give me a heart-attack someday."

I roll my eyes, not sure that's even possible for a God. When the wound is finally cleaned, I feel the soft press of his lips against my lower back. I shudder in his grasp, unsure if I want to move away or lean into his touch. Instead of doing either, I turn around to face him.

Thorne stares up at me, his eyes shifting with a myriad of emotions. There's lust there, but also so much more.

"Can I stay?" he asks softly.

My heart stutters.

"Just to hold you?" he explains quickly, a hint of vulnerability creeping into his tone. "Only until you fall asleep. Then I'll go."

From the sound of it, I don't know if he's trying to convince me or himself. Still, I find myself nodding at his request. His eyes go round as his mouth falls open, as if he truly didn't expect me to agree. My gaze flits to the door. Maybe I shouldn't have... I know it's not smart, but at this moment, I'm not sure I care.

Stepping into the bathroom, I shut the door behind me before I remove my tattered dress. Quickly going about the business of rinsing off, I wash away the dirt and blood that covered my body. My hands tremble as I think about who's waiting for me in my room.

The idea of spending the night with Thorne is far more tempting than it should be. I open the cabinet that houses my sleepwear and find myself selecting a wine-colored nightgown. The thin material is practically sheer, hiding little of my body underneath. My palms sweat as I stare at the result in the mirror, searching for the boldness that usually comes naturally to me.

Forcing my feet toward the door, I crack it open slightly and peek through the gap. Thorne stands with his back to me, and my mouth falls open at the sight of so much bare skin. His shirt lies discarded on the nearby chair, but his pants remain on, hanging low from his hips. My eyes are immediately drawn to the dark ink splayed across his shoulder blades, the lines forming the shape of wings. My eyebrows shoot up as I realize this is where he hides them when they aren't being used.

My heart cracks as I notice the slightly raised scars that linger around the top of the tattoos. It takes a lot to leave a mark on an immortal. Hatred boils within my veins, heating my skin as I think about how I'd punish the men who did this to him. They'd beg for death before I was through with them.

The savagery raging inside of me cools slightly as I notice the hunched set to his shoulders as he stares at my bed. He almost appears unsure of himself. Insecure...

Sleeping next to someone is something he's probably never had the opportunity to do. It would be too dangerous since his skin could accidentally brush against theirs. The idea of him lying in bed next to some hypothetical person has my face scrunching up with a mix of jealousy and disgust. Gods, I need to get a hold of my emotions tonight...

He turns at the sound of my approach, his brows shooting up as his gaze crawls over my body, lingering in all the most interesting places. My cheeks turn pink as my nightgown has its intended effect.

"You're the most beautiful thing I've ever seen," he breathes.

His words make me strangely shy. He doesn't seem to be the kind of man who hands out compliments like that often, so receiving them from him feels important. Special.

And that makes me so deeply nervous. The last time I believed someone thought I was special, I was wrong. And I wasn't the only one who paid the price for my poor judgment.

I lock those worries behind the bars of my mental prison. Scurrying over to the other side of the bed, I climb in and pull the blankets up to my chin. After a few moments, he follows my lead and slips into the other side. Several minutes pass as we both remain silent, neither of us touching each other as we stare up at the ceiling. Taking a deep breath, I summon the courage to ask the question that has been weighing heavily on my mind all week.

"Why did you ask for my freedom?"

The bed shifts as he tenses next to me.

"I'm not trying to argue," I clarify quickly. "I genuinely want to know why you chose that when you could have asked Baylor for anything."

It's quiet for a few moments before he responds, his voice brimming with soft sincerity. "Because I wish someone had stepped in to help my mother."

The simple answer makes my heart ache for him. The guilt he still carries over what happened to her is palpable.

"What was she like?" I ask quietly, unsure if this is a subject he feels comfortable discussing.

He remains silent, and for a moment, I think he won't answer me, but then he takes a deep breath and speaks.

"When she was herself, she was warm. Funny." I can hear the smile in his voice, but it fades with his next words. "But once the *enchanter* started giving her his potions, she changed. She became prone to these sudden changes in mood. She'd swing from one emotion to the next, unable to calm herself down. It was like that for a long time before everything finally ended."

"What happened to the *enchanter* after you got away?" I ask.

"He serves the God of Life now."

"Leland?" I gasp, rolling over to face him as I recall the adviser who accompanied Foley to the ball. "It was him?"

He nods, his jaw tight. "He's worked in many courts over the years, but right now, he serves Eyrkan."

I wonder if the God of Life knows the history of the man he's employing. Perhaps that's where the tension between Foley and Thorne stems from?

We fall silent in the wake of the tense conversation, both of us lost in our thoughts. I roll onto my back again as my mind returns to what I learned from Maebyn. Does Thorne know who Baylor is going to ask him to kill?

"Can I ask you a hypothetical question?"

"Alright."

I take a deep breath. "What would someone gain from killing a God?"

He turns his head on the pillow, raising a brow at me. "Should I be nervous about this line of questioning?"

I roll my eyes. "Hypothetical, remember?"

"Of course." He grins as he rolls onto his side. "*Hypothetically*... I'm guessing this person already has the means with which to kill said God?"

"Let's say for argument's sake they do," I say, turning to face him. My pulse quickens as I notice the limited number of inches separating our faces.

"I suppose there are many ways someone could benefit from the death of a God," he muses. "But if a person were determined enough, there is a way they could take the God's place."

"What?" I ask as a cold chill creeps over my entire body, causing me to pull the blankets closer. "You mean they could become a God?"

"It's possible." He nods, adjusting his position to narrow the gap between us. "Very few know this, but when a God dies, their Heir doesn't fully ascend right away. The process can take weeks or even months. And in that time, the Heir is incredibly vulnerable. Their body and powers are growing stronger, but they can often be unpredictable. If, hypothetically, someone were to kill an Heir during their ascension, they could claim the Heir's destiny as their own."

My mind buzzes as his words spark a myriad of thoughts. "That's..."

"Terrifying?" He raises a brow.

"And more." I shudder. "Has it happened before?"

"Only once that I know of," he says as his leg brushes against mine. "I was told it was only a few centuries after the Gods first came to power. Supposedly, the one who intervened and killed the Heir was severely punished by the Fates."

"*Some Heirs were fated to rise, others to fall,*" I murmur, repeating Maebyn's words.

"Hmm?" he asks as his hand slips under my nightgown to rest against the bare skin of my back.

"Nothing," I whisper as my body erupts in shivers. "If the Fates killed that person, then so much for your theory that they appreciate a little defiance."

"Maybe it's a case-by-case basis," he says softly as he pulls me closer, curling me into his body as he slides one of his legs between mine. "We never truly know what the Fates have planned for us. There could come a day when they want a new bloodline to take over one of the Isles."

"I suppose," I say, thinking of Foley. Would the Fates actually punish someone for saving the world from the likes of him?

His face nuzzles into the crook of my neck, avoiding my collar as he inhales my scent. I lift a hand, brushing my fingers through the soft strands of his dark hair, enjoying the sigh of contentment that escapes him.

"So, if I was wanting to replace a God," I say, turning the conversation back to my original question. "I'd have to know the identity of their Heir?"

"Correct," he murmurs. "Otherwise, you'd risk the Heir completing their ascension before you ever found them. Most Gods are extremely skilled at hiding their children..." His words trail off for a moment as his mouth parts on a wide yawn. "It would take years of searching to even find a single lead."

Which means that if Baylor is finally ready to end Maebyn's life, he already knows where her Heir is hiding. With that terrifying thought, my eyes drift shut as I wrap my arms tightly around Thorne. No matter what comes later, here in this moment I feel safe.

CHAPTER
THIRTY-SEVEN

I find myself standing outside the doors of the royal temple with no idea how I got here. My brows pinch as I glance down at myself, realizing I'm wearing an extremely large white gown with a full skirt made of tulle. The style reminds me of the gowns the other ladies wear at court.

"There you are." Bellamy's voice steals my attention. He's gliding toward me, his face pinched with worry. "I was afraid you were going to be late."

Confusion ripples through me. "Late for what?"

The corners of his eyes crinkle with mirth.

"Very funny, Ivy." He grabs my arm and pulls it through his, leading us toward the double doors. "Come. We don't want to keep them all waiting."

I start to ask who he's referring to, but suddenly the doors swing open. Hundreds of people rise from the pews and turn to face us. I recognize most of them as prominent high fae, many of them nobles. Every single eye is focused completely on me as my brother pulls me down the long aisle.

"What's going on, Bel?" I ask, my voice too high. "What are we doing here?"

"See for yourself." He points toward the end of the altar where a man waits alone.

Baylor.

His eyes shine with victory as he tracks my movements, marking each step that brings me closer to him.

Oh Gods... This is a wedding. Our wedding.

No. My heart races in my chest as my vision goes blurry. I was supposed to have more time. I was supposed to find a way out. It's too soon. I'm not ready.

I try to shake my head, but for some reason, I can't turn away from Baylor. Words travel up my throat, halting on my tongue as I'm unable to speak them.

This isn't right. I don't want to be here.

Panic curls around me as I try to scream, but my mouth won't open. I can't move my face at all. It's locked in a serene expression. My lips are curved into a pleasant smile, my eyes radiating false joy. Inside, I scream for my body to respond to my commands, but all I'm able to do is watch as the distance between myself and the king gets smaller.

I'm nothing but a puppet, unable to pull my own strings.

When we're within a few feet of the altar, Baylor reaches out and takes my hand from my brother. Bellamy disappears into the crowd as the king leads me up the steps and places us directly before the temple priest.

"You look lovely," he whispers.

My cheeks stain with a blush. "As do you."

Stop! I don't want this. I don't want any of this! Doesn't anyone care?

"Iverson Pomeroy, do you take this man to be your husband for the rest of your days. Do you promise under the Fates to be loyal and obedient to him in all things?"

I'm screaming at myself to say no, but instead I open my mouth and say, "I do."

Please, I beg the Fates. Please intervene. Don't abandon me to this fate.

Baylor's voice is distant as he speaks his own vows. My brain is unable to latch onto any of his words except the final two.

"I do."

My stomach drops.

"Then, with the power vested in me by the holy sisters, I now pronounce you husband and wife, bound together for all eternity. My King, you may now kiss your bride."

The crowd erupts into cheers as Baylor's mouth lowers to mine. Acid burns in my stomach at the taste of him on my tongue. The collar tightens, squeezing my throat in its iron grasp.

"Now you're mine," *Baylor whispers, his eyes feverish.* "Forever."

I SIT UP, gasping as I clutch my throat.

The sheets are in disarray, completely tangled with my legs. I kick them away, needing to escape the sensation of being trapped. Usually, my nightmares are memories. This was the first time since I was a child that I've dreamed of something that hasn't actually happened to me.

But hasn't it? Haven't I lived that way every day for the past year?

As my pulse slows, I realize even though the dream may not have been real, the emotions were. Everything in that dream was a mirror of my situation here. My gaze moves to the other side of the bed, confirming what I already know.

I'm alone.

Thorne must have left at some point in the night. Not wanting to confront the loneliness blooming in my belly, I force myself out of the bed. My feet pad across the floor, and I pull back the curtains to find that the sun has barely woken up. I quickly hurry through the process of dressing myself, not wanting to wait for Alva or Morwen to arrive in a few hours. I'll be gone by then.

I have no desire to be alone today. Unfortunately, Della likely hasn't forgiven me for what I said the last time we spoke. And Remy is off searching for the *almanova*, which is what I *should* be doing. The thought of ripping through people's homes today sounds even worse than sitting alone in my room.

There's always Darrow?

I shudder. Willingly spending time with Darrow would truly be hitting a new low.

With nowhere to go and no friends to visit, I find myself roaming the halls, something I haven't done since childhood. Servants and courtiers give me respectful glances and stilted bows as we cross paths. All of them are likely trying to make up for their previous behavior now that I'm going to be the new queen.

Nausea twists my insides as thoughts of the dream return. Perhaps that's why I find myself standing in front of Baylor's office. With no destination in mind, my feet must have carried me to the source of my frustration.

Huxley and Doral both bend at the waist as they exchange nervous glances.

"The king is in a meeting right now, Lady Iverson." Huxley announces. "Though, I'm sure you'd be most welcome to return later."

I start to tell him it's alright, but I'm cut off as the door opens, and Bridgid rushes into the hall. Huxley's cheeks turn pink, and I suddenly understand the guard's reactions to my arrival. I imagine covering up your boss's affair is incredibly stressful. Not that they need to bother.

Bridgid halts in her tracks when she notices me, her damp eyes brimming with accusation.

"You must be pleased with yourself," she spits. "You got everything you wanted."

A feeling I never thought I'd associate with Bridgid settles in the pit of my stomach. Pity. Overnight, she went from having everything she'd ever wanted, to suddenly being shunned by her entire community. It doesn't matter that much of her pain was brought on by herself. In some ways, she's also a victim of Baylor's cruelty.

"I didn't want any of this," I tell her honestly.

She sneers, pushing past me to storm down the hall. Some of the weight that's been sitting on my shoulders all morning lessens. It's strangely invigorating to tell the truth instead of reciting whatever lie will produce the best outcome.

"My lady?" Huxley draws my attention. "Did you still want to see the king?"

Do I?

Usually, stepping into this room sends a wave of nervous energy barreling through me, but it's strangely absent today. Being here almost feels like a continuation of my dream, as if I'm not truly here, so what I say or do doesn't matter.

I nod and Doral opens the door, announcing my arrival. "Lady Iverson, Your Majesty."

As I walk into the room, I find Baylor standing beside his desk, flipping through an obnoxiously large pile of folders.

"Have you seen Kaldar?" he demands, not bothering to glance up from his task.

His demeanor is frantic, and based on the unbrushed state of his hair, I'd guess he's had quite the morning, thanks to the absence of his adviser.

"Not today," I tell him honestly.

He doesn't question my vague answer as he flips open one of the folders and scans its contents before chucking it aside with more force than was necessary.

"He picked a pretty fucking selfish time to disappear," he complains. "That whole family has been causing me too many problems of late."

Instead of pushing down my annoyance as I normally would, I roll my eyes, not caring if he notices my disrespect.

He points to the pile that reaches his chin. "It's his responsibility to organize this mess and summarize the important details. But now he's up and disappeared, leaving me to sort through all of this."

I help myself to one of his plush chairs as he continues ranting. Usually, I would wait for him to invite me to sit, but I don't give a fuck about ceremony or decorum today.

"As if I don't have enough on my plate with all the Angel of

Mercy fanfare," he continues. "Not to mention that business with the *almanova*. Which, by the way, I'm very disappointed in your friend Remard. This should have been handled already. I need this fucking alliance settled."

"Then maybe you should deal with it yourself," I point out.

He chuckles, grabbing another folder. "Very funny."

"I'm not joking."

He goes quiet as my words register. Glancing up from his papers, he watches me carefully. "Everything alright, pet?"

I take a deep breath, steadying myself. "Do you know what yesterday was?"

"No." He shrugs. "But you can send my apologies if we missed some event."

"It was the one-year anniversary of your wife's death."

His body goes completely still. "Why are you bringing that up?"

The flippancy in his tone grates against my skin, opening all my barely healed wounds.

"Because I cared about her," I tell him, my voice thick with emotion as I stand up. "You *knew* I cared about her."

He puts his folder down, stepping around the desk to move closer to me. "Iverson, whatever has you so ups—"

"What will you tell the God of Death?" I cut him off as I take a step back, not wanting him anywhere near me.

His eyes narrow into slits. "Don't mention that man to me."

His tone warns of danger ahead, but for once, I continue down my path with no care for the consequences.

"Will you agree to his terms?" I ask. "Will you remove the collar?"

"I'll do whatever I think is best," he says evenly.

A humorless laugh bubbles out of me. That response is so *Baylor*. "Were you ever planning to remove it?"

He cocks his head, observing me. "What has gotten into you, Iverson?"

My eyes roll again, this time catching his notice. "Answer the question, Baylor."

He bristles at the disrespect in my tone, his fists balling at his sides. "If I did that, how would I keep you safe?"

"Don't you mean caged?"

"That's not—"

I raise my voice as I speak over him, not wanting to listen to his grating tone. "Did you honestly believe nothing would change between us after what you did?"

"What happened with Bridgid was a mista—"

"I'm not talking about poor Bridgid! I couldn't give a single fuck who you take to your bed." His eyes flare with anger, but I don't care. I take a step closer, raising an accusatory finger at him. "I'm talking about what you did to Leona."

He goes still. "What do you want me to say?"

"The truth. Try it, Baylor. It might even feel good."

A dark chuckle flits through my mind. I only just started embracing honesty, and I'm already holding it over people's heads.

"You want the truth?" he asks. "Leona was standing in my way, so I had her removed. There. Are you happy?"

A burning rage tears through me, sending sweat beading down my skin. "And what will you do to me? Will you kill me too if I get in your way?"

"Never." He shakes his head, lifting his hands in a placating gesture as he tries to come closer. "You're different, pet."

"Don't call me that!" I scream.

He stops mid-step, his face going white.

"The only difference between me and Leona is that I haven't outlived my usefulness yet," I seethe. "Once I do, you'll order someone to kill me the same way you ordered Kaldar to kill her."

Questions enter his gaze. He's probably assigning new meaning to his advisers sudden absence.

"You don't believe any of this," he says gently, attempting to pacify me. "You've been through a lot in the past few days."

I shake my head. "I mean every word. I don't love you, Baylor," I announce, giving life to a truth that's been trapped on my tongue for a year. "I never truly did."

Navy eyes flash crimson. His temper lashes out swiftly as he strikes my face with the back of his hand. My skin stings as the taste of blood fills my mouth.

Baylor's eyes instantly fill with regret, shifting back to their natural blue shade. "Iverson, I didn't—"

I spit at him, leaving a red stain on his pristine white shirt. A deranged smile pulls at my lips as he begins to shake with rage. Before he can react, the door opens again.

My gaze flits to the new arrival, thinking it's Doral or Huxley, but my brows pinch together as I see the last person I was expecting.

Worry seeps through my anger, gnawing at me as I get a good look at Remy. He's far thinner than the last time I saw him, his armor now swallowing his sickly frame. The dark circles under his eyes are stark against his pale face.

"Remy—" I start to ask if he's alright, but he cuts me off.

"I apologize for the interruption, Your Majesty," he says, his tone urgent. "But this couldn't wait."

Baylor waves his hand, his body still tense with unspent anger as he keeps his eyes on me. "Get on with it."

"I have learned the identity of the Angel of Mercy," Remy announces.

Baylor's head snaps toward the captain. Every ounce of heat abandons my body at once, leaving me with nothing but ice in my veins.

"Give me their name," Baylor sputters. His claws are already extending as his fury finds a new target. "Tell me who it is!"

Remy's gaze flits to mine, and I spot a familiar hostility there. The same one I saw in Grell Darby. His attention drops to my collar as a cruel smile overtakes his face.

"Iverson Pomeroy."

CHAPTER
THIRTY-EIGHT

Silence hangs in the air in the wake of Remy's accusation. I don't move. I don't even breathe. All I can do is stare into the face of the man I love like a father, begging the Fates to let me wake up from this nightmare.

Remy belongs to the whisperer now.

When did it happen? I rack my brain, trying to remember the last time we spoke? He's been so busy searching for the sword, I don't think I've truly spoken to him since the night of the ball.

The night my father was murdered.

No. No, that couldn't have been Remy. Memories of him glaring at my father that night make their way to the front of my mind, forcing me to see what I should have noticed then. He wasn't himself. I assumed it was because he was exhausted, but I was wrong. The *almanova* had already latched onto him.

Remy is one of the Forsaken.

Baylor's hand snaps out, snagging my wrist in a tight grip. His claws prick against my skin in warning. "Have you any proof of this claim, Captain?"

Remy nods. "There are several witnesses who can place her at each crime scene."

I'd bet my life those *witnesses* are all Forsaken.

"But what made me suspect her in the first place is the fact that I saw her exiting Lord Pomeroy's room around the time of his murder," Remy adds. "And she had blood on her clothes, Your Majesty."

My fists clench at my sides as I pull against Baylor's hold. "That's a lie."

"Why did you wait until now to bring me these concerns?"

Remy lowers his gaze, his features twisting with false sorrow. "Forgive me, my king. I was conflicted about turning in someone who's been like a daughter to me."

I bark out a laugh.

"Do you deny these claims?" Baylor raises a brow.

"Yes!" I insist. "I didn't kill my father."

"And what of the others?" He tilts his head. "You didn't kill those people in the city, did you, pet?"

I open my mouth to deny it, but I can't bring myself to lie. Not anymore. Still, there's no way I'm admitting to more than I have to.

"My hands may be filthy with blood," I admit, hating how true the statement is. "But none of it belongs to Nigel Pomeroy. I was in my room that whole night."

"If only someone could verify your whereabouts." Baylor sighs dramatically. "Wasn't that the night you refused to come to my chambers?" He tsks as his fingers squeeze my wrist tighter and his claws break the skin. "What a pity. If you'd simply done as I asked, I could have been your alibi."

"You know I didn't do this," I tell him, ignoring the pain.

"I don't know any such thing." A vicious smile breaks across his face. He's enjoying his revenge after our earlier conversation. "Captain, it appears we'll need to keep my dear fiancée under supervision until we can get to the bottom of these matters. Take her to her chambers and station a guard outside her door. And tell no one of her involvement in these crimes."

Panic sets in. Pulling on my power, I begin to wrap myself in an illusion, but Baylor yanks on my arm. He pulls me closer as his hand darts out to grip my collar, his thumb pressing into the rubies.

"No so fast, pet," he orders. "Drop the illusion."

I comply immediately, unable to deny any order given while his hand is touching the collar.

"That's better," he croons. "I prefer you obedient. Now, you're going to be good and let Captain Remard escort you to your chambers. You will remain there until I come get you. Tell me you understand, Iverson."

The order settles over my skin, leaving it tight and itchy.

"I understand," I whisper.

"Good." He moves to hand me to Remy but stops at the last second. "One more thing. You need to decide how you want the rest of your life to play out. We can continue on in the way we've always done, or I can take away your illusion of free will and show you just how much of a prisoner you really are. The decision is yours, but you'd better make it quick, pet. You know I can't stay away from you for long."

Finished with his threats, he allows Remy to drag me out of the study. The guards give us curious glances as we pass but say nothing. Reality mirrors my dream as Remy leads me through the halls. Inside, I scream at myself to fight back, but my body refuses, unable to disobey Baylor's order.

"When did the *whisperer* claim you?" I demand.

He ignores my question.

"I know you're still in there, Remy. You can fight this."

He gives me a cold glare. "I stopped fighting it the moment I murdered your father."

"You killed my father because you still care about me," I insist. "I know you do."

He shakes his head. "You're wrong."

"You did it to protect me."

He doesn't answer.

"I know somewhere deep down you still want to help me, Remy. You have to fight."

He opens the door to my room, tossing me inside.

"I'm done fighting. *He's* coming for you, Ivy. When you hear the whispers, you'll know he's close."

He slams the door, leaving me to face my fate alone.

CHAPTER

THIRTY-NINE

The events of the past twenty-four hours weigh heavily on my shoulders as I pace across the rug in my room. I rack my brain, trying to think of a plan that would get me out of this mess but coming up empty. With the collar forcing me to obey Baylor's order, I'm trapped here.

Without warning, the door swings open, and my lady's maids enter the room.

"Thank the Fates," I breathe, grateful to see friendly faces. "You have to help me. Baylor has me trapped here."

A warm smile breaks across Alva's heart-shaped face. Her blonde hair is pulled back today, showing off her round ears. "The king was the one who sent us here."

Confusion wrinkles my forehead. "Sent you here?"

"We're supposed to help you get dressed," Morwen answers as she opens the armoire and digs through my gowns.

I shake my head, unable to keep up with the conversation. "Dressed for what?"

"For the wedding, of course!" Alva beams, her eyes dipping to my collar momentarily.

Warning bells blare through my mind.

"Just as I thought," Morwen complains as she slams the wardrobe shut. "There's nothing here that'll work, but I think I know where I can find something that will. I'll be right back."

She scurries to the door and disappears into the hall.

Swallowing thickly, I turn to Alva and ask the question I fear I already know the answer to. "Whose wedding am I getting ready for?"

"Yours, silly." She grabs my shoulders, pushing me toward the vanity. "The king announced that you two will be married today."

My legs give out, and I all but fall into the chair. The mortal maid begins brushing through my hair, combing out the thick waves.

"Please Alva," I beg her, my eyes filling with tears as I catch her gaze through the mirror. "I can't marry him. You have to help me get out of here."

Her head tilts to the side, a confused smile on her face. "Why would I do that?"

My brow furrows. "Because I'm your friend?"

She laughs. "Oh, Ivy, you're nothing but a rat masquerading as a queen."

The words hit me with so much force I nearly slide out of the chair.

"Besides," she continues, "this is exactly where *he* wants you."

I swallow, my mouth suddenly dry. "*He?*"

"The one who whispers."

I squeeze my eyes shut as she continues styling my hair. *No*, I beg the Fates. *Not Alva too. Not after I already lost Remy.*

The door slams behind Morwen as she rushes back in, her arms overflowing with a bundle of white fabric.

"I found it," she announces, a wide grin on her face.

Alva claps, bouncing up and down excitedly. "Let's see it!"

Once they've unraveled the swath of fabric, I realize it's a dress that's eerily similar to the one I wore in my nightmare.

"Where did it come from?" Alva asks.

"I remember Tess down in the kitchens bragging about how she swiped it from the late queen's closet after she died."

My hands tremble. "This was Leona's?"

"And now it's yours."

I shake my head, desperate to wake up from this nightmare.

"Morwen," I keep my voice low as I pull her a few feet away. "You have to help me. I need to escape before the ceremony."

Her eyes narrow. "But this is where he wants you to be. The one who whispers is coming for you tonight."

My stomach drops. *No. Not Morwen too.*

How many does he have? Who all has been warped by the sword? Thorne's face flashes through my mind, and a sharp bolt of fear pierces my heart. Where is he? What if he's not safe? What if the Forsaken find him and force him to touch the almanova?

Stop.

Thorne is a God. He can take care of himself. But right now, I need to focus on saving myself.

"Exactly," Alva pipes in. "How would he find you if you weren't where you're supposed to be? You're being so silly today, Ivy."

I try to smile. "Must be the nerves."

"Cold feet," she agrees. "My sister had those."

My heart constricts. She's exactly like herself right now.

"What does the one who whispers want from me?"

"That collar doesn't belong to you," Morwen answers. "It's time for you to give it back."

Usually, I would be all for that plan, but somehow I don't think *he* intends to simply remove it. I have a sinking suspicion he plans to take my head along with the collar.

"Come." Alva pulls me back to the vanity. "Let's get you dressed. You have to look beautiful for your wedding."

With nothing else to do, I let them carry on with their task, even though I have no intention of getting married. No matter what, neither Baylor nor the *almanova* are taking me tonight.

Footsteps approach from the hallway, alerting me that the time for my escape has come. My back is already pressed into the wall as I wait next to the door. I've spent the morning mentally going through my options, searching for any loophole in Baylor's commands.

You will remain there until I come get you.

Which means that as soon as he steps into this room, the command should lift, and I'll be able to escape. Unless he gets his hands on my collar again and gives me a new order... But without being able to see me, that's not going to be easy for him. When we were in his study, he commanded me to drop the illusion. However, he didn't specify that I wasn't allowed to create another one. Which is exactly what I've done.

My eyes are glued to the brass handle as it turns, and the door swings open, revealing Baylor on the other side. He stays where he is, not entering the room.

"Hello, pet. Have you had time to think over your options?"

His words are directed at Rose, who's currently sitting on the edge of the bed with her back to the door. In this moment, I've never been more sure of my decision to keep my *eidolon* a secret. A shudder passes over me as I remember all of the times I almost told Remy. My heart aches at the thought of my mentor, but I push the emotion aside. Sadness has no place here. Only determination.

"I have," she says softly, an exact replica of my own voice.

A few red strands have escaped her elaborate updo, dropping down the back of her gown like blood stains over snow. Worry blooms in my stomach as I pray the imagery doesn't foreshadow what's to come.

As soon as Alva and Morwen left, I created Rose to be the perfect blushing bride they'd polished me into. With their hard work preserved onto my likeness, I slipped out of the tent of white lace and tulle, choosing a pair of dark pants and a fitted black tunic. Removing the pins from my hair took at least ten minutes, but it's now hanging down my back in a practical braid. Before the king arrived, I strapped every blade in my collection to my body, knowing I might need them all before the day is through. Though I did spare one for Rose, tucking it into her garter for safekeeping.

"Well," Baylor replies, "what have you decided?"

Rising from the bed, she turns to face him with her eyes cast down in a submissive gesture.

"I will marry you willingly," she says. "And things will return to how they have always been."

The corner of his mouth lifts. "I'm glad to hear that, pet."

My pulse hastens as Baylor lifts his foot and steps over the threshold. I hold back a sigh of relief as I feel his command release me.

Baylor steps deeper into the room, and I shoot forward, ready to be free of this place. My path is blocked when Doral and Huxley enter behind him. I push myself flat against the wall again, my heart racing at the near collision. Bumping into them would have given away my true position and ruined the entire plan.

Their large frames linger in my path. Doral is stern, but Huxley shifts uncomfortably as he watches Rose for any signs that she might attack. He doesn't appear happy about the prospect of subduing her. Is it because he's afraid of me? Or is it possible the idea of having to harm me doesn't sit right with him?

I save those thoughts for later. There's no room for any of that now. All my focus needs to be reserved for my escape. With my back wedged against the wall, I carefully slide toward the doorway. From the corner of my eye, I see Baylor approaching my *eidolon*.

"You've made the right choice, pet." He grabs her shoulders and pulls her into an embrace. "You won't regret this."

"I know," she whispers.

Finally, he steps back and loops her arm in his. "Come. The guests are already arriving at the temple."

As Baylor leads her to the door, Doral and Huxley finally step aside, allowing them to pass through. As soon as they've crossed over the threshold, I make my move. Darting between the couple and the guards, I finally slip into the hall.

Relief floods through me as Baylor leads Rose away, both guards trailing behind them. Not wasting any time, I hurry toward the servants' stairwell at the end of the hall. My time is limited. I have no idea how long I will be able to hold my illusion. I've never sent Rose further than Baylor's room before.

As the distance between us expands, I sense my connection to her growing thin. The moment she disappears, Baylor will discover that I've escaped. Then it will only be a matter of time before he begins tracking me through the collar.

And likely choking me as well.

I push that worry aside. Dwelling on my fear will only slow me down. Besides, there's nothing I can do to stop the inevitable pain he will inflict. However, if I hurry there may be something I can do to prevent him from tracking me.

If the Fates are on my side, Darrow will still be at MASQ. For an *enchanter*, creating a ward to hide my location should be simple. Even if the king sends guards to search the premises, I can hide in the crawl space under Della's office. I discovered the secret room years ago when I used to accompany Leona on her visits to MASQ. Back then, the idea of stepping foot down there was terrifying, reminding me too much of the memories I tried to bury. But now it may be my saving grace.

When I come to the bottom of the stairs, I dash into the kitchen. Thankfully, the noise and bustle from the servants chopping vegetables and boiling water is enough to mask my rushed steps. The back exit is within sight, but halfway there a large man enters my path, nearly whacking me in the head with a tray of golden-brown pastries. Spinning around to avoid him, my elbow accidentally tips over a bag from one of the nearby shelves. A dozen potatoes spill out, falling to the ground and rolling across the floor.

"Ugh, look at the mess you made, Jon," an elderly mortal woman complains. "I've told you before to be more careful."

"I didn't even touch it!" the man insists as I navigate the minefield of fallen vegetables, careful not to trip.

Finally, I make it to the door and sprint outside. The temple is on the northern side of the palace, I head for the southern gate that will bring me closer to MASQ. Baylor's voice echoes distantly in the back of my mind, filtering through my connection to Rose.

"You're quiet, pet," he whispers as they stand outside the golden doors. "Not regretting your choice, are you?"

The silence stretches a beat too long before she responds. "Just nervous."

Her voice is almost monotone, lacking any emotion or conviction.

The faster I race through the gardens, the more frayed our connection becomes. A pounding ache begins in my temples, warning me I need to cut her loose soon.

"I'll be at the end of the aisle," he tells her, his eyes cold. "Don't keep me waiting."

A tingle along the back of my neck has my eyes lifting to the sky. In the distance, black wings flap overhead as Thorne rushes toward me. Tears well in my eyes at the sight of him and my chest swells with gratitude. He came. He found me.

Blood drips from my nose, and I know I can't hold on to the connection much longer. Any moment now, Rose is going to disappear before their eyes. Hopefully, they mistake her vanishing for simply becoming invisible. I'd rather they curse me for being a *wraith* than suspect I might have fooled them with an *eidolon*.

I grit my teeth as I'm forced to give up my invisibility, no longer having the strength to hold both illusions. My skin stretches thin and I stumble to the ground. Thorne is close enough now that I can see the concern on his face. But even with him flying us to MASQ, there won't be enough time before Baylor begins tracking me.

Rose finally makes it to the altar, coming to stand beside the king, and a reckless plan forms in my mind. At that same moment, Thornes arms sweep me off the ground, and we leap into the air. I'm vaguely aware of guards shouting, but in my mind, the priest is asking Rose to repeat after him. The connection ripples, seconds away from giving out. Mustering the last of my strength, I know what I have to do.

Rose's hand wraps around the cool metal blade at her thigh as she pulls it free. Baylor doesn't even have time to flinch before she drives it into his eye. Shock erupts through the temple as the king stumbles back and drops to his knees.

His scream is the last thing I hear as the connection fades and Rose disappears.

"Talk to me, Angel," Thorne's voice is desperate. "Tell me what's wrong."

"Get me to Della," I beg him, too weak to lift my head from his shoulder.

His arms tighten around me, and my eyes drift shut as we soar through the skies.

CHAPTER FORTY

The sound of shouting filters through the edges of my consciousness, followed by a loud banging.

"Open this door or I'll kick it down!"

The growled threat comes from somewhere nearby, but the words mean nothing to me. My mind is a distant haze. The desire to open my eyes is strong, but my body is far too weak to comply. Muffled noises reach my ears, metallic clicks followed by a scraping sound.

"Pipe down, you—" The woman's words end on a gasp. Where she came from, I have no idea. When she speaks again, her tone is far more serious. "Bring her inside. Now."

"What's happened to her?" a new voice asks, another male.

"I don't know. I found her running for her life outside the palace. By that point, she was already bleeding from her eyes and nose."

"Fuck," the woman curses, her cool fingers brushing against my forehead. "She pushed herself too far, and now she's depleted. Always so reckless."

"Can you fix it?"

That voice... It stirs a comforting warmth in my chest. I latch onto the sensation, hoping it will lead me out of this haze. My mind clears slightly, allowing the world to press in on me. Dull pain radiates through every inch of my body. Each breath I take feels heavy and hard won. Am I dying? I try to pry my eyes open, but they don't respond, leaving me trapped in darkness.

At least I'm not alone, I remind myself as I become aware of the strong arms wrapped around me, cradling me against a hard chest.

Thorne, I realize. *I think his name is Thorne.*

"Place her on the table, and open her mouth," the other man orders.

A whimper climbs up my throat as Thorne's body disappears, replaced by a cold surface.

"I'm right here, Angel." His touch finds me once more, his fingers gently brushing over my face.

I focus on the feeling of his skin against mine, praying he doesn't stop. Without this connection, I fear I'll drift into the ether and slip away.

"I'm not leaving you," he whispers, his warm breath tickling my cheek.

"Found it!" The other man returns as his footsteps race toward us. "I knew I had a bottle stashed here."

"Hold her mouth open," the female voice orders sharply. "This won't taste pleasant, but she needs to drink all of it."

Strong hands grip my chin, forcing my lips to part. I twist against his hold as a cold bottle touches my lips and a bitter liquid hits my tongue. My body jerks as I try to cough it up.

"Easy." Thorne's thumb gently brushes over my jaw. "This is going to make it better, I promise. Just keep drinking for me."

I do as he asks, hating each disgusting gulp. Finally, when I'm sure I'm going to vomit, the bottle disappears. Soothing fingers brush over my hair, gently pushing the wayward strands away from my sweaty forehead. It feels nice.

"You're touching her," the other man says. There's a strange tone in his voice as he speaks the words, almost as if he's awed by this fact.

The fingers go still against my skin. "I am."

"She's your—"

His sentence abruptly cuts off as my eyes flutter open. Thorne, Darrow, and Della gaze down at me with varying degrees of concern. For a single moment, I feel at peace, but it's broken the second the haze clears from my mind, and my eyes flare wide, landing on the *enchanter*.

"He's going to track me," I say desperately, my voice rough.

"Shit." Darrow curses as he rushes to the cupboards on the other side of the room, pulling out various vials and bowls. Distantly my mind registers that we're in the kitchen at MASQ. "How long has it been?"

My mouth goes dry as I try to remember.

"Maybe fifteen minutes from the time I found her to now," Thorne answers for me.

My gaze flickers to where he stands over me on the other side of the table. His face is pinched tight with concern as a muscle jumps in his jaw. It takes a considerable amount of effort to lift my heavy arm and stretch my fingers toward him. Barely a second passes before his warm hand closes around mine.

"We may be too late," Darrow mutters. "He might already be on his way."

"Who?" Della demands. She stands at the end of the table, placing her hands on her hips. "What's going on?"

I force my head to lift off the table, allowing me to see her better. "Baylor. He's going to come for me."

Something dark flashes in her eyes as determination hardens her delicate features. "He can try."

I tell myself not to think too deeply about the reaction. It likely stems from her hatred of him rather than a desire to protect me. Still, I can't stop the wave of gratitude that rises within me. I pray her decision not to throw me out doesn't come back to bite her.

"I don't think he's searching for me yet," I tell them as I try to push myself onto my elbows, earning me a disapproving scowl from Thorne.

Darrow barks out a humorless laugh as he returns. A blond curl falls into his eye as he stirs something in a large basin. Based on the smell, I'd guess it's full of crushed up herbs and likely a few other things I'd rather not know about. He sets the bowl down next to me and pushes up his sleeves.

"I doubt he has more important matters to attend to," he says, pushing me back down as he takes my arm.

The memory of screams echoing through the temple rushes back, filling me with sick satisfaction. "I stabbed him in the eye."

His movements halt as his eyes go round. "I stand corrected."

"Help her!" Thorne growls from my other side.

Spurred on by his fear of the God of Death, Darrow quickly dips his fingers into the green mixture and uses it to draw swirling symbols along my arms. He whispers words in a strange tongue I don't recognize, and I want to ask him if it's one of the old languages, but now isn't the time for questions. When he's finished, he steps back and the symbols disappear, sinking into my skin and leaving no trace behind.

"It's done," he announces.

"He won't be able to find her?" Thorne asks, standing over me like some sort of avenging angel. I roll my eyes as I push my torso up, supporting myself with both hands.

Darrow shakes his head as he wipes his fingers on a towel. "Not unless he started tracking her before. But if that were the case, I think he'd be here by now."

My shoulders relax, but the relief doesn't last long. Only a second passes before a loud bang hits the back door, and all of us freeze as our minds go to the same place.

"Miss Della?" Nolan's cheerful voice calls. "Can I come inside?"

No one moves.

"It could be a trap," I whisper. A flash of grief hits me as I think of his fiancée Morwen. "He could be Forsaken."

Della's eyes widen as her head swings toward me. "You think they've already spread this far into the city?"

I don't bother questioning how she learned about the effects of the sword. With Darrow staying here, he likely warned her of the danger.

I nod. "Alva and Morwen are with them now." Every eye in the room turns toward me, but I tuck my chin and avoid their gazes. "And Remy too."

"Ivy," Thorne breathes, his hand wrapping around mine once more.

I glance up to find Della watching me with a softness I haven't seen from her in years. "We'll make it right," she promises.

I'm saved from having to answer when Nolan pounds against the door once more. "Is everything alright? I thought I saw Ivy being carried inside earlier?"

Without warning, Thorne drops my hand and barges over to the door. He throws it open, dragging the half fae inside before slamming him against the wall. Della runs to close the door and slide the locks into place.

"Shut your godsdamned mouth," Thorne snarls, his face inches from Nolan's. "Say her name again and it will be the last thing you do."

The room darkens as shadows creep up the walls. Della squeaks as the snakes slip past us, heading for the new arrival.

"What in the Fates is this?" she cries.

Darrow throws his arms up as he grumbles petulantly, "*This* is the reason I showed up at your door in the middle of the night and never left. But now, it seems they're going to ruin this place too."

I narrow my eyes at him as one of the snakes slithers into my lap, nudging it's head against my stomach as it begs for attention. I quickly comply, petting it's scales.

"They're actually sweet once you get to know them," I tell Darrow.

His horrified gaze drops to the creature in question before flitting back to me as he shakes his head. "I don't think I'll be doing that."

Nolan whimpers as the rest of the snakes wrap themselves around his legs, hissing as they give him a glimpse of their sharp fangs. Thorne holds out his hand, summoning the weapon only a reaper can wield. Every eye in the room flares wide as the scythe materializes, its silver blade radiating an unnatural shine.

"How—" Della's question dies on her tongue as Thorne drags the tip of the curved blade over Nolan's arm, sending a few drops of blood splattering to the floor. The reaction from the snakes is immediate as they pounce, hissing at each other as they lap up the blood with their forked tongues.

Darrow gags at the sight, raising his brows at me with concern. "And you let those things touch you?"

I shrug. "They like me."

"Well," he huffs, his face slightly green as he turns back to the action. "There's no accounting for taste."

I roll my eyes as Thorne raises the scythe to Nolan's neck, letting it rest gently against the apple of his throat.

"One wrong move, and they will rip you apart," he says, his voice low. "Do you understand?"

Nolan's chin quivers as he watches the writhing snakes, who are now eyeing the bleeding cut on his arm with interest. "Y-yes," he stutters. "I understand."

Thorne nods, stepping back while keeping his blade in place.

"Bring him here," I tell him as a plan forms in my mind.

Thorne's head whips in my direction, his eyes hard. "Want to rethink that statement?"

"Not particularly," I shake my head. "But I'll repeat it, since you seem hard of hearing. Bring him here."

He rolls his eyes. "Awake all of five minutes and she's already making demands."

Annoyance flares. "Fine, I'll come over there."

I swing my legs over the edge of the table, swaying dangerously when my feet hit the floor.

"Dammit, Angel," Thorne grumbles as he leaps forward to catch me, trusting the snakes to keep Nolan in place. "Why must you always do things the hard way?"

"I've been asking myself that question since she was ten years old," Della mutters.

I glare at both of them as he uses one arm to lift me onto the table again, keeping a hand on my shoulder to stop me from falling forward. Thorne twists his head toward the prisoner, holding out his scythe once more.

"You," he barks. "Come here."

The baker's face is pale with terror as he steps over the shadow snakes. Several of them nip at his heels as he passes. When he stops in front of us, Thorne positions himself slightly in front of me. Apart from the fear shining in Nolan's eyes, the young man looks the same as he always does. He shifts awkwardly on his feet, curling his shoulders inward as if to protect himself. I'm about to tell Thorne to release him when his attention suddenly dips to my collar. Something dark and covetous briefly flashes in his eyes, there one second and gone the next. But I caught it.

"He's one of them," I say softly, hating the words as I speak them. "He's Forsaken."

His eyes widen innocently as he shakes his head. "Ivy, I swear—"

Thorne cuts him off by slamming a fist down on his head. Nolan eyes roll back as falls to the floor and the snakes wrap around him, ensuring he can't escape when he wakes up.

"How did you know?" Della comes closer, staring down at our friend's limp body.

"They always look at my collar." I shiver as I recall the way Remy kept staring at it during the ball. "It's as if they can't help themselves."

"That's a useful tell," she murmurs.

"Yes." Darrow nods, leaning against the table next to me. "Very kind of them to out themselves like that."

Thorne shifts his attention to the *enchanter*. "Is there anything you can do to stop Baylor from activating the collar?"

My stomach twists. It won't be long now before the noose around my neck flares to life once more. I squeeze my fingers, balling them into fists.

Darrow shakes his head, meeting my gaze. "I can give you something to try to manage the pain, but there's nothing else I can do." I notice that the dark circles under his eyes are more prominent than usual. He looks truly worn down, and I can't help but wonder what these last few weeks have been like for him. "I'm truly sorry, Iverson."

I nod, unsure what else to do.

Somewhere inside of me, I know that the time has come to follow the advice I was given and *accept my fate*. Baylor is going to activate the collar no matter what. All I can do now is try to be prepared when that time comes. Pushing my shoulders back, I turn to face Della.

"Is anyone else here?"

She shakes her head, making her long curls bounce. "After everything Darrow told me about the *almanova* I decided to close the place until this mess is sorted. The city is too dangerous right now to have random people coming in and out every night."

"That's probably smart," Thorne comments as his hand comes to rest on my lower back. Its presence is a comforting weight, giving me the strength to speak my next words.

"Not having to worry about other people makes things easier," I say. "But I think it would be best if I hide in the crawl space."

Della's thin eyebrows shoot up. "Why? You always hated it down there."

I'm surprised she remembers how I used to avoid it as a child.

"Just because Baylor can't track me anymore doesn't mean he isn't going to be searching." My mouth turns dry at the thought, but

I force myself to keep going. "Once the collar activates, I'm going to be in too much pain to be able to move quickly if any guards show up."

"Ivy—" Thorne interrupts, but I keep going.

"It's better to hunker down in a secure spot and try to ride it out."

"Alright," Della agrees softly. "I'll get it set up for you."

My skin crawls at the thought of going underground again, but I'll face worse things tonight than a little claustrophobia.

THE CRAWL SPACE is a depressing seven-by-ten-foot room. Thankfully, Della has added on a small bathing chamber since the last time I was here. When you pull back the rug in her office, there's a hatch underneath connected to a narrow staircase that leads down here. With no windows, the only light comes from oil lamps and a few of the blood-red candles I recognize from our meetings. It would make sense to keep them down here since any noise would easily carry upstairs. If the guards show up to search MASQ, those will come in handy.

Thorne insisted on carrying me all the way from the kitchen. I wanted to fight him, but truthfully, I wasn't sure I'd be able to make the trip without falling down. Now he tucks me into a small bed situated in the corner of the room. The only other pieces of furniture are a stool and a wooden chest with extra blankets.

"Let me know if you require anything else," Della says before pointing to the steaming mug of tea she placed on the floor next to the bed. "And drink that. It will help."

Darrow told me earlier that while the tea won't erase the pain, it should knock the edge off. On top of that, he said it would hopefully prevent my trachea from collapsing under the pressure of the collar.

Hopefully being the operative word.

At least it smells nice. Citrus and rose coat my tongue as I take a sip, letting it warm me from the inside out. The door shuts behind

Della, leaving Thorne and me alone. So much has happened over the past twenty-four hours. Was it just last night that we had lain together in my bed? It feels as if years have passed since then.

"Do you want to tell me what happened?" he asks, dragging the stool closer to the bed. He looks comically large on top of the tiny seat.

Normally, I would avoid answering his question. Or I would simply make up a lie. But I'm trying to be different now. The things he said about me before were true. I do have a tendency to isolate and punish myself. But I don't want to be that way.

I want to let him in.

So, I tell him everything. My nightmare. The conversation I had with Baylor. I spare no details, even sharing how alone I felt when I realized everyone I loved in the palace was a stranger to me now. All of them lost to the Forsaken.

"I'm so sorry," he whispers, leaning forward. "I can't imagine how isolated you felt."

His hand skates over the thin sheet on the bed and grabs hold of mine. A shy smile plays at my lips as I realize it's something he's done often since that night in the alley. He's always finding a way to touch my skin somehow.

"The thing is..." I trail off, summoning the courage required to share such vulnerable emotions. "I'm not alone. You came for me. When I needed you, you were there." My eyes grow damp as I stare into his. "I saw you flying toward me, and I knew I didn't have to be alone anymore, that you'd always be reaching for me."

He opens his mouth to speak, but I cut him off as I use his hand to pull him off the stool. The bed dips under his heavy weight, but thankfully, the frame doesn't give out. Pushing him down flat, I position myself on top of him, my thighs straddling his middle.

Those pale blue eyes are wide as he stares up at me. "Ivy, I should—"

"Don't." I shake my head. Taking a deep breath, I allow myself to admit a little bit more truth today. "I'm so afraid."

His hands move to my hips as he sits up, bringing our faces only inches apart.

"I'm terrified." My voice shakes and tears form in my eyes. I swallow, clearing the emotion from my throat. "But there's nothing I can do to stop what's coming, no matter how much I want to. I have to be strong enough to accept that."

"Shhh," he whispers as his hand brushes over the back of my hair, pulling my forehead to his. "You're the strongest person I've ever met."

Those words settle against my chest, making me feel as though maybe, just maybe, the sentiment is true.

"Let me be here with you until it starts," I whisper. "Please don't let this be the moment you stop reaching for me."

"Never," he swears, leaning forward to taste my lips.

The kiss is gentle at first. He cradles my face, his thumbs brushing against my cheeks as he tentatively explores my mouth. My fingers move to the hem of his shirt, desperate to remove the barrier. He pulls back briefly, pulling the offending garment over his head and tossing it aside.

I bite my lip as I run my hands over his broad chest, marveling at the perfection of his body.

"You're beautiful," I say softly. "Perfect."

There's an uncharacteristic shyness hiding in his eyes as I explore him, but it's quickly replaced by all-consuming desire. He leans forward, taking my mouth again, but this time, there's nothing gentle about it. His hands slide down my back, moving to cup my ass as he pulls me closer. Desperate for friction, I rock myself against him, enjoying the sounds that escape him with each move I make.

I can't get enough of his taste. My tongue entwines with his as my fingers dig into his hair, reveling in the softness of the silky strands.

"Ivy," he whispers against my lips. "I—"

Whatever he was about to say is cut off as the collar springs to life, squeezing my throat with a vengeance. I jerk as my body goes rigid. My head tilts back, mouth open wide in a horrific visage as I try to gasp for a breath that won't come.

"Please, Angel, don't hurt yourself." Thorne pulls at my wrists, trying to stop my nails from frantically clawing at my neck.

I slip off him, landing on the mattress as my back arches from the strain of suffocation. As gently as possible, he manages to roll me onto my side and wrap his arms around me from behind. I jolt against him, trying desperately to pull an ounce of air into my lungs.

More than a minute passes before the collar eases its grip, finally granting me a precious breath. I take full advantage, swallowing gulps of air as fast as I can.

"Is it over?" His voice is strained as he whispers against my ear.

I shake my head, trying to slow my racing pulse. "This is only the beginning."

As if spurred on by my words, the collar seizes again. Just like I knew it would. Baylor is playing with me.

And the game is just getting started.

CHAPTER
FORTY-ONE

Hours pass this way.

My entire world shrinks down to the movements of the collar as it traps me in an endless cycle. It only knows two actions: contract and release. But the delay between the two is constantly expanding as Baylor pushes me to my limit.

My head spins from the lack of oxygen. My fingers went numb earlier, and their feeling hasn't returned. My vision isn't faring any better. The edges of the world have grown dark, covered in a permanent vignette. Strange figures dance in the corners of my eyes, creeping closer each time the collar is activated. My mind whispers that they are lost souls, sensing my imminent demise. *That's not possible*, I remind myself. As long as the veils are in place, a soul could never be lost. More likely, they are simply hallucinations.

Though I'm not sure that's any better.

Thorne holds me through all of it. I track each rise and fall of his chest, imagining the air he breathes is somehow able to be shared between us, passing from his lungs to mine.

Silent tears trail down my cheeks, but I no longer bother fighting against the collar. My body simply doesn't have the strength anymore. Besides, nothing I do has any effect. Instead, I lie here and count the time between breaths.

Black spots dot my vision as the seconds stretch on. My throat is raw and aching. Surely it will snap, and my windpipe will collapse.

One hundred sixty-seven.

One hundred sixty-eight.

The sound of my rattling gasps fills the room as the collar releases its hold. I suck in as much air as I can, knowing my reprieve will be brief. Thorne rubs my back, whispering encouraging words in my ear. Baylor only allows me ten seconds of air before the cool metal tightens again.

Please.

My mouth forms the word, but no sound comes out.

Stop. Just let it be over.

"Count with me, Angel," Thorne whispers in my ear.

One. Two. Three. I mouth the words along with him. I want to tell him I will be okay, but I promised myself I wouldn't lie anymore.

"It will end," he says, unbound by any such promises. "You will breathe again. I swear, Ivy."

And he's right. I do breathe again. Scattered gasps every few minutes are all Baylor allows me to have. Still, I keep counting the seconds between each breath as they expand into an eternity. In the darkness, I begin to understand what Maebyn meant about time having little meaning.

Please, I send another silent plea into the ether. *Let it end.*

It doesn't.

It stops shortly after midnight.

I'm counting during a reprieve when, for the first time all night, a full minute passes without the collar starting up again. My heart pounds as I wait for it to happen, but it seems that Baylor is finally taking a break from his attacks.

A cruel smile curls my cracked lips. No matter how terrible I feel, I know Baylor isn't faring much better. Using the collar, even in small increments, is draining. And with the injury I gave him earlier, he's probably suffering greatly.

Good. May his pain have no end.

Air passes unrestricted into my lungs, but each breath burns. Still, I drink them down gladly. The dampness on my face is a mixture of both sweat and tears. Every muscle in my body aches, leaving me feeling as though I've been trampled by several horses. Still, I force myself to roll over and face Thorne.

His head rests on the pillow next to mine, but the lines of his face are pulled tight with strain. His entire body is rigid, as if he's currently exercising every ounce of his restraint to stop himself from flying back to the Palace and ripping Baylor apart.

"It's over." The strangled whisper is barely audible.

"Shhh," Thorne brushes my hair out of my face. "Don't try to speak. Just nod, okay?"

I do as he orders, hating the way the movement pulls at my tender skin.

"Scratch that." He grimaces at the sight of my pain. "No nodding." He reaches for the hand that rests between us. "Just squeeze my fingers for yes."

I do as he asks.

"That's right, Angel." He leans forward to kiss my brow. I close my eyes, hating how my heart clenches at the tender action. "Will he start again?"

The fear in his voice makes me want to lie, but I don't. Instead, I softly squeeze his fingers, making his jaw clench tighter.

"How long? Days?"

My hand doesn't move, and his face pales.

"Hours?"

I squeeze again.

"Drains him," I whisper. The words scratch my throat on their way out and I immediately regret trying to speak again.

"Shhh." He gently brushes his soft lips over mine. "No talking, remember? Just try to get some rest."

I have every intention of staying awake, but somehow, my eyes drift shut as I slip away.

∽

I wake up gasping for air, my gaze flying around the room, searching for danger.

Strong hands grab my arms, and a deep voice whispers in my ear, "It's ok, Angel. You're alright."

I find him in the darkness, sitting on the stool next to the bed.

"You've only been asleep for half an hour," he whispers. "You should try to rest more."

While you can.

He doesn't need to say the last part. We both know it's true.

The door creaks open, and Della appears at the top of the stairs, another steaming cup of tea in her hand.

"I thought you could use this," she says as she makes her way down to us. "Darrow said to tell you he's much better at removing pain than preventing it."

I pray he's telling the truth because I'm not sure how much more I can take.

She hands me the mug, and I take a sip, savoring the flavor on my tongue. The warm liquid coats my throat, and I can feel it working immediately.

"He mentioned it would start healing the internal damage right away."

It does. The worst of the pain begins to ease. It still hurts, but it's much more manageable now.

"I believe some friends of yours have arrived," Della says to Thorne. "A man and a woman. They're waiting for you upstairs."

"Griffen and Fia," he explains. "I summoned them earlier."

My brows pinch together.

"Through the tattoo," he explains, lifting his wrist to display the burning rose etched onto his skin. "It's why everyone on my council has one made from the same enchanted ink."

Distantly, I realize that's how Griffen was able to summon him the night we were trapped in the alley. A frown pulls at my lips. I probably should have put that together earlier, but to be fair, I've had a lot on my mind.

"I can stay with her if you want to go say hello," Della offers, glancing back and forth between us. "I believe they've already begun interrogating poor Nolan."

Thorne shakes his head. "I'm not leaving her."

It's fine, I mouth. *Go.*

His gaze turns skeptical, and I roll my eyes. Eventually he relents, rising from his seat at my bedside and offering it to Della.

"Do not get out of this bed," he orders as he pulls his gloves from his pocket and slips them on. "You need to rest." His stern gaze lands on Della next. "Come get me if anything changes."

She nods.

He disappears up the stairs, and Della and I are alone together for the first time since I said those awful things to her. Shame burns in my gut, and I wash it down with another gulp of tea.

"I added honey," Della says, her tone shockingly gentle. "I remember you always refusing to drink your tea unless it was sickly sweet."

I've thankfully outgrown that habit, but I can't deny that it tastes delicious.

Thank you, I mouth.

We sit in silence for a few moments, neither of us sure what to say. Her back is straight as she perches on the stool, her fingers digging into the material of her trousers. The sight of her in anything but a dress is strange and unfamiliar. I didn't even think she owned pants.

Her brown eyes settle on the bruises at my neck, and her full lips twist into a grimace. "He's done that to you before?"

My shoulders stiffen, but I nod.

"I'm sorry." The force behind her words tells me she's referring to more than just my injuries. She shifts uncomfortably on the stool before standing up and pacing back and forth through the tiny room.

"I should have done more to help you," Della whispers, her gaze cast down. "It's what *she* would have wanted."

I flinch as her voice cracks.

"But I was so furious," she continues, coming to stand before me as her eyes meet mine. "And I blamed you for something that wasn't your fault."

I stare at her, completely dumbfounded. Those are words I never expected to hear from Della. I feared she would regard me with civil hatred for the rest of our lives. My fingers dig into the sheet covering my lap as I force myself to be brave enough to accept her apology, instead of insisting I don't deserve it. Still, I can't stop myself from offering my own confession.

"I'm sorry too," I croak, my voice horrible and raw. "I was a fool."

"Shh," she whispers, her soft fingers brushing through my hair. "So was I."

My eyes drift shut as she continues her gentle ministrations, and I slip into my dreams once more.

CHAPTER
FORTY-TWO

Sometime later, I wake to the sound of people filing down the stairs. My eyelids feel like sandpaper as I pry them open to find everyone crowding into the cramped space.

"What's going on?" I ask, the words quiet but not as breathy as before.

Thorne is at my side in an instant. "We think we might know where the *almanova* is being kept."

"Where?" Surprise has me trying to push myself up, causing my head to spin. Thorne places a hand on my back, offering his silent support to keep me from tumbling out of the bed.

"He said he'll only tell you." Fia steps forward, dragging a bloody and broken Nolan with her.

My heart breaks at the sight of the sweet baker. His nose has clearly been broken and both of his eyes are black. The way he's hunching forward and clutching his ribs tells me they're likely broken. Despite the fact that I know this was necessary, I still hate to see him this way.

"Tell her what you told us," Griffen orders him. His typical light-hearted nature is gone, leaving a calculated warrior in its wake.

Nolan's hateful gaze connects with mine. "*He's* going to kill you tonight."

In a flash, Thorne is across the room, the back of his hand smacking against Nolan's face. "Say that again, and I will end you."

Everyone in the room goes still.

"Now tell her what you said earlier," Thorne growls as he grabs a fistful of the man's hair and forces him to look at me.

His lips pull back and when he finally speaks it's through clenched teeth. "He's waiting in the place where he first saw you."

My nose scrunches. *Where he first saw me...* I turn the words over in my mind, trying to decipher their meaning. A memory flashes of a dark silhouette standing in a window, watching me as I passed by on the street below.

"*The house*," I whisper, my gaze connecting with Thorne's. "The one in the Lowers where the woman attacked me."

His eyes widen. "You were right all along. Darby did go there."

My thoughts race, and I swing my legs over the side of the bed. "We need to go. Now."

Thorne steps in front of me, his hand on my shoulder stopping me from standing up. "It's most likely a trap."

He glares down at me, but I merely shrug.

"That's never stopped her before," Griffen adds unhelpfully.

I peek around Thorne to scowl at the high fae.

"There's a first time for everything." Thorne pulls my attention back to him.

"You and I both know this reprieve won't last forever," I tell him, not raising my voice above a whisper. Darrow's tonic may have helped, but my throat has still been through a lot. "The longer we let this continue, the weaker I'll become."

"I won't let that happen," he argues, but we both know he can't follow through on that promise.

"The only way to end this is to remove the collar. And for that, we need the *almanova*."

He takes a deep breath, closing his eyes. When they open again, I know I've won.

"Fine," he grinds out.

My shoulders slump with relief, but before I can say anything else, Fia steps forward.

"The sword can remove your collar?" she asks, her body tense as she glances back and forth between me and Thorne.

I nod, and a strange expression passes over her face. Next to her, Griffen crosses his arms over his chest.

"You should have told us that," he says to the God beside me, his forehead wrinkling with worry.

Thorne stiffens. "We can discuss this upstairs. Ivy needs to rest."

I open my mouth to argue, but he cuts me off with a hard glare. The trio disappears up the staircase, causing unease to swim in my stomach. Why would Thorne have kept that a secret from his council? Did he think I wouldn't want him to share it? Was he trying to protect my privacy?

I push my guilt aside, choosing to focus on happier things. Such as the fact that I didn't feel a single spark of jealousy as I watched Thorne leave with Fia. While I can't say exactly what's growing between us, I do know that loyalty isn't something I need to worry about. Thorne has proven many times over that he only has eyes for me.

"Ivy." Darrow's voice pulls me from my thoughts as he sits on the stool next to my bed. "Do you have a moment?"

My lips turn down at his polite tone. I observe him closer, noticing the way he's holding himself too straight.

"You should know, the enchantment I placed on you is tied to this building," he says, refusing to meet my eyes. "Once you leave, the king will be able to track you."

Deep down, I think I already knew that. Leaving is a risk, but doing nothing is even worse. "Thank you for telling me."

With that said, I expect him to head back upstairs, but instead he stays seated.

My eyebrows pinch together. "Was there something else?"

His eyes meet mine, clouded with self-loathing. "I wanted to apologize."

"You've apologized to me before," I remind him. "Recently."

"I know." He nods, his throat bobbing as he swallows. "But it will never be enough."

I want to tell him that's not true, but the words won't come out. Still, whatever animosity I've harbored toward him in the past seems to have subsided.

"When I was desperate and afraid, I came here," I admit quietly. "I knew I could count on you to help me when I truly needed it. Whatever was done in the past, I'm ready to move on."

His head rears back as shock splashes across his face. "That's a very mature answer, Lady Iverson."

I shrug. "I'm a very mature woman."

"Eh, I wouldn't go that far."

"You're just jealous." I roll my eyes.

"I'm unfamiliar with that emotion," he says snobbishly. "Perhaps you could describe it to me?"

I roll my eyes. "Let me guess, it's because you're too beautiful to be envious of anyone?"

His hand flies to his chest dramatically. "Ivy, I'm flattered, but I think of you as the little sister I never had."

I arch a brow.

"Fine," he grumbles. "The annoying younger cousin I'm only vaguely fond of."

"I don't think of you at all," I whisper proudly.

"*I don't think of you at all*," he mimics my tone.

"Break it up, children," Della says as she returns from the bathing chamber. "And you." She points at me. "You're supposed to be resting your voice, not getting into pointless arguments. Go clean up."

Darrow's laughter follows me into the bathroom, and I pause to offer him a crude gesture before shutting the door.

All my amusement dries up when I catch sight of my reflection.

My skin is deathly pale. Bruises cover my entire neck in varying shades of black, blue, and purple. My lips are chapped and bleeding, but I think the worst part may be my eyes. They are completely bloodshot, making my amber irises appear darker.

Frankly, I look like a monster.

I'd love to take a bath, but there's no time. Instead I splash water on my face and use a rag to wipe down my body. Once I'm done, I borrow a brush I found in one of the drawers and comb through my hair, frowning at the state of it. While it's usually a vibrant shade of copper, now the color appears flat and lifeless. It's as if the collar is sucking the life out of me, bleeding me dry each time it's activated.

I force myself to take a deep breath and push aside my paranoid thoughts. My fingers shake as I untangle the mats in my hair and fashion it into my usual braid. With one last glance at my reflection, I decide it's best to avoid mirrors for the foreseeable future.

I'd be lying if I said I wasn't afraid of what's to come tonight. I'm usually confident during a fight, some might say overconfident, but I know I'm not at my best right now. My reflection alone is proof of that. After the events of the last twenty-four hours, my body is drained and calling on my illusions will only drain me further. Which means I won't have my *eidolon* or invisibility to fall back on. Tonight, I'll have to rely on my strength alone to get me through.

When I return to the room, I find Thorne waiting for me by the stairwell. He doesn't carry any weapons, but I suppose there's no reason for him to do so. His shadows and scythe are just a summons away. And of course I can't forget about the flames he summoned at the ball. Those will make an impressive weapon.

"Where is everyone?" I ask as I head for the bed. It seems Della left my blades and sheaths waiting for me on the pillow.

"They already left," he says, scanning my body for signs of weakness.

Anger stirs in my veins as I strap the sheaths to my thighs. "You can't seriously be backing out of our agreement."

"I'm not." He crosses his arms over his chest as he leans against the wooden rail. "They left without us because they're going on horseback."

I narrow my eyes. "And we're not?"

He shakes his head. "You and I are flying. Once we're outside these walls, Baylor will be able to track you. Flying will make that more difficult."

"Oh." My head cocks to the side. "That's actually smart."

One corner of his mouth kicks up in a half smile. "The tone of surprise isn't appreciated."

"My sincerest apologies, oh so intelligent God of Death." I roll my eyes as I move around him to get to the stairs.

He darts in front of me, blocking my path. "You don't sound sorry."

I take a step closer, crowding his space until my chest is brushing his. "What would you do if I told you I'm not?"

Shadows curl around the outer rim of his eyes. "There are many things I could do."

"Such as?" I glance up at him innocently as my teeth sink into my lower lip.

"I don't think I should say."

I trail a single finger across his shoulder. "But I want to know."

"You see, if I tell you, I'll have to show you." His arm wraps around my waist, pulling me closer. "And then we won't be leaving this room tonight. Is that what you want, Ivy?"

My heart gallops as my breathing turns heavy, this time having nothing to do with the collar. A shiver skips up my spine in anticipation, but I force myself to step back. His arm falls away immediately.

My shoulders slump as I heave a regretful sigh. "Later?"

"Always," he promises.

Taking my hand in his, he leads me up the stairs. As we make our way to the roof, I send silent prayers to the Fates that "later" will still exist for us after tonight.

CHAPTER
FORTY-THREE

Wind blasts against us as we circle above the city. The roaring sound of it makes speaking to each other impossible. Thorne's arms are tight around me as I cling to him with all my strength. The other times he took me into the sky with him, I was too weak and disoriented to really appreciate the experience. This time, I find myself wishing that was the case.

I squeeze my eyes shut as Thorne takes us higher. The air is thinner up here, making it difficult to breathe. Cracking one eye open, I glance down and immediately regret it. Solmare is barely visible beneath us. A thick layer of fog hovers over the city, distorting everything. The moment I realize how far off the ground we are, my entire body tenses, and I shove my face into the crook of Thorne's neck again.

His body shakes as he laughs against me. I want to smack him, but I don't dare move at this height. My indignation is slightly mitigated by the feeling of his large hand gently rubbing against my back. Dampness settles in my eyes, and I tell myself it's just a side effect of the wind as I nuzzle deeper into his warmth.

"There," he says directly into my ear.

Before I can ask what he means, we're suddenly diving toward the city. My stomach falls into my throat and I can't stop the scream that forces its way out of me. Black feathers curl around us, tickling my nose as we fall through the sky. Each second brings us closer to the hard ground. Just as quickly as it began, our steep decent screeches to a halt as Thorne spreads his wings wide.

"Don't *ever* do that again!" My throat burns as I shout over the raging wind.

"No promises, Angel." His lips brush over my ear, and a shiver passes through me that has nothing to do with the chilly night air. "Over there."

Pulling my face out of his neck, I scan his features and realize he's staring at something below us. I swallow my rising fear and peek down. Squinting through the fog, I catch a brief glimpse of horses galloping across the bridge that separates the Dockside District from the rest of the city.

"It's time," I whisper, too quiet for even my own ears to hear over the heavy breeze.

Thorne carries us lower—thankfully, not diving this time. His wings glide gracefully over the currents of air as we descend, coming to a stop in an alley between two brick buildings. The moment his feet land on solid ground, I release my death grip and unwrap my legs from his waist as I throw myself onto the cobblestone. I've never been so grateful for the existence of gravity.

"Not a fan of flying?" Thorne asks, an undeniable edge of humor in his tone.

I narrow my eyes. "I wasn't built for the skies."

"Really?" He arches a playful brow. "I rather enjoyed the way you clung to me."

I open my mouth to respond, but the biting words die on my tongue as footsteps pull our attention to the left. The others appear at the mouth of the alley, silently filing into the narrow opening.

My brows pull together. "Where are the horses?"

"We figured they'd be too conspicuous, so we left them a few blocks away," Fia whispers, her eyes scanning for threats.

"Glad to see you survived the flight." Griffen grins in my direction as they all join us in the back corner, Della and Darrow appearing slightly out of place among the odd group.

"It was a close call," Thorne answers for me, earning him a scowl.

"It will be a close call for *you* if you ever take me up there again," I grumble.

"Please settle down," Darrow says, his lip curling with disgust at the sight of mud staining the hem of his velvet trousers. "I don't want to have to be the responsible one here."

I roll my eyes. "Trust me, no one thought you were."

He sends me a glare as Della speaks up for the first time since they arrived.

"What's our plan?" she asks, a small hint of fear underneath her even one.

While Della knows how to handle a weapon, she isn't a warrior. She can fight off an enemy if she has to, but she's never taken on a large group of them. My palms grow damp at the thought of her having to swing the sword strapped to her hip. I should never have gotten her involved in any of this...

Thorne steps forward, taking charge as our small group circles around him. Fia hangs back, keeping watch at the front of the alley with a crossbow in her arms. Strapped to her back is a cylindrical container full of arrows. I've trained with a bow before, and I'm a fairly decent shot, but I've never worked with one like hers. My fingers itch at the thought of pulling the trigger. Perhaps she'll let me borrow hers sometime?

"Our destination is one block over," Thorne tells us, his features once again shifting into the emotionless mask he so often wears around others. "We stick together as a group, and no one breaks formation. Assume anyone who approaches us is an enemy."

"What do we do if the Forsaken join us?" Della asks.

"Oh, they're definitely going to show up," Griffen chimes in, his fingers resting on the pommel of his broadsword.

"Go for the kill," Thorne answers coldly.

My stomach churns. Memories surface of the alley lined with the dead bodies of the Forsaken. In my mind, their faces morph with those of my friends, shifting into Alva, Morwen, and Remy. The thought of hurting one of them is unbearable.

"Shouldn't the goal be to incapacitate them?" Della argues, mirroring the thoughts running through my own mind. "They are innocent people, after all."

I glance at the others. The carefree gleam that usually shines in Griffen's eyes is nowhere to be found. Instead, I find only determination, as if he's preparing himself to do whatever must be done. Surprise flares through me as I take in Darrow's down-turned eyes and clenched jaw.

"Whatever they were before is gone now," he whispers. "None of them are innocent anymore."

"But it's not their fault," I insist as something hot and ugly roils in my gut. "It makes them do those things. It controls them."

"This isn't the same as what Baylor does to you with the collar," Thorne says, not unkindly. "Whoever they once were is gone now. They'd kill their own family if the sword told them to, and they'd do it with a smile on their face." His gaze moves around the group, landing on each one of us. "If they approach, we don't hesitate to end their lives."

I blanch at his words.

"I told you, Ivy," he says softy, a flash of emotion rippling behind his pale eyes. "I'm not good like you."

That night in my room, he said the lines he's willing to cross would shock me. Is this what he meant?

The situation is ambiguous. They're our enemies, but not by choice. I wrestle with the rising tide of guilt that threatens to swallow me whole. My hands are stained red by the lives I've taken, but most of those weren't my decision. Not the innocent ones, at least. I held the blade, but Baylor issued the commands.

This is different.

There's no way to absolve myself this time. No one is forcing my hand. If I choose to kill these people, the weight of that decision will rest on my shoulders alone.

"Couldn't we at least try to knock them out or something?" I suggest as I grasp for some loophole. "Hurt them just enough to make them back down?"

"You could try," Darrow says softly, meeting my gaze for the first time since this conversation began. "But consider what might happen if you fail."

Ice drips down the back of my neck as his meaning settles in.

Failure means death. Not only mine, but my friends as well. The whole city maybe. If we don't stop the *almanova*, how far will the Forsaken spread? Am I willing to slaughter these innocents to spare everyone else?

I thought I knew each dark corner of my soul, but apparently, I was wrong. It turns out there are still new facets of myself left to discover, all of them just as ugly as the rest. *But is it really new?* I ask myself. *Isn't this who I've always been? Someone willing to do the hard things and live with the consequences.*

My jaw clenches as resolve settles over me. I don't have to revel in the lives I'm going to take tonight; I only have to accept that it's necessary. Cassandra's haunting comments from the ball drift back to me again.

The truth cannot be fought, child. Only accepted.

Determination mixes with shame as I force myself to meet Thorne's gaze. "I can do it."

He nods, watching me for a few moments before addressing the group again. "We need to move."

We establish our formation quickly, positioning Thorne and me at the front of our small group with Della and Darrow right behind us. Fia and Griffen bring up our rear. The night air ripples, growing thicker as Thorne's shadows settle around us. While they don't hide our party completely, they do provide a small degree of camouflage as we move into the open street.

The quiet of the Lowers is eerie and unnatural. At least half of the streetlamps are out since the city doesn't bother refilling the oil that fuels their flames. That kind of privilege is reserved for the wealthier districts, leaving Dockside to rely on moonlight to chase away the darkness.

As we round the corner, stepping onto the street where the gray house waits for us, an icy chill runs down the back of my neck. It turns my blood cold even as the collar flares with warmth. The hairs on my arms stand on end, telling me we're being watched.

"Are you guys seeing this?" Della whispers behind me.

Glancing over my shoulder, I find her gaze locked on one of the nearby houses. The windows are boarded up, but between the gaps in the wood several pairs of eyes watch us without blinking.

"They're over here too," Fia says, pulling our attention to a house on the other side of the street.

Dread curdles in my stomach as I scan the surrounding homes, finding the same situation at each one. There must be dozens of people watching us. "They're everywhere."

"What's the plan here?" Fia asks as she aims her crossbow at one of the windows, her finger resting against the trigger.

"We don't engage unless we have to," Thorne orders from beside me as a muscle flexes in his jaw. "We stick together and keep moving. As long as they stay inside, they aren't our problem."

His gaze finds mine, holding it for a moment before we're forced to continue on our path. We push onward, but the sound of scraping metal has me glancing over my shoulder. Darrow unsheathes a thin rapier, its gold handle encrusted with emeralds the size of my eyeballs. His blond curls are held back by a ribbon and his white long-sleeve shirt is untucked. I can't help but notice that he's leaning into the pirate theme lately. Shaking my head, I shift my attention forward again.

Only twenty yards stand between us and our destination when Griffen's voice breaks the silence. "Looks like they just became our problem, boss."

My forehead wrinkles as I turn to ask what he means, only to be halted by the sight of dozens of people filing out of the nearby houses. They flood the streets from every angle, boxing us in from the sides and at our backs, leaving only a ten-foot-wide trail leading to the grey house.

"It's like a parade," Darrow murmurs before grunting as Della elbows him in the ribs.

"Shut up," she whispers.

Thorne edges closer to me as he takes in the situation. If I didn't already know things were bad, the sight of fear clouding his eyes would leave me with no doubts about our current state. My fingers curl tightly around the cool metal of the blades I hold in each hand.

"Stay in formation," Thorne orders, the side of his arm pressing into mine. "We're almost there."

Fear pierces my chest as I take in the sheer number of Forsaken surrounding us. Every instinct in my body is on high alert as I realize we're animals caught in a trap.

"We've got movement," Fia calls from behind us.

Apparently, we aren't walking fast enough for them because the ones at our backs have begun edging closer.

"They're herding us," I whisper as claustrophobia traps the air in my lungs and tightens my bruised trachea. Old fears surface, making me feel as though imaginary walls are closing in around us. The taste of dirt fills my mouth. In my mind, I'm choking once more as I claw out of my own grave.

"Stay with me, Angel." Thorne's voice pulls me back to the present. "I need you to hold on."

I swallow, nodding as I meet his worried gaze. He holds my stare for a few seconds before dropping it. With the enemy closing in at our backs, we're forced to increase our pace. Our feet hasten over the jagged cobblestone. Della nearly trips on an uneven area, but

Darrow's quick hand reaches out to steady her. I keep my gaze on the Forsaken, hating how familiar some of their faces are. I recognize several of them from my time at the pub, but now their eyes burn with hatred as their lips twist into cruel, taunting smiles.

"Watch them," Thorne commands. "If any Forsaken makes a move, you put them down. No hesitation."

I steel myself, pushing aside whatever pity I may harbor for these poor souls. Mercy has no place here tonight. There's no one to avenge, no one to save. Tonight is about one thing.

Death.

In this moment, I desperately wish I could summon an illusion to help me slip through this crowd of enemies. I've been stripped bare of my most valuable weapon. All I have now are the blades strapped to my body.

And years' worth of muscle memory and fighting instincts, I remind myself.

Sure, I've never taken on this many enemies at once, but I've also never had a group of allies at my side either. I may be without my illusions, but I'm not alone.

As one, the Forsaken shift their attention away from us, their heads snapping in unison toward the gray house. It's almost as if they share some sort of hive mind... But Taron, the one from the alley, was different. He was cruel and violent, but he disobeyed the orders he'd been given when I taunted him. So, while they've all been warped and twisted by the *almanova*, perhaps some of them are able to hold on to a small measure of their own will.

Those thoughts fall away as a dark silhouette passes over the threshold of the gray house, stepping onto the porch. The sword is nowhere to be seen as Grell Darby scans the crowd before him, yet the pulsing heat at my neck tells me it's close. The former guard looks slightly worse for wear tonight. He's lost weight, making him appear gaunt as his skin seems to sag off his bones. I suppose being controlled by the *almanova* for several weeks would be bad for anyone's health.

"Thank you for delivering the *wraith* to us," he says, his deep voice easily carrying over the quiet street. "You've saved us the trouble of collecting her ourselves. Send her forward, and we'll allow the rest of you to leave in peace."

"Thank you for the kind offer," Thorne replies coolly. "But we decline."

Relief wars with guilt as I do my best to show no reaction to Thorne's words. I didn't think he'd hand me over to them, but I also know it would be the smartest option.

A smile plays at the corners of Darby's mouth. "I hoped you'd say that. May the veil welcome your souls."

"Is it just me," Griffen mutters behind us, "or does he not seem upset about our refusal?"

My lips twitch, but the amusement promptly fades as Darby turns to the Forsaken, apparently done addressing us.

"My friends," he calls out. "Tonight, what was broken will be remade. The first pieces will be reunited as we usher in a new era. *He* thanks you for offering your lives in service to his mission."

A hand touches my shoulder as Darrow leans forward to whisper in my ear, "If this goes badly, you run. Whatever happens, you can't let them get the collar."

My head whips toward him, searching for answers as questions race through my mind. I catch sight of Thorne's stony expression. A muscle flexes in his jaw as he narrows his eyes at Darrow's proximity to me.

I'm about to ask the *enchanter* what the fuck he's talking about when movement from the Forsaken steals my attention. Chills skate across my skin as they each raise their right foot and stomp it against the ground in unison.

Darby's fevered gaze settles on me once more. "It's time."

The words set everything into motion. As one, the Forsaken begin closing in on us. They prowl forward, their faces twisted with loathing. Just like in the alley, their weapons are a mix of blades and other crude objects. It's as if they've armed themselves with whatever they had lying around. My mouth goes dry as my attention catches on a tall man clutching a mallet. The idea of him using it to crack open my friend's skulls makes my teeth grind. I bend my knees and press my back against Thorne's as I prepare for the incoming swarm. They've almost reached us when their advance is suddenly halted.

A great wall of fire springs to life, its flames roaring as they ignite in a circle around our group and drive back the Forsaken. Several of them scream as the blaze licks their skin, filling the air with the smell of burning flesh. Heat snatches the oxygen from my lungs, warming my body instantly.

"That was..." I trail off, unable to describe the sight before us.

"Impressive?" Thorne suggests at my side, one eyebrow raised as he stares down at me. "Awe inspiring?"

I give him a bland look. "Perfectly average is what I was going to say."

One corner of his mouth kicks up in a half smile. "I'm sure."

The amusement fades quickly as the reality of our situation presses in. "I need to get inside."

He shakes his head, his eyes glued to mine. "You aren't going alone."

My jaw clenches at his commanding tone.

"To be fair," Griffen pipes in as he squeezes to the center of our small group, "I don't think any of us are moving anytime soon."

Ignoring the blond fae, I keep my focus on Thorne. "Can you fly us over the flames? We could try to enter through the roof?"

He opens his mouth, but before he can speak, Fia steals our attention. She stands at the back of our huddle, her face frozen with horror as she looks toward the other houses.

"Archers!" she cries. "Get down!"

My head whips toward the sky, where I spot a dozen arrows heading straight for us.

CHAPTER
FORTY-FOUR

Barely a second passes before I'm pushed to the ground, a large body covering mine. The others fall around us, but I can't see anything as Thorne's large frame blocks out the rest of the world.

Arrows ping off the cobblestones, dozens of them landing one after another. A feminine scream cries out, echoing over the roar of the fire. My stomach drops. I twist my neck painfully, but I can't see anything over Thorne's shoulder. His body goes rigid, straining as a pained grunt rises in his throat. The sound turns my skin to ice despite the inferno surrounding us.

"Thorne?" My heart gallops against my chest, each beat sending another shudder through me as I wait for him to respond.

"It's nothing," he grumbles, shifting above me. "The bastards have shit aim."

His words pound through my skull, and I feel as if I'm sinking deeper into the ground beneath us.

"Where are you hit?" I manage to ask.

"My leg. It's only a graze," he says, as if that somehow makes it better. "Hold on."

A few seconds later, his weight disappears from my back, and I quickly push myself onto my knees. Glancing up, I find a blanket of shadow forming a few inches above our heads. Inside the darkness, snakes slither and hiss, snapping at each arrow that threatens to fly past them. The inky cloud hangs low, forcing us to stay close to the ground but providing enough cover to crawl around.

The sound of a quiet whimper pulls my attention behind me where I find the others gathered around Della. My heart stutters as I spot the arrow lodged in her left shoulder.

"No," I breathe, moving on my hands and knees to reach her.

This can't be happening. She can't d—I squeeze my eyes shut as I stop the thought in its tracks, unwilling to even entertain the notion. Taking a deep breath, I force myself to assess the situation calmly.

Della lies on her side, cradled in Darrow's arms as he applies pressure to the wound.

"I'm fine," she says through gritted teeth.

"That doesn't look fine." He nods to the arrow sticking out of her shoulder.

"It will be once you pull it out," she snaps.

"Can you heal her?" I ask Darrow, praying he's got some enchantment up his sleeve.

"I can stop the bleeding, but it will take time to fully heal." He pulls a vial of white powder from his pocket.

"Do it," Thorne orders from beside me. His warm hand against my back is an anchoring weight. "Quickly. I'll need to lower the flames soon."

"What?" Darrow squeaks, his head shaking back and forth. "That sounds like a terrible idea."

"With all of us in here, we're a flashing target," he explains. "They have the numbers, so we need to draw them apart into smaller groups. And it will be much harder for the archers to get a clean shot if we're mixed in with the Forsaken."

"Besides," Griffen says, pulling at his collar as a bead of sweat drips down the side of his face, "it's getting warm in here."

He's not wrong, I think as I wipe the dampness from my forehead.

"How long can you hold the flames?" I ask, knowing that's part of the reason he's suggesting this plan. Controlling a fire this large must be eating through his energy at a rapid pace. If he keeps going for too long, he'll burn himself out. I'm not sure how deep a God's magic reserves are, but we still have a big fight ahead of us. With the graze on his leg and the shadows he's using, he's already pushing himself.

His shoulders tense as he meets my gaze. "Long enough."

Darrow gets to work quickly. Della cries as he pulls the arrow from her flesh. The sound makes me want to vomit. Thankfully, her screams fade as he shakes the vial over her bloody shoulder, sprinkling the enchanted powder onto the wound.

"It should help to numb the pain," he says gently, taking her hand in his.

Not for the first time, I wonder about the history between those two. While I don't know if it's romantic in nature, they definitely have some sort of connection.

I insist Thorne allows Darrow to sprinkle some of the powder over his wound too, which he's not happy about. When he lifts up his pant leg and exposes the long, jagged gash, I'm filled with the deep urge to break something. My knuckles bleach white as I squeeze my fists tightly.

"Fia," Thorne calls as Darrow finishes with his leg. "I need you to take out the archers."

She nods, pushing her shoulders back as she accepts his order without argument.

"Find cover and try to get a shot," he continues. "I'll send the snakes to search the houses, but that means they won't be with us to stop any arrows that make it through."

"We're running out of time," Della gasps, her horrified gaze fixed a few yards away where several of the Forsaken are throwing themselves into the flames, creating a gap with their bodies.

"What are they doing?" Darrow grimaces.

I gulp down the nausea that rises in my throat. "Making a bridge."

"We have to move now." Thorne pushes himself onto a crouch. "Focus on driving the Forsaken away from the house. We need to create an opening for Ivy and me to get through."

Everyone prepares themselves, checking their weapons and getting into position. I crouch next to Thorne, and his bare hand reaches for mine, entwining our fingers for a few fleeting moments.

"Be careful," he whispers, his crystalline eyes reflecting the flames.

I nod, but the gesture is too stiff to appear natural. "You too."

Please, I beg the Fates. *Let my friends survive.*

As usual, my prayers drift into the ether without any response. Still, I hope they hear me.

His hand slips from mine as the fire extinguishes. Within seconds, the battle has swallowed us whole, cutting off my view of the others. Forsaken come at me from all sides as I dodge their attacks. Lunging forward, I deliver a death blow to a young man. His hateful eyes blaze right until the moment their light fades. A helpless rage pulses through me as I let his lifeless body fall to the ground.

The sword, I tell myself. *Once we have the sword, we can end this.*

The dead pile at my feet. There's nothing merciful about the way I slice through the Forsaken, taking their lives with each swipe of my blades. Hands reach for me from all directions, their numbers endless. I push down every ounce of humanity as I become an instrument of death. Cocking my arm back, I send one blade flying toward a Forsaken, my empty hand immediately unsheathing another.

Footsteps crunch behind me, and I spin, striking out only to halt an inch from my target as I catch sight of a familiar face. A memory pushes through the murderous haze of my mind as I take in his features. The *mendax* appears far more haggard than the last time I saw him, standing outside his shop in Midgarden. His shaggy brown hair is matted with blood, his eyes teeming with hatred as he stares down at me.

Unfortunately, my moment of hesitation costs me. His hands shoot out, grabbing the sides of my head and squeezing it tightly as his magic pours into me. The sounds of the battle fade as reality slips away, and I lose my mind to his illusion.

∽

When I open my eyes, I find myself lying on a picnic blanket in the field near Pomeroy manor. The afternoon sun beats down on me, warming my skin with its comforting rays.

"Ivy!" a feminine voice calls. "You're here!"

I sit up to find Clara, my former governess, running through the grass as her sage-green dress billows around her. Bellamy follows close behind, snagging her hand in his own as he intertwines their fingers.

"We've been waiting for ages," he says, a wide smile stretching across his face.

Confusion wrinkles my forehead as I watch them approach. "Waiting for what?"

Clara tilts her head, a patient smile on her lips. "For you, silly."

The sound of shouting echoes from somewhere in the distance, but I find no signs of distress as I scan the field around us. I open my mouth to ask what we're doing here, but another voice pulls my attention.

"There's my girl!"

I tense as Lord Pomeroy approaches, appearing out of nowhere as he pulls me into a tight embrace. His hand cups the back of my head, running over my hair as if I'm precious to him.

"We've missed you, daughter," he whispers in my ear before releasing me.

My eyes flare as I pull back. "What's going on?"

Everything about this scene is perfect, but the too tight feeling creeping over my skin tells me something is very, very wrong. I'm not supposed to be here.

"What do you mean?" Bel asks, concern leaching into his tone. "Are you alright, Ivy?"

"Do you want to lie down?" Clara wraps an arm around my shoulder, her familiar scent clouding my mind and pulling me back into the haze. "I could tell you a bedtime story. You always loved those."

I open my mouth to say yes, when a voice shouts again, this time closer.

"Iverson!"

I turn around, searching for whoever is calling my name. "Did you hear that?"

"I'm sure it's nothing," my father says. "Come sit down and have some of the berries."

"I picked them fresh from the garden this morning," Bel says as he pops the blue fruit into his mouth. "I wanted today to be special for you."

With no reason to object to their request, I trudge toward the flannel blanket. I'm only a foot away when Clara steps in front of me, blocking my path. I glance up to ask what she's doing, but the sight of her face sends me stumbling back in horror.

The pleasant expression she wore earlier melts away as her eyes grow unnaturally wide. White light bursts from behind her irises, glowing like moonlight. It radiates throughout her whole body, emanating from somewhere within her.

"Wake up, Ivy," she says, her voice deeper than I've ever heard it. "You need to—"

Her words cut off as the tip of a blade suddenly pushes out of her forehead. A scream rises in my throat as her face contorts, and the world around us melts away, being replaced by chaos. Smoke tickles my throat. The sound of weapons clashing is everywhere as a mob of people battle in front of the rotting gray house.

Instead of Clara, a man stands before me with a sword through his head. *The mendax*, I realize as the blade is pulled free, leaving the *Illusionist* to fall lifelessly before me.

"Are you alright, my lady?" a shaky voice asks.

Looking up, I find Calum standing in front of me, his chest heaving up and down as he catches his breath. My focus snags on the bloodstained sword clutched in his trembling hands.

"What are you doing here?" I ask, trying to make sense of what's happening.

"We aren't lettin' these bastards take our home from us," he curses, his rheumy eyes shining with determination. "The Lowers may not be much, but it's ours. And we'll defend it."

My gaze flits over the chaos once more, and I realize he's right. All around us, mortals are battling the Forsaken. When did they show up? How did they know to come? Questions swirl through my mind as my attention drops to the man lying dead at my feet.

"You saved me," I whisper, glancing up at my friend once again.

"Of course." He waves me off with a shaking hand. "Ya can always count on me, my lady."

My brows shoot up as my mouth falls open. "You know who I am?"

"I may be old, but I'm not daft," he grumbles, his shoulders hunching forward as he struggles to hold up the weight of his rusted broadsword. "It's not hard to guess the identity of the invisible lass from the pub when you live in the same city as a wraith."

Shock barrels through me, nearly tipping me over, but he reaches out to steady me. I never realized he knew who I was when we would sit together and chat over a pint of ale. In all honesty, I always assumed he thought I was just a voice in his head, not someone real...

"We need to mo—" His words cut off as his eyes go round.

The lines of his face tighten as he falls to his knees, and I spot the hilt of a dagger sticking out of his back. The world shudders around me as I notice the person standing behind him, a gleeful smile twisting her wrinkled face.

The old woman who attacked me a few weeks ago.

The one I spared.

"*He said all the rats will bleed and die,*" she sings her haunting song, jumping up and down as she claps her hands. "*When all the stars fall from—*"

Her voice abruptly cuts off when my blade pierces her throat, but I don't bother watching her die. Instead I turn back to Calum, sinking to the ground as I roll him onto his back. His head falls limply to the side, his cloudy eyes seeing nothing as they stare at the battle raging next to us.

"No," I whisper, the sound going unheard as it's eaten up by the clashing of swords.

My fingers shake as they press against his neck, searching for a pulse I already know I won't find. Death has been my constant companion over the years, haunting every step I take. I've met many iterations of it, yet somehow, this one feels the most unfair. I know Calum lived a great life. He married his childhood sweetheart, and they spent fifty-three years together until she passed. He was ready to follow her through the veil, but it shouldn't have been like this. Not here, where he's just another body piling up on a battlefield. He deserved to be warm in his bed, surrounded by his family.

Something wet trails down my face as I close his eyes and position his hands over his chest. He almost looks as if he could be sleeping...

Air swooshes toward my cheek, and I duck seconds before a sword slices over my head. Turning, I find a man standing above me, his eyes burning with wicked delight as he raises his weapon to swing again. I roll out of the way, tossing a knife at his chest as I shoot to my feet. He falls to his knees, his wound spewing blood all over the ground, but I don't have time to care.

Forcing myself to leave Calum's body behind, I push aside all the emotions swirling within me, leaving only a cold, righteous fury to fuel my fight. Scanning the crowd, I find a large group of mortals gathered near the porch as they try to fight off the Forsaken. I search their faces for a glimpse of my friends but come up blank. There's too much chaos to find anyone in this mess.

Knowing I'll never make it through that mass of people, I take off running around the side of the house. Several Forsaken try to stop me as I sprint through the raging battle, but all of them regret that choice as the light leaves their eyes. There's no room for mercy tonight. Only death.

It's eerily quiet as I reach the left side of the house, finding it free of any fighting. A frisson of unease curls around me as I search for a way inside, unable to stop myself from glancing over my shoulder every five seconds. The windows on the bottom floor are boarded up, but most of the ones on the second story are wide open.

A truly stupid plan forms in my mind, but with limited options, I latch onto it. Grabbing a nearby trash bin, I tip it upside down and place it directly under one of the second-floor windows. I thank the Fates that it holds steady under my feet as I climb on top. Even with my arms stretched above my head, there's still about twelve inches of space between me and my target.

I take a deep breath, steeling my spine as I bend my knees. Relying on every ounce of muscle I've built over the years, I push off the can and jump. Uneven wood digs into my fingers as they latch onto the windowsill. My arms and shoulders protest painfully as I hang against the side of the house, my feet kicking wildly. Fire burns in my core, but I manage to pull myself over the ledge and tumble into the room.

I lie on the floor, my breathing ragged and heart racing from the exertion.

"I told them you'd come."

The air gets thinner as his scratchy voice echoes through the room, more familiar than my own. Scrambling to my feet, I turn to face him. My mentor. My friend. My Forsaken enemy.

Remy.

CHAPTER
FORTY-FIVE

He sits with his back against the wall, his position eerily similar to the woman who sat there the last time I entered this house.

The one whose life I just ended.

But none of that matters now, not when there's an arrow sticking out of Remy's chest. My face pales at the sight of blood soaking the front of his uniform, the same one he was wearing when I saw him yesterday. His body jerks with a wet cough that leaves his lips stained red.

"Punctured a lung." He grimaces as he gestures to the arrow resting right above his heart. "Fucking archers. They can't aim for shit."

I step forward on instinct, my hands outstretched. "Remy, I—"

Faster than I'd expect given his injury, he reaches for the sword lying at his side and points it toward me. "You come any closer and I'll cut that lying tongue from your mouth, *rat*."

I stop in my tracks, my lips parting on a gasp. Hearing such ugly words from someone so gentle, so kind... It's unbearable. Backing away from him, I push myself into the opposite wall.

"You need to at least pull the arrow out," I mutter. I know I shouldn't linger, but I'm unable to force my feet toward the door. "Otherwise, it won't be able to heal properly."

He rolls his eyes, his shoulders shifting uncomfortably. "I survived having my throat slit, Ivy. This is nothing."

My gaze falls to the pale scar on his neck, the one I've asked him about many times. "I don't suppose you're finally going to tell me how you got that?"

The ghost of a smile pulls at his lips. "Maybe another time."

Heat prickles behind my eyes. Everything about the reaction is perfectly Remy. How can he truly be lost to me when there's so much of him left behind? Sounds of the battle rise from beneath the floorboards, but for a single moment, we exist here together in a silent reprieve. Two soldiers resting in opposite corners, readying ourselves to return to the fight.

The moment of peace fades as his gaze falls to the collar and something hot flashes behind his eyes. "That doesn't belong to you."

"I never asked for it," I remind him, hating how meek my voice sounds. "I'd gladly give it away if I could remove it."

"Doubtful." He shakes his head. "Your kind are all the same. Every word out of your mouth is a lie."

"My kind?" My brows raise. "You mean high fae?"

He chokes on a laugh, wincing from the movement. "High fae, half fae, mortals. This whole planet is a cesspit. And soon, *he* will wipe us all away."

A door slams shut down the hall and footsteps pound against the floorboards. Our time is running short, but I need answers.

"Who is *he*, Remy?" I press him. "Who do the Forsaken serve?"

His eyes turn glassy as his stare shifts to the window. "The *almanova*," he whispers. "The *Soul of the Star*."

Soul of the Star.

That's what Darrow said *almanova* translated to in the old language. But how does that make sense? Surely the name is merely meant to be poetic, right? It can't refer to an actual soul trapped within the sword.

The train of thought is cut short as a symphony of screams ring out beneath us. Time stands still as a single male voice rises above the rest as its owner cries out in agony. I know that voice...

Thorne.

A second later, I'm sprinting from the room. Remy's wet laugh follows me through the halls as I leap over rotted pieces in the floorboard and race down the stairs. I reach the bottom and turn the corner into the living room, halting at the sight before me.

Like some sort of unholy tableau, bodies are scattered throughout the room in various displays of death. Mouths gaping and eyes wide, their faces are frozen with the terror of their final moments. A crack forms in my chest at the sight of Alice Darby's lifeless eyes gazing at the ceiling.

In the center of the room, Thorne stands over a fallen Grell Darby, pointing a blade at his throat.

"Please," the mortal begs. "You don't have to—"

His words end in a bloody cough as Thorne drives the weapon through Darby's neck.

That's right, a horrible voice whispers. *Kill him for what he's done to you. End his miserable life.*

No. I stumble back as my gaze drops to the sword in Thorne's hands. It's not the scythe he usually uses, but I recognize it all the same. The once white bone handle has faded into a stale gray, contrasted by the glimmering rubies that sparkle along the pommel. The matching gems hanging from my collar burn at the sight of it.

The almanova.

Thorne lifts his head. Not a single ounce of recognition shines in his glacial eyes when they connect with mine. There's no stopping the pitiful cry that falls from my lips at the hatred simmering in his gaze.

No. This can't be real. He's not one of them. He's not gone.

You know you want to do it, that cruel voice whispers.

Thorne rolls his neck, and I spot a few drops of blood trailing from his nose and ears. He takes one step toward me before coming to a halt, his eye twitching from the strain.

He's fighting it!

A bolt of relief shoots through me, sending life back into my limbs. He's fighting against the sword's hold. I search my memory, trying to recall Darrow's words from weeks ago. He said a God or an Heir would be able to withstand the sword's influence for a short time, but it would take all their strength. Based on the rigid way Thorne is holding himself, I'd say that strength is waning.

"Thorne." His eyes flare at the sound of my voice. "You don't want to do this."

His spine twists as a shudder racks through him.

She makes you weak, Killian Blackthorne. She'd never understand the things you've been forced to do. The choices you've had to make.

I bare my teeth, hating every whispered lie that bastard utters. In the past twenty-four hours, my body has been pushed to its breaking point. I've taken hit after hit with no time to recover. But the years of brutal training Remy put me through have taught me to push aside the pain, the heartbreak, the terror. All of it. I clear it from my mind, leaving only blind determination behind as I take a step closer to Thorne.

To the *almanova*.

His eyes widen at my movement, a hint of fear flashing behind their cold disgust.

"Nothing that thing whispers is true," I promise him. "You and I make each other stronger."

Lines appear around his mouth as he pulls his lips back, forcing a single word through gritted teeth. "Run."

"No." I shake my head as I lift a trembling hand between us, holding it out to him. "This is not the moment I stop reaching for you."

She lies! When she learns the truth, she'll turn away from you. She could never accept you for who you truly are.

Despite the *almanova's* ugly lies, hope expands in my chest as Thorne lifts his hand toward mine, but it's quickly dashed as his shadows wrap around my legs. They pull me down, forcing my body to hit the floor so hard that a few of the rotted pieces of wood crack under the impact. The wispy snakes take advantage of the moment, slithering over my limbs and binding my arms behind my back. I cry out as one of them pulls on my braid, twisting my head to the side at a painful angle.

End her now! Punish her!

Thorne's arms shake from the strain as he lifts the blade, his eyes glued to mine. His jaw is clenched, his beautiful face twisted into a grimace. My heart stutters inside my chest as its beating becomes erratic. The unfairness of it all presses in on me. Why would the Fates bring him into my life only to cut our thread short in this moment? We were supposed to have more time.

"It's okay," I whisper, keeping my eyes on his as tears fall freely down my cheeks. A sad smile pulls at my lips as his words from a few nights ago drift back to me. "I'm not frightened of the violence inside you, Thorne. I know who you are."

End her! Do it!

Determination shines in his eyes as he swings the blade. My gaze is locked on his as the sword drives through the air, straight toward my throat. I jerk from the impact, the force of it causing my head to bounce against the floor.

Screams fill my ears as something hot and vicious unleashes within me. A scalding heat rips through my veins as it both destroys and remakes me. My body convulses uncontrollably. It's as if every part of me is being swallowed whole.

Deep within my mind, a cage door swings open.

Not the one that houses my painful memories. No. The beast within this prison is far more deadly. A monster both ancient and inevitable. And now, thanks to the sword, it's been set free.

Finally.

When the fire beneath my skin cools, I'm left weak and exhausted. The world is nothing but a blurry haze as I crack my eyes open, my gaze settling on a single object lying before me.

A broken collar.

It lies on the dusty floor, its opulence completely at odds with the grimy environment. The silver metal of the clasp has been sliced in two. Those rubies that once sat against my skin now flicker with the moonlight that peeks through the open door.

I'm free.

The shock of the realization makes my head spin. After years of praying for freedom, finally, it's here. My muscles protest as I trace my fingers over my bare neck, gingerly brushing the place where the collar sat. It can't be real, yet somehow it is.

Everything around me is silent. Like all battles do eventually, this one has reached it's inevitable end. Worry creeps into my mind as my friends' faces flash before my eyes. Are they alright? Did they survive? Della, Griffen, Fia, Darrow, and Thorne.

Thorne.

The name is a horn blaring through my mind, spurring me into action. My body is stiff as I roll onto my side and push myself to my knees. Scanning the destroyed living room, I find him lying a few feet away. His chest moves steadily up and down, but there's a puddle of blood dripping from his nose and ears. Fighting against the whispers for that long must have drained him completely.

My gaze drifts to the sword, lying a few feet away from him. Darrow always said there would be a cost for using the *almanova*, but Thorne paid that price for me. Instead of bending to the sword's will and taking my life, he used it to remove my collar.

He freed me.

An unfamiliar emotion blooms inside my chest, more powerful than anything I've ever felt. Somewhere in the back of my mind, my subconscious knows what that emotion is. It's what spurs me forward, giving me the strength to crawl toward the God who nearly gave his life for mine.

I've almost made it to him when footsteps pull my attention toward the door. My mouth opens wide as I gape at the man on the other side of the threshold.

"Hello, *pet*."

Baylor looks terrible. His skin is sallow and thin, as if it's been stretched too tight over his bones. Bandages cover his ruined eye, a bit of blood seeping through the gauze. His only remaining eye has shifted crimson, the bloodshot veins making it appear as if his irises are leaking. The color is a bad sign, telling me he's dangerously close to revealing the monster he keeps tucked away. The *other* that hides beneath his skin.

My hands move to my sheaths, only to find them empty. My blades have all disappeared throughout the battle, leaving me without a weapon as I sit at the feet of my greatest enemy.

His gaze falls to where the sword lies between us. "What do we have here?"

I push myself across the floor, but he's faster. His fingers wrap around the hilt, and he snatches it up. A low growl rises in my throat when he points the tip directly at Thorne.

Baylor tsks, cutting me a glare. "One wrong move and I'll drive this through his chest. Sit back down, Iverson."

With no choice but to do as he says, I drop to my knees once more as I brace myself for Baylor to turn Forsaken.

"Mmm," he murmurs. "How nice to have you back where you belong."

At first, I think he's speaking to me until I realize his attention is on the *almanova*.

"Did you know this has been in my family for a very long time?" he asks, his gaze reverent as he runs a finger down the length of the blade. I shiver when I notice that his claws are fully extended. "My grandfather used to keep it on display, allowing his guests to covet what could only ever belong to him. He alone was unaffected by its influence."

His words send a wave of apprehension through me. Something about what he's saying is familiar. Important.

"You see," he continues, "before the Fates raised my grandfather from obscurity, he was an *enchanter*. And *this* was one of his creations."

My eyes flare as my mind makes the dangerous connection. No. He can't be...

"You see, Iverson, only those born from my grandfather's bloodline are able to withstand the whispers."

When I'd asked Darrow if anyone would be able to use the sword without consequence, he'd said only the Goddess of Illusion.

Or one of her descendants.

I shake my head, trying to deny it. When I'd asked Maebyn if she knew Baylor before all of this, she'd said she hadn't seen him since he was a boy.

"That's right, pet." A cruel smile reveals razor-sharp teeth. "*I am the Heir of Illusion.*"

At once, his skin shifts to a sickly translucent gray as horns grow from his head, curving into dangerous points. The fingers wrapped around the sword elongate into talons so sharp that one slice could disembowel someone. His spine hunches and his shoulders curl inward as horrible, membranous wings rip from his back and expand across the length of the room.

This is the version of him that has haunted my nightmares. His *vetere* form. The one they call the Beast of the Battle.

A choked laugh pulls my focus away from the monstrous king. Thorne's gaze is locked on Baylor as he uses what little strength is left in his body to push himself to his knees. He sways, and for a moment, I think he's going to fall back down, but he catches himself on his hands.

Hatred burns in Baylor's gaze as he edges closer to Thorne.

"You can't kill him!" I cry, desperate to stop him. Terror builds through me as I watch Thorne struggle to keep his eyes open. He's far too drained to even attempt to summon his shadows or fire. The sword took everything from him.

"Watch me." Baylor positions the tip of the blade at Thorne's throat.

"The *almanova* in the hands of a God becomes a God Slayer," I repeat Darrow's words, praying Baylor actually listens to me. "Even if you are an Heir," *And that's a big if*, I think privately. "He is still a God, meaning only another God can kill him."

"I've always wondered about that," he murmurs, tilting his head as he gazes at Thorne with disgust. "Who's to say an Heir couldn't do the same? To my knowledge, the theory has never been tested but now seems like the perfect time to try."

"You're no Heir," Thorne spits, his eyes locked on the monster before him. "I'd sense it if you were."

Baylor chuckles darkly. "You would think so, wouldn't you, boy? Usually, you'd be able to sense anyone with divine blood, but the Fates do love to dole out their little punishments."

"What are you talking about?" I ask, trying to keep him talking in the hope I can distract him long enough to stop him from hurting Thorne.

"I angered *them*." His upper lip curls. "And now those three vindictive bitches are teaching me a lesson by trying to deny me my birthright." He pounds his free hand against his chest indignantly. "My fate!"

"Because you locked your own mother in a cage?"

His crimson eyes flash to me. "I see you've been sneaking into places you shouldn't, pet. We'll have to talk about that after we've put your collar back on."

"You won't touch her," Thorne growls, his whole body vibrating with a mixture of rage and exhaustion.

"And you're wrong, Iverson," Baylor says to me, completely ignoring Thorne's threat. "*I* didn't imprison my mother. That was my father's doing."

Triston? Maebyn's husband?

I shake my head. "Why would he do that?"

"Jealousy eats away at us all," he answers. "Even the Gods and their mates aren't immune to it."

"You killed him," I murmur, pulling on the knowledge from my history lessons. "When you marched on the palace and took the throne, you killed Triston. Your own father."

He shrugs, but the gesture isn't as convincing as he wants it to appear. "I saw an opportunity, and I took it. Besides, he'd gone mad. Someone had to stop him."

"You could have freed your mother at any time," I insist.

"And then what would I do?" he snaps as his rage builds. "Return her crown and expect her to welcome me with open arms?" He barks out a hollow laugh. "That bitch never wanted me. She sent me away the day I was born and never let me return."

"So instead, you plotted to kill her?"

"I chose to forge my own path!" he shouts. "The Fates can try to deny me my destiny all they want, but once Maebyn is dead, her power will shift to me. I will ascend into the God of Illusion, whether they like it or not."

"Clearly madness runs in your family," I sneer.

"Sometimes we have to make hard choices," he says, his voice low. "You'll understand that soon enough."

I open my mouth to ask what he means, but the question dies on my tongue as Baylor pulls the sword back, arching his body as he prepares to strike.

Time slows down, each second stretching into a thousand. There's no debate. No hesitation. My body moves faster than it ever has before as I slide in front of Thorne just in time for the sword to drive straight through my chest.

My eyes go wide, my mouth opening on a silent gasp.

"No!" Thorne's voice echoes through the room, shaking the very foundation of the house.

Everything darkens as his arms come around me, holding my back to his chest to keep me from tipping forward.

"Why would you do that?" Baylor whispers, true despair entering his voice as his frantic gaze bores into me. "It wasn't supposed to be you."

"*Run*," Thorne growls behind me. "*Now*."

Fear clouds Baylor's face before it's replaced with determination. His gaze flits back to mine, and I know exactly what he's going to do a moment before it happens. With his hand still gripping the hilt of the sword, he rips it free from my chest before fleeing for the door.

This time, there's nothing silent about my reaction.

Screams tear from my throat as red-hot agony flares through me. My entire existence has been one painful encounter after another, but this... this is different. Not a single ounce of it is dull. The pain crashes over me again and again in razor-sharp waves that leave me weak and breathless. It's endless. A greedy monster, spreading outward from the wound and infecting every part of my body.

I try to breathe, but the air gets clogged in my throat as the taste of blood fills my mouth.

Air. I need air.

My body convulses as that old, original fear rears its ugly head once more. Of course, fate would bring me back to this feeling again, the misery of being denied life's essential substance.

Strong arms lower me to the ground. I think I hear someone talking, but the roaring in my ears is too loud. A wet, racking cough claws its way up my throat, clearing away some of the blood that was choking me. Gasping, I pull air into my lungs, gorging myself on the precious oxygen.

"You're okay," Thorne assures me, his voice louder now. "You'll be okay."

The rest of the room disappears as my world narrows down to a single vignette with his face at the center. New voices chime in from the shadows, but their words mean nothing to me as I keep my gaze on Thorne.

"What happened?" Griffen demands.

"*Baylor*."

"Will she make it?" Fia asks quietly, kneeling on my other side.

"She has to," Thorne insists. "I won't lose her. Not now."

The fire in my chest is endless, blazing furiously even as the rest of my limbs go cold. Somewhere in the back of my mind, I know that's a bad sign. *The blade must have nicked my heart*, I realize distantly through the haze. High fae are resilient, but the heart is where all life stems from. Once it's damaged…

"Angel," he whispers. "Please open your eyes. Please don't leave me."

I do as he asks, finding his beautiful face immediately, only now it's twisted with horror as he stares down at me. Not an ounce of blue is left in his irises as they are overtaken by dark shadows. I open my mouth to tell him it will be alright, but there's too much blood. My body jerks in his arms. It feels as though the veil itself is tugging at my soul, trying to pull it free from my body. Can it sense how close I am to death?

Tears land on my cheeks, and it takes me a few moments to realize they aren't mine.

"Stay with me, Angel," he begs, his tender fingers wiping the wetness from my face.

I try again to let him know I'm not going anywhere, but the words refuse to form.

Through it all, I keep my eyes locked on his.

Even when my heart stops beating.

CHAPTER
FORTY-SIX

I'm nothing.

At least, I think that's what I am. The rest of the world is tangible and solid, but I'm something else. Something bodiless. A phantom on the wind. Not even gravity deems me worthy of holding onto. Instead, I float through the ether disconnected from everything.

That's not true, a voice whispers. *You're tethered.*

I don't know what that means, but I suppose it doesn't matter. Strangely, there's something familiar about being nothing.

That's because you've done this before, the voice speaks again. *Once a very long time ago and again just recently.*

Having no way of knowing if that's true, I take the voice's word for it. Maybe *I've* been here before, but I don't think the *others* have. They float around me, all of us being pulled in the same direction. But there are some who don't float. Instead, the Dark Ones linger in the shadows, tracking our movements.

Don't go near them, the voice says harshly. *They aren't like you anymore. They shouldn't be here.*

The others grow antsy as we approach the stone archway. We all sense its wrongness. One by one, they are pulled through the veil, disappearing to somewhere unknown. The giant, gaping mouth swallows them whole, leaving nothing behind but the echoes of their screams. Whatever lies on the other side, it isn't peaceful.

The air between the pillars ripples in anticipation as it pulls me closer. I've almost reached it when, all of a sudden, I'm pulled to a halt. The others continue their procession, disappearing into the veil without interruption.

What's happening to me?

You're tethered, the voice repeats.

A moment later, something tugs me backward, away from the veil. The world flashes by me in a blur. Before, I was floating slowly, but now I'm racing through the air. Deep within the nothingness, I sense something growing. A connection of some sort. Whatever it is, I think it's the reason I didn't pass through.

Is this what happened to me when I floated before?

I wait, but the voice stays silent, offering no further explanations. I suppose I'll find out soon enough.

Perhaps then, I won't be nothing anymore.

When my eyes open there's only darkness.

I blink several times, and the world expands around me, taking the shape of an unfamiliar bedroom. At least, I think it's unfamiliar. My mind is currently too disoriented to be sure. The bed I'm lying in is soft, yet my back aches. The skin there is sore and itchy. I twist my arm to scratch it, wincing as my nails brush against the tender flesh. Was I in some sort of accident?

It takes me several moments to realize the darkness I'd seen was just the black curtain of the canopy above me. My back protests as I sit up and stretch out my neck. The only source of light comes from the fireplace, it's flames casting a warm glow on the maroon walls. I roll my eyes when I realize everything about the decor is dark and moody. Whoever lives here must be very dramatic.

As my thoughts begin to clear, a bone-deep panic sets in.

Where am I? Who brought me here? I glance down at myself, sighing with relief when I recognize the clothes I'm wearing as my own. At least no one changed me while I was unconscious.

My relief quickly fades when the sound of a door slamming and raised voices come from the other side of the wall. *The room next-door,* I realize.

"Are the two of you just going to sit there silently?" a male voice demands, his words immediately followed by the sound of an object crashing against the floor.

"What do you expect, Clyde?" another man responds. "They'll back him no matter the cost. They always do."

"Tell him to calm down!" the first one, Clyde, insists. "Tell him he can't seek revenge."

Deciding it's time to move, I push myself off the bed as silently as possible, ignoring the tightness in my back. Moving toward the large dresser, I quietly search for some sort of weapon I can use against whoever's out there. Frustration fills me as I pull open the drawers, finding nothing but folded men's clothing.

"Hey!" Clyde shouts as another crash echoes through the room. "You need to figure out what our next move is now that he has the *alm*—"

His words are cut off as something large slams against the shared wall, rattling the door that separates us.

"Stop talking," a woman orders, her voice sounding familiar. "He doesn't care about that right now."

Realizing I'm out of time, I abandon my search and settle for a crystal vase sitting on a side table.

"He doesn't care?" Clyde asks incredulously. "We have backed him throughout this entire insane scheme! We followed every plan, no matter how impossible. And now when we're so close to getting what he promised us, he's going to ruin it all to avenge some woman? Some whor—"

"She's dead!" a deep voice growls, one I recognize with every fiber of my being.

As I turn toward the door, my gaze snags on the sight of my reflection in the ornate mirror above the dresser. Time stands still as my eyes flare wide at the sight of my neck.

My bare neck.

Flashes of the battle assault my mind, one after another. Calum's lifeless eyes. Thorne killing Darby with the *almanova* and then using it to remove my collar. Baylor—

I swallow thickly as the image of Baylor driving the sword through my chest rips through me. The memory is so sharp that I feel an echo of that searing pain. The others continue shouting, but I can't listen through the roaring in my ears. My gaze falls to my chest, but no sign of the wound remains on my skin. A giant hole has been ripped in my tunic where the sword pierced my chest, but other than the blood stains, no trace of the fatal injury remains.

Fatal.

My body trembles as the past reawakens, rearing its ugly head as it collides with the present. I flash back to the day my father drowned me in the lake. As I'd sunk to the bottom, I convinced myself that my brother had jumped in to rescue me. I told myself everyone only believed I had died because my pulse was too faint to hear. My breathing too shallow to see.

But like so many things in my life, it wasn't true. I've always been a skilled liar, able to manipulate almost anyone. Including myself.

Another vision plays in my mind, this one more recent. I'm standing before the veil, trying desperately not to tumble over as Kaldar drags me down with him. I told Thorne that I'd been able to twist over the side at the last second, that I hadn't gone through the archway, but that was a lie too.

Deep down I've always known the truth, but I refused to acknowledge it. Every time those events came up, my brain carefully skirted around them, never letting me look too deeply at why they haunted my dreams relentlessly.

The vase slips from my fingers, shattering against the floor as Thorne's shouts replay through my mind.

She's dead.

The fighting on the other side of the wall goes silent at once. A few seconds later, heavy steps pound against the floor, and the bedroom door is thrown open. Several people file in, their expressions filled with varying degrees of shock as they catch sight of me standing beside the dresser. Multiple gasps fill the room, but I ignore them all as I'm caught in the snare of Thorne's crystalline gaze.

Dark hair falls in a mess across his forehead, as though he's been running his hands through it in frustration. His lips are parted, his head tilted to the side as he watches me warily, as if he fears I might disappear any second.

"Ivy."

My name is a prayer on his lips, sending chills through me.

He moves in a blur, appearing before me faster than my eyes can track. His hand reaches toward me, hovering an inch from my cheek, as if he's scared to close the gap and discover I'm only an illusion. His gaze flits to the bed momentarily before shifting back to me. "How are you..."

"Alive?" Griffen asks, finishing Thorne's question.

My gaze flickers to the others briefly, finding Griffen and Fia standing by the door with three people I don't recognize. Two men and one woman.

"How?" Thorne asks, his gloved fingers finally connecting with my skin. He turns my face back toward him, as if he's unable to have my attention directed at anyone else.

A cold jolt of fear strikes in the center of my being, sending me shuffling back a few steps. Hurt flashes in Thorne's eyes, there one second and gone the next as his hand falls between us. I want to throw myself into his arms and tell him everything, but a bone-deep fear holds me back.

I've been so honest with him. I've shared my pain and regrets and shame. I've given him every piece of myself. But this is one truth I can't offer.

I lick my lips, my mouth suddenly dry. When was the last time I had a drink of water?

"I must not have been as badly injured as everyone thought," I whisper.

I can't force myself to meet Thorne's eyes as I utter the lie, but at least my voice sounds steady. Still, my stomach churns.

"You weren't injured, Ivy," Fia speaks up, her eyes watching me warily. "You were—"

"Dead," Thorne finishes her sentence as he closes the distance between us, coming to stand only a few inches away.

I shake my head as I stare at my feet. "No, it must have only appeared that way. My body just needed time to heal."

"Thorne."

My attention flits to one of the new faces, a tall man with dark hair. I recognize his voice as the person who was shouting before. Clyde.

"She was dead and now she's not," he continues, his brown eyes brimming with suspicion. "You know as well as I do what that could mean."

Thorne stiffens, his fists clenching at his sides. I summon all of my bravery and meet his gaze again, finding it locked on me. The blue of his eyes is glacial as suspicion creeps into them, making my forehead wrinkle. I open my mouth to ask him what's wrong, but Clyde's insistent tone rings through the room again.

"We need to see if she has the—"

Thorne silences him with a glare. The man purses his lips, his body practically vibrating with unspent anger as he crosses his arms.

"Lift up your shirt," Thorne commands, his attention focused on me once more.

My head snaps back. "Excuse me?"

"You heard me." There's not an ounce of warmth in his voice as he speaks. "If you are who Clyde suspects you to be, the evidence on your back will be undeniable."

My brows shoot up at that statement. Who the fuck do they think I am? And what evidence is he referring to?

"But," he continues, "if there's nothing there, then you're free to go."

Something ugly twists in my stomach. "Go?"

He nods, his jaw clenched tight.

"But I—"

"You what?" he demands, his tone full of ice.

I take a step back as I realize the mask he used to wear has slipped back on. He's cold again. Indifferent. Completely the opposite of the person I've come to know over the past few weeks. The person I've come to—

I cut that thought off as I force myself to ignore the painful cracking in my chest. Now isn't a safe time to acknowledge vulnerable emotions. Not when the lines of friendship are so quickly shifting around me.

He arches a brow. "What will it be, Angel?"

My stomach shifts uneasily. The way he said my nickname just now felt wrong. A taunt instead of an endearment.

"Why are you acting like this?" I whisper, wishing I could take the words back immediately. They give far too much away.

Something flashes behind his eyes, but he doesn't respond.

"Why are you waiting for her permission?" Clyde demands as he stomps toward me. "We should just hold her down and look for ours—"

"No one touches her," Thorne growls.

His menacing stare stops the man in his tracks. The space around him darkens as shadows stretch across the hardwood. The protective reaction has a spark of hope flaring in my chest, but when he turns back to me, his gaze is even more frigid than before.

"If you have any hope of leaving this room again, you will show us your back. Otherwise, we'll keep you here until you comply."

Air catches in my throat as the threat falls from his lips. This can't be the same man who risked his life to free me... What's changed since he used the sword to remove the collar? What's made him become so cold toward me? Is this all because of one little lie?

I glance toward to the others, searching for an ally among the crowd. Griffen and Fia keep their faces blank as they stare impassively at the scene before them. For a moment, I think I spot a faint trace of guilt swirling beneath Griffen's cool exterior, but it's gone before I can be sure. The reality of my situation sinks in, making my limbs heavy and weak. Deciding it's better not to drag this out and give them a chance to change their minds about holding me down, I turn around and lift up my tunic, exposing my back.

Gasps echo through the chamber immediately.

"No," Fia breathes. "It's not possible."

"The proof is right there," Clyde argues.

Turning my back to the ornate mirror, I twist my head around to see what has them so shocked. My eyes go round as I find a giant red tattoo covering most of my back. The crimson lines span from shoulder to shoulder, creating a symmetrical design. It takes my brain longer than it should to realize they are in the shape of wings.

My body jerks as I drop my shirt immediately, as if removing it from my sight will make it disappear. The air in my lungs is too thin as my heart pounds against my chest. I whip my head toward Thorne, recalling the way his wings always fold against his skin to become a tattoo when he no longer needs them.

This can't be real. I can't have wings. I'm neither God nor reaper, so it's not possible.

"You said she was *Maebyn's* Heir," Clyde accuses Thorne.

"Maebyn?" My head snaps around as I turn to gape at him. "Why would you think that? Baylor is her Heir. He's got her locked away in an underground prison."

"What?" the new woman exclaims, her gaze narrowing on Thorne. "You didn't tell us that!"

"By the time I learned that fact, it no longer mattered," he responds coolly.

Griffen watches the argument anxiously, his hands flexing at his sides. "Thorne, what exactly did Maebyn say when you spoke to her?"

I stumble back, hitting the dresser as shock blasts through me. He spoke to the Goddess?

"She claimed to have no knowledge of a female Heir in the Seventh Isle," he says, not turning to face his friend as he keeps his eyes glued to mine. "I assumed she was lying to protect her child."

Child?

I gulp. Something Maebyn said when I was in the tunnels takes on new meaning.

When the other one came to see me, he asked about you. Wanted to know who you came from. But if he were smart, he'd have killed you the moment he laid eyes on you.

At the time, I assumed she was talking about Baylor... But I was wrong.

No, I shake my head as reality bends around me, twisting as it reforms into unfamiliar shapes. None of this is true. It can't be.

"But she wasn't lying, was she, Angel?" He prowls closer, his eyes simmering with hidden knowledge. "Because there's only one way you could have come back to life."

"I didn't," I argue, trying desperately to hold on to my lie as everything else slips away from me. "As I said before, I must have not been—"

"You were *dead*," he cuts me off, a shudder passing through him. "While I usually find your lying tongue amusing, now is not the time to push me. You were dead and now you're not, which means your soul must have been *tethered* to your body, preventing it from being pulled through the veil when you died."

My eyes go wide. Somewhere in the recesses of my mind, that word stirs at a memory.

You're tethered, a voice spoke to me.

My spine snaps straight as an image of the veil flashes before my eyes, its pale stones taking on a sinister edge. I have no idea where those thoughts came from, but they're quickly pushed aside when Thorne speaks again.

"There's only one person who could have done that. *Desmond*."

My brow furrows. The former God of Death? My heart races, and my mouth goes dry. "I never met your father."

The smallest hint of sadness flares behind his eyes, but it fades so quickly I'm sure I imagined it. "Desmond wasn't my father, Ivy."

I shake my head, my brain struggling to understand his words. "That doesn't make sense. If he wasn't your father, then you wouldn't be—"

"The God of Death?" he finishes my sentence, a cruel smile pulling at his lips. "Did you know there are many similarities between a God and a reaper? When the Fates created the Gods, they even based many of their physical features off the reapers they were always jealous of."

"Yeah, right before they made the reapers obsolete," Griffen grumbles.

Thorne shrugs. "The Fates have a bad habit of hating everything they didn't create."

"More like everything they can't control."

"That too." Thorne chuckles darkly before he continues. "It wasn't hard to pass myself off as Death's Heir. The people of the Fifth Isle were desperate for Desmond's offspring to show up and rule them. When I arrived and called myself his son, they hardly even questioned it."

"But you said your father was—"

"My father *is* a God. Just not Death," he corrects me as he removes one of his gloves. "But who I came from doesn't matter right now. Because there's only one person Desmond would have gone to the trouble of tethering a soul for."

His body presses in against mine, our gazes locked as he gently brushes his bare fingers against my cheek. When he speaks again, his warm breath tickles my ear.

"His Heir," Thorne whispers.

My head snaps back, frantically shaking back and forth. Time slows down once more as reality stops shifting and a new world is born. I may be a liar, but Thorne is something so much worse. An impostor.

Everything he's saying is madness, and yet when he speaks his next words, they hold an undeniable ring of truth.

"You're the Heir of Death, Ivy. And your ascension has just begun."

Acknowledgments

First, I want to start by saying thank you so much for reading this book. Please know that I am truly honored by the love and support my readers have already shown. It means more to me than I could ever say. Thank you.

I'd also like to thank my friends and family, for their continuous support. I wouldn't be here without you. Thank you for always unequivocally supporting my irresponsible and delusional ambitions. And to my incredible book besties who have welcomed me with open arms, thank you so much. I'm forever grateful for your support and friendship.

I'm thankful to have worked with so many amazing people in this industry. Thank you to Maddi Leatherman for being a supportive and amazing editor. Thank you to Bianca at Moonpress Designs for the most beautiful cover. And thank you to the wonderful team at Nerd Fam who handled my ARCs.

To MacKenzie, who has talked me off every ledge, I love you forever.

I'd also like to thank my dog, Eleanor, for always snoring very loudly while I was trying to write. You're the true Angel of this story and you deserve all the credit. And the treats.

And finally, I would like to thank Sertraline, without which I most likely would not have had the mental capacity to finish this book.

All my love,
Madi.

About the Author

Madeline Taylor is a fantasy romance author with a degree in English Literature and Creative Writing. She loves to escape reality whenever possible, so reading and writing are great outlets for her. Her other notable hobbies include maladaptive daydreaming, listening to Taylor Swift, and being bossed around by a senile pug.

Made in the USA
Monee, IL
16 August 2025